BURIED

# BURIED

## CIRCLE OF THE RED LILY

# ANNA J. STEWART

CAEZIK
ROMANCE
**ARC MANOR**
ROCKVILLE, MARYLAND

SHAHID MAHMUD
PUBLISHER

www.CaezikRomance.com

Cover Designer: Authors on a Dime

ISBN: 978-1-64710-138-1

First Edition, First Printing, July 2025
1 2 3 4 5 6 7 8 9 10

An imprint of Arc Manor LLC

www.CaezikRomance.com

*For Lezli Robyn.*

Editor extraordinaire. Warrior woman.

For helping me find my voice.

# PROLOGUE

*4 Years Ago*
*Outside New York City …*

HE smelled blood.

Strong. Metallic. As if he had a handful of pennies shoved in his mouth.

*She can't be dead.*

FBI Special Agent Mitch Keaton pressed his back against the brick wall, the chilly wind of a New York winter shooting through his windbreaker like bullets of ice. His right hand tightened around the grip of his Glock-19.

"NYPD is fifteen minutes out."

Mitch turned his head just enough to see SA Lynda Prince, his partner of six years, move in behind him. "Cassia doesn't have fifteen minutes."

*She has to be alive.*

Lynda pulled out her weapon. "We go in then. Keep your head straight in there." She released the safety. "We don't want Internal Affairs crawling up our asses because you surrendered your Boy Scout card."

Too late. Boy Scouts didn't turn off cameras in interrogation rooms or make Faustian deals with serial killers.

1

Mitch took a deep breath and instantly regretted it. Beneath the stink of blood lay the tangy decay of death. Panic and desperation pulled at him, but surrendering to either would get Cassia killed.

If she wasn't dead already.

Mitch turned and kicked in the graffiti-tagged sheet of plywood covering the entrance. It landed with a dull thud, a sound covered by that ear-piercing music. "Remember to be prepared for anything."

"You're the one who needs the reminder, not me." Lynda peered past him for a view of the warehouse's dimly lit interior. The stench burned his eyes and scorched a permanent imprint inside his lungs.

"I've got point." Mitch headed down a hallway strewn with debris and trash, passing empty offices, only to stop short at a dead end. "Damn it!"

"This way." Lynda was already headed down a branch in the hallway he'd passed.

His feet followed in her wake. Where she stepped, he stepped. They had a pattern, a routine. Safety a priority.

Mitch fought down the urge to rush in. It had been more than ten hours since Cassia's abduction. Ten hours she'd spent in here, in this … place.

Bile rose in his throat. His stomach churned. He swallowed the anger and tightened his grip on his weapon.

*Is she alive?*

His shoulder brushed against the wall. His jacket caught. Tugged.

Mitch spun, trigger finger twitching. The hallway behind them was empty.

"You okay?" Lynda's voice barely carried over the din.

"Yeah." He stared into the darkness, fighting his imagination. "Yeah, I'm good."

One more turn. One more hallway.

The music grew louder. And there was light. Strobing light.

At the end of the corridor, Lynda stepped to one side, Mitch the other. They glanced in.

The main part of the warehouse had been transformed. The cavernous space echoed with the repetitive, screeching music. Cold air blew in through the broken windows near the ceiling. But it couldn't blow away the stench of blood and death.

A bank of enormous televisions propped up on concrete blocks formed a circle about forty feet around in the middle of the space, screens facing inward. Through the gaps in the televisions, Mitch saw flashes of black and white movement onscreen, like old film caught in a stuttering loop. But inside the circle …

Inside the circle he could see shapes. Large boxes. Tables. The silhouette of a man moving.

*Whittaker.*

Mitch could practically feel Lynda tense, like a cat prepared to pounce on its prey. He wasn't as coiled.

*Where is Cassia?*

He became aware of shouted words—*pleas for mercy*—rising from those screens. Those cries pierced the shrieking guitar notes. And there were screams …

Agonizing, staccato screams punctuated the music like a drumbeat.

"Alive," Lynda said as if to remind Mitch of their objective.

Taking Whittaker alive meant answers. Answers for the victims' families. Answers for the judicial system.

Mitch had taken an oath to uphold the law. To stand for justice.

*But that was before Cassia …*

Mitch strove for calm, for control. as Lynda slowly made her way around the screens and out of sight.

As she circled around, Mitch moved forward, firearm at the ready, and slipped through the gap between two screens. He entered the arena of death like a gladiator ready for battle.

Near the opposite side of the circle, Whittaker towered over a gurney, looking like he'd fully embraced his inner psycho. Shaved head, smiley face boxer shorts, his chest and legs coated in flesh, gore, and ropes of blood as if he'd chosen to wear nothing but the evidence of his victims' suffering.

Mitch blinked, trying to reset his brain when he saw the gurney rocking and squeaking against Whittaker's whirring bone saw. As he saw Death carve up his latest prize.

*God, please, no. Don't let it be …*

Whittaker drew back the saw, took a step away, far enough for Mitch to catch sight of long, blood-streaked blond hair draped over the edge of the gurney.

Finger on the trigger, Mitch's gaze instantly shifted to the woman's bare thigh.

No double helix tattoo.

*Not Cassia.*

His knees nearly buckled. His finger moved away from the trigger.

If she wasn't there … where was she?

The back of his neck prickled. Lynda shifted into sight as she continued around the perimeter of the television screens.

There was only one other item in the circle—a red rectangle the size of a coffin sat atop a fabric-draped platform in the middle of the televisions.

A coffin covered almost completely in blood.

The stench of blood and death nearly overwhelmed Mitch once more.

*Whose blood?*

He clung to his training, to his oath. To his sanity. If Cassia was here, she was in that centerpiece. He was certain of it. As a forensic scientist, part of the team tasked with capturing the monster responsible for these deaths, she'd be the star of his gothic horror show.

Whittaker bent over the body on the gurney once more, the electric saw adding its whine to the chaotic symphony of sound.

Lynda was nowhere to be seen.

Pulse pounding, Mitch crept forward, keeping one eye on Whittaker and one on the coffin.

He swiped his free hand across the glass lid, smearing an arc of blood, beneath which he saw legs.

Legs that moved!

Adrenaline surged. Mitch used his jacket sleeve this time and smeared away as much of the gore as he could up to where her head lay.

His breath lodged in his chest. He stared down into Cassia's pale, dazed, disconnected face.

"*Mitch.*" Her voice was muffled, slurred. She pressed her palms against the glass, as if uncertain if what she was seeing was real.

*Quiet. Please be quiet, baby.*

Gripping onto calm, Mitch felt for hinges. Realizing they were on the other side of the glass coffin, he crept around to set the woman he'd fallen in love with free.

4

Cassia's eyes went wide as she focused behind him.

Mitch's gaze shifted down, to the shimmer of movement reflected in the dripping blood. The movement of a madman coming up behind him, revving the saw the way a motorcyclist revved his engine before taking off.

"Freeze! FBI!" Lynda's voice cut through the chaos, reverberated up and into the pitched high-beamed ceiling. "Gavin Whittaker, you're under arrest!"

Mitch turned, an odd calm washing over him as he raised his weapon.

"Put the saw down!" Lynda yelled as she ran forward and yanked the power cord out of the generator. The saw went dead. "Your brother gave you up, Gavin. He's the reason we found you. You're both done."

Whittaker came to a halt in the center of the theater, as if confused about what was happening. He opened his mouth in a silent scream, looking like an overworked Grim Reaper, divested of his robes.

He stared with blank, stark hatred, aimed not at Mitch but at the coffin.

And the woman inside.

"Mitch!" Cassia's muted voice broke through the glass.

The fog.

The rage.

"This is your last warning, Whittaker!" Lynda stepped into the spotlight of overhead lamps. "Put down the saw and raise your hands."

Whittaker laughed, a villainous chuckle that sent shivers down Mitch's spine.

"Mitch." Cassia said again, drawing his gaze. She pressed her palm flat against the coffin's lid.

Mitch laid his hand on the glass over hers. He stared into the desperate eyes of the woman he loved.

Time slowed into one perfect moment of clarity.

*Whittaker won't stop. He'll never stop.*

Whittaker let out an unholy sound drawn from the deepest level of hell.

Mitch turned. Gaze colliding with livid, pale eyes.

He widened his stance. Raised his weapon.

And fired.

# CHAPTER ONE

"INHALE pink." Dr. Cassia Davis filled her lungs with a long, controlled breath and held it for a count of four. "And exhale blue." Another four seconds. "In with the good." *Hold, two, three, four.* "And out with the bad." *Inhale ...*

Her eyes narrowed against the rays of the rising sun reflected against the Hollywood sign in the distance. An ideal late March morning in the Cahuenga Valley meant cloudless skies and radiant sunshine that could erode the darkest moods and Los Angeles smog. But—Cassia frowned. Only half her face felt the incoming warmth.

"Come on." She shifted slightly, hands fisting on her knees. "Almost there. Just another few ..." Static filled her ears as the H in the Hollywood sign pixilated before vanishing completely. "Damn it!"

Cass snatched VR goggles off her face and rubbed her eyes. Good thing she wasn't on anyone's timetable than her own when it came to this new virtual crime scene analysis program.

She sighed and the peace she sought—the peace her friend Laurel Fontaine insisted was possible—evaporated beneath frustration.

Cass's gut had been right. Building a meditation space in a closet had been a complete waste of time. On the other hand, doing so had been less irritating than listening to Laurel continually comment on Cass's TPD—Terminal Perfection Disease. Such a diagnosis, according to the high-priced defense attorney, required serious emergency treatment that began with breathing in and ... letting go.

Cass's lips twitched with actual inspiration. "Now I know what to sing at Temple House's next karaoke night." Even as she said it, the knot of anxiety she'd been trying to rid herself of for years balled back up and tightened in her chest. She hadn't been to a karaoke night since last summer. Riding the dual roller coaster of post-traumatic stress and agoraphobic tendences that more times than not left her paralyzed within these four walls meant shifting one's perspective. And priorities.

*Progress. Not perfection.*

Little steps, she reminded herself. Not marathons.

As if sensing her unease, Elliot, her constant companion in Golden Retriever form, stood at attention. He let out his familiar whine of concern before he padded over and pushed his furry head into her empty hands.

"I know." Cass pressed a kiss to the top of his fuzzy head and absorbed the comfort he offered. "I'm hopeless, aren't I, boy?"

She sighed. Laurel and her other friends meant well. The miniature Zen sand garden, dull-sounding gong, and the laughing Buddha statue had all been purposely arranged and looked beautiful. As for being inspirational and invoking some calm into Cass's life?

*Yeah—no.* She grimaced as she shoved herself to her feet. She found more peace reading the latest issue of *The Polymathic Pathologist: Advanced Studies in Interdisciplinary Forensics.*

Barefoot, she stepped out of the meditation zone and into her open floor-plan apartment—an apartment that looked more like a scientific laboratory than living space. Out of habit, her gaze landed on the small bank of computer screens across the room, flashing through the security cameras that kept the common areas of Temple House under constant surveillance. Neighbors hustled and bustled about their Friday morning routines. All, it seemed, was well.

Reassured, Cassia shifted her attention back to her own dwelling. Some people filled their homes with trendy or antique furniture. Others, like her upstairs neighbor and friend Mabel Reynolds, opted for cozy, mismatched pieces intermingled with family mementoes that immediately triggered a feeling of welcome and warmth.

As Cassia was neither showy nor homey, practicality played the primary role in what she called techno-chic. The description had the added bonus of making Laurel's eyes roll back in her head.

The large round, recessed sofa and huge coffee table took up most of the space in what was laughingly called a living room. It suited both her taste and her needs as it was big enough to host her friends, comfy enough to sleep on those nights she couldn't drag herself away from the trio of wall-mounted eighty-inch computer screens hanging over her workstation, and durable enough to tolerate Elliot's shed-inducing, leg-splaying naps.

While her best friend Sutton O'Hara, who lived downstairs with her adopted niece and nephew, preferred to create culinary magic with her favorite movies or TV shows on in the background, Cass thrived within the constant hum of white noise: whirring computer fans and server racks, alert tones from various software programs processing, and the clunking and mechanical pressure release of the new DNA sequencer that had been running pretty much non-stop for the past three weeks as victims found buried up in the Hollywood Hills were identified.

That all felt like home to her.

Her heart only jumped slightly when her front door popped open. Nox, Cass's long-time assistant, caught sight of her from across the room.

"You lasted a whole seven minutes." They glanced at their watch and smirked as they closed the door behind them. "That's close to a personal best for you, isn't it?"

Their pixie-cut hair gleamed in a rainbow of pinks and turquoise against the late morning sun streaming through the clerestory windows overlooking the Hollywood Hills. Aside from the makeshift recording studio and guest bathroom, Nox had created themselves a—for want of a better term—lair in her apartment.

Since the programming genius and former hacker was around one credit shy of earning their super villain degree, the word seemed appropriate. As did their décor—from the collection of mini-voodoo dolls made out of discarded computer parts, to the recently acquired digital frame displaying a rotating array of photographs of Nox with their plethora of friends. Nox's personality was front and center in their comfortable space.

"More mail from your number one fan." Nox plucked out a pair of postcards out of the stack of mostly junk. "You want to look at them?" They turned the cards over in one hand, inclined their head.

"Not really." But Cass held out her hand, determined to deal with things as healthily as possible. Her stomach clenched. The cards had started arriving a little over a month ago. Seemingly innocent messages like *It's been too long* to *Let's catch up soon.* No signature; nothing indicating who they were from. The postmarks were local and the address they'd been sent to was her current PO Box at the annex post office two blocks from Temple House. "Someone's got too much time on their hands." She walked around her desk and pulled out the plastic evidence bag in which she'd been keeping the cards. Just …

Well, just in case.

"You don't think those are creepy?" Nox asked.

"Doesn't matter," Cass stated as she swallowed her unease. "The only prints we found on the first few were ours and postal employees." She'd put a lot of crazies away over the years. There weren't enough hours in the day to even attempt to narrow down who may have developed a fixation on her.

"You looked stressed," Nox said. "Maybe you should try meditating again."

"Nah. I've bested my record of four minutes ten seconds. I'm good." And on that note, Cass's mood improved. Definite progress. She slammed the desk drawer shut. "I'm thinking of having Blake install a heavy bag like Mabel has in her guest room. Something tells me beating the crap out of one those things would work better for me than ohm-ing and … uh, breathing."

Elliot wandered to his cushioned bed under one of the windows. He stared at the wall for a long moment, whining and scraping a paw against the floor before he circled around, and curled up, his ears twitching.

Nox looked down at the goggles Cass set on the end of their desk. "How'd they do?"

"The program glitched again." Cass appreciated the irritation in Nox's purple contact accented eyes. "Same place. When the sun hits the H."

"I don't get it." Nox glared at the goggles as if wanting to set them on fire. "They were working fine a couple of days ago. That last update should have taken care of any problems."

"The issue must be deeper in the program. Don't worry." Cass knew Nox did not do well with imperfection which they equated with failure. "What?" She added at Nox's frown. "Don't tell me you're still ticked I didn't use Hawai'i as our test image for the new program?"

Nox shrugged. "It would have been nice to use a place we can't see every day from the roof. Or that window."

"I needed to use someplace familiar so we could easily spot errors with the imaging." Not entirely true. A little over a week ago she'd been unable to open her front door without her lungs freezing in terror. But recognizing she and Nox couldn't proceed with their new project without getting those images had been the key to Cass reclaiming control of her mental state.

After weeks of self-imposed seclusion, work had been the reason she'd flipped the trio of deadbolts on her front door and stepped outside her apartment. It was because of work she'd forced herself up the stairs to the roof of Temple House where she could take the photographs they needed and to feel actual sunshine and fresh air on her face for a good long while.

When all else failed, work was the only thing that could sway her to leave her apartment. To plan and execute. Her scientific approach was finally pushing her out of her comfort zones.

As a result, she'd begun to crack the foundation of those mental blocks extreme trauma had set in place four years ago in New York.

Since her trip to the roof, she'd set herself a different kind of schedule. Monday nights she went to Laurel's for a glass of wine. Wednesdays, she and Elliot went to Mabel Reynolds's apartment for a doggie playdate with Barsky. Fridays were ... open, but most weeks she was the one opening her doors to her family of friends.

Not this week, though. Everyone was a bit helter-skelter with their schedules these days.

"Maybe next time we use Hawai'i for our test run?" Nox pressed.

"Maybe," Cass lied. Walking up to the roof was one thing. Flying across the ocean was quite another. "In the meantime, I have faith you'll figure out the programming glitch."

"Don't know how much deeper into the program I can go," Nox muttered as they sank into their chair behind their elaborate, mind-bending computer system and tapped a few keys. "Might have to rewrite the entire thing." The networked printer near Cass's desk wheezed to life and spat out pages. "I went through and cancelled or rescheduled the lectures you marked on your calendar."

The printout could wait; she knew Nox would have already made the update to her digital calendar. "You get any pushback from any-one?" Normally she accepted every speaking engagement she was offered, but she needed to shift most, if not all of her attention, to the hills.

"Pfffth." Nox waved off the idea and set their silver rings to glint-ing. "I wouldn't be a very good assistant if I couldn't play 'dragon at the gate.' Besides, working for one of the foremost forensic scientists in the country gives me serious cred in dealing with irritated aca-demics." Their back straightened with pride as they beamed, their disappointment about Hawai'i forgotten.

Cass's internal communication system beeped its telltale alert and brought the overhead center flatscreen to life. "Probably helps that you used to be an irritated academic yourself once upon a time." She retrieved the enhanced Bluetooth headset from her own desk, slipped it on, and tapped to answer.

"You've got Cass."

"It's Linnea."

Cass's head snapped around at the tense tone in the older wom-an's voice. She hit a button on her own keyboard and stepped back as the feed on the center screen went from Loading to Complete.

Dr. Linnea Crawford appeared on the enlarged screen at the "Red Lily" mass-grave excavation site, the stress lines on her mid-dle-aged face starkly visible, showing definite signs of annoyance.

"What's going on?" Cass tapped the screen of her cell, noted the time, then caught movement behind her co-worker. Co-*in-charge*-worker, Cass corrected herself. "What in the hell are the police doing up there?" The idea of people stomping around their crime scene flipped Cass's bitch switch.

"They are here,"—Linnea didn't attempt to keep her voice down. If anything, she raised it—"because the private security firm the mayor and DA agreed to hire for overnight guard detail isn't worth crap." Over Linnea's shoulder Cass saw one of the uniformed officers flinch slightly before he moved out of camera range. "Someone broke into the site last night. They cut their way through the chain link back by grave twenty-four."

Cass took a bracing breath. *One, two, three, four ...*

"They tossed the evidence tent and smashed their way into the office," Linnea went on. "Poor coffee machine didn't know what hit it. They tried to access the refrigeration lab. Bashed the hell out of the electronic keypad. Not that there was anything in there to be worried about. We'd transported the day's evidence back to the main lab at the LAPD already."

"Well, shit." Cass's flexed her hands, wishing she had that heavy bag to punch. This case was already a quagmire of political sensationalism. District Attorney Johanna Eichorn was in serious butt-covering mode after her less-than-above-board activities that resulted in one of her investigators nearly getting blown into the next world. The mayor was playing suck up to the media rather than addressing actual concerns in getting the mass grave case closed as quickly as possible. If word that the gravesite had been compromised leaked, it would add another layer of controversy—and delay—to an already complicated investigation.

In the meantime, the remains of more than sixty individuals were being used as political fodder for yet-to-be-determined purposes.

Irritation slipped in as Cass's mind raced. She had never, in all her years as a forensics investigator, encountered such interfering stalling tactics when it came to closing a case of this magnitude. Nor had her competency ever been called into question. But she was getting hit with both barrels where this case was concerned. Sure, she might not conduct her investigations in the expected way, but she'd created a system, environment, and procedure that produced refined, unadulterated, unquestionable case-making results.

They, whoever they were, could throw as many obstacles in her way as they wanted. Nothing was going to stop her from getting answers. Not only for herself, but for everyone who had lost a loved one.

Cass swallowed hard, thinking of Mabel, whose twin sister had recently been identified as one of the bodies buried in the hills. Mabel who, despite her heartache or maybe because of it, was counting on Cassia to find whomever was responsible not only for her sister's death, but the dozens of other victims whose voices had been silenced.

Cass had made a promise. To Mabel, to the other families, to do whatever it took to see this case through. Even if that meant …

The past shivered up her spine like a ghost.

Even if that meant asking for help from the one person she never wanted to see again.

She squeezed her eyes shut, but that only made the image of FBI Special Agent Mitch Keaton shift from black and white to full Technicolor in her mind. Hearing his voice the other night, despite him speaking only a few words, made Cass's heart skip into a rhythm meant only for him. A rhythm she'd had to force herself to forget.

A rhythm that even now made her wish she could go back in time and rewrite the past.

For a blinding second, her lungs seized, forgetting how to breathe. The same way they had …

*Stop! Stop now!*

She had a fight on her hands. A fight to not only keep control of this case, but to preserve her reputation. The toxic combination of politics, media sensationalism, and Cassia's unique *situation*, publicly called into question her reliability and effectiveness. The accusations and suspicions had left her with only one solution.

She'd made the call she'd dreaded, even though doing so meant she hadn't had a good night's sleep since. Cass almost snorted. Like she slept.

Nox walked over, tablet in hand, and gently nudged Cass back into the conversation with Linnea. Gratitude swept over her, but they both knew her acknowledging her slip in concentration would only embarrass them both.

"What's the security company saying about the break in?" Nox asked as Cass pulled herself together. They began to type notes as they always did when Cass began a video call. "Did they at least catch who did it or were their guys asleep on the job?"

"Apparently the two guards who had been up here for the past two weeks called in sick last night," Linnea responded. "That left three on the job who are, let's just say, far from competent."

Now it was Cass who flinched.

"They also stomped all over the scene which left us with little to nothing to look to for in trace evidence," Linnea ground out.

"Awesome." Cass's entire body itched in a way that could only be scratched by her going down there and looking over the scene with her own two eyes. But … yeah. She flexed her hands to the point of pain. That wasn't an option so long as her mind refused to release her from the mental prison she'd been trapped in the past four years. Wandering around Temple House like a ghost haunting her own life was one thing. Walking out the building was another.

That said, there was little that offended Cass more than interfering with or desecrating a grave site. And that gave her something to focus on.

"On the bright side," Linnea said. "This could end up working to our benefit. You and I both pushed for LAPD oversight out here, but we were overruled. Maybe now the mayor and city council will reconsider."

"Yeah," Cass glanced at Nox who met her gaze with an arched brow. "Wouldn't count on that. Is anything missing?"

"Couple of metal detectors," Linnea said. "The new stereoscopic microscope you ordered for us. And three cameras."

All things easily replaced. But, Cassia thought sourly, it would slow down their work.

*Maybe that was the point.*

Restless, Cass walked around to her desktop computer, typed for a few minutes and craned her head to look at monitor number one as it displayed the video camera feed from the burial site. Static. "They either got my surveillance camera, too, or the feed's been cut. Double check when you can, yeah?"

"Of course," Linnea said. "We should probably keep an eye on social media," she suggested. "See if any videos pop up. Something like this could have been some kind of clickbait exercise."

"Cap lock crusaders."

"What's that?" Linnea's brows knitted and Cassia realized she'd spoken out loud.

"Nothing." Her face warmed and she found herself turning away from Nox. Dammit! Now was not the time to reminisce about Mitch Keaton's verbally entertaining dissection on the evils of social media.

A dissection that tagged nearly every participant as a graduate of the University of Unsolicited Opinions. "Thinking about … something I heard once."

"Cops say it'll be another few hours before they've finished here," Linnea said. "We can't start putting stuff back together and moving on until they are. Add to that, we've hit maximum overtime on hours this week so this weekend will be two, three people max. I'm supposed to be overseeing the testing of the evidence we've already collected but I can't be in two places at once."

"I know." Guilt surged despite knowing Linnea didn't intend the comment as a personal criticism.

That said? Their hurdles weren't entirely Cass's fault. Despite the multi-departmental push, the powers that be refused to approve overtime or additional staff which made absolutely no sense given the rabid public scrutiny. Plenty of other cases with far less attention pinned on them received ridiculous amounts of budget-busting money. It was as if someone didn't want the case solved.

If the city, the mayor, the beleaguered and compromised District Attorney wanted to, they could have tripled the team size and approved a 24/7 work frame. Cass and her team could have been finished by now and she wouldn't have had to call …

*Stop!*

"Okay." Time to focus on the positive and stop thinking about Mitch. Situations like this were why Cass always built in time buffers and contingency plans for every case she oversaw. "Let the police do what they have to do." She was already on thin ice with the higher ups at the mayor's office not to mention the LAPD; she couldn't afford to alienate anyone with her ongoing complaints, but Linnea was right. "And we'll hope this break-in is a silver lining of sorts."

"I know bringing in the Feds wasn't your idea." Linnea stepped closer and looked up at the camera as if looking into Cass's eyes. "When your FBI agent gets here—"

"He's not *my* FBI agent."

"Wow," Nox muttered. "That was your outside voice."

Linnea held up her hands in surrender. "Didn't mean that the way it sounded but understood. Whatever federal assistance we're allowed, chances are they can pull some strings we can't."

"Maybe." Cass took another deep breath. "I only agreed to call in the Feds so we could keep control of the case. Not so they could come in and take over." After speaking with Mitch to make certain he was amenable, she'd called the FBI to make her request official. They'd told her the agent assigned would arrive by Monday at the latest. That gave her time to get her head wrapped around the notion of seeing Mitch again. Ironic that his subsequent shift from behavioral science to forensics put him in the perfect, if not inconvenient, position of being able to ride to her rescue. Again. "In the meantime, we keep doing what we can do." She gnashed her back teeth to the point of pain, but she forced a strained smile. "Just keep on going, Linnea. Get to the lab when you can, make sure our people are safe at the site. That's all we can do. When are we expecting the latest round of dental X-rays?"

"Should be sometime today or tomorrow," Linnea said. "Weekend might slow them down."

"If you can push that, I'd appreciate it. The sooner we get those records uploaded into the system the better." There was little that gave her more satisfaction than feeding information into her specialized ID program and getting answers. The more victims they positively identified, the more closure they'd find for the families. "Hey, Linnea?" She called to Linnea's back.

"Yeah?" Linnea faced her again. For a blink of a moment she saw the shadows of exhaustion and stress in the older woman's eyes.

"As irritating as this forced break in is, they left the graves alone. It could have been a lot worse."

"I suppose." Linnea shook her head. "The whole thing makes me a little sick. You know what they've started calling this case, don't you?"

"Burial Boulevard? Yeah, I heard." Cass steeled herself against the disgust. She'd given more credit to the twenty-first century media to be far cleverer dubbing horrific crimes. "Personally, I would have gone with Horrorwood Hills."

"Now that one hits home." Some of the tension faded from Linnea's face. "I'll text once we're back up and running."

"I'll be here." Cass clicked off, removed her headset and tossed it on the desk.

"You okay?"

Cass glanced up at Nox's uncertain tone. "Yeah." She scrubbed a hand across the back of her neck. "What's one more complication?" She gave herself a hard mental shake as Elliot stood up and pawed at the wall. "What is going on with him?"

Nox sighed. "He's been doing that the last couple of days. Maybe he's just over stressed?"

"Possibly." Another layer of guilt for Cass to absorb. Elliot had flunked out of canine cadaver recovery school as a puppy and was subsequently diagnosed with trauma—one of the reasons she and Elliot had bonded so completely. Never in her life had Cassia so instantly connected with another living being.

*Well.* She swallowed the sudden lump in her throat as another image of Mitch floated through her over-stimulated mind. *Maybe there had been one other.*

She went into the kitchen, made a racket opening up the nearly empty doggie treat jar that always brought Elliot to her side.

He approached, but not with his usual enthusiasm. The way he kept looking over his shoulder made Cassia wonder if she wasn't the only one dealing with ghosts. "Here you go, bud." She crouched and offered the homemade peanut butter snack.

While he chomped, Cass stroked his fur, hoping, willing his emotional state to get back on track.

"Has there been any activity on that private page on the Scheherazade website?" The Los Angeles gentlemen's club, or at least their website, had been linked to the last disappearance and murder that they knew of: Eva Hudson. Custom-made invitations found in Eva's apartment could—emphasis on could—lead them deeper into the ill-deeds of the secret group Cass and her friends believed to be behind the abductions and murders. Crimes that went back decades, to as far back as the earliest days of Hollywood.

But that was all they'd discovered on that branch of the investigation. So far, anyway.

"I've got a bot running that monitors the site." Nox waggled their phone in the air. "As soon as any changes or updates are made, I'll get an alert."

"At which time we'll be able to access the private page?"

Nox went wide-eyed innocent, then winked. "That's the plan."

"Hmmm." Cass left it at that.

Nox came over, leaned their arms on the counter and rocked up on their heels. "I think I'm going to call Wally and suggest we postpone our weekend in San Diego."

"Don't do that." Inwardly, Cass cringed. She'd forgotten about Nox and Detective Wallace Osterman's long-planned first weekend away together. "You've earned some time off."

"Yeah, but …"

Elliot finished munching his treat and nuzzled Cassia's hand in a silent beg for another. She didn't even try to fight it. "No buts. You need to go. Get out. Decompress. Have some fun." One of them deserved to have some. "Like Linnea said, it's Friday. Things'll slow down for the weekend. And I managed to handle things on my own before you were around."

Nox scoffed, rolled their eyes. "Not very well, you didn't."

"Well, I can handle a couple of days."

"What about walking Elliot?"

Elliot stopped mid-crunch and looked between the two of them.

"Ah." Cass held up a finger. "I've already got that worked into my plan. Riley said she'd walk him—I just have to take him upstairs." That stomach jolt didn't hit quite as hard as it had even a few days ago. She wasn't in love with the idea of leaving her apartment and climbing the two flights of stairs. It was a lot further than walking across the hall to Laurel's, or up one flight to Mabel's, but she was determined to conquer another challenge. She and building manager, Blake Redford, had gone out of their way to make Temple House the most secure apartment building in the city. At some point she was going to have to trust in that.

*If I'm not safe here …*

She fisted her hands to stop them from trembling.

"Wally wouldn't mind waiting until we're done with this case," Nox pressed, but they sounded far from convinced.

That, in addition to the concern Cassia saw on their face, pushed her own worries away. "Hey." Cass took hold of Nox's shoulders and looked down into their wide eyes. "Thank you for worrying about me. It's appreciated. But you've got a life to live. I'm not letting my issues erode your future. You need this time with Wally. You want to find out where this is going with him, remember?"

Nox shrugged. "Yeah."

Cass had always been selfish with her affections. Few people slid into her heart without reservation, but Nox had, within moments of their meeting, become the younger sibling she'd never had. The one she never realized she'd needed. "You know what I want more than anything?"

"For that FBI agent you called not to show up?" Nox's brows rose up so high they almost disappeared under the shock of pink hair falling across their forehead.

Cassia couldn't help it. She laughed despite silently admitting it was true. "I want you, Nox Kessler, to be happy. So please. Go have your weekend with your cinnamon-roll detective. Eat at all the food trucks. Spend time at the beach." Nox's second favorite place on the planet after the aquarium. "I'm even going to go a step further and suggest you turn off your phone."

Nox couldn't have looked more horrified if Cass had suggested amputating an arm, but the doorbell chimed before Cass could tease them further. She bypassed the video screen connected to the video bell, forcing herself to focus on the fact that anyone with access to her front door had to get through those aforementioned security measures.

She unsnapped the trio of locks and pulled the door open.

Immediately her heart lifted and whatever sour mood had descended with Linnea's call evaporated.

"Well well." She leaned against the doorframe and looked down at the trio of kids bunched together, all three of them wearing various versions of the Summercrest Academy blue blazered uniform.

Mabel Reynolds's almost ten-year old daughter, Keeley, stood in the middle, her pigtails regimentally braided, holding a familiar covered cake dish in her hands. Keeley was flanked by Sutton's niece, seven-year-old, Addie, and nine-year old nephew, Lucas. It wasn't surprising to see them all together as Keeley had been staying with Sutton while her mom and Paul Flynn were in New York dealing with selling his apartment. "To what do I owe the pleasure of this early morning visit?"

"Hey, Aunt Cass." Keeley smiled and exposed slightly crooked teeth that would, one day soon, require bank-breaking braces. "Aunt Sutton sent us with cake."

"She said you've been cranky," Lucas added without any hint of trepidation.

"Did she? Have I?" Cass glanced over her shoulder in time to see Nox nod in agreement before they turned away. Elliot barked once before toddling over to the door. "And what kind of cake cures the cranks, I wonder?" She accepted the plate and motioned them inside. She sniffed, but didn't need to. Sutton rarely baked her anything that wasn't chocolate related. "Are you her new delivery service?"

The door clicked shut.

"I have something to give you," Keeley announced as Cass set the plate on the counter. "Aunt Sutton said cake might help you say yes." She dug a folded envelope out of her blazer pocket. "It's an invitation," she said as Cass accepted it. "To my birthday party next weekend."

Cass looked down at the marker and crayon creation that had clearly been crafted with a heap of love.

"We helped!" Addie announced. "I made the tacos there because there's gonna be a taco bar! And Lucas drew the picture of Barksy on the back."

"Well then." Cass pulled the invitation free and quickly scanned the details. She should not be feeling those pinpricks of panic and dread for a child's birthday party, but—yeah. Cass sighed. Even the idea of a birthday party gave her the shakes. "I'd heard your Aunt Riley and Miss Moxie agreed to let you have it on the back patio," Cass said. "I bet it's going to be fun."

"I'm inviting everyone in the building," Keeley announced. "Miss Moxie said we can get a big pinata to hit. Mom said it was okay as long as we have some healthy food to eat, too."

A given, Cass thought, considering Sutton was doing the catering. "Have you talked to your mom recently?"

"Uh-huh." Keeley nodded so hard she rocked back on her heels. "Last night."

"Are she and Paul having a good time?" Cass hung the invitation on the refrigerator with a magnet in the shape of a double Helix.

Originally Paul Flynn, once a prosecutor back east, had come out to temporarily oversee the investigation into the missing women now located in the burial site Cass now supervised, but falling for

Mabel—and Keeley—quickly changed his life plans into something far more permanent.

"They're coming home on Sunday." Keeley bounced on her toes. "Mom said they're bringing me a surprise. So can you come?"

Cass blinked.

"To my party," Keeley pressed. "You don't have to buy me anything. I don't need a present."

Cass's gaze drifted to the front closet where she'd stashed the state-of-the-art telescope she'd ordered weeks ago after Keeley expressed interest in the astronomy club at school. At the time Cass had wondered if that might be enough to get her back out onto the roof. "Kee—"

"Just think about it, please?" Keeley leaned over and tilted her head, aiming those big eyes at Cass like high beams in the desert. "I know mom said we shouldn't push you, but it would be the best thing *ever* if you could come. Even for a few minutes."

Nox slipped their bumper-sticker covered messenger bag over the kids' heads and moved to stand behind the trio, adding their own silent wide-eye plea to the group.

Cornered, Cass forced a smile as her heart fluttered. "I'll see what I can do." She reached out and brushed a hand down Keeley's cheek. If there was anyone worth expanding her safety boundaries for, it was this little girl. "Thank you for the special in-person invitation."

"She didn't say no!" Keeley did a little boogie in a circle as they moved to the door. "Come on! Let's go tell Aunt Sutton!"

"You heading out?" Cass asked Nox.

"I guess." They didn't look at all enthused. "You're sure you're okay with me—?"

"Don't make me fire you." Cass grabbed her friend by the shoulders and pivoted them around to follow the kids out. "I don't want to hear from you or see your face until you're back on Monday."

"What if I need your advice about something …Wally related?" Nox turned at the door, uncertainty springing into their gaze.

"Wallace," Cassia corrected despite knowing that Nox had been given special permission to use the shortened version of the detective's name. "I'll give you that exception. Have a fabulous time. Eat all the things and be safe. And by safe, I mean—"

"Way ahead of you." Nox's cheeks went bright pink. "We are definitely locked and loaded where that's concerned. And now the guest bath is well stocked with condoms."

"Good to know," Cass laughed, gripping the edge of the door, watching as Keeley, Lucas, and Addie headed upstairs while Nox made her way down.

Hallway empty, Cass closed the door, stepped back, and nearly tripped on Elliot. He sat, eyes locked on the collection of leads hanging on one of the hall hooks.

"You want Aunt Riley to take you for a walk?" Cass didn't stop long enough to let herself think. She embraced the leftover energy provided by the kids, along with the promise of the homemade chocolate cake that awaited her. She retrieved her sneakers from her bedroom closet before returning to grab one of the leashes.

Elliot circled around her, moving out of reach, barking once, twice, and scratching at the door.

"Hey, stop that." She tugged on his collar. It wasn't like him to be so … excitable. "Elliot. Come on. Settle down."

She didn't have time to panic or overthink or worry about stepping outside. All her attention was on Elliot when he stepped closer, pressed his nose against the door. He whined then barked twice.

"Give me a second." She could feel the panic begin to build, but she shoved it down even as it stole the air from her lungs. Her hands shook when she clipped the leash in place, but she ignored it when she twisted the knob and pulled the door open again.

A yelp caught in her throat. She got lightheaded with the surge of adrenaline.

She saw the feet first. Practical, heavy lace-up black boots. As she dragged her eyes up, familiarity sank in around the surprise even as her heart beat faster than a hummingbird's.

Elliot bolted forward as FBI Special Agent Mitch Keaton dropped a duffel bag off his shoulder, crouched down, and sank his hands into the thick fur at Elliot's neck to give the dog a good scrub.

"Hey, Elliot. Man, you're a lot bigger than the last time I saw you. It's good to see you."

Mitch's voice sank though her, comforting and instantly warming as if she'd slipped into a perfectly filled tub of heated water. The last four years vanished beneath the wave of longing and desire, of memory and contentment.

Before the terror slammed back at her with the force of an eighteen-wheeler.

Her ears rang; that dull, warning mix of phantom music throbbing into her head. Her stomach pitched, then dropped as all thought fell out of her head. For a moment—the briefest, longest moment—all she could see was a bloody haze of glass inches away from her eyes.

She glanced over Mitch's head as Blake Redford appeared, climbing the last two stairs with an expression of guarded suspicion on his face.

"It's fine, Blake." She didn't recognize the forced carefree tone of her own voice. "Mitch is … he's the FBI agent I told you about."

Mitch shifted to look over his shoulder, brows knitting before he returned his attention to the dog. Blake met Cass's gaze, waited an extra beat before he nodded and gestured to indicate he'd be just downstairs before he turned and headed back down to the lobby.

"Bodyguard?" Mitch asked.

"Building manager," Cass corrected before adding, "And friend."

Mitch's brow shot up. "Attentive."

Joke? Cass wondered. Or …? "Cautious." And dedicated. Blake Redford's attention to security was one of the primary reasons she'd felt safe in Temple House after an attempt on Riley Temple's life in the basement shortly before Christmas.

Elliot jumped and licked and finally dropped to the ground before he rolled over and unashamedly displayed his belly.

"Now that's what I call a greeting." Mitch complied with Elliot's bidding and scratched the dog's stomach with both hands.

"I didn't think—" Her toes curled in her sneakers to the point they cramped. Cool air wafted down the hall on the other side of the threshold she couldn't bring herself to cross. She hated that feeling—a feeling she'd been working so hard to overcome. A feeling she wasn't about to share with Mitch.

Thankfully, Elliot had blocked any possible path out. "I, um …" She tucked an invisible strand of hair behind her ear. "I hadn't heard my request for your coming was approved."

*Oh, God. I'm not ready for this. Not even in the slightest …*

"Yeah, well. It took you four years to call me." Mitch lifted his chin and locked his eyes on hers. His very blue, very tempting, oh-so-familiar blue eyes currently straining with humor on his now-bearded handsome face. "I wasn't going to take the chance you'd change your mind, so here I am." That familiar, grating concern flashed for only an instant. "Is there a problem?"

*Oh, only a massive six-foot-two one with bright blue eyes and hands that ….*

She shook her head. "Of course not." Only a little more than a minute in and she was lying to him already. That boded well. "Like you said, I called you."

Elliot continued to squirm and demand affection. Mitch's laugh tugged at Cass's heart and shot her, for a brief instant, out of the past.

He ruffled his hand down Elliot's fur. "I wasn't sure Elliot would remember me."

"You gave him to me," Cass managed. How could she both breathe and not? "Of course he remembers you." Just as she remembered every moment she'd spent with the both of them. And with Mitch. Alone.

Elliot nuzzled Mitch's hand and looked as if he'd hit the doggie lottery. His absolute joy made Cass smile even as seeing Mitch again made her heart weep. She was reminded how her initial doubts about Mitch's "good guy" reputation four years ago had been put to rest immediately upon meeting him. Doubts that were permanently erased when he'd turned up the next day, Elliot's lead in hand, insisting she needed the canine protection and companionship after … well. She felt the blood drain from her face. *After.*

Now, watching their reunion, every cell in Cass's body sparked with electricity.

She flexed her hands over and over, trying to dilute the sensation as her fingers tingled and her breathing quickened. The vastness of the exterior hallway behind Mitch loomed, pulsing in and out in a kind of heartbeat she couldn't get under control. Everything felt too intense.

The hallway. Outside. The world.

Mitch.

"I've read the information your friend Paul Flynn sent over." Mitch didn't miss a beat with Elliot as the dog scrambled to his feet and pushed his head into Mitch's stomach. "I figured the sooner we got down to business and you filled me in on what isn't in the file, the faster I can get to work."

"Now?" She couldn't quite wrap her brain around the concept. She wasn't ... ready for this. "You want to talk *now?*"

"Bad time?"

"Actually." Cass almost didn't recognize her own voice. A sudden headache pulsed behind her eyes as her chest tightened. "I'm, um ... I've got something I need to finish for another case." She pointed uselessly behind her to work that didn't exist. "Might take me some time to finish up. Would you ...?" She had to push the words out. "Would you mind taking him for a walk? There's a dog park—"

"Down on the corner. I saw when my ride-share dropped me off." Mitch stood back up, that frown of his still in place. "Are you okay? You look pale."

"I just need an hour." Or ten. "Seriously, you'd be doing me a favor." She motioned to the leash that had been pulled out of her grasp. "I didn't hear a buzz from downstairs when you got here." How had she missed that?

"Oh, yeah." Mitch's smile was pure Mitch—charming, disarming, and now that he wore a full, neatly trimmed beard, exponentially more masculine and appealing. He picked up his bag and set it down inside the door. Cass clenched her toes to keep from stepping back. "There was a woman with a grocery cart that was giving her trouble. She let me in on her way out."

"Mrs. Yan." Obviously, the tenants needed a refresher reminder when it came to letting strangers into Temple House. Nothing about Mitch's appearance screamed law enforcement, let alone FBI. He shouldn't have been let in. "This ... thing I'm working on, it's going to take a while, so you can take your time with him." She offered a trembling smile. "Seriously. Just ... I'll see you when you get back."

"Okay." That frown remained. "How about I take your—"

She closed the door in his face.

"Key."

Only when she'd snapped the three locks back in place did the tight band around her chest ease. She waited, forehead pressed against the door.

"Okay, boy," Mitch said to Elliot on the other side of the metal door. "I guess I've been given my first marching order. Let's you and me take a walk, huh? Just like old times."

Cass turned her head so she could peer out the peephole. Her insides did a bit of a flip when Mitch looked back at the closed door. How had he gotten *more* handsome? She squeezed her eyes shut, unable to continue looking at him.

It still made sense for him to be here; for her to have called him. Professionally, at least. Reminding herself of that acted as a tether to reality. She had to keep that in mind in order to continue to think straight.

But personally? She shook out her suddenly stiff hands.

Work. She needed to work.

Her hands shook as she grabbed her cell phone, scrolled through her library of music before landing on her go-focus music, *Clair du Lune* by Debussy.

The instant the piano centric tune started playing over the built-in speakers, the band around her chest loosened. She breathed in, shaky at first, then out.

*In … two, three, four. Hold, two, three, four. Out, two, three …*

She took deliberate steps to her desk, sat behind her desktop and reminded herself that this was her safe place. This was where she belonged. Yes, Mitch was back. It was just a fact now. One she needed to move past and accept.

She could do that. She'd done far more difficult things.

Hadn't she?

Her screen blinked to life and she quickly clicked on Nox's custom built, secured email system.

Three new messages waited for her, two of which she'd been expecting from attorneys she'd recently sent lab results and analyses to. But the third, dated just five minutes ago, was from Nox and read, "Recommended upgrades to VR program."

"Dammit, Nox. I bet you weren't even out of the lobby before you sent this."

Cass clicked on the email. The screen blinked, the expected website popped up, then it seemed to refresh … and redirect. Her screen blacked out, then blinked back on. The background was blurred.

A man shifted into view. Polished. Presentable. Disturbingly good looking. All in cool contrast against the intense, dark, dead eyes in the face that filled the screen.

Cass leapt up. Her chair crashed into the cabinet behind her.

She stared at the screen, unable to blink. Unable to move.

"Hello, Cassia."

Her head spun. Her ears roared.

He was in one of the most secure prisons in the country. On lockdown twenty-two hours of every day.

This. Wasn't. Possible.

And yet …

She held her breath as Jonathan Whittaker sat down. He leaned in and offered that slow, disarming smile that had lured numerous victims into his and his brother's deadly, torturous trap.

"It's almost time." He touched a finger to the camera and trailed it down the screen as if caressing her skin. "Can't wait to see you."

The screen flashed once, as if a picture had been taken.

Her monitor went black.

# CHAPTER TWO

ALL in all, Mitch thought as he led Elliot down the stairs, the re-union with Cassia hadn't gone ... too badly.

*Well*, he grimaced, *not as badly as it could have.* Whatever hope he'd had that he wouldn't see shadows in her eyes had been dashed the instant she'd opened the door.

Seeing her again erased the four years between them. For him, at least.

Her physical appearance had changed. She'd darkened her hair and added burgundy streaks. Her brown eyes were filled with the past, her skin missing that appealing tint of pink that popped on her cheeks when she smiled. Her face was makeup free and, other than small diamond earrings, she wore no jewelry—probably, he remind-ed himself, because she constantly had her hands in earth, a machine, or attached to a keyboard. Her curves on the other hand? Her curves were definitely ... curvier. His fingers itched to explore the new-to-him terrain and commit her flesh to memory once more.

As if reading his mind, his arms ached in need to hold her, to feel her wrap around him again. To fold into him as if she never wanted to step away. He'd done everything he could think to put Cassia and his feelings for her in the past, but hearing her voice again had proven beyond a shadow of doubt that doing so was not going to be possible.

As for Cassia's reaction to him?

He might not be a profiler any longer, but he recognized the ghostly presence of trauma when it stared him straight in the eyes.

Trauma that had left a Grand-Canyon-sized gap between them.

"At least you're happy to see me." When Mitch glanced down at Elliot, he found the dog gazing up at him with a combination of glee, anticipation, and concern. Maybe the concern was projection on Mitch's part, but Elliot looked to Cassia's apartment as if part of him thought they should go back. "I don't think that's a good idea, bud."

Cassia had shut that door as firmly as if she'd been locking up Fort Knox. Her face had drained of color to the point she blended with the ivory paint of the hallway walls. Each flip of the lock had echoed like a gunshot in his ears.

"Would that you could speak, my old friend," Mitch murmured as they rounded the landing and headed down to the lobby. He'd had a lot of questions about Cassia even before he'd gotten on that plane. Questions he honestly hadn't allowed himself to entertain. But now that he'd seen her?

Anxiety curved its sharpened talons around the control he'd spent years learning to hone.

Now he had even more.

The spinning that felt like a tornado in his chest nearly pitched him off balance, but focusing on Elliot and the pooch's clear determination to breathe fresh air—and relieve his bladder—gave Mitch a respite.

The last time he'd seen Cassia, Mitch had watched her climb into the back of an NYPD patrol car designated to drive her to the airport for her flight—her move—to California. He thought of that day a lot. More than was healthy. But he'd kept the most important promise he'd made to himself.

He hadn't left anything unspoken. He'd told her, flat out, if she ever needed anything, to call and he'd be there.

At the time, the blank, haunted look on her face in response convinced him she'd never take him up on the offer.

Which meant the level of shit she currently found herself in must be seriously deep.

Still. She'd heard him. Better yet, she'd believed him.

She'd called.

He'd take that as a win.

Mitch wrapped his hand more securely around the leash and rounded the landing to the lobby.

Finding the man from the stairs waiting for him at the bottom, arms folded over his weight-lifting-defined chest and looking like a soldier on sentry duty was the least surprising thing to happen to Mitch in months.

"Blake, right?" His initial impression held. Definitely military. Dark cargo pants, dark shirt. Neat haircut and a trimmed beard that gave Mitch momentary coiffing envy. Building manager by title, Mitch reminded himself. Friend by circumstance. "Mitch Keaton." He held out his free hand. "Cassia and I used to—"

"You don't need to explain." Blake accepted the greeting as Elliot stepped forward and pushed his nose into Blake's palm. "She trusts you with Elliot. Tells me everything I need to know. I saw Mrs. Yan let you in."

"Will she be given demerits?" It was, Mitch thought, a poor attempt at humor. "Sorry. I've been on three flights in the past four days. I'm punchy stupid." Even as he said it his body drained like a cell phone with its brightness turned up too high. "Cassia asked me to walk Elliot since she has work to do."

Blake's expression didn't shift.

"What branch did you serve in?" Mitch offered a verbal olive branch.

Blake arched a brow. "Naval intelligence."

"The Navy? Really?"

Blake merely stared. "Coffee?" He walked off before Mitch could answer.

Mitch and Elliot followed Blake across the lobby decorated with Hollywood highlights ranging from intimate, flash of the moments between the likes of Bogart and Greenstreet, Garland and Kelly, Brando and Gardner. It was, Mitch thought, a bit like walking through a museum of the Hollywood greats. He nearly tripped over his own feet when he caught sight of a shadow box containing an actual Maltese Falcon.

"It's real," Blake said before Mitch could ask. "It's not one of the lead ones, though. It's plaster. Everything in Temple house is part of Moxie's personal collection and every item has been authenticated."

"Moxie …Temple? Moxie Temple owns this place?" He'd grown up watching replays of the Sally Tate movies, entertaining murder mysteries featuring the spunky, independent woman working in a factory during WWII. His grandmother had adored those films and by extension so had Mitch. It made sense of course, considering the apartment building's name.

"Moxie and her great niece own Temple House."

"Riley." The name had been part of the digital reports Paul Flynn emailed to Mitch the day after Cassia had called. Scattered puzzle pieces slipped into place. "The paparazzo." The woman who had started the whole picture kerfuffle.

"Former," Blake said as he stepped behind the expansive bar at the far end of the lobby. "Riley does private work now. She lost the taste for the other last Christmas."

When her penchant for lost film nearly got her killed, Mitch thought. Yeah, he imagined that would do it.

"I'll get you set up with an access code for the front door," Blake said in a way that sent a bit of a chill racing down Mitch's spine. "Security's a big deal around here. Especially these days." He motioned behind Mitch to a pair of twenty-something women making their way down the stairs, arms loaded with boxes.

"Only two more loads to go," one of the women called to Blake as they passed. "We'll be out of your hair soon."

"Take your time," Blake reassured her. "Riley hasn't even advertised for new tenants yet. Let me know if you want help."

"We will," the other woman said with a tight smile before they elbowed their way out the front door.

The apartment building struck Mitch as a definite throwback to when hotels and apartment buildings were destinations unto themselves. Rich attention had been paid to architectural interest and design. It seemed a bit of a mish mash of styles including Art Deco and California chic. But there was an instant comfort he found appealing along with a sense of history that called to his classic Hollywood enchanted heart. So much more character than his barrack-style house in Virginia. "You get a lot of turnover here?"

"They're the second tenants to move out since I've been here." Blake set the state-of-the-art coffee machine to brewing. "Estie just got a part on a TV show shooting in Vancouver, so she and Heather are northward bound."

"Another Hollywood success story, then." The addict-triggering aroma of freshly brewed caffeine drifted into the air and filled Mitch with a bit of promise. The airplane coffee had been straight up terrible and couldn't have caffeinated a flea.

"Hope so." Blake busied himself beneath countless bottles of alcohol lining shelves locked behind gold wired doors.

Elliot whined as if reminding Mitch he was still there. "Best make it in one of the to-go cups," he added and cast an apologetic look at the dog.

"Will do," Blake said.

So." Mitch leaned an arm on the bar. "How does a former Naval Intelligence officer become a building manager in Hollywood?"

"Luck." Blake met his gaze in the mirror over the bar. He shook his head, a bemused smile quirking his lips at Mitch's surprise. "Defying expectations is a hobby. How do you take it?"

Why did Mitch feel as if this were some kind of test? "Straight." Like the Scotch he'd been too fond of for too long. "So." He waited until Blake set the filled cup in front of him. "You and Cassia."

Blake didn't even blink. "Me and Cassia what?"

Mitch didn't have time to formulate an answer before the sound of racing footsteps pounded down the stairs had him turning around. A trio of children seemed to move in well-rehearsed choreography as they tumbled around one another.

"Come on, Addie! Trade chores with me." A boy aged somewhere around ten wearing khaki chinos and an almost too small blue blazer embroidered with a badge identifying him as a student of Summercrest Academy whined in desperation. "I hate doing the dishes."

"So do I!" One of the girls shot back.

She was younger than the boy, by a few years at least. Smaller and slighter, too. Her own version of the Academy's uniform featured what he'd heard referred to as a skort—half shorts, half skirt in the same blue as her blazer. Her strawberry blonde hair was arranged in a geometric pattern of braids and knots merging into a single rope down her back. Prim and proper, Mitch's mother would have said.

"We trade next week, Lucas. It's on the schedule."

"I can help with your chores."

Mitch recognized the second girl immediately from the photos in the files. Keeley Reynolds, daughter of Mabel Reynolds. Mitch could see Mabel in Keeley's round face, right down to the glimmer of mischief in her bright eyes. From what Mitch had read about Mabel, the part-time record-keeper had spent the last eight years of her life not only as a volunteer helping victims of violence, but making herself a huge pain in the ass for Los Angeles law enforcement where her sister's long-ago disappearance was concerned.

Keeley wore the same uniform as Addie, but where Addie wore plain, practical white sneakers, Keeley wore bright pink tennis shoes Mitch suspected weren't on any approved uniform list on the planet. Either that or Summercrest Academy was quite … lenient.

"You're our guest, Kee," Addie said in such a grown-up voice Mitch wondered if she was projecting her adult self from the future. "Guests don't do chores. Aunt Sutton said so."

Keeley didn't look convinced. "But—"

"I'll let you play my video games if we trade now," Lucas bolstered his offer to his sister.

Mitch bit his cheek so as not to grin at the temptation crossing Addie's face.

"For how long?"

Mitch couldn't recall ever hearing someone so young voice so much suspicious doubt.

"An hour," Lucas offered.

Addie rolled her eyes. "You have swim practice after school, and I have chess club. We won't get home until late and Aunt Sutton doesn't let us use screens after six. Try again."

"Awwww, man." Lucas clomped his way over to Blake as the building manager rounded the counter, pulling his cell phone out of his back pocket. "Aunt Sutton said to check with you about an update to our keychains." He offered Blake a mock salute before handing over a small plastic lion on a short chain. Addie and Keeley lined up behind him.

"She's working out a new recipe and needs peace and quiet," Addie told Blake with a wary eye pinned on Mitch's hold on Elliot. "Who are you?"

"I'm Mitch," Mitch responded easily, appreciating her distrust.

"Mitch is an old friend of Cassia's," Blake said. "He's taking Elliot for a walk."

"We should go get Barksy," Keeley suggested. "They can have another playdate!"

Addie's eyes narrowed in disapproval. "Then we'd be late for school."

"So?" Keeley didn't seem offended at the idea.

Blake tapped open an app on his phone. "Tell your aunt peace and quiet is overrated."

Mitch moved just enough to be able to see the app Blake was working with. He immediately recognized the prototype tracking system, a joint venture between the military and federal law enforcement that had been under development for the past few years. He hadn't heard anything about it being made available to the general public.

He watched Blake send an update to Lucas's lion. The lion's plastic eyes blinked once before going dark again.

"Okay." Blake tapped his phone a few more times and handed the lion back. "Good to go, Lucas. Keep it close. Addie?"

"It's here." She tugged on the small plastic kitty clipped through one of her blazer's buttonholes. She wasn't quite as ebullient and excitable as her brother and, to Mitch's eyes, appeared far more cautious.

"Got you. And Keeley."

She unclipped a purple octopus from her own jacket. "This saved my mom's life," Keeley told Mitch. "We found where the bad man took her because she had it."

"That's … great." Mitch didn't know what else to say. He imagined Mabel's abduction had caused a fair amount of trauma for the girl, but he didn't see a trace of it looking at her. That told him she had a really good support system in place.

Another few seconds and the octopus was back on Keeley's jacket.

"Should be good through the weekend. Hit me up on Monday for another check, yeah?" Blake instructed them. "See you all when you get home from school."

"Okay!" Lucas yelled before spinning on his heel and racing back to the stairs, Keeley right on his heels. Addie followed at a slower pace as she looked over her shoulder at them.

"Cute kids." Mitch said when Blake faced him again. "You're good with them."

"They make it easy." Something in the other man's eyes told Mitch he'd hit a nerve. "Addie and Lucas live with their aunt on the first floor. Keeley is—"

"Mabel Reynold's daughter," Mitch finished for him. "I got the rundown from Paul Flynn."

Blake's eyes sharpened. "Did you?"

He'd bet Blake was syphoning through whatever else Mitch might have been made privy to, which meant a change in subject was needed.

"How'd you get your hands on HawkEye?" Mitch asked. "Last I heard, it was still in testing."

"Connections," Blake said. "And necessity. I called in a few favors when Mabel was threatened."

"From what I read, it's a good thing you did. So are Addie, Lucas, and Keeley part of field tests now?"

Blake simply blinked. "Something like that."

Right. Small talk it was then. "How many residents live in Temple House?" Mitch asked. If he wasn't going to get details about one thing, he'd ask about others.

"We have twenty-two apartments." Blake's tone shifted to a less guarded one. "Thirty-six tenants all together, not including pets. Well, by the end of the day it'll be thirty-four." He glanced toward the stairs.

Elliot whined.

"You'd best get him to the park," Blake told him as he headed off. "Buzz the manager button on the pad outside when you get back and I'll get you set up with that personalized entry code."

"That would be great." Good to know others understood he'd be around for a while. "Thanks." Mitch toasted him with the coffee cup. "And for this."

"You bet."

Mitch looked down at Elliot after Blake had gone. The dog quirked his head as if doubtful he might actually get his walk.

"Okay, enough delays. Here we go, boy."

The flood of people Mitch had seen in the lobby upon his arrival had slowed to a trickle. He held the door open for Estie and Heather upon their return and they offered him a passing smile.

Mitch forced himself to walk slowly and take in the cool air of the late March morning.

It wasn't his first time in Los Angeles, but this time he might have the chance to see something other than the inside of the local FBI office building. On the few cases he'd worked in LA while a field agent, none had allowed for any kind of appreciation of the city or, heaven forbid, a day of sightseeing.

In a lot of ways, this Los Angeles neighborhood reminded him of where he'd lived in New York. The mish mash of various size buildings, businesses, residences along with mom-and-pop shops intermingled with the show-offy aspect of California's Mecca of movie making and stardom.

Elliot might have flunked out of cadaver school, but he must have excelled at obedience training. The Retriever seemed content to saunter alongside him, stopping easily when Mitch did but also taking his own lead to stop and sniff the tree trunks and bushes along the path to the dog park.

Mitch had been so amped up during and after his last flight, wondering what seeing Cassia again after all this time might entail, that it was only now he felt as if he could breathe. Not completely. He hadn't done that for four years. But the energy felt different here. Maybe, he thought, because he'd finally been presented with the opportunity for closure.

Mitch rolled his eyes. As if there was such a thing.

After reading Paul Flynn's abridged report detailing the burial site Mitch had been asked to help supervise, Mitch was stymied as to why his expertise was needed. From what he read about the setup and planned exhumations and recovery, Cassia had been handling everything perfectly fine, even if she wasn't on the premises. In his experience, the more specialists assigned to the case the more room there was for contradictory testimony, not to mention a potential battle of egos.

No one, especially Mitch, was on the same level as Cassia when it came to forensics, but then it wasn't his forensics ability she'd been interested in, was it? It was more his continued thread-bare connection to the FBI. He'd found it impossible not to keep up with her professionally, especially after his career shift. Whoever it was calling her abilities and reputation into question was either straight up stupid or looking for a fight they were never going to win. He wasn't anyone's puppet and if it came down to a choice between his career and Cassia …?

He swallowed the bile-tinged guilt that rose whenever he stepped a little too close to memory lane. There had to be more going on out here if his assistance was being requested.

And it had to be pretty big to have Cassia herself do the requesting.

The long city block eventually led him to the black wrought iron gated dog park. With its well-manicured grass acting as a wide-open space for over-energized canines. It was larger than Mitch originally thought, taking up a good portion of what a building might. The back corner boasted a continually running fountain low enough to the ground for even the smallest of dogs to partake in with the landscaping so canine friendly he imagined most pooches wouldn't want to leave.

He unlatched the gate that squeaked when he pushed it open. Two other dogs, a puffy Pomeranian and ragamuffin mutt, played an excited game of keep the ball away from one another while their owners had their faces stuck in their cell phones.

Elliot whined again, just loud enough for Mitch to quickly un-hook his lead. The dog took off and immediately relieved himself on the base of a large Black Oak. Mitch stood where he was for a good long while, drinking his coffee, enjoying the morning breeze. Pushing his mind forward rather than sinking into the past.

He nodded in greeting as the two dog owners collected their pets and quickly made their way out of the park.

Poor Elliot looked a bit forlorn at being left alone and bounded back to Mitch, dark eyes filled with expectation. At first, he lamented not having anything to toss for Cassia's dog to play with, but he quickly located a branch on the ground that would do the job.

When Mitch set it to soaring, Elliot hopped into the air before bounding after it.

They were on their sixth round when the gate squeaked. Mitch turned to the woman standing just inside the gate, hand wrapped securely around the leash of a grey dog that clearly only had eyes for Elliot.

It wasn't until Mitch saw the three kids behind the curvaceous, sandy-blonde-haired woman that he realized this must be their Aunt Sutton. Given the curiosity-tinged suspicion in her brown-eyed gaze, she'd come here for a purpose. He felt pretty certain that purpose was him.

She wore comfortable, casual business clothes with a name badge on her shirt denoting her position as lead nutritionist at The Golden Age Retirement Home.

The guarded expression on her face reminded him instantly of the one worn by her niece Addie earlier.

Elliot immediately forgot all about their stick and fetch game and trotted over to the dog as Sutton unclipped the leash.

"Okay, Barksy." She patted him on the rear and the dog shot off, dodging around Elliot as the two scooted over and around one another. "Keep an eye on him, okay?" She told the kids. "We're leaving in ten minutes!" She approached, wariness giving way to borderline acceptance. "Hi. I'm Sutton O'Hara." She didn't offer her hand. "I hear you're a friend of Cass's."

Was that so difficult believe? Mitch approached but kept some distance between them. "Mitch Keaton. Cassia and I worked together in New York a while back."

"Did you?" Doubt mingled with surprise. The sun caught the gold highlights in her light brown hair. "Funny. She's never mentioned you."

Mitch would have been surprised if she had. "She called me last week. Said she could use my help with a case she's been working on. The Burial Boule—"

"I wouldn't use that phrase around here." Sutton cut him off. "It's just crass. Not to mention disrespectful."

"Noted." And agreed. Mitch would have apologized except for the fact that Paul Flynn had used that reference in his email. Probably because it made the case more searchable online when Mitch did some additional digging. He distracted himself for a moment with the dogs. "Barksy and Elliot seem well acquainted."

"They should be," Sutton said. "They're best friends. Did, um,"—she tucked her hair behind her ear after a breeze picked up—"Cass ask you to take him for a walk?"

"Yeah. She was on her way out when I got here, said she had some work she needed to finish." As he spoke, he saw confusion rise in Sutton's brown eyes. "What?" What had he said wrong? "What's that look for?"

"Sorry. It's taking some getting used to." At his blank expression, she went on. "She's only just started leaving her apartment again." A delivery van backfired as it drove past. Sutton jumped. She pressed a hand against her heart but quickly gathered herself. "Did she seem okay? I mean … was Cass—?"

"I'd say finding me on her doorstep was definitely a surprise." Despite the fact she should have been expecting him.

"I'll bet it was," Sutton said slowly as she pulled out her phone. "Lucas! Addie! Kee! Let's go, please! Sorry." She avoided Mitch's gaze as she waited for her call to connect. "I just want to check … dammit."

Mitch frowned. "What's wrong?"

"Cass isn't picking up. Now, guys!" The tone shift had not only the kids running, Barksy right on their heels, but Mitch calling for Elliot as well.

"I don't under—" But Sutton was already headed back to Temple House. He quickly clipped the lead back to Elliot's collar.

Dread and uncertainty tumbled around one another in Mitch's chest as he followed. He grabbed the door from Sutton the second she keyed in her code and it popped open. He gestured Addie and Lucas inside before he stepped in.

"Are you going to tell me what's going on?" Mitch asked in a low voice, but Sutton only shook her head.

"Blake!" She called the second their feet hit the lobby.

The building manager appeared immediately from around the corner. "Yeah."

"Cass isn't answering her phone." She swung on Mitch. "She was in there when you left, right?"

"Yeah."

Blake barely glanced at Mitch before he shifted into action, taking the stairs two at a time ahead of them.

*What on earth is going on?*

"Lucas, Addie, go back to the apartment please," Sutton said to the children. "Wait for me there."

"But we're going to be late for school," Addie said, her brows knitting.

"I know, but I need to check on your Aunt Cass." She pushed them ahead of her up the stairs and handed off the leash. "Keeley, take Barksy with you."

"Should they take Elliot as well?" Mitch suggested as the kids ran ahead of them.

"No." Sutton shook her head. "I think we're going to need him." She rifled through her keys as they made their way upstairs. "Is she answering?" She asked Blake as they reached the landing on the second floor.

"No."

"I've got the key." Sutton handed it over but when Blake inserted the key into the deadbolt and unlocked it, the door still didn't budge.

"She's engaged all the locks." Blake looked over Sutton's head to Mitch. "We can't get in."

# CHAPTER THREE

HE'D found her.

Somehow, some way. He'd found her.

"Keys. Painting. Mirror. Hook." Cass pressed a hand against her chest, struggling to draw in breath that refused to cooperate. She'd almost made it to the hallway before her legs went weak and she dropped to the floor. The images returned, flashing, a kind of film-strip of jagged memories cutting through her mind against the continuous splashes of red.

What was happening? Why … how had Whittaker gained access to her email? How did he *know*?!

She shivered so hard her teeth hurt.

She was cold. So cold.

"Keys." She pushed out the air, dug her fingers into the wood flooring. "Painting." She dragged her gaze from object to object. Her nails scraped into splinters that made her wince. Just a little further … the door wasn't that far away.

And yet it felt as if it would take her years to reach it.

Her body froze at the mere idea of touching that door. She lost track of the minutes, time folding in on itself as she tried to regain any semblance of focus or control.

"Mirror." She had to force herself to move her eyes to look at the mirror across from her. "Hook." The hook containing Elliot's walking paraphernalia. In the distance she heard the humming and buzzing of her machines, sounds that normally brought her comfort. "Keys." There they were. Five useless sets of keys that, for the most part, had been gathering dust for years. Keys that gave her access to her friends' apartment and the private roof. "Painting." The ethereal image of a woman in white walking down a moonlit path in the darkness. The woman she desperately wanted to be. "Mirror." Hanging too high to see her own reflection. Thank God. She inhaled as hard as she could and … focused. "Hook."

Finally. The pressure released. Not completely, but enough for her to drag in enough oxygen to reignite her brain.

Her hands trembled as she tried to focus on the sounds she could identify. The beeping and gentle whine of her computers. The click-click-click of a program attempting to reboot. The scanners humming in an unpredictable tune.

And there. Beneath it all. Beneath the ringing in her ears …

Her cell phone rang again.

Cass turned her head, feeling as if she were caught in the undertow of a full moon tide. Her heart continued to race, and her skin went clammy even as she struggled through the disorientation and abject urge to run away. Except there was no running. He'd found her. From his cell in a maximum locked down prison, Whittaker had found her.

There had been no hiding after all.

There was no way to push her arms and legs into doing anything beyond being pulled into her body like a turtle pulled into its shell.

She blinked, again and again, a kind of staccato reboot one of her therapists had recommended. They had suggested she should think of herself as a computer that simply needed restarting when one of the attacks hit. The idea would have made Cass laugh had she the energy. Anger surged around the periphery of her panic. She'd almost, *almost* forgotten what this felt like and she couldn't fathom ever having a panic attack this bad. It shouldn't be happening! She should be beyond this. Except …

The image of Mitch shifted in front of the spatters of blood she couldn't erase from her mind. *Mitch.* He'd been the only positive thing to be found in those nightmare weeks. "Fucking bad luck," she whispered on a sob. He'd shown up today. Today of all days. What were the odds …?

She gasped, sat up straighter as the thought lodged in her mind like a thorn.

*What were the odds?*

Tears filled her eyes. Aggravated tears filled with pent up rage that never had a place to go. She could not, would not go back! Maybe … she blinked again, reason crashing through the residual fog. Maybe she'd imagined the email. The video. Maybe her mind had finally turned on her in order to drive her over the edge of control.

Maybe she was finally losing her mind.

None of that was logical and it was logic she desperately clung to. Even as she heard the barely-there strains of screams and music she'd been forced to listen to in those endless, trapped hours.

Something was broken inside of her. Something she began to fear she could never, ever fix.

"Keys." She took an extra beat and blew out a breath. Drew it back in. "Painting." Another inhale. Another exhale. The terror cracked along the edges. "Mirror." The glass shimmered against her blurry vision. "Hook."

Someone banged on the door.

She jumped. Her body tensed so hard and fast she thought her bones might snap. Hands pulled in tight against her chest, she turned her head to the locks she'd bolted back in place.

"Cass! Cass! You need to open the door!"

Sutton! Sutton was someone safe. Sutton was … safe.

A sob caught in the back of her throat as she pushed herself over and onto her knees.

Unfolding her arms, she dropped her hands to the floor, gripped the wood planks with her barely-there nails until she felt another splinter wedge beneath her skin.

The door was only inches away, mere inches and yet the distance felt as if a marathon lay before her.

"Cass, we need to know you're okay. Please. Either answer your phone or open the door."

There were other voices mingling with Sutton's. Cass could hear that now. But it was the solitary bark from Elliot that finally broke through the fog.

She dragged herself forward, reached up with one hand and grasped the doorknob.

Her hand went numb as she pulled herself up. Every cell in her body screamed in protest. But she pushed through and slowly unlatched the three bolts preventing anyone from stepping inside her zone of safety.

No sooner had she unlocked the last one than the door burst opened.

She flew back, that sob escaping her control as she huddled against the wall, hands clasped at her mouth as the warmth of blood drained from her face.

"Cass." Sutton moved into her line of vision. Sutton with her girl-next-door beauty and calm demeanor. Sutton who rested gentle hands on Cass's upper arms and guided her away from the door, back into the safe haven of the home Cass had built for herself.

The fact there was no sympathy on her friend's face, only concern and determination, helped shatter the last vestiges of terror and break her free of the attack. She was not going to give in and lose what progress she'd made.

Was she?

"Breathe, honey. Come on. You know what to do. Breathe in." Sutton did this with her as together they made their way to the sunken living room in the center of the apartment. "Breathe out. That's it."

"Close it," she whispered to her friend. "Close the door."

Sutton pivoted Cass and gently pushed her into the cushions. Only when Cass heard the gentle click of the door closing did her lungs begin to open up again. Dammit!

Elliot pressed his head up and into her belly, his soft whine of worry bringing a new rush of tears to Cass's eyes. "I'm sorry," she managed, hating, loathing the idea she was causing anyone—even her dog—concern. "I couldn't stop it. I couldn't—" Her breath was shaky when she tried to inhale again.

"It's okay." Sutton sat beside her. "Can one of you get her some water, please?"

Cass squeezed her eyes shut, but not fast enough to avoid the sight of Mitch stepping into her sanctuary. Alarm bells clanged, inaudible to anyone other than her.

She immediately chastised herself. It wasn't Mitch.

This wasn't his fault. It wasn't his presence that caused this.

But the memories he brought with him?

She should have been ready. She should have prepared. She should have realized …

She covered her eyes with one hand, unable to stop the tears from escaping. She hated this so much!

"Tell me what I can do." Mitch's voice sounded like an echo from the past as Blake stepped down to push a glass of water into Cass's hand.

"Nothing. P-panic attack," Cass managed as she dropped her shaking hand onto Sutton's leg. "I'm okay." Or she would be. Even now she could feel exhaustion creeping up on her, but she slapped it back as hard as she could. She would not surrender to the fear. Not today. Not ever. "I'm okay." She was trying to convince herself as much as she was the others. Water sloshed over the rim of her glass, but she drank and sank her free hand into the thick coat of Elliot's fur. "I'm okay, boy."

"I'm not so sure," Sutton murmured. "You haven't had one this bad in a while."

"It's been that kind of day." Out of the corner of her eye, she saw Mitch wince, as if her words had hit a easy-to-find target. She had no energy to apologize or to explain, not only because she knew a barrage of questions would follow, but because she'd see the one thing she'd never be able to withstand.

Pity in the eyes of the man she'd loved.

"This would be why you're here," Cass said and earned a spark of anger instead of sympathy from Mitch. "My state of mind where this case is concerned has been called into question. They want … someone else involved. In case I tip completely out of my rocking chair and blow up the case."

Sutton squeezed her hand. "I don't think that's—"

"That's the short explanation." She could feel the adrenaline draining and that damned fog of depression descending. "I don't have the mental bandwidth to deal with the long version at the moment."

"What can I do?" Mitch's query was asked in a quiet voice Cass didn't recognize. Maybe that was a good thing considering she was questioning every thought that passed through her mind at the moment.

*Can't wait to see you.*

Cass's stomach rolled as she choked back bile. She didn't know what terrified her more: seeing Whittaker's face again.

Or the idea she'd imagined it.

Her phone rang again. She glanced at the screen with something akin to fear surging through her system, but she pushed it down and snatched up her cell. She answered the call from Linnea as if it were a lifeline to sanity.

"Yeah, Linnea."

"Whoa. Who pulled out your plug?" Linnea's surprised sarcasm almost, *almost*, made Cass smile.

"Is there an update?" Cass didn't have to see a video to know her co-worker was frowning. "Are the police still there?"

"Are the police still where?" Mitch asked.

Cass turned her back on him.

"Still taking statements and examining the scene," Linnea said. "Feels like they're never going to leave."

Linnea wasn't far off. Cass was well-aware how long it could take law enforcement to clear a scene and release it. And there was a lot of scene up in the hills to cover.

"Were you able to talk to the higher-ups about getting us some more feet on the ground?" Linnea asked. "Cleanup is going to be a bigger job than we thought."

"I haven't had a chance to call yet." Cass honestly didn't want the details. She glanced over her shoulder. "Our federal liaison just got into town," she said. "I'll bring him up to speed and send him your way. It's the best I can do today." Especially when she wasn't convinced she could put together a coherent sentence. "But it should free you up to be able to get back into the lab."

"Okay, that sounds good, actually. Thanks. I'll touch base again at our usual conference call time. Hey, get some rest, yeah?" Linnea said with concern in her voice. "You sound wiped."

Cass hung up, closed her eyes briefly. She tilted her head from side to side, trying to get rid of the kinks that had formed in her neck.

"There was a break in at the site overnight." She mentally reached for the stability of work and held on tight. "Police are just finishing up, but the place is a mess." She turned on the sofa to look at Mitch. "Last week the higher ups told Paul they no longer have confidence that I can lead from … here." She waved her hand around her apartment. "I told Paul I could bring in someone with forensics experience at the FBI to act as a kind of surrogate on site. Someone," she added slowly, deliberately as she finally met Mitch's gaze. "I can trust."

His brows lifted slightly, but what that meant she couldn't be sure. Surprised or not, disbelieving or not, he was listening. Right now, that was all she needed.

"Since then, my lead forensic anthropologist has had to shift from examination and testing at the lab to being at the site. Apparently, my long-standing system of observing and directing over video isn't going to cut it. I need Linnea back doing what she does best." No one made evidence sing better than Linnea. "Which means I need you up there."

"I would have thought having Linnea involved would have mitigated you having to call me," Mitch said. "She's one of the best. Same as you."

An odd bubble of relief popped in her chest. "You know her?"

"We met at a forensics conference a few years back. We're friendly." He nodded as if anticipating her next question. "I can work with her, no problem."

"Good." Now for the hard part. "What do you need to—?"

"Exact location and an Uber," Mitch cut her off. "It'll give me a chance to get a lay of the land. So to speak."

"I'm going to text Quinn—let him know what's going on. Detective Quinn Burton," she explained to Mitch. "He's working—"

"He's the detective who investigated the attack on Riley Temple. And Eva Hudson's and Mabel Reynolds's disappearance. I've memorized pretty much Paul Flynn's entire report. Where is Flynn, by the way?"

"New York, ironically enough," Cass said. "He and Mabel went back for a few days to get his apartment listed. He thought Mabel could use a change of scenery." The after-effects of her abduction were taking their time abating. "Keeley said they'd be back by Sunday, so I'd rather you not bother him about the break in," Cass said. "There's nothing he can do. No point in ruining their trip." Mitch didn't respond, but she recognized the way he was chewing on the inside of his cheek. "You don't agree?"

"You're in charge. It's not my place to argue. If I was in his shoes and got back to hear—"

"He can get mad at me, then." Cass changed the subject. "Wait. Why do you need an Uber? The agency didn't arrange a car for you?"

Mitch glanced away. "Must have slipped their mind."

"Well, arrange for one," she told him. "I'd rather not have my right hand reliant on rideshares."

"Yeah," he said quickly. "I'll take care of it."

"I'll drive you up now." Blake's deep voice broke the growing tension and reminded Cass they weren't alone. "I'd like to see what setup the security company had in place that allowed for the break-in to happen." He shifted unreadable eyes to Cass. "I'd be happy to up my recommendations if Axiom Security is no longer going to be involved. Since they dismissed my earlier suggestions about improvements. The mayor's office might be more amenable to your recommendations now."

"That's what we're hoping. Thanks, Blake." Nerves made her stomach tremble, enough to make her worry about rejecting the cake she'd eaten earlier but she and Mitch needed to address the flying pachyderm in the room. "We'll talk later, okay?"

*Please don't argue with me. Not now. Not in front of …*

"Count on it."

She chose to believe he wasn't still able to read her mind. "Keep your eye out for the press, social and otherwise," she told Mitch and Blake when they turned to leave. "They're buzzing around like blow flies on a corpse. Hearing about the site being broken into is only going to invigorate their sensationalist tendencies. Doesn't help that we're working the site with a skeleton crew."

"So to speak," Sutton muttered and winced at Cass's raised brows. "Sorry. I've been hanging around Riley too much. Her sarcasm and inappropriate commentary seems to be contagious."

"We might luck out," Cass went on. "It could take a while for word to get out, but we can only move as fast as we can move. We've lost time with the IDs with Linnea being on site. Dental X-rays on the remains are top priority for when she can get back into the lab." She shifted her attention back to Mitch. "Linnea can walk you through our schedule and procedures and setup when you get there. It'll make for a long day."

"Don't worry about me," he said easily. "I can pick up takeout for when I come back for my stuff if you want."

The question unexpectedly warmed her from the inside. Some of their happiest times together had been spent in bed, gobbling up takeout in an effort to try every local hole-in-the-wall in her uptown New York neighborhood.

Their gazes locked.

In that moment, their thoughts may as well have been synchronized by memory.

"I'll bring something up." Sutton's comment broke the moment. "I've only got a half day at Golden Age, so I'll come back and cook." She looked to Mitch. "Do you have any food allergies I need to know about?"

"No." Mitch and Cass answered at the same time before Cass's cheeks went flame hot.

Sutton glanced between them, her lips twisting as if to keep from smiling. "Well, okay then."

"You're sure about this?" Cass's question to Mitch sounded more loaded than a double-barreled shotgun.

"I wouldn't have come if I wasn't sure, Cassia." The almost blank stare of his eyes left her feeling oddly chilled.

She could see hesitancy in his eyes. A tamped-down concern to what he'd witnessed when he'd walked through her front door moments before. But there was also the promise of the discussion to come. A discussion she wasn't entirely sure she was ready to have.

"Then I guess we're off." Mitch flashed another smile, but it didn't come close to reaching his eyes. "Boss."

"Boss. Please." She rolled her eyes, appreciating the good-natured ribbing and the attempt to move past that which felt insurmountable.

"Plan for a discussion on new locks for your door," Blake tossed over his shoulder. Elliot continued to nuzzle Cass's legs.

"Great." Today had been an important lesson. Locks might make her feel safer but the easily kept out the people she looked to for help.

Cass didn't move until the door closed behind them. Only then did she give in to the urge to sag back into the soft cushions of the sofa. Elliot jumped up beside her, rested his head on her stomach.

"I can call Riley and have her take the kids to school," Sutton said. "You know. If there's anything you want to talk—"

"There isn't." The response was automatic, practiced. Self-protective. She petted Elliot, surrendering to his comforting presence. "Not now. I appreciate the offer," she lied. "But there's a lot more to the situation than a simple conversation can resolve." Even with her best friend.

"He's the guy, isn't he?" Sutton sat forward, her open face a billboard of understanding and compassion. "The one you left back in New York."

"He is the guy." Cass ignored the waves of curiosity coursing off her friend. It was so tempting, the idea of surrendering herself to a good-old-fashioned confession session but there was no way Cass could see of addressing her history with Mitch without needing to talk about other … events.

*It's almost time.*

Her stomach rolled and her desperation for being left alone amplified tenfold. "Go, take the kids to school. Go to work. Cook up a storm. Don't spend the rest of the day worrying about me. I'm going to eat some of that cake you made for me and get myself back into peak capacity." She stood up when Sutton did and welcomed the quick hug of comfort her friend offered. "There's no other choice. I've got a birthday party to go to next weekend."

Sutton smiled. "I'm not going to stop worrying about you." She touched Cass's hair, the sympathy she'd no doubt been couching ever since she burst through the front door finally shining through. "No matter how hard you try to stop me. How's lasagna for tonight?"

"Depends," Cass said cautiously as Sutton pulled away and headed to the door. "Are you going hide a bunch of vegetables in it?"

"Of course I am," Sutton snort-laughed. "Getting actual nutrition into you is part of my life's work. By the way,"—she pulled open the door and faced Cass again—"don't scarf down that entire chocolate cake in one sitting, okay."

That was an odd warning. "Why?"

"Let's just say it'll up your fiber intake for a while." Sutton's eyes went Lucas-innocent wide. "Pace yourself."

Cass frowned after her, staring at the closed door, unable to decide if Sutton had been joking. Probably not. The woman took her devotion to nutrition seriously.

Then again, that could have been Sutton's attempt at breaking the last of the tension filling the now empty room.

"Guess we'll find out soon enough," Cass muttered as she grabbed the remote and, turning back to the overhead screens, began clicking through the various feeds at the burial site.

The monitors flickered, just for a second, as if caught in some kind of feedback loop.

She smacked the remote, as if that would do any good, but the pictures readjusted and settled.

Frowning, Cass turned her focus away from the past. Away from the panic attack she wanted to pretend didn't happen. Away from Mitch.

She tossed the remote onto her desk, went into the kitchen and opened her medication cabinet.

Cass stood there, fingers tensing against the wood as she stared at the lineup of bottles filled to varying levels. She could have opened her own pharmacy given the various anti-anxiety, anti-depression, anti-emotion drugs lining her shelves. Pharmacists could write masters theses on her maneuvering through the pharmaceutical industry on her quest for mental peace.

But as she scanned the labels, her brain ran through every side effect. That one made her irritable. This gave her brain fog. Another made her throw up. She snatched up the bottle on the end, the one that made her sleep. Sleep. The idea promised everything she needed, most importantly an escape from the spinning and panic that continued to circle inside of her like a cyclone. Her knuckles went white around the bottle. Her thumb inched up to touch the lid.

"No." She practically threw it back on the shelf, slammed the door shut.

Sleep might be an escape, but it was only delaying the inevitable. She could already feel the buzz of hyperactivity descending. Normally she wanted nothing more than to tune it out.

But now? Today? This moment?

She spun around and looked at her desk. At her computer. At the screen that had flashed a nightmare so terrifying it had sent her crashing into the past to a time when she hadn't been able to get out of bed. Not even to feed Elliot.

Elliot whined, walking around her legs as if trying to remind her that he was there.

"Not this time," she told herself. Told the dog. Told the universe. "He doesn't win. Not again."

She yanked open her tool drawer, pulled out a screwdriver and the small bag filled with additional tools. Returning to her desk, she hit the music app on her phone again, sending the strains of music through the speakers once more before she walked around her desk.

She shoved her desk chair away, dropped down to the ground and pulled the CPU out from under the desk, spun it around and glared at it, anger dissolving the last of the terror.

"Let's see how you got into my system, you son of a bitch."

# CHAPTER FOUR

MITCH could count on one hand the number of times he'd taken an emotional sledgehammer to the gut.

He'd been seven the first time. Barely. He'd come home from second grade to discover his mother had gone off to Vegas to live out her actual dream of being a card dealer. The second hit much later when his father died of a heart attack the week Mitch started the FBI Academy.

And the third?

His thumb tapped against his thigh, the therapy-trained auto response to stress kicking into overdrive.

The third had been finding the woman he loved encased in a glass coffin smeared with blood.

He'd convinced himself he'd never see that haunted, stricken, terrified expression on Cassia's face again and yet …

He was so damned tired of being wrong.

Mitch locked his jaw and turned his blurry attention out the window of Blake Redford's SUV. Mulholland twisted and turned its way into the Hollywood Hills, a place synonymous with the glitz and glamor of movie making. Now a place revealing the far seedier aspect of not only the business but the city itself. A city where dreams were built on the shoulders of naivete and desperation.

He powered down his window and turned his face into the early afternoon air to clear away the exhaustion and guilt-ridden cobwebs of the past.

The scent of jasmine hit first, followed by the familiar aroma of sage and other native, woody plants. One didn't think flowers and fauna where Los Angeles was concerned; they thought of style, sprawling estates, and never-ending parties attended by the "it" stars of the moment. But Mitch was old enough now, with enough miles behind him, to know beauty was often found in the smaller things. The unexpected. Not in the flashy and over the top existence so many lived.

"You didn't know, did you?" Blake broke the silence Mitch had gotten used to. "About Cass's ... situation."

"No." He'd heard rumors of course. Rumors and rumblings he'd chalked up to petty gossip and even pettier jealousy. He knew Cassia. *Knew* her. He'd been up close and very personal with a woman who personified resilience and strength. He hadn't believed ... but it seemed the rumors had barely scratched the surface of the truth.

He knew a virtual shut-in when he saw one and therefore the panic attacks didn't come as a surprise. Discovering her home looked to have been designed either by a Bond villain or Mr. Robot was one turn of events he'd ever anticipated.

Mitch had to stop the mental spiraling that threatened to drag him into inescapable depths. Nothing good waited for him down there, especially when what he needed to do was help Cassia. Professionally, he reminded himself. He was here to work, not make up for the past.

Rationally, Mitch knew he couldn't blame himself for her current state of mind or her inability to move beyond that which they'd shared, but he'd never been rational where Cassia was concerned. As evidenced by the fact he jumped on a plane due to a thirty-second phone call.

"How long has she been ...?" Mitch couldn't stop himself from asking and part of him hoped Blake wouldn't oblige him with an answer. "How long has she been like this?" He felt shitty for asking. She'd had therapy; he'd recognized some of the behaviors she displayed as coping mechanisms for severe panic attacks, but he'd bet good cold cash that panic attacks were the least of her issues.

Not with all those locks on her doors.

Jonathan Whittaker might be locked away in a maximum-security prison in Utah, but it seemed to Mitch that Cassia was the one in prison.

"As it's none of my business," Blake said slowly. "I've not asked too many questions about her situation. But since you need to know." Blake glanced at Mitch. "Cassia hasn't left Temple House since she moved in."

"But that's ... four years." The words escaped on a painful rush of air.

So much made sense now. Realizations and answers dropped into place one after another.

Her video-only presentations at forensics conferences and new technology introductions. Her lectures were pre-recorded and any Q&As were virtual. He couldn't recall the last alert he'd received about her lecturing on a college campus or attending high school career weeks, something she'd told him had always been her favorite things to do. No book signings. No personal appearances or interviews. Everything about the life she'd lived four years ago had shifted into a remote presence. Given the state of the world the last few years it wasn't entirely unusual, but ...

Her ability to connect and socialize with people had always been her biggest strength. There wasn't anyone she couldn't speak to or converse with, about pretty much anything.

That said? Other things hadn't changed one iota. Her classes were still mandatory for various degrees, certificates, and fellowships; her science and results remained unquestionable. Her testimony in dozens of criminal and civil cases continued to be unrivaled and—a majority of the time—uncontested. And her continued advancements with inventions and new forensic techniques? There were times even Quantico lagged behind in their abilities for processing and evaluating as she pushed science at a relentless forward-moving pace. Her mind had the ability to capture and store unlimited bits of information as if it were a superhuman processor.

That she'd kept up her professional pace while hiding from the world was either the saddest thing he'd ever heard or ...

More likely she was hell-bent on proving her circumstance had nothing to do with her intellect and abilities.

Yeah. He'd lay even odds on the latter.

"Cassia appears to have a solid support system at Temple House," Mitch said finally. "Sutton seems like a good friend."

"She has a lot of friends," Blake confirmed.

"Including you." He wasn't about to acknowledge the very thin sliver of jealousy stabbing at him.

Blake smirked. "Come at me with that question from any direction you want. You aren't going to get a different answer. Told you before. Cass is a friend." He shook his head slightly. "Nothing more."

Mitch would have responded, maybe even apologized, but Blake went on.

"I'm not the one you have to worry about, Mitch. Whatever she's going through today, she'll pull herself together if for no other reason than because when Laurel, Riley, and Mabel hear about Cass's episode—and, believe me, they will hear—those four will descend like a flock of furies protecting their sister. No one gets to Cass without going through them." He looked at Mitch for an extra beat. "No one."

"Consider me warned."

Blake veered left onto what at one time must have been a private road. The overgrowth had since been shoved aside rather than cut back and the collection of tire tracks left deep and wide impressions in the soil. The area was still wild though, and no doubt contained even more secrets than the graves that had been dug up here.

A uniformed officer stepped into sight, one hand held up, the other resting on the butt of his gun. His blue uniform was pristine, right down to the shiny badge on his chest. Blake shifted the car into park.

"You got your FBI badge with you?" Blake asked.

"My badge?" Anxiety prickled low in his chest as Mitch reached into his back pocket. Now wasn't the time to admit—to anyone—that he no longer possessed the magic key everyone assumed he carried. "No. But I've got my ID."

Blake stopped the car and powered down the window. "Officer."

"Road's closed." The thirty-something Black man eyed Mitch and Blake with caution. "Restricted access. You need to turn around."

"FBI Advisory Agent Mitch Keaton." Mitch flipped his Quantico ID open and leaned forward. "I'm working with the forensics team on the case."

The officer's eyes barely flickered with acknowledgement when he shifted his questioning gaze to Blake.

"I'm his driver."

The cop stepped back as a second SUV pulled up behind them.

Mitch looked over his shoulder as a tall man wearing a crisp blazer and slacks stepped out of his vehicle. With the dark Aviator glasses and a jaw of steel, he looked as if he'd just stepped off the screen of the latest hit procedural.

He turned to the cop. "Officer Yarrow."

"Detective Burton." Yarrow's voice drifted through the open window. "Sir. Officers Callahan and Myers are still on-site taking statements about the break-in. They should be done soon. Sergeant Fox and officer Tiptin left a little over fifteen minutes ago."

"Good. I was hoping to get a breakdown from someone." The new arrival stopped at Blake's door, bent down and pulled off his sunglasses, looked directly at Mitch. He was clean shaven, slightly tanned and carried himself with a self-assuredness and confidence denoting his more than a decade on the job. "Special Agent Keaton? Cass texted and said you were on your way up."

Some things never changed, Mitch thought. Cassia always, *always* did what she said. "Mitch, please, Detective."

"Quinn. Good to meet you." He shifted back to Yarrow who had relaxed his stance; his arms were well away from his weapon now. "Heard we had some visitors last night, Yarrow. Who was on duty?"

"The private team from Axiom, sir." Disapproval rang clear in Yarrow's voice. "My partner and I offered to work overtime, but—"

"But?" Mitch asked Blake under his breath.

"Police commission has stood firm on the private company taking lead on overnight security," Blake said.

"Even with overtime," Mitch wondered out loud. "Wouldn't it have been cheaper to use the LAPD?"

"Yes," Blake said without looking away from Quinn and Officer Yarrow. "It would have."

58

And with that statement what Mitch had read between the lines of Paul Flynn's report/rundown shifted into focus. There was definitely something more to the case than what had been officially released. Or that he'd been told.

"What did you see when you got here?" Burton asked the officer.

"Nothing out of the ordinary," Yarrow said. "Didn't realize anything was wrong until Dr. Crawford's team headed toward the office and saw the damage. Can't blame her for being pissed. No one should have gotten through and now they can't do their jobs as long as we're here." Yarrow's jaw tensed. "This wouldn't have happened had LAPD been in charge."

"A statement I intend to make certain my LT conveys to the commission." Quinn earned a tense smile from the younger man. "You see anyone lurking around since you've been here? Any issues with reporters or social media hounds?"

"Not that I've seen. Officer Deacon hasn't reported any sightings either. She'd have let me know."

"And she's patrolling where exactly?" Blake asked and earned a wary look in response.

"Southern perimeter that's over the hill. Only two of us per eight-hour shift."

"Doesn't make it easy for you to serve and protect, does it?" Quinn muttered. "Appreciate your feedback, officer." He gestured to the car. "They're with me."

"Yes, sir." Yarrow gave them a curt nod before walking to his vehicle and moving it out of the way so they could pass.

Quinn tapped his hand twice on the open window. "I'll follow you in, Blake."

Blake put the car back in Drive. Gravel rattled in the wheel as they moved forward. "How much do you know about the history of this place?" Blake asked.

"Besides what I've read in the files I received, not much," Mitch responded as a haunting silence pressed in. Only now did he notice that birds had stopped chirping. Even the breeze refused to venture past the tree line. "I tried to do some additional research on the way out, but the countless rabbit holes of conspiracy theories and verbal suppositions online were impossible to filter through." Still, there was a lot he felt confident in knowing. "The main building is an abandoned film production studio where Mabel Reynolds was held after being abducted by Orson Berwick a few weeks back," Mitch recited the details from memory. "This is also where Berwick murdered Eva Hudson after kidnapping her from the hospital and—if the media can be believed—dozens of other women whose bodies have since been discovered on the property. Yeah," he said with a smirk at Blake's snort of disbelief. "Don't worry. The media and I are not on friendly terms. Most of the time they could tell me the sky is blue and I'd question it." Considering Mitch still had a restraining order in effect against one obnoxious social media bloodhound who made the mistake of getting in Mitch's face after his disciplinary hearing regarding the Whittaker *incident*, he definitely had no affection for those in the profession. "What is the latest on Berwick, by the way?" Mitch asked. "Didn't see a lot of notes on him about what happened after his arrest."

"Berwick's been in solitary since he was taken into custody," Blake told him. "It'll be a year, probably more, before he's brought to trial." Blake winced as a branch caught in Mitch's open window. "*If* there's a trial."

"What makes you think there won't be?" Mitch asked.

"Experience," Blake responded.

Mitch knew a loaded answer when he heard it. Instead of pressing, he simply waited. He was good at waiting.

"Does the circle mean anything to you?" Blake finally asked.

"Circumference or diameter?" He didn't even earn a smile. "Not what you were talking about, I'm sure. Feel free to expound."

"You'll have to discuss that with Cass," Blake said. "Some of the bodies they've found are decades old. Berwick's in his forties; no way one guy off his nut is responsible for all the killings. Same goes for the Redrum twins who tried to kill Riley last Christmas," Blake said as if reasoning things out for himself. "Sorry. That's what Quinn calls the now dead Tompkin siblings. Even if they were still alive, with the nonsensical shit they were spouting at the end they wouldn't have been any help. Plus they were younger than Berwick."

"Acolytes." It was, Mitch thought, the best way to describe any of them. Holden Tompkin had thrown himself off a freeway overpass to avoid being arrested while his even more unhinged twin sister died trying to drown the aforementioned Riley Temple in an underground ceremonial pool.

Riley's impressive Temple House aside, given Mitch's views on the paparazzi, Mitch wasn't entirely sure he was looking forward to meeting the photographer who had stumbled across lost evidence that started this steel ball rolling. Sounded to him as if the woman had a penchant for finding trouble.

"Additional details beyond established facts were … sparse." Mitch paused, frowning. "The only reason I can think to hold back additional information would be concern over who might have access to official reports."

"Then you're as smart as Cass said you were." Blake made his way through the twists and turns with ease. "In a non-specific way," he added. "She just said she called someone she knew would see and understand what we do. More importantly, that you'd be someone we could trust."

It was, Mitch thought, the best ego boost he'd had in a long while.

"The most recent owner of record for the two thousand acres of property we're currently driving on comes back to a production company called Touchstone that went out of business ages ago," Blake went on.

"So this Berwick guy was what?" Mitch asked. "Some kind of psychopathic Scooby-Doo caretaker?"

Blake shrugged. "Touchstone was represented by Young & Fairbanks, a law firm with a very long history in Los Angeles. Interesting fact." He glanced over at Mitch. "One of their former attorneys is representing Orson Berwick."

"The world gets smaller every day," Mitch muttered.

"This town's borderline incestuous when it comes to their business dealings," Blake said. "You ever build one of those murder boards like you see on TV? With pictures and notes and strings connecting everything together?"

"Kind of." He preferred creating his own kind of mind map on his computer.

"You'd need a board about the size of Temple House to display all the players potentially involved with this thing," Blake said. "Or computer screens if you're Cass."

Cassia. Truth be told, as intrigued as Mitch was with the looming work, he was anxious to get back to her. He wanted, needed, to make certain she was all right. And to explore her incredible collection of machinery and equipment. Technology wise, he reminded himself quickly.

"You were up here the night Mabel Reynolds was rescued, weren't you?" Mitch asked, recalling details from the reports. "You saw Berwick."

Blake's knuckles went white around the wheel and for an instant Mitch recognized the darkness that crossed Blake's face. "We met."

Mitch understood that far better than Blake would probably be comfortable with.

"The place might look empty and innocent in the daylight," Blake said. "But you can't imagine the death that surrounds us here."

"Sure I can." There wasn't a day that passed when Mitch didn't think about death. "I appreciate the ride up."

"Like I said, ulterior motives." Blake made another turn and parked the SUV next to a muddied lime green Prius. A half-dozen other cars parked in the area had been left in such a way as to easily drive back out. "Protecting this site is vital for any possible future prosecution, not only of Berwick but anyone else he might be working with or for. We can't take any chances, especially with break-ins. Every time someone unauthorized steps foot on the property, it gives a new argument for the defense of contamination of evidence. And the second they call one piece of evidence into question, the entire case could fall apart."

"Sounds like you have some experience with that sort of thing."

Blake didn't answer.

A short distance away, the large, dilapidated ranch style structure both loomed and sagged behind six-foot panel fencing. Window glass had been smashed long ago. Stained planks and boards crisscrossed over frames, leaving huge gaps for the wind and weather to seep through. The stucco was cracked and filled with mold, with parts of it having crumbled off in chunks. Insects had infested areas that left big gaping holes in the sides of the building.

"Place looks as secure as a chicken coop." Mitch earned a nod of agreement from Blake as they climbed out of the car. "Considering how much lip service the city is paying to this case with the press, I'd have thought there would at least be barbed wire on the fence line." Not to mention more than a pair of uniformed officers on patrol during the day from a pretty far distance. Different city, same shit. The bureaucratic disconnect between results and funding—be it local, state, or federal—never ceased to frustrate him. "You know anything about this Axiom Security the city hired?"

"Word around City Hill is one of the members of the police commission pushed for them. Lots of former cops working for them."

"Kickbacks?" Mitch guessed.

"Possibly." Blake paused. "Probably."

Greed. It infected pretty much everyone at some point, didn't it?

Quinn's SUV rounded the back of Blake's car and parked nearby. He pulled off his glasses this time when he got out. "Good to meet you, Mitch." Mitch shook the offered hand. "I called Paul on the drive up," Quinn said. "I wanted to let him know what happened overnight and that you're on scene now."

"Cass didn't want him bothered," Blake mentioned.

"Yeah, well, Cass isn't the one who'll catch holy hell from our special investigator when he gets back," Quinn defended himself. "Don't worry. Paul and impulse don't live in the same universe. It's not like he jumps on a plane seconds after getting a phone call." Quinn pinned him with a look. "No offense."

"Took me a little longer than a few seconds." Even now the thought of those unending hours waiting on approval from his bosses broke his irritation meter. "But I'm not the type to wait around when someone I care about has asked for my help."

Blake's eyebrows shot up. Approval, Mitch wondered? Or surprise? Hard to tell with this guy.

"Good to know," Quinn said. "Shall we?" He gestured to the divided fence section with an open padlock that had seen better days. "I used to use one of these to lock up my bike when I was ten." He snatched the lock off the link, held it up. "You taking notes?" He asked Blake before he tossed it to the ground.

"It's why I'm here."

Mitch was more than happy to let Blake view the scene with his personal slant. It meant Mitch didn't need to pay attention to the clearly negligent way the security company had been addressing their assignment. He could focus on the job Cassia needed him to do. Which was … what exactly? He supposed he'd find out soon enough.

He saw the two uniformed officers immediately, off to the side, speaking with a group of individuals in civilian clothing wearing white badges clipped to their collars or waistbands. Behind them sat the large white evidence tent where, Mitch assumed, initial examination and bagging of evidence commenced. His initial impression was that the site had been set up efficiently and professionally, two words that definitely described Cassia.

But while the evidence team looked both irritated and frustrated, it was the pair of men wearing bright blue uniform shirts embroidered with Axiom Security over the right breast pocket that Mitch felt the vibes of anxiety. Personally, Mitch gave them a modicum of credit for staying on scene, but both looked young, inexperienced, and shell-shocked.

Not ideal qualities for private security. Especially a case of this magnitude.

Another of those oddities Mitch filed to ponder later.

He spotted a third officer walking the perimeter of the fence line erected around the entirety of the dig site. Fat lot of good that fence had done. Despite the flimsy padlock, Mitch seriously doubted anyone would have simply walked through the main gate. As incompetent as the private security company appeared to be, not even they would have taken their eyes off the primary way in.

Which meant access had to be found elsewhere.

"Command post over there?" Mitch pointed to the converted cargo trailer a good forty feet away from the back of the main structure of the production studio. Plywood boards now covered the openings where the windows had been broken.

"Yeah. Equipment storage, too." Quinn clarified. "Shared offices with the security team, something Linnea wasn't thrilled with. She's even less happy now."

"She would be," Mitch agreed. Coming into an already established forensics team that, from everything he'd heard, had been functioning perfectly fine, was always one of the trickier parts of being an FBI agent. He didn't like ruffling feathers although in his experience, most local law enforcement personnel were more than happy to accept help. Territorial fights happened far more in Hollywood scripts than they did in the real world.

Still, you never knew what you were walking in on. Knowing a friend, apart from Cassia, was part of this team definitely eased his mind.

"The team is working mainly out of the evidence processing tent and cold storage," Quinn said. "Transport of evidence takes place every forty-eight hours. That could change," Quinn added. "I imagine Cass is going to be requesting a number of them after last night."

Mitch glanced at the long, narrow tent with virtually transparent plastic sides. Nearby sat a pair of portable restrooms. "How's the power holding up, other than the generators?"

"The city turned the power back on weeks ago, but it gets sketchy." Quinn ducked his head. "Could explain why the security cameras went out last night."

"I'm sorry, the security cameras what?" Mitch balked. "You're shitting me."

"If only," Quinn countered easily. "I've already had a conversation with the managing partner at Axiom Security. Skittish little guy for a security professional. There's no video record from six o'clock on last night. Add to that, shortly after they were hired, they removed all but one camera Blake installed at Cass's request."

"Did that camera catch anything?" Mitch asked Blake, assuming the building manager had installed it. Blake glanced away in an action Mitch identified as a tell. "What?"

"Plug your ears." Blake told Quinn. "I might have forgotten to remove two other cameras Cass originally had me place."

Quinn snort-laughed and ducked his head.

"Only issue is," Blake said as he checked his watch. "I couldn't power them through the same feed as the one Axiom allowed her to keep. Battery life isn't horrible, but the WiFi out sucks here. The feed should have already loaded into cloud storage by now assuming everything was working properly. Happens every twenty-four hours. I'd suggest keeping this between us for now," he added, "until we know what or who we might be dealing with. I'll download the recordings as soon as I'm back at Temple House. You can start listening again now," he told Quinn.

Quinn simply blinked in wide-eyed innocence, an exaggerated expression that actually made Mitch's lips twitch.

He prided himself on being a good and instant judge of character. So far Detective Quinn Burton and former Naval Intelligence officer Blake Redford had soared to the top of his approved list. Honorable, he thought. Dedicated. And willing to cross lines they probably shouldn't—not because it was thrilling or dangerous but because it was the right thing to do.

*I doubt either of them would have shot a murder suspect at point blank range.*

Mitch's hands fisted at his side as he pulled himself back from the edge. "Can I have copies of the recordings?"

"Sure."

Mitch turned his attention to the pair of generators situated between the makeshift office and refrigeration trailers. He recognized the brand as a reliable one, especially for use in the field. GPR, laptops, and flood lights were often reliant on portable power. "Shifts are running between what times?""

"One shift. Seven to seven and rotating to quarter-staff on weekends," Quinn said. "Preserving DNA evidence is our primary concern." He gestured to the larger of the generators. "That said, identifying the remains is top priority, so that stays hooked up and running for constant backup. Cass has been downloading the results as they come in. Fifteen positively identified so far. Next step is contacting next of kin, but given some of the remains are decades old, it's proving problematic. And before you ask, every bit of evidence is catalogued and processed either by Cass or through the networked system she's hooked into at LAPD central."

So far Mitch couldn't see anything wrong with how the scene was being addressed. Before he'd seen Cassia in person, he couldn't fathom why anyone would question her position as lead investigator. Now it was clear the concern had little to do with the actual handling of the evidence and everything to do with her mental state. And that, he admitted through gritted teeth, was seriously irritating.

"Blake mentioned the property owner is dead."

"Yeah. Died about three years ago," Quinn confirmed. "After his estate went into probate, the court appointed his attorneys as custodians. Young & Fairbanks. I swear that firm represents more dead clients than live ones." He straightened. "Kian! Val!" He called out to two scene workers breaking away from the group speaking with a pair of officers. "Linnea or Connor around?"

"Conner's doing an inventory of the damage," The leaner and more athletic of the two pointed behind him into the tent. "Whoever it was took a bat to pretty much everything we'd left out in the tent. Thankfully we keep our really expensive equipment in either Linnea's or Jay's vehicle. They're inside there." He turned toward the single refrigerated trailer, his jet-black ponytail falling over one shoulder. "Whole thing's been damned inconvenient but like Linnea said after she talked to Dr. Davis, it could have been a lot worse."

"You could have missing evidence," Mitch clarified. "Sorry." For a man who wasn't prone to apologies, he'd done so twice in the space of minutes. "Mitch Keaton. I'm with the FBI."

"Oooooh, yeah, we heard we were getting some federal help. Kian Nakamura." The young man gave him one of those chins-up of welcome. "Good to meet you."

"You guys doing okay?" Quinn said. "Can't be easy thinking about someone invading your scene."

"It is what it is," Kian said, but Val seemed to think otherwise.

"It's damned creepy," she said, touching a hand to the collection of hoop earrings arcing down her right ear. "Makes me glad we weren't approved to work overnight."

"I hear that," Quinn said. "We're going to do what we can to make sure you feel safe again. Susie says hey, by the way, Val."

"Best boss I've ever had," Val said and earned a nudge from Kian. "Other than Linnea and Dr. D of course." She hugged a clipboard against her chest. "Do us all a favor, Quinn? When you find whoever did this, lock them up long enough to make an impact?" The scowl on her face reminded Mitch of his stern and rather intimidating fourth-grade teacher. "Place is already creepy enough without us worrying about being attacked."

"You don't have to ask twice," Quinn promised as the three of them headed to the trailers. "What are you thinking, Blake?"

"Nothing's changed since the first time I came down to offer my opinion on security," Blake said. "If anything, they pulled back on what I was told they'd set up. Video cameras are crap brands and there are too many areas out of sight. At the very least, I'd suggest changing out all locks to key access cards and pads."

"Doubt the city will spring for that." A rotund woman in her early forties, with dark blonde hair knotted at the base of her neck, stepped out of the refrigerated trailer. "About time you got here, Quinn. I was about to call—Mitch!" She turned surprised blue eyes at him as a smile widened her small mouth. "What are you …? Wait. You're Cass's fed?"

Wording aside, Mitch smiled. "Guilty as charged." He accepted the quick hug of welcome. "It's good to see you again, Linnea."

"You, too." She rubbed his arm in comfort. "Guess now we know what it takes to drag you out of the depths of Quantico, huh?" Her greeting was warm enough to ease any anxiety he had about coming out here. "You're going to be Cass's eyes and ears and hands, then?" If there was any resentment on Linnea's part, it certainly didn't show. The mayor had wanted a Fed assigned to the case and, despite all of Linnea expertise, one thing she could not claim was a federal connection despite being frequently called in to consult on cases.

"Details to be worked out," he said easily. Whatever Cassia wanted or needed him to do, that's why he was here. A chill raced down his spine and prickled the back of his neck. He turned, looking at the cordoned off markers outlining the various graves that had been discovered.

For a moment, the entire world went silent, as if he'd been pulled into a forced reverie of sadness.

Eight years as an agent, another four as a forensics specialist, meant he'd walked onto a lot of crime scenes, most of which were disturbing in their own right.

But here? He nearly shivered against the ghosts shifting down his spine.

He blinked at the chillingly large space filled with crisscrossing low-lying lengths of bright twine twisted around plastic industrial strength stakes. Brushes, trowels, and stacks of large wooden box sifters lined the graves, while fine metal mesh sat nearby, awaiting their use in straining every single speck of dirt for potential evidence. Red plastic flags flapped in the wind, noting location information as well as other details necessary to identify one grave from another.

Technology only got them so far; in most instances, the old ways worked best.

To Mitch's eye, the configuration of the outlined graves seemed obsessively straight, oddly ... planned. As if whomever had left the bodies had done so in an organized, very meticulous manner.

A filing system for bodies? He might have rolled his eyes had the idea not been so macabre.

"Everything okay?" Quinn asked him.

*No*, Mitch thought. *Mass graves exist.*

"I'd like to walk the scene, if that's okay?" He asked Linnea. "Not much I can do in there until you all are set back up. I need to ..." His voice trailed off, at a loss for words.

"Go on. We trust you with them," Linnea said quietly. "It's good to have you here, Mitch."

"Thanks." He hoped that feeling remained. "Give me a rundown on what the officers say?" He asked Quinn who nodded.

Mitch left the trio behind, his boots sinking slightly into the dark, damp earth beside the heeled imprints of the officer he'd seen earlier.

Since receiving the files, he'd spent hours poring over photographs. But nothing prepared him for the vast, cold emptiness of reality. After the last four years behind a desk in the lab at Quantico, running equipment and processing evidence, he felt jumpy. Out of his element.

His skin itched. His fingers flexed.

He didn't belong in the field anymore.

No. That wasn't right. He didn't *want* to be here. "And yet, here you are." Because Cassia had called him.

Every step he took into the long-hidden graveyard felt like an invasion of sacred space. The scientist part of him pushed back, reminding him there was a job to be done. But the other part of him? The side that had joined the FBI to ensure justice prevailed? That man couldn't quite push past the weight of responsibility and obligation to the dead.

He wasn't a man of faith. He didn't ascribe to any particular religion or tradition. But he believed in spirit; in the power of the soul housed by the fragile shell of humanity every person wore. More so every day, as a matter of fact.

He crouched, touched a reverent hand against the earth, and bowed his head as if in genuflection at the feet of suffering.

Staring into one of the graves that had been meticulously excavated, he couldn't help but imagine who had slept beneath the dirt or for how long. But he'd bet, with his very last dollar, Cassia knew every single name so far confirmed, ever single face.

Every single life.

It was part of why he'd fallen in love with her. Her devotion not only to the science that directed and guided her life, but her utmost respect for the lost lives she'd been given—and accepted—responsibility for. Helping the field helped everyone, which was no doubt why she hadn't stopped.

Every murder victim, everyone who knew and cared about them, were entitled to answers that allowed them to grieve. Whether they could move on was beyond his and Cassia's remit.

Despite having every reason, opportunity, and ability to walk away from forensics after New York, Cassia had instead dug her heels in and, as Stephen King wrote so eloquently, stood.

Off to the right, yellow crime scene tape had been tied around the cut rungs of the fence indicating where the intruders had gained access. The sloping hill on the other side of the fence acted as a concealed entry point, at least from the vantage of outside the property. Whoever had been ballsy enough to break in, they hadn't exactly concealed their means of access.

From where he crouched, it occurred to Mitch that nature had, intentionally or not, added a touch of beauty to the darkness. Long neglected trees arced and mingled with one another, creating a canopy over the intentional graveyard. Or, Mitch considered, perhaps the branches were simply bowing in honor to those lying beneath their protection.

Dead leaves rustled in the barely-there breeze. Mitch brushed his hands on his jeans before pushing to his feet to resume his walk down the makeshift path designated by simple twine. Every open grave had been carefully cleared of its contents, numbers and notations scribbled on the flapping plastic flags snapping in the breeze.

Ground Penetrating Radar had been utilized, a standard of examination that had been set in place years before. GPR helped to identify not only where remains might have been buried, but, in this case, how many waited for identification. Bodies buried on top of one another three or in some instances four deep.

Knowing Linnea and Cassia as he did, Mitch wasn't surprised by the steady and consistent progress they'd made together. Linnea especially would have paid particular and extra attention to details where the evidence was concerned before she proceeded with entering it into the system for processing.

When Mitch had met Linnea two years ago at a conference in Chicago, he'd learned that her primary experience was the result of working in the Sudan where countless mass graves had been unearthed. She had seen the absolute worst humanity was capable of inflicting upon one another. It made sense she was part of this team, especially given her home base was Los Angeles.

He remembered she'd laughed off how Los Angeles was her safe place; nothing like what she was used to dealing with would ever rear its ugly, inhuman head where she often only saw light.

So much for jokes.

Blake had said Mitch couldn't imagine the death that surrounded this place. Now that Mitch stood surrounded by so many innocent victims, a bit of him felt chipped away, lost forever in the swirling morose that felt like a blanket of grief draped over these hills.

His ability to compartmentalize had vanished in the instant of a single shot four years ago. It was the reason he'd walked away from the field. *Well,* Mitch chided himself, *one of the reasons.*

Turning the empathic part of his brain to silent, he shifted his attention to his natural curiosity for answers that continued to keep him employed and given him the guise of purpose. Looking at this place through a filtered lens would allow him to process and convey back to Cassia precisely what he saw. And thought.

He stepped out of the cover of trees, off the damp soil and onto the mostly untouched graves buried in far more solid ground.

Sporadic weeds and flowers had sprouted, but every explosion of life seemed a struggle, as if they'd immediately surrendered to that which lay beneath. Funny, Mitch thought. Plants and flora often thrived around decaying bodies, but here …

Something red shifted in the breeze a number of yards ahead.

Mitch frowned, looked around, unable to pinpoint precisely what struck him as off.

"Find something?" Blake's deep voice seemed to fit this place as he stepped silently up behind Mitch.

Mitch shook his head, half in an attempt to clear it, the other half an uncertain answer. "You were right," he said, lowering his tone. "There's no understanding this place." Even after being here.

"As if anyone would want to."

Before Mitch's agreement could be voiced, his attention was pulled back to the red flag in the distance. Only …. He frowned, turned one way then the other, taking in every detail of the outlined plots. "They put up red flags when they're done with a grave." He'd made the mental note shortly after looking at the graves behind him. "Yellow indicates what the GPR showed. Blue means the graves are waiting to be excavated." He pivoted and zig-zagged toward the flag. Blake followed, his heavy footfalls a dull echo in Mitch's ear. The ground here was cakey and dry, as if starved of thirst. His shoes no longer left an imprint but instead kicked up fine dust and dirt as he moved his feet.

It wasn't until he was standing over the grave marked number forty-six that Mitch saw it hadn't been a red flat at all.

It was a solitary red flower.

"Don't!" Blake grabbed his shoulder and pulled him back when Mitch leaned down to pick it up. "Leave it."

"It's just a—" He stepped back when Blake shook his head. "I think it's a lily. Odd color." Had he known they could be red? The fence line had narrowed back here, keeping close to the edge of where the graves had been marked. To the right, the sloping hill beyond the fence rose above his eye-line and led off the edge into the sky. To his left, more flat, wooded land stretching for as far as he could see with the fence dead-ending maybe thirty feet ahead.

"Linnea needs to see this," Blake said as Mitch turned in a slow circle.

Something was nagging at Mitch. "The officer."

"What officer?" Blake asked in an absent tone.

"When we first got here," Mitch explained. "There was a uniformed officer walking around the graves." An officer who, now, was nowhere in sight.

"That would make five uniforms in total, and the Sergeant who reported to the scene," Blake clarified, his gaze narrowing.

"Okay." Mitch didn't understand the confusion.

"According to Quinn, only two cars which means four officers were dispatched to deal with the break-in."

Mitch shook his head. "There wasn't a third car?"

"Quinn was just talking with them. Four officers. Plus the sergeant." Blake followed Mitch's lead and looked around. "You're absolutely sure you saw a uniform out here?"

"He was right … come on." He led the way back, scanning the dirt and then damp soil as he retraced his steps. He stopped and held out his hand to keep Blake from coming closer. "Here. See? This is my footprint." He pointed to the ones his work boots had left. "This isn't. Different heel impression. Someone was here and he was wearing a uniform."

Blake pulled out his cell, dialed and faced the evidence tent. Behind the transparent "windows" shadows moved. They weren't so far away that Mitch didn't hear a cell phone ring.

"Quinn, Mitch found something you and Linnea need to see." Blake hung up at the same moment Quinn poked his head out of the tent. He walked out, Linnea and two others close behind.

"What?" Quinn yelled as he approached. "What is it?"

"How many officers came out about the break in?" Blake asked as if to appease Mitch's doubts.

"Four. Callahan and Myers just left. I should get copies of their report in a few hours." Quinn rested a hand on his hip. "What's going on?"

"I saw a fifth officer out here, when we first arrived," Mitch repeated. "Walking the fence line. Linnea?"

"I wasn't counting officers," she told him. "I was trying to figure out how much of our equipment we were going to have to replace."

"There." Blake pointed to the footprints. "One set is Mitch's."

"And this is supposed to be an officer's?" Quinn bent down as Linnea took the long way around to stand beside Mitch. "Neither are police issue boots. That heel doesn't match." He looked up at Mitch. "Where did you see him exactly?"

Mitch pointed in the general direction. "I just assumed …" He cut himself off. One of the first things he'd learned as an Academy recruit. Never assume anything.

"Footprints are the least of it." Blake looked at Mitch. "Show them."

"Okay." What was he missing? But he did as Blake requested and returned to the flower.

The four of them stood over the marked grave.

"Son of a bitch." Quinn planted his hands on his hips and stared down at the red lily with such loathing Mitch had to look twice to make sure he wasn't seeing things.

"Someone want to fill me in?" Mitch asked. "It's just a flower. Our trespassers maybe? Perhaps they left it—"

"Someone left it all right," Quinn said. "Linnea?"

"This wasn't here earlier," she confirmed. "Both Jay and I walked the entire scene before the officers got here." She crouched, tilted her head as if examining the flower from all angles. "I'll need to get it under the scope to confirm, but I'd be safe in saying it's probably a match to the pollen of the flowers we've found in each of the graves so far."

"Awesome," Quinn muttered. "Now they're taking up flower delivery."

"Would someone please," Mitch said, as he looked between the detective and Blake, "explain the significance of the flower? And who is the 'they' you're talking about?"

"Not here," Quinn said when Blake opened his mouth. "And not now." He touched a hand to his ear, as if telling them they might not be alone. "Linnea?"

"We'll take care of it," she assured them. "And we'll take casts of the prints. We'll need your shoes for elimination purposes, Mitch."

"Fine, whatever." Frustration built around irritation. "One of those missing details from the reports?" He finally asked Quinn.

Quinn nodded. "Blake, you need to get back to Temple House and look at that security footage."

Blake looked at Mitch.

"Go on. I'll find my own way back," Mitch said. He had the feeling Cassia wasn't ready to see him again just yet and considering he was feeling like a jet engine on overdrive, now was not the time to go barreling back into her apartment demanding explanations. Besides, he had his own mystery to solve.

Where in the hell had that 'officer' gone?

# CHAPTER FIVE

CASS tapped her ear and ended her call with Warden Taggart. Part of her felt utterly ridiculous for even thinking about making the call to the man in charge of Falcon Ridge Federal Penitentiary, but seeing Jonathan Whittaker's face on her computer screen pretty much erased any resulting embarrassment.

The ultra-maximum-security prison, nicknamed The Nest, was carved into the red rock cliffs of Devil's Canyon in Utah. Surely if anyone, let alone one of their most high-profile inmates, had escaped, not only would she have been notified personally, but the details would have been on every news chyron on every network.

She stood at her desk, glaring down at her unassembled CPU, a nervous hand tapping against her unsteadily beating heart. She'd heard the forced patience in Warden Taggart's voice after he'd listened to her concerns. He'd responded by assuring her he was looking at the live 24/7 camera feed running in Jonathan Whittaker's cell.

The convicted multiple murderer was right where he was supposed to be.

She'd even pressed to speak to three of the prison guards to confirm nothing was amiss.

Cass's subsequent request to see Whittaker for herself had probably offended the lot of them, but the warden had tapped his cell phone in order to display Whittaker's surveillance camera so Cass could see him with her own eyes.

As much as she despised the idea, the sight of Jonathan Whittaker reclining on his cement bed, reading a copy of Seneca's *Letters from a Stoic*, brought her enough relief that the fear abated.

She was assured, twice more, that he had not been granted computer privileges and that any move he made around the facility was observed and recorded. None of the men she spoke with were particularly polite, no doubt unappreciative of their professional performances being questioned. Cass didn't care.

She only cared that Jonathan Whittaker was exactly where he was supposed to be, under the restrictions the prosecutor had requested and the judge had granted.

Utter and complete lockdown.

She wanted to breathe easy. But ... the assurances only presented dozens of additional questions. She had not imagined the email. She hadn't imagined it. Hadn't imagined *him*.

But as the minutes ticked by, doubt crept in.

*Was it possible ...?*

The answer might be found in her private server, or behind a broken firewall. That meant running security checks. On everything. Multiple times. "Perfect time for Nox to be away."

Actually. Cass bit the inside of her cheek as she thought about it. The timing was perfect. While Nox was aware of the basic information regarding Cass's past—that she'd been targeted and abducted by a pair of killers—Cass was not in the right frame of mind to go sharing the details of her personal interactions with the more unhinged of the two Whittaker brothers.

She didn't want Nox knowing that information. She didn't want anyone knowing. Not now. If Cass had her way, not ever.

She knew Mitch and his then partner Lynda had called in a lot of favors to keep Cass's name out of the reporting on the events in that warehouse outside New York City. Nothing had changed that made her want to undo all that.

If anything, she was more determined to put it all behind her.

Jonathan Whittaker didn't belong out here, in this new life of hers. Where she'd started over. She would not give him the satisfaction of blowing up her world yet again.

Her hands still trembled.

Elliot whined and this time clawed his paws against the wall and hardwood floor.

Cass sighed and stepped to the side, hugging her arms around herself against a sudden chill. "I don't know what's going on with you," she called to the dog and got barely an ear twitch in response. "But if you don't stop acting weird, I'm going to have Nox take you to the V-E-T when they get back on Monday."

Elliot's looked back at her with one of his "you wouldn't dare" expressions before he turned in a circle, sighed, and curled up in his bed, and tugged his stuffed Lambchop stuffie under his chin for a pillow.

Cass retreated into her bedroom for a sweater. Only when she returned to her desk did she notice the sudden silence in the apartment. She stood still, turned in a slow circle. It was so quiet. And cold.

It took her longer than she was comfortable to with to realize the white noise, the constant background hum of technology had gone dormant.

"What the …?"

She did a quick visual check of her machinery, much of which typically remained in standby mode.

They weren't on now though.

She double checked plugs and connections but had to flex her hands again against the cold after each machine.

It was so cold!

Snapping to attention, Cass grabbed her cell and clicked open her thermostat app. "Fifty-nine degrees?" She frowned. No wonder her equipment had shut down. She had most everything save her computer, the mass spectrometer, mini-refrigeration unit, and the micro-DNA sequencer set to go into automatic shutdown should the apartment's temperature drop below sixty-five or above eighty. Given the southern California climate, it had been an over-precaution given the amount of electricity her apartment pulled in.

"Programming glitch." Had to be. She hurried over to the thermostat, rebooted it and, once it was back on quickly reset the default temperature to seventy-four. Irritation crept in as she made a mental note to add a thermostat check to her daily routine and returned to her workspace. She quickly wrote down her plan to run a diagnostic and security check on the entire system including her personal secured server, just in case. Something just nagged at her, but she couldn't put her finger on it.

Yet.

She had just pulled the plug on her last machine when someone rang the bell and then knocked.

Her heart leapt into her throat and she froze, staring at the door.

"Cass?" Riley Temple's voice sounded timid enough that Cass frowned. "Can we talk?"

As much as she wasn't in the mood for company, she dropped the power cord and headed to the door. One thing she'd learned living in Temple House: her friends weren't the type to stand back when they knew she was having a rough go. Even if she and Riley had recently argued, the fact her friend was reaching out made it impossible for Cass not to respond.

"Just a second!"

Abandoning her computer for a while might be a good thing. She'd been unable to backtrace the email that had somehow vanished from her system. If she was honest with herself, she simply didn't have the emotional pennies to withstand the mental gymnastics it would take to come at the problem from a different direction.

The closer she got to the door, the dread and anxiety spiraled again, but she refused to surrender. "Not this time." She let it all move through her as she walked down the short hallway and practically dived at the door.

Her hands shook as she unlatched the locks. It was the cold. Nothing else.

"Hey." She managed a tight smile that faded at the concern on Riley's face. She repressed a sigh. "Sutton told you about my panic attack, didn't she?"

"No," Riley said immediately then winced. "Maybe. She was worried, Cass. I am, too."

"You can both stop. I'm fine, Riley." Elliot came up behind her and nudged her with his nose. She stretched out her hand to pet him. There was no greater comfort than the presence of her dog. "I promise."

"Okay." The blithe response sounded so rehearsed Cass wondered if Riley had been practicing with her Great Aunt Moxie for the octogenarian's upcoming stage performance in 12 Angry Women. "Just thought you could use some company. And a friendly ear. And maybe some empanadas." She drew her hand from behind her back to show a grease-soaked white paper bag. "It's your favorite. Carne Asada. Carmen made these extra spicy today."

Coming from anyone else, that statement might come across as a nosy kind of bribe. But Riley had never been one to sneak around the point. One reason she'd earned a reputation as a paparazzo with a heart. She simply didn't abide bullshit.

Truth be told, in this moment their past argument didn't matter. They'd become instant friends the moment Cass had called from New York asking about one of Temple House's apartments that had just been listed as looking for a new tenant. It was the perfect location, a good-sized building that would allow her to live, and hopefully disappear amidst a crowd. The best thing? It was as far from New York as she could get.

After what happened at the warehouse, Cass found it impossible to stay in the city she'd loved living in. New York had a vibrancy and energy that was impossible to replicate. Coming across the online listing for the recently vacated apartment in Los Angeles was the sign she'd been looking and hoping for.

Cass had immediately called the number and explained some of her situation to an open-minded and sympathetic Riley. Within the hour they'd agreed to a long-term lease and whatever upgrades Cass believed were necessary for her to work out of her new home and, more significantly, feel safe.

They'd been friends ever since.

Her move might have been triggered by trauma but she'd ended up finding the best friends she'd ever had. She hadn't lost the entirety of her independent streak, but she had to admit, she had quickly learned that Laurel, Mabel, Sutton, and Riley made her life so much better.

She almost hadn't had the time or inclination to miss Mitch.

Almost.

Cass stepped back and waved Riley in, eying the empty hallway beyond her. Cass guardedly waited for the anxiety to surge back, but when it didn't, she breathed a small sigh of relief. She closed the door and resisted the urge to snap the locks.

"It was the empanadas that did it, wasn't it?" Riley sounded as if she were talking on eggshells. Cass could only imagine the focus that required of the typically sarcastic and loquacious photographer.

Dressed in her usual snug jeans and a grey-green Stevie Nicks t-shirt out of her seemingly unending collection of classic rock attire, Riley had her dark hair pulled back in a practical tail and her fingers were stained and a bit burned due to the photographic chemicals she used in developing film. That hobby had become an obsession since walking away from her job as a celebrity stalker photographer, but Cass knew it also served as a distraction from having very little to do investigation-wise until the burial site was completely excavated, and the evidence was in.

Other than lending her voice and opinions, whatever role she had to play in the mystery had become a bit of a supporting one. Probably for the best, Cass thought, considering her last foray into a wrongful conviction and decades' old murder had almost gotten Riley killed.

"The empanadas are a bonus." Cass touched a hand to her grumbling stomach, recalling she had chocolate cake waiting for her. "I could do with the protein."

"Brrrr." Riley shivered. "What the hell? Is your heat not working?"

Ah, Cass thought. *There* was the Riley she knew and loved. "I just rebooted my thermostat," Cass said and led her inside. Elliot followed, his nose pointedly aimed at the bag in Riley's hand. "Should be back up to temp pretty quickly."

"I'll have Blake check the fuses when he gets back. Just to be safe." Riley set the bag down on the kitchen island, jerked a thumb at the fridge and the invitation Cass had hung up. "Did Keeley take you on a guilt trip when she dropped this off?""

"I wouldn't say it was guilt," Cass hedged. "It was more like a desperate plea."

"What did you tell her about going?"

It wasn't like Riley to be cagey. "I told her I'd think about it." She shrugged. "I'm leaning toward maybe." If for no other reason than to keep moving forward. She'd already missed so much. The part of her that wanted to break forever free of this, at times, paralyzing anxiety was growing by the minute.

"Maybe?" Riley's brows went up. "Guess now we know who has the most influence in this building."

"Maybe doesn't mean yes," Cass corrected her. Right now the idea of attending an apartment building party felt like hiking to the top of Mount Everest, but that didn't mean it was impossible.

"Well, it's not a no and that I will celebrate." Riley's smile was somewhat sad. "So." She cleared her throat. "I heard FBI Special Agent Mitch Keaton is in town. Funny,"—was that hurt or curiosity in her gaze?—"I'm not familiar with the name."

Cass snatched the bag away from Riley and grabbed a couple of paper plates. "We'd better eat these quick. Sutton's bringing up lasagna for dinner."

"Mmmm. Veggie, I bet." The tilted brow let Cass know Riley was well aware she'd changed the subject.

"As long as I can't tell what's actually in it, it'll be fine." Not that Cass was vegetable adverse, she just preferred her food more … calorie and carbohydrate dense. Case in point, the steaming empanadas sitting on her counter.

The flaky pastry was still warm as she pulled one out of the bag. Her stomach rumbled louder as she tossed the pastry from hand to hand. "One of the best things about you dating Quinn is that he introduced you to this place. Kind of out the way for you though, isn't it?" Cass bit in and, despite the steam erupting into her mouth, nearly swooned at the spicy flavors of the beef and buttery, crumbly pastry.

"Mmmm." Riley all but buried her nose in the bag to pull out another. "I took Merle to physical therapy today," she explained, referring to one of her late grandfather's long-time friends who had been seriously injured in an attack last year. "I was in the area. Besides,"—

she broke one of the empanadas apart and sent fragrant steam wafting into the air—"I wanted to talk to Carmen about catering part of my wedding."

Cass coughed, sucked down some of the beef the wrong way, and choked.

"Not the reaction I was hoping for." Riley got up and immediately grabbed a glass for water, pushed it into her friend's hand as Cass dragged in a breath. "You okay?" She pounded a hand on Cass's back.

Eyes watering, Cass nodded and drank deeply. "W-what …? Wedding? Quinn proposed?" She didn't see a ring on Riley's finger. "You're getting *married*?"

"No." Riley grabbed a bottle of red wine out of the fridge and poured herself a healthy glass. "He doesn't think I'll say yes." She shrugged. "So I've mostly decided I'm going to propose to him." She took a drink, examined the glass's contents as if it were a complete unknown. "What do you think?"

Hope and happiness descended in unexpected waves. The news gave Cass the perfect cover to let her tears flow free. "I think that's probably the most Riley thing you could ever do." She wiped her eyes and laughed as she continued to cry. "Quinn's gonna love it."

"Thought maybe you could do with some good news," Riley said, her always observant eyes narrowed in a way that made Cass feel like one of her microscopic samples.

"You aren't going to stop there are you?" Cass demanded. "Details please. When are you going to do this? How are you—?"

"Absolutely no idea." Riley tilted her head before returning to her seat, but the self-satisfied smirk on her face kept Cass's mood bolstered. "The idea came to me the other day and I haven't been able to get it out of my head. To be honest, I never really thought I even wanted to get married." She took a healthy bite of her own empanada. "I know it's something Quinn wants but he won't ask me unless he's sure I'll say yes."

"Smart man," Cass said.

Riley shrugged. "I know his parents would be thrilled. His father even offered to walk me down the aisle. Quinn was mortified," she added on a laugh. "But I could see it in his eyes. He wants to be married."

Anyone who looked at the two of them could see they belonged together. "But you want to be married, too, right?" Cass pressed. "This isn't about wanting some big wedding party."

"I do." Riley's frown didn't match the surprise in her eyes. "Like I said, I never really thought marriage was a me kind of thing. But if it's to Quinn? Hell yes. Besides, I don't think there's anyone else on the planet who could put up with me and ... all this stuff." She gestured to the equipment still in power up mode. The overhead screens flickered flicker to life, going through their usual software reboots. All of which were running in conjunction with the mystery and murders Riley was responsible for exposing. "With me almost drowning at Christmas and then with Mabel's abduction, I can't help but think about the future and ..." She shrugged. "Forget the fact that we've kicked over a hornets' nest in this town. We've got the Melanie Dennings' case being reopened, a conviction called into question, and a hill filled with bodies." She shrugged again. "Puts things in perspective. We never know how long we have. I mean, it could all be taken away in a second. Be it by psychopath or a fast-moving bus."

In Cass's experience, she'd lay odds on the psychopath.

Her food turned to a lump in her throat.

For an instant, Cass was back in that glass coffin, barely able to breathe, her mind foggy because of the drug she'd been dosed with that kept her just aware enough to see everything that was happening around her.

*The screams. Sometimes she couldn't stop hearing the scr ...*

"Cass?" Riley reached out, touched her hand.

Cass jumped before quickly covering by pulling away and tucking an imaginary strand of hair behind her ear. "Sorry." She managed a weak smile and blinked away the past. "You're right. We never know how long we've got." She paused. Realized. "Wait. Am I the first person you're telling about this proposal thing?"

"Other than Carmen and her empanadas." Riley's eyes filled with concern but made the topic shift Cass suggested. "The whole idea is weird. I don't think this way. I'm not a romantic."

"Do tell." Cass couldn't help but enjoy this conversation. Seeing different angles to her friends always piqued her interest and left her viewing them with new eyes. It was just the distraction she needed.

"Maybe it's stupid. Or maybe it's fear." Now Riley sounded as if she might be trying to talk herself out of it. "Things have just been really unstable lately. And we don't know what's coming at us next."

Cass pressed her lips together. Oh, she had a pretty good idea of what was coming down the pike.

"We need some happy to balance out the crazy, you know?" Riley said. "And I'll admit it: the last couple of months have made me think about what I want my life to be filled with."

"Love," Cass suggested at Riley's eye roll. "You want it to be filled with love." And her friend got that in spades with Detective Quinn Burton. "You can say the word, Riley. Especially since you're about to propose. It's not going to hurt you."

Had they been outside, Cass might have looked up for an errant lightning bolt strike. It was one of the lessons she'd learned, wasn't it? That even the *word* love could hurt.

Something akin to envy slipped around inside of her. It wasn't jealousy necessarily, just a kind of sadness shining a light on the idea that Cass's life had stopped spinning four years ago. She missed the excitement of falling in love, of being in love. Of the promise of the future.

Funny. She'd thought she'd been in love plenty of times. But then she'd met Mitch and instantly realized she'd had no concept of what love actually was until him.

She'd had to let go of so many things when she'd left New York, including the idea of being someone's other. Of having someone who would, no matter what, have her back; someone who looked at her as if there was simply no other person in the world who could fill the void so many waited a lifetime to fill.

Riley—and Mabel, too, thanks to Paul Flynn—had both found that.

So many emotions cycled through her, but thankfully, whatever Cass felt didn't include anything but absolute happiness and joy. One of her best friends was pushing forward, grabbing hold of the life she wanted and wasn't letting go. No matter what surrounded them.

They'd overcome their traumas and moved on, proving what Cass had suspected early on: her friends were far stronger than she would ever be.

"Well." Cass cleared her throat. "I love this whole idea of a surprise proposal and if you need help arranging"—she waved a hand in the air—"whatever you plan to do to pop the question, just say the word."

"I'm still mulling ideas," Riley said. "It'll come to me. The one thing I do know is I want Moxie to walk me down the aisle. But it was nice to know Quinn's dad is willing to do it if I need backup."

Cass couldn't have erased the smile on her face if she'd wanted to. "Moxie is going to love giving you away to Detective Sexy Pants." Riley's great aunt had bestowed the nickname on Quinn almost as soon as he and Riley had met.

"Seriously might have to have a special cake made just so we can put DSP on it," Riley said. "You think Sutton will forgive me for not asking her to cater, if I ask her to make the cake?"

"Sutton will do anything and everything you want her to. But you're getting ahead of yourself, aren't you? Planning the wedding before you're even engaged?"

Riley shrugged. "Like you said, it's me."

"Just do me a favor with Sutton?" Now it was Cass who grabbed Riley's hand. She squeezed. Hard. "Promise me you'll make sure she uses sugar."

"Can you even call it cake if it doesn't have sugar?" Riley frowned. "But good point. If it's too much for her, I'd rather hire it out to someone else. I don't want my bridesmaids overwhelmed. I'm going to need them at peak performance." She eyed Cass. "Including you."

Cass blinked.

"It's going to be here," Riley rushed on. "At Temple House. In the garden patio, same as Keeley's party, so maybe you can consider that a dress rehearsal. Or we could have it here. In your apartment."

Cass rolled her eyes. "You can't be serious." But one look at her friend told Cass that Riley was, indeed, serious.

"I want you there. However it has to happen. If that means getting married at Radio Shack lite, then so be it. It'll just be close friends and family. Not a lot of people. And it won't be until all of … this is behind us. It would be a nice gift since the idea of registering anywhere makes me itch."

If Cass didn't know better, she'd have thought Riley had been getting pointers from Keeley. "Couldn't I just get you an InstaPot?"

They looked at each other for a long moment before they both burst out laughing. Hands clinging, they leaned over, gently knocked their heads together.

"I can't believe you even know what an InstaPot is." Riley swiped happy tears from her cheek.

"Me, either." But the moment wasn't strong enough to break the chains of fear locked around Cass's heart. Perhaps they weakened a little but … they were still there.

The very idea of stepping foot outside the apartment had dwindled back once again to one of absolute impossibility. But she didn't want to erase that bare hope on her friend's face that she'd be willing to at least try. For Keeley. And Riley.

"I'll give you a maybe," she said finally as the burden of change landed squarely on her shoulders. She needed to step up her mental rehabilitation routine. "Same as I gave Kee."

"I'll take it." Riley brightened. "Oh, one more thing. I need to keep this between you and me for now. I needed to tell someone and, well,"—she shrugged, but there was something knowing in her gaze—"I think you're probably the best of us at keeping a secret."

If Riley only knew. "Laurel's a lawyer. She keeps secrets for a living," Cass reminded her of one of the other spokes in their five-friend wheel.

"Yes, but Laurel's secret-keeping comes with strings like laws and stuff and I'd rather not be left to her mercy while I'm happily mulling. Okay, what the hell is with the buzzing?" She snapped and Elliot whined. Riley spun on her chair and looked at him staring at the wall. "That's new for him. What's going on?"

"He's stressed," Cass said. "We all are. Including my equipment." But now that Riley mentioned it, the buzzing had settled into a constant drone along the edges of her hearing, making her head ache. With all her equipment turned off, only now did she notice it. Like she needed another mystery to solve. But she added it to her ever-increasing list of things to do once Riley left. Again there was a whisper of …something—a little hint of fear at the back of her mind. She was getting paranoid, after what happened today. *Time to get a grip, woman.*

"So now that I've elevated your mood with my news," Riley teased, turning to face her again, "FBI Special Agent Mitch Keaton? Well well. Finally, we've got a name for the guy back in New York."

"You make it sound as if I tossed him into the lost and found." She hadn't meant to sound snippy. Maybe she just needed more food.

86

She took the last empanada out of the bag and bit in, attempting to come up with a succinct, painless way of explaining hers and Mitch's past. "Don't get all judgy, Riley. He's a good guy."

"I figured," Riley said. "Otherwise you wouldn't have called him for help."

"Exactly," Cass said. "So please get that 'I'll hurt him, if I have to' glint out of your eye." She circled a finger in front of Riley's face. "Seriously. He can help us. Beyond what he can do to keep me on the job, he's a phenomenal profiler and we could use his expertise." Pressure began to build inside of her, pushing whatever desire she had to finish the empanada away. "You can trust him because ..." God. She was so going to regret saying this. "You can trust him because I trust him."

And that could very well be a big problem.

It was the one memory she refused to venture down. Trusting him had been the greatest feeling in the world; a feeling she'd waited a lifetime to experience.

Except ...

Trusting him had almost gotten her killed.

Riley tilted her head, doubt shifting to surprise. "I've never heard you say that about anyone except us."

"Yeah. Well." Cass attempted to shrug it off. "Suffice it to say, I can count on both hands the number of people I'd stand for and they all, except him, live and or work in Temple House. Yes, Mitch and I have history, and it's complicated." Massive understatement and she couldn't help but think she was rambling a bit. "But there's a reason he's who I called when they wanted to pull me off the case. And for the record, I ended things between us, not him." If it had been up to Mitch they'd have ridden into the sunset together on the back of a white horse, leaving the past as far behind as they could.

Instead the past had been locked around her like the unbreakable chains of Sisyphus.

"I can't wait to meet him." Riley seemed almost convinced. "Sutton says he's hot."

Cass laughed, surprised yet again that she could find amusement in anything regarding this situation. "Sutton spends too much time in front of an oven. She thinks gingerbread men are hot."

"And Blake," Riley added with a smirk. "She thinks Blake is hot, too."

"We aren't supposed to notice that." Cass pressed her lips together, refusing to take the bait about their mutual friend's crush on the building manager. Whether it was mutual wasn't entirely clear. Blake was as easy to read as a book in the dark.

"So I'm not the only one who sees it." Riley sounded vindicated. "I mean, I get that Blake's past is complicated—"

"He lost his wife and son," she reminded Riley. "That's more than a complication." It was a tragedy. Blake rarely mentioned the family he'd lost, but on the few occasions Cass had watched him with Sutton's niece and nephew, or how protective he was of Keeley, she could see a pain behind the mask of cool control.

Masks were easier to see when you wore one yourself.

Riley scrunched her mouth. "I swear those two are swimming around each other like a pair of Beta fish trying to decide whether to kill each other or—"

"Just because you're happy living in connubial bliss with DSP doesn't mean it'll happen for everyone." That didn't mean she didn't agree with Riley's observation though. Even earlier today, when Sutton and Blake had been in her apartment, Cass felt the tension between them.

She'd never seen two people so ... cautious around one another. Unless she counted herself with Mitch in the days following the warehouse incident. He'd been so concerned, so worried ... she'd almost suffocated from it.

It wasn't that she didn't appreciate him trying to take care of her, but she'd had other issues simmering beneath the surface she couldn't let herself think about let alone deal with.

But where Sutton and Blake were concerned, she clung to a thread of hope, however thin, that something might shift and they realized what possibilities they had in front of them.

"Do me a favor," Cass asked Riley. "Don't turn me and Mitch into some kind of thing or one of your special projects. It was really difficult for me to call him and it's going to be even harder having him here. I don't need to be thinking about the four of you having gossip sessions about us."

"Pfffth." Riley waved off her concern and drank more wine. "We wouldn't have a gossip session. We're always happy to talk about you guys right to your faces." She paused. "Question."

"Since when do you ask permission?" She so wanted a glass of wine, but with the way she'd upped her anxiety medication lately, it wasn't worth the risk. Besides, she had work to do and wanted to still be in a productive state of mind when Mitch came back to pick up his things.

"Are you okay?" Riley winced as if debating whether to clarify. "Really okay? The panic attack—"

"I thought we were done talking about this."

"No. You avoided the topic," Riley countered. "We're worried about you. Especially now that this Mitch guy is back. Sutton said this one was bad."

"It was." No point denying it. The reasons behind it on the other hand …? "The attacks work like pressure valves, Riley. I was due for one with everything that's been building up. And seeing Mitch again brought a lot of stuff back." It was, Cass told herself, the worst lie she could have told. Mitch's appearance might have gotten the ball rolling, but it was the email that sent her careening over the edge. An email she couldn't explain to anyone without confessing the entire truth of her past.

"Is Mitch part of the reason you're …" Riley looked around the apartment. "Stuck."

Cass couldn't believe her ears. Was that Riley Temple attempting to be diplomatic? "Not Mitch specifically."

"We've never talked about what really brought you out to Los Angeles. Not in any detail, anyway," Riley said quietly.

"No." Cass hoped her voice sounded stronger than she felt. "We haven't."

"Just know, whenever you're ready to—"

"I know." Her voice broke and she could only hope Riley heard and took it for the warning it was. "I'd appreciate you not pushing me about it. I'm dealing with it." The only way it was safe to do so.

Alone.

She had come to a point where she could handle her friends being protective and concerned about her mental and emotional proclivities. If they knew the details of the reasons behind her issues?

Cass hadn't fully been able to come to terms with what had happened herself. She didn't want to burden the people she cared about most with a truth that was hers to carry alone.

She'd have thought her ultimate nightmare had come true when she'd found herself looking Jonathan Whittaker in the eye over her computer screen. No.

Her biggest fear was that everyone—her Temple House family in particular—would learn the truth. They'd never look at her the same way again. They'd only see her as a victim and that she knew for certain she'd never survive.

"It might help, you know," Riley urged. "Talking it out. And this isn't me pushing it's just me saying—"

"Have you asked your aunt if she's ready to talk about what happened to her back in the day? When she got that tattoo on the back of her neck that she refused to talk to you about?" It was a horrible question to use as a shield. Cass loved Moxie Temple as much as she did anyone in her life, and she kicked herself for crossing a line she'd refused to cross before. "I'm sorry. That wasn't fair."

Riley took a very long drink of wine. "Actually." Riley blinked as Cass grabbed her hand again. "It's entirely fair. And, as Quinn has been working to convince me, trauma is trauma. We all ... have it." The ghost of Christmas past crossed across her eyes. "It goes deeper for some of us than others. I don't know how to talk to Aunt Moxie about whatever it is that happened all those years ago. But I do know I'm running out of stalling tactics. She knows something about The Circle. Some ritualistic element that is a part that is a part of the deaths. The lily."

"Yes," Cass agreed gently. "She does."

Riley frowned, a light of acknowledgement shining in her dark eyes. "Maybe I'm the wrong one to approach her. Quinn suggested he or Mabel might be better suited because of their training and experience when it comes to dealing with survivors of violence, but now ..." She took a deep breath. "Now I wonder if you're the best choice."

"Me?" Cass couldn't have hidden her surprise if she'd tried. "You want *me* to talk to Moxie?"

"If you're willing." She lifted her gaze to Cass's. A gaze that Cass now saw was filled not only with doubt, but concern and fear for the woman who had helped raise her. "As someone who's been through what I can only assume is something … similar, would you be willing to get her to open up?"

Cass bolstered herself against the wave of self-doubt. Managing her own trauma had been difficult enough. Helping someone else through theirs?

"She can help us put the pieces together in this mess." Riley went on quietly, as if trying to convince herself that what she was suggesting was right. "The way she reacted when we first noticed the mark on her neck? I've never seen her so scared. I'm surprised she didn't shut completely down."

"She shut you down instead," Cass recalled from what she'd heard from Mabel. Moxie had not only dropped a new bottle of red wine, she'd vehemently protested any conversation that even tiptoed around the origin of that lily-shaped tattoo she kept hidden under her dyed red-orange hair.

"I've lived with Moxie since I was five years old," Riley whispered desperately. "I have never seen her so scared. We haven't been able to find any additional answers in weeks, Cass. I can't help but think we're running out of time to keep ahead of whatever else is coming at us."

Whatever guilt Cass felt over hers and Nox's inability to come up with any more answers than they've already found was instantly swamped by determination. It was time, she realized, to let Nox loose for that deep dive into the dark web that they'd been pushing to take. A dive that terrified Cass to the marrow of her bones.

It wasn't so much what they might find, but what kind of target they'd make of themselves by even daring to look deeper.

But they were being outpaced by all the threads of the investigation that as of now was only circumstantially connected. Riley being targeted after she'd developed those photographs, the attack up at the Tenado estate that revealed it to be a meeting place of sorts for people on the other side of the disappearances. Then there was Mabel's abduction after digging for answers on her sister's disappearance, not to mention the various unanswered questions revolving around Dean Samuels, the man held responsible for Melanie Dennings's murder more than twenty years ago. A man who had disappeared almost immediately after stepping foot in the federal prison system.

Cass's gaze shifted to the windows and the Hollywood Hills. The dozens of bodies that were finally being unearthed. They were all pieces to the same increasingly enlarging puzzle they couldn't quite decipher.

As determined as Cass was to identify all the bodies and put that part of the investigation to rest, she could feel an urgency to address the other issues—Dean Samuels, in particular—in order to finally put it all to rest.

"I agree that we need to know what Moxie does," Cass agreed slowly. "But I don't want to take the chance of losing Moxie in exchange for answers. And you were so resistant to her being questioned before now."

"I was. I think it was in part because of my own fear. Worried about the trauma it could bring her to talk about it. I wouldn't be asking for your help if I didn't think you were best suited to the conversation," Riley said. "I think you'd be a kind of preserver for her to cling to," Riley said. "I trust you with her, Cass. If that helps at all."

It didn't.

If anything, the confidence Riley placed in her felt like an anchor that, if they weren't careful, could drag them all under.

Cass was lucky to maintain her own mental equilibrium. Was she in any position to take Moxie down a road the older woman had declared no interest in walking?

But, as with Riley's pre-planned wedding request, Cass couldn't bring herself to deflate the balloon of hope she saw rising in her friend's guarded gaze.

"I'll do what I can." She knew what it took to dive into a past you couldn't face and had spent years trying to forget. Riley might be convinced Cass was the right person to make the connection with Moxie, but was that true?

Cass wasn't so sure.

# CHAPTER SIX

IF Mitch hadn't left his duffle at Cassia's apartment, he may have begged off dinner and headed directly to the hole-in-the-wall hotel he'd found on the cheap. According to its meager website that looked as if it had been designed by someone in the porn industry, the seen-better-days Silver Screen Motel offered the three things he was looking for: it was only a mile and a half away from Temple House, there was a vacancy and, most importantly, the rooms were cheap enough for him to pull actual money out of his wallet in order to pay for it.

He wasn't exactly in a position to claim expenses. But—he shifted uneasily in his seat—a call like Cass's was what built-up vacation time was for.

Headlights blared bright in the rearview mirror, making him flinch.

Mitch shielded his eyes before he reached for the flip tab on the rearview mirror, but there wasn't one. The rental agency hadn't had a lot of choice and most of the vehicles hadn't been built in this decade, but the transaction was cheap and fast. In the growing darkness, Mitch couldn't quite get a read on the vehicle on his tail. Black? Blue, maybe. Definitely dark. And it was so damned close he couldn't read the blasted plate.

"Nuisance driver," he muttered.

The giant SUV made his rented one looked as if it had been crapped out of the other's tailpipe. With the way it sped up and backed off, it was clear the driver was used to having the road to his—or her—self. Or they liked playing vehicular chicken. Either way, he was not amused.

"Get off my ass," he muttered as the car behind him sped up. "Go around for Christ's sake!" For one instant, he was convinced the car was going to simply plow over him. He gripped the wheel, preparing for impact. He looked for somewhere to turn off, but spaces were full and parking lots inaccessible from the middle lane. Too many other cars around.

Other horns blared as the SUV swerved but remained behind him as if Mitch was some kind of pace car. He sat up, spine stiffening as the SUV screeched over into the right lane and barreled past him, blasting through a red light.

"Idiot." Mitch eased to a stop and flexed his hands. "They'll be scraping him off the sidewalk before he hits the freeway." Well— Mitch sighed and rubbed tired fingers across his forehead—he was awake now. One of the best tactics he'd learned in the Academy, and in the field, was how to compartmentalize. He found it hard to do so since that incident four years ago, but he did so now, shifting the incident into the file under one seriously shitty day.

Five minutes later, he pulled his rental car into a clear spot across the street from Temple House and killed the engine.

He sat there, hands on the wheel, forcing himself to relax. The adrenaline rush he'd been riding the past thirty-six hours had drained out of him around the time he found a reasonably priced car rental, but apparently he'd found an additional supply.

The silence that settled around him was far more comforting than at the recovery site. But it also acted as a kind of meditative blanket, reminding him that quiet could be soothing. But it wasn't completely silent, was it? The streetlamps hummed and buzzed that almost imperceptible droning.

Moving from New York to Quantico, Virginia, had been a bit of a shock to his over-charged and stressed system. But the peace he'd found there—between the forests and the Potomac and Quantico Creek, one of his favorite places for a long, solitary hike—soothed his soul. Hell, he'd practically become a walking commercial for the small town. It might have been the last thing he wanted, moving out of his beloved New York, but it had definitely been what he'd needed.

Any concerns he had about being able to hold a coherent conversation with Cassia were now gone. That flipping car may as well have been a six pack of Red Bull.

He sighed, unbuckled his belt and shoved the door open. A car whizzed past, horn blaring and he pulled the door closed again. "Unbelievable," he muttered to himself as he checked the side mirror before trying again.

It was just late enough that complete darkness hadn't quite descended yet and the historic tenant building clung to the barest hints of the gold and pink shadows of the past.

If he let himself, he could imagine this place forty or fifty years ago. The swanky people he'd find inside, toasting new deals among Hollywood's elite. Starlets and wannabe movie stars mingling with power players that would promise to make their dreams come true.

It was a simpler time in so many ways, but in others far more complex than anyone of this day and age could understand. But it was nice to think about, the history of this place, as a reminder of the truly remarkable things the human race was capable of. There was beauty buried beneath the darkness.

Sometimes it just took extra effort to unearth it.

He focused on the line of named buttons beneath the intercom and not-so-subtle video camera overhead. Mitch may have leaned a bit too heavily when he pushed Blake's intercom.

It wasn't more than a minute before Blake appeared at the door to let him in. "You look like shit."

Mitch actually smiled. Clearly they'd established a probationary friendship if Blake was being that honest with him. "Feel like it." Now that he said it, he was back to thinking begging off dinner and crashing for the night was the best idea. "I'm just going to head up and grab my bag—"

"I've gone through the security recordings from the cameras at the site," Blake said from behind him. "I didn't spot anything helpful. You ask me, they knew what to avoid, surveillance wise, which means I have more questions than answers. If you want to look yourself—"

Mitch shook his head. "Keep it in reserve. If you didn't see anything to raise an alarm, I'm not going to waste my time."

"Plus, you don't look up to processing any more information tonight."

"Truth." Mitch gave him a thumb's up as he dragged himself up the stairs. He'd seen the curiosity on Blake's face. The unasked questions lurking behind a demeanor that was too polite to push for any information as to what he and Linnea had accomplished at the scene.

Not much, if Mitch was honest with himself.

Other than collecting the lily, cleaning up the mess the intruders had created and going through Cass's meticulous schedule Linnea insisted on following to the letter, Mitch had once again found himself irritated that anyone, no matter how high up in power, found Cass's oversight of the scene to be anything but competent and productive.

He supposed, however, that he owed them his thanks. He'd have grabbed any chance to see her again, but that didn't mean he didn't resent the passive-aggressive attacks against her. The world, he'd long ago accepted, was full of idiots and malcontents.

They were behind schedule, but he felt confident they could make up the time over the weekend even with a skeleton shift. The victims were waiting; nothing was going to drive him harder to recover them than finally giving them back to their loved ones.

It was, he recalled with pride, the one thing he and Cassia definitely had in common.

Regret surged around exhaustion and snuck in. How different life might have been had things not happened the way they did. If he'd paid closer attention, not been so self-assured in his profile of Jonathan Whittaker that turned out to have one glaring error. An error that had very nearly cost Cassia her life.

"At least one of them's dead." That said ... while the bullet he'd put through Gavin Whittaker's skull had stopped the murders, it had also killed any future he and Cassia might have had together. "Enough already." Self-pity annoyed the crap out of him.

He grabbed hold of the railing and dragged himself up to the second floor. He pushed the video-doorbell outside Cass's apartment, stepped back and waited, already mentally rehearsing what he was going to say to cut the evening short.

When the door snapped open, it took Mitch a second to convince himself that the unfamiliar woman standing in front of him was real.

Tall, elegantly shapely, with dark hair and equally dark eyes, she wore a figure-hugging pair of leggings and a bright-blue oversized, wide collared sweater. She leaned a shoulder against the open frame and crossed her arms over her chest. The look she pinned him with made Mitch wish he'd donned protective gear.

"You must be Mitch Keaton." She smirked. "You're shorter than I expected."

Mitch resisted the urge to tilt his chin up. "One of the furies, I take it?"

Her gaze narrowed and sharpened. "Excuse me?"

"Ah, never mind. Just something I ... heard." His mind raced through the list of friends Blake had mentioned in the car. Mabel was still in New York and besides, she was blonde. He'd met Sutton, and the pictures he'd seen of Riley Temple didn't match this woman who, in her rather elegant attire, looked as if she'd stepped out of a very high-end fashion magazine. Which meant she must be ...

*Oh. God.* Mitch actually swallowed hard. He definitely should have worn a cup.

"It's a pleasure to meet you, Ms. Fontaine." He offered his hand despite thinking he wouldn't be surprised if she snapped it off at the wrist and gave it to Elliot as a chew toy. "Just ... picking up my bag. And checking on Cassia."

He looked behind Laurel to where he assumed his bag still sat on the floor. Long dark waves of her hair cascaded over her shoulder. "And dinner," she added for him. "Don't forget dinner."

Mitch wasn't often at a loss for words, but Laurel Fontaine's ruthless reputation far exceeded the boundaries of California. She had a license to practice law in seven states, including New York, which she'd visited frequently with her wealthy clients footing the bill. She was the kind of attorney that sent shivers down the spine of prosecutors and litigants. In person, she struck him as the kind of woman who didn't take shit from anyone—status or perceived power be damned.

Laurel was, Mitch instantly surmised, precisely the kind of friend Cassia needed.

When women like this found one another, they tended to form an unbreakable bond that could withstand even the biggest emotional hurricanes. Suddenly, he was very grateful that Laurel was solidly—and unequivocally—in Cassia's orbit.

He shoved his hands in his pockets, rocked back on his heels. There wasn't a chance in hell he possessed the ability to charm this woman, which left honesty and humor as the only weapons in his interaction arsenal. "I'm curious."

She arched one perfect brow.

"Should I expect to be vetted by every person who lives in Temple House where Cassia is concerned," he asked. "Or are you and the dragon downstairs the only trials by fire?"

For a moment he doubted whether leaning into the joke had been the right call, but as a smile slowly stretched across her face, he noticed a spark of amusement in her eyes. His apprehension eased slightly.

"You're going to be fun, aren't you?"

"Remains to be seen," Mitch admitted.

She stepped back and stopped blocking his path. "Cass? You've got company. Oh!"

Elliot streaked past Laurel and skidded to a paw-splaying halt at Mitch's feet. Mitch crouched and grabbed the dog for a wiggly hug that left him with a wet face and a full heart.

"You never disappoint, do you, boy?" He held the dog's face in his hands and pressed his nose to his. "This dragon loves me," he told Laurel as she shut the door behind him.

"Yes, well, you're on probation with this one," Laurel warned, one elegent finger pointed at her chest. "Cass!"

"I heard you the first time you bellowed."

It was the first time he heard a hint of the Cassia he'd fallen for back in New York and the sound was like a balm across his heart. She'd changed into snug jeans and a dark turtleneck. The red tips of her hair rested against what he imagined to be soft fabric. The trepidation in her eyes when she saw him, however, cut his elevating mood off at the knees.

"Mitch." Her smile was quick and polite. "You're back."

"Just to get my bag." He gestured to the duffel by the door. "Thanks for keeping it for me."

"Sure yeah. Of course." She shifted the grip she had on a screwdriver "Come on in."

"I don't have to." Even as he resisted the urge to follow her request, he caught a whiff of a delicious, onion and garlic-based aroma that made him mentally swoon. "I saw a vacancy sign on a motel about a mile down the way." He'd have to have been blind to miss the disbelieving looks the women exchanged. "I know it's nothing special—"

"Heaven help us—he plans to book a room at the Silver Screen." Laurel reached down to give Elliot a solid scratch behind the ears. She flashed a quick, oddly deadly smile at him. "Partial to bedbugs and Legionnaire's disease, are you?"

"Come on," he actually chuckled. "It can't be that bad." He'd definitely spent his fair share of time in crappy motels.

"No one jokes about the Silver Screen." Laurel actually shuddered. "Riley's grandfather petitioned to have the place declared a hazard and get it torn down over twenty years ago. It hasn't gotten better since then." She glanced at Cassia. "We need to find him someplace better."

"Yeah." Cassia's brows went up before her nose scrunched in that way when she was puzzling out a problem. "Sure."

"Listen, honestly," Mitch insisted, feeling unsettled by the sudden protection. "I just need a bed and a shower. Besides, I'll barely be there." He caught Cass's gaze when she shifted her attention to him. "I'll be up at the site most of the time."

"What the hell is going on with the FBI's budget these days?" Cassia scowled. "First they forget your rental car. Now they can't afford more than seventy-nine a night?"

"Actually, it was fifty- … never mind. It's really not that big a deal." He couldn't exactly come clean about what the Agency was willing to cover, when admitting the truth risked breaking whatever fragile trust Cassia had in him. "I just—"

He went instantly silent when Laurel held up a finger.

"We have enough on our plates without wondering whether you're going to survive the night in a place that makes the Bates Motel look like the White Lotus." Cassia waved him inside so casually he actually had to force himself to recall her earlier panic attack.

She seemed so … calm now. So completely unaffected by not only the open door, but his presence. Not that he was going to question it. He much preferred this welcome than his previous one. But it did leave him curious about her day-to-day behavior.

"Laurel?" Cassia asked. "You joining us for dinner?"

"I don't think I will." Laurel followed Mitch. "Something tells me you two have a lot to talk about." She plucked up an empty wine glass off the counter and set it in the sink. "I'm just across the hall. If you"—she looked pointedly at Mitch—"need anything."

"It's your loss." Cassia clearly didn't catch the expression on Laurel's face. "Sutton made lasagna."

"That's what smells so good," Mitch said before he thought to catch himself. "Sorry." He glanced down at his stomach that sounded like a post-hibernating bear's. "Haven't eaten much today other than a protein bar I found at the recovery site."

"Recovery site." Laurel frowned. "I've never heard anyone call it that before."

"It's always a recovery where bodies are concerned," Mitch said. "We're bringing them home, aren't we?"

"Yes," Cassia agreed with a slow, appreciative nod. "You are indeed."

"Well, damn, Special Agent Mitch Keaton." The tension lines around Laurel's eyes melted away as the ice in her eyes thawed. "I'm beginning to understand your appeal. Well said. Oh." She snapped perfectly manicured fingers and pointed at Cassia. "That file you're going to get me on Granger Powell."

"File?" Cassia blinked blankly for a moment. "Oh! Of course. Yeah, I'm working on that." She gestured to the desktop computer that appeared to be under a current state of repair. "Still compiling background information. I should have that soon. Sorry."

"Not a problem," Laurel said slowly. "I'd just like to have my arsenal stocked before I make my final approach."

"Approach for what exactly?" Mitch asked.

He waited for Laurel to tell him to mind his own business, but he could see the wheels turning in her head, as if every word he spoke added to the picture she was building of him.

"Granger Powell is the head of Powell Studios," she said. "He's also leading the charge to reboot the Sally Tate film series."

"They've made a couple of offers to Moxie about a co-starring role," Cassia added.

Mitch didn't understand their less than anticipatory tone. "Why is that a bad thing?"

"Depends on what strings they attach to the offer," Cassia said.

"Granger Powell has been actively trying to buy Temple House ever since he took over running the studio," Laurel added. "Part of his re-building the family name and fortune plan. Suddenly they're bringing Sally Tate back and dangling the carrot of returned stardom in front of Moxie's nose." That steel returned to Laurel's dark eyes. "I'm not a fan of emotional manipulation."

"The last offer he made Moxie coincided with a substantial bump in Granger's offer for Temple House as well as a producing credit for the movies," Cassia explained. "We don't think that's a coincidence."

"Sure doesn't sound like it." And with that, he silently bade Laurel good luck in her showdown with the media mogul, whose reputation was just as intimidating as hers.

"Really sorry for the delay," Cassia told Laurel. "Brain blip."

"You're entitled." Laurel brushed a hand down Cassia's arm. "I'll leave you to … dinner. In the meantime, I'll find you some place tolerable to stay, Mitch."

"You really don't—" Mitch cut himself off at her look. A look he felt fairly certain the defense department could implement as a counter-active laser beam should they so desire. "Thank you."

Her smile widened in a way that made him feel a bit like Elliot after the dog was praised for obeying. "You're welcome."

Mitch watched her leave, partially feeling as if he'd been run over by that SUV after all. "Honestly, Cassia, if you'd rather I leave—"

"I wouldn't actually." She spun away from him even as she said it. There were those ghosts again, swimming in her dark eyes. Ghosts and caution and … more than a little hesitation. But in true Cassia form, she was pushing through all of it. "If it's all the same to you, for tonight at least, I'd like to stick to talking about your work here and nothing else."

Not entirely surprising. It wasn't as if he had planned on delving back into an examination of the mistakes they'd made back in New York. Or the time they'd shared. Didn't mean he wasn't disappointed, though. If they were going to work together effectively, they were, at some point, going to have to talk about New York. "That's fine."

"I had some of that beer you like delivered." She grabbed a bottle out of the fridge, held it out. "Lasagna's just staying warm in the oven so we can eat anytime."

He looked at the bottle, old temptations rising before he could shove them aside. "Thanks. I stopped drinking a while ago." It wasn't an admission that embarrassed him. Far from it; he was proud of his hard-won sobriety. He just wasn't fond of explaining himself. "Water's fine."

She pivoted back to the fridge, exchanged the bottle for a bright yellow can. "Fizzy okay? It's …" she turned the can around to read it. "Mango. Personally, all I taste is sulfur, but Nox is addicted to the stuff."

"That's perfect." He took the can and popped it open. "Nox is your assistant, right?" He'd seen the name scribbled on various items on the L-shaped desk in front of the windows.

Cass grabbed a bottle of water for herself and nodded. "Yeah. They'll be back on Monday morning."

"I seem to recall you being assistant averse," Mitch remembered.

"Things change." Her dismissive had him moving on.

"How'd you two meet?" Mitch cast his gaze around the apartment and noticed the distinctly different décor in the area by the window. If Cassia was scientist chic, Nox was more Silicon Valley meets an apothecary supply shop. "I'm guessing it wasn't a college mixer."

"Nox was a student in one of my cybercrime forensics classes a few years back. Virtual, of course."

"Of course," Mitch agreed.

"I don't think I even saw Nox's face the first few weeks of class. They always had their nose buried in a book or something. Suddenly, during one lecture, their head pops up when I'm talking about RAM dumps and analyzing volatile artifacts that vanish when power goes off—"

"As one does." Mitch tried not to grin. She really was in her element with the techno-babble.

"After class Nox emailed me and pointed out an error I made. Nothing snotty. Just informational and they presented it in a way

102

that opened up a new avenue on a project I was working on. I was impressed, not only with their knowledge, but with the fact they chose to come to me privately rather than call out my mistake in front of the entire class."

"Honorable." Mitch took another drink. He hadn't met Nox, but he was already pre-disposed to like them.

"And trustworthy," Cassia agreed. "Not to mention bloody brilliant. When the patent on that project came through, I added their name to it and offered them fifty percent of the profits."

"It was that good an idea?" It wouldn't surprise him if Cassia was simply that generous.

"You tell me." She took a long drink of water. "Ever heard of EchoLock?"

Mitch almost spit out his drink. "Holy …" He covered his mouth. "EchoLock was implemented by the nuclear division at the Pentagon."

"As well as the banking industry and, I do believe the FBI uses it as well." She smirked. "Nox had their student debt paid off with their first check and I believe most of what they get is invested in various startups around the world."

"Impressive." It said a lot that Nox stuck around long after, considering they wouldn't need to work probably for the rest of their life. Not surprising to learn that Cassia continued to inspire loyalty from just about everyone she met.

Mitch met Cassia's gaze. "Does Nox know about New York?"

"I'd be surprised if they didn't." Cassia winced. "Nox's hobby is infiltrating various un-crackable computer systems to keep their hacking skills up to date. But they've never asked me about it." She paused. "That means a lot."

That loyalty thing went both ways. Always had with Cassia.

"So people," he pressed. "Nox and Sutton, for instance. Them coming in isn't so much of a problem as you going out." It wasn't particularly typical for those with shut-in tendencies.

"Once you've been kidnapped and held in a blood-covered coffin for twelve hours, your trust in the outside world erodes."

"I suspect it would," he said quietly, paying attention to the guardrails he saw rise in her eyes. Her hand tightened around her water bottle in a familiar gesture. "I don't mind if you drink," he told her, but she waved off the comment.

"Doesn't mix well with my meds." She took another drink and when she set the can down on the counter, she looked at him.

Looking into her eyes felt like coming home after a lifetime away. Being here, with her—no place had ever felt more perfectly suited.

He could read so much in her gaze. So much he didn't want to see, actually. Including the conversation she was determined not to have with him. It was as if the past sat in the background, dimly lit by a spotlight on a stage of memories. Memories neither one of them had been able to fully address or deal with back in New York.

None of that mattered now, though. He was here for her. What he wanted didn't mean crap. Instead of pushing or prying, he simply stepped back and mentally shut the door on all the things he should to say to her.

"So." He took a long drink of the bubble water, covered his mouth when he burped. "As New York is off limits, how about you tell me who the hell you pissed off that you had to call me?"

Her smile was flash-bulb quick. "The short answer? Any number of people. The longer one?" She shrugged. "Possibly … everyone." She inhaled deeply and leaned her arms on the kitchen island. "Riley opened a massive can of worms with those photographs she found. The second she developed that film, the conviction of Dean Samuels was immediately called into question."

"Dean Samuels is the cab driver who was convicted of murdering Melanie Dennings, what … twenty years ago?" Even living on the east coast, he'd found himself caught up in the sensational and infamous Hollywood murder of the young woman who had come out to seek her fame and fortune as an actress. She'd ended up in the headlines for months, but not remotely in the way she'd hoped to.

"Closer to twenty-five." Cassia took another sip of water. "Riley's pictures show a newspaper where you can see a date that proves Melanie was alive, or at the very least still being held, well after Samuels was in custody. None of that was known at the time, when the case went to trial. A lot of careers were made or bolstered on that arrest and conviction. Officers, prosecutors, the mayor at the time who went on to serve in the State senate. And"—she flinched slightly—"Quinn's father."

"Police Chief Burton?" Mitch let out a low whistle. "You don't think he—?"

Cassia held up a hand with almost as much effectiveness as Laurel had done earlier. "There are few certainties where this case is concerned, Mitch, but there's absolutely no way Alexander Burton is involved with any kind of cover up. He's as straight and dedicated as they come."

"You're sure?" The optimism she'd often accused him of wearing on his sleeve had been tarnished long ago by the realities of his job. And the world.

Cassia tapped a restless finger along the edge of her water can. He could practically see the comic book thought bubble appear over her head as she debated options.

"You're the one who brought it up," Mitch pressed. "Convince me." Was she reticent because she didn't have actual proof of her convictions? Or was it that she didn't trust him enough to confide in?

"Hypothetically," she said finally, slowly, "it's possible that Chief Burton is the one who leaked the Dennings photos to the press when his request to reopen the case was slow walked up the chain of command." She tilted her head, narrowed her eyes. "You don't look surprised."

"I've met Quinn." Those three words seemed to earn him some respect. "That honor he wears on his sleeve had to come from somewhere. Or someone. On the flip side …" His next thought was not going to win him any points. "If Chief Burton was responsible for the leak, it would give him some plausible deniability as to whether he was involved. No chief of police is going to push– "

"And there's the profiler," Cassia muttered.

If she meant it as an insult, he didn't take it that way. Their minds worked differently, his with a bit more suspicion and hers with more logic. That said? She was more than justified in her doubt in behaviorists considering how he'd let her down four years ago.

"I'm an outsider looking in, Cassia. But it doesn't take a behavioral scientist to see multiple angles of motivation for surprising actions taken, especially when it comes to something that sounds rather … expansive." He didn't know a lot, but she'd told him enough that it was obvious conspiracy theorists were going to have a field day with this case once it finally, hopefully, came to a close. "If the Chief of

Police was anyone other than Quinn's father, would you have eliminated him as possibly being involved?"

Her mouth twisted. He'd struck a chord.

"He could very well have leaked the story to keep suspicion off him," Mitch continued. "Especially if he's put safeguards in place—"

"Do me a favor." Cassia smirked and her eyes sparked. "Run this half-assed theory by Quinn the next time you see him. I dare you."

He definitely would rather not. "I'm just saying—"

"Don't say it again." Cassia waved away his protest. "Chief Burton had no power at the time this case went to trial and while the case might have put him in a position to elevate his professional status in the department, he's always been one of the good ones." She shook her head, irritation shining clear in her eyes. "The chief is an ally, our ally—maybe our only ally in that department when it comes to whatever the hell we're dealing with. And he's the reason the DA hasn't been obstructing our investigation. Chief Burton and Paul Flynn both stood up for me with the mayor when he wanted to disqualify and fire me. Chief Burton wants me on this case, probably because he knows I won't stop until I find the truth. That alone tells me he doesn't have anything to hide."

"Okay." Mitch reached across the counter and caught her hand, slipped his fingers through hers because, for that fraction of a second, he saw her drop her guard. And ... because he needed the grounding contact himself, he held on tight. "I'm convinced." But he wasn't shutting the door on anyone's possible involvement. Even at Cassia's behest. "Dean Samuels initially pleaded innocent to Melanie's murder, didn't he?"

"Vehemently and repeatedly." She stared at their joined hands for a beat before she pulled free and gripped the edge of the counter. "He changed his plea before the defense began their case. Took life in prison without even returning to court. Since then?" Cassia lifted her gaze back to his. "Dean Samuels has vanished into the prison system."

Mitch actually scoffed. "That's not possible."

"It shouldn't be," Cassia confirmed. "But I think we both know the prison system isn't as well run and organized as it should be. Inmates get away with things they shouldn't. They get privileges they shouldn't. And if they go in with a target on their back, it wouldn't be hard to miss."

Mitch frowned. "I suppose that's one way to look at it."

"We've scoured the names and photographs of every inmate in the country at this point. And by we, I mean Nox and Riley and—to the extent she can—Laurel. Paul even called in favors within the prison system as well as the US Marshals. No one can locate Samuels. But"—she lifted her hand—"Dean Samuels isn't why I brought you out here. He's a side bar at the moment, and one Paul is taking care of. We need to focus on the women in those graves. There's evidence up there that will steer us in the right direction of whomever is responsible. The fact roadblocks keep going up to stop us shows me we're onto something. Someone's not happy with us looking into things and I believe they'll do whatever it takes to make that happen. Including discrediting me."

"Coming from anyone else that might sound paranoid." All the more reason she'd want this case solved. The only thing Cassia would appreciate less than her reputation being smeared was being tagged as incompetent.

"Coming from *me*, it sounds paranoid," Cassia agreed. "Doesn't mean I'm wrong."

Mitch chewed on the inside of his cheek, debating. She hadn't mentioned the red lily he'd found near the vandal's entry point up at the site. Either Linnea hadn't had time to tell her or Linnea had decided to wait. Or Cass knew and wasn't willing to share whatever it meant with him. She trusted him enough to bring him out here, but maybe not enough to bring him completely inside. At least not yet.

"You're convinced that's what's going on then?" He asked. "That you're being purposely pushed off so the investigation falls apart?"

"Those women were not meant to be found," Cassia said flatly.

"You've eliminated people, but do you have any actual suspects? People, names, anything to go on?"

"We're working on it." And there it was again, that curtain of secrecy she very effectively pulled across her face. "The killings haven't stopped. They may have shifted, but they haven't stopped. They came after Riley, and then Mabel. Coming after me shows the pattern is holding. If we don't expose them now, there are going to be more victims buried in this city—only this time it'll be someplace we never find."

That puzzle piece that had been floating around Mitch's head since his conversation with Blake earlier finally slipped into place. "This group you're talking about. Are they by any chance called The Circle?"

The slight twitch in Cassia's left eye told him he'd hit it in one. "Where did you hear about The Circle?" She took another drink, but he could tell by the sudden set of her jaw she'd put up some kind of shield, be it emotional or mental. She narrowed her eyes in a way he could see the wheels turning. "Blake's not usually so chatty."

He hadn't been here long enough to warrant throwing Blake Redford under whatever bus might be passing by at the moment. "You going to tell me about them?"

"That's not why you're here." She glanced away. "I need you focused on the burial site."

Was she trying to convince him of that? Or herself.

"You want me locked down on lab duty while I'm here, that's fine," Mitch said. "I told you when I got here, I'm here for whatever you need me to do. Boss," he added and earned a flicker of a smile. "But,"— he tapped a finger against his temple—"like you said, the profiler goes where I go." No matter how hard he'd worked to silence that part of himself, there was no turning that off. Especially when it could work to her benefit. "It's probably difficult, thinking of asking me for help in that capacity, considering how wrong I was the last time." Sadness hit him hard. "Sorry." He held up both hands again, surrendering at her frown. "I know, you don't want to talk about all that."

"You're right. I don't." Her brow furrowed before she rubbed restless fingers across her forehead. "Whatever else happened that day, you found me, Mitch. When Whittaker …" Her voice broke. "You found me. I know we haven't talked about how or exactly what went down that made that possible, but I'm here. Because of whatever choices you and that profiler brain of yours made." Only now did she look back at him. "Let me bounce some ideas off you."

"Okay." The change of topic helped to settle his surging emotions—the impact her words had on him.

She took a deep breath. "I seem to recall you had a fascination with secret societies. The Freemasons, the Illuminati, the Golden Dawn. Groups with a large and vested interest in themselves, lurking in the shadows, keeping their activities under wraps while they work to achieve their desired goals."

"It's a hobby." And it had been for most of his life. It was one of the few interests he had shared with his father, researching the history and legends of various groups.

"Well, suffice it to say The Circle, or at least the information we've gathered so far, could be considered stiff competition for any one of those groups."

"In the abstract, perhaps. Fiction and legend have built those societies into everything from boogey-men to power-hungry megalomaniacs bent on world domination." He'd meant it as a bit of a joke, but there was no humor in her gaze.

"We've got more than sixty bodies, all women as far as we know, buried on property owned by a dead man, maintained by a law firm that represents dozens of clients with various ties to crimes and disappearances going back decades." Her eyes narrowed. "I don't think it's out of the realm of possibility there's an organized aspect to their activities."

Okay, Mitch thought. He'd give her that much. Generations of victims implied more than a single serial killer. But an entire secret society of killers? His mind reeled.

"We're going to keep digging and we're going to find out the truth, but truth isn't always a welcome revelation, is it?" Cassia proposed. "With groups like this."

"No," he agreed. "I'm not sure bringing in a federal agent is going to go very far in keeping whatever investigation you're running quiet, however."

"But I didn't call just any FBI agent," Cassia reminded him. "I called you. Because despite … everything"—there it was again, the past that loomed between them like a wall of shadows—"I can trust you to get the job done. Even if I'm taken off this case, I know once you get your hands on the evidence, you're going to follow it no matter where it goes or who it involves. That's why I called you. The rest is pretty much a bonus."

*The rest?* So she needed all of him. That may very well be the best thing he'd heard in a very long time. He resisted the urge to reach out again and catch her hand as it moved restlessly across the counter.

"If that's the case, you're going to need to bring me in, Cassia. All the way in. On all of it. Including this circle thing. I need to know everything you know, if only so I can be prepared for whatever might come flying at me."

"I brought you here to work the hills," she said quietly. "First and foremost, I need you up there with them."

"For now."

"For now." She pulled her hands behind her back. "It occurs to me I didn't thank you earlier. For coming all this way. You didn't have to. You could have said no. Or hung up on me."

"You didn't really expect me to do either of those things, did you?"

"No," she admitted with another small smile. "No, I didn't."

And that may very well be the most important thing she'd said to him since he'd arrived. "I told you before, Cassia. I keep my promises." Maybe now she'd believe him. He could see she was struggling, the way her eyes shifted back and forth, as if uncertain whether she could look him straight in the eye. "Now, considering we've both had a very long day, I think we set the heavy stuff aside. Just as soon as I ask you one more question."

"Okay." Suspicion rose back into her eyes.

"What did your computer do to deserve that?" He pointed over his shoulder to her desk.

"What?" She looked to the area that had earlier been tidy and organized, just like her.

"It looks like you're punishing it for something." The spilled and pulled wires and electronics lay discarded like the insides of an animatronic frog after a biology class. "What's wrong with it?"

"Um." There she went, debating again. Now she yanked her hand away, tucked her hair behind her ears. "Not sure. Maybe nothing. Just some …" She shook her head. "Just had some issues earlier, is all. I wanted to make sure nothing was …" she cut herself off. "I'll get it put back together after you leave."

"Anything I can help with? I've gotten pretty good with—"

"No." The answer came so fast he almost got whiplash. "Thanks, but I've got it." She turned to the oven. "You ready to eat?"

"Sure. What can I help with?"

She pointed to the fridge. "There's a bag of salad in the crisper drawer. Dressing in the door. I'll just get the bread in and let this cool for a few minutes."

It took him all of five minutes to put the salad together and set it beside the plates she got out of the cabinet. She didn't really seem to be in a chatty mood, so rather than pushing her into conversation, he turned his attention to Elliot, who while he was sitting in his very plush and padded dog bed, seemed intently interested in the brick wall.

"Elliot." The dog looked back at him as he approached and let out a soft whine. "What's up, boy?"

"He's been doing that all day," Cassia told him. "I hope he isn't getting sick."

Mitch sat on the floor and, after a bit of coaxing, welcomed Elliot into his lap. The dog wasn't small by any stretch of the imagination. Sixty-five pounds of solid fur-ball was a lot to manage, but it was clear by the way Elliot snuggled into him that Mitch wasn't the only one feeling off kilter or in need of comfort.

Cassia had put a pre-emptive kibosh on them discussing the past, which probably meant her panic attack earlier today was off the discussion table as well. That left ... surprise, surprise, *work* as the safest topic of conversation. Or at least the work she'd officially called him for help with.

"You put together a good team for the hills." He kept his focus on Elliot while Cassia continued to putter in the kitchen. "A good mix of experienced and newer technicians."

"My own Clue Crew," Cassia said and made him smile. "Isn't that what your old college professor used to call you and your fellow science students?"

"You remember that, huh?" He continued to scrub Elliot as a distraction. He shouldn't be surprised. Cassia remembered everything. "I'm not thrilled at the idea of being a glorified babysitter-slash-spy."

"I don't expect you to spy. You're here to fulfill the mayor's request that a federal agent be on oversight duty. Besides, I did a deep dive into all the people I've approved. Nox and I are working on something that will alleviate the concern I'm not hands on enough at the site. Which reminds me." She walked past him to the tri-platform desk by the window next to Elliot's bed. She yanked open a drawer and pulled out a custom narrow black wooden box. "Here." She handed it to him. "It's a new prototype that needs field testing. If you wouldn't mind?"

"Ah, sure." He withdrew his hold on Elliot to take the box, popped it open. "They're … glasses." He frowned. "I don't wear glasses."

"They're not prescription. See there, in the top corner of the frames? Those little holes are micro cameras. When they're connected to my server, they'll record and upload everything you see. Providing you're wearing them, of course."

"And this?" he indicated the larger button on the earpiece.

"MicroBluetooth." She looked rather pleased with herself at that information. "Everything's better with Bluetooth. There are other features, but those are the two important ones for now."

"So you'll literally be in my head and my ear while I work."

"Yep." She pointed to the screens across the room. "I've set the center one to auto display whenever the glasses are activated, which they are as soon as you put them on. They're water and shatter proof. But be careful, we've only gotten the battery up to eight hours so far. Oh, and there's a microscopic zoom feature along with voice documentation. The idea is you can verbally dictate while you're working."

"Not big brotherish at all," he murmured. "Clever."

"It's Nox's and my second joint invention. Expanding on other models already on the market, of course. These are attuned specifically for forensics and field work which is why we're working on including infrared readings and multispectral scans. No doubt there are a lot of bugs to work out, but you can help us kill two birds with one … stone. So to speak." She offered a quick smile. "The hope is that in the future they can be used not only in forensics but also in medicine during surgery."

"What could go wrong?" He wasn't thrilled at the prospect of having his every move watched, but what was he worried about if he was doing his job correctly? "Slippery slope."

"Slippery slopes are everywhere. We just need to learn how to navigate them. There's a charging cable in there. Make sure it's powered up before you head out to the site tomorrow, yeah? And please be careful with them. They cost a fortune."

And just like that, she'd shifted back into boss mode.

"Yes, ma'am." He put the glasses back in the box. "This case really is important to you." It had to be, otherwise she wouldn't be investing so much time, effort, and money into it. He lay back as Elliot nosed him back so he could splay himself across Mitch's chest.

She returned to the kitchen. "This case is going to be talked about, written about, whispered about for years. It's the Black Dahlia times a thousand, and with a rabid press and social media following. It needs the best overseeing its resolution. I don't want any questions remaining—at least not where the evidence is concerned. I want it closed to supposition and rumor. We've got a pretty good video record of everything we're doing up there. Adding the glasses to the mix will mitigate any issues for the future."

She had a point. There were already a handful of podcasts dedicated to the various mysteries surrounding the burial site and the mostly closed lips of the authorities. Nothing fed a media sensation more fervently than rumor, supposition, and innuendo.

"I actually meant that it seems personal for you," Mitch said. "Your friend, Mabel Reynolds. Her sister was one of the first set of remains that were recovered."

When she didn't respond, he tilted his head back, found her frowning down at the sliced open loaf of bread about to be slathered with butter and garlic.

"Mabel spent years looking for Sylvie. It's why she moved to Los Angeles in the first place," Cassia finally said. "I'm in a position to get her the answers she's been waiting for. Including the name of the person or persons who killed Sylvie. I know how important it is for her. Which means it's important for all the families."

Every answer she gave him only made him more curious. "Has she seen the pendant?" Mitch asked, thinking of the evidence log he'd reviewed this afternoon. "It's what you've used as Sylvie's initial ID, isn't it?"

"She's seen it. But Mabel never had any expectation Sylvie was still alive."

"She didn't?" Mitch frowned. Odd. Without a body, most people wouldn't give up the hope their loved ones would or could return.

"No." Cassia slapped the bread onto a cookie sheet and slid it into the oven. "I don't think she'd mind me telling you." She walked around, sat on the edge of one of the bar stools. "Mabel dreamed of

Sylvie. For years after Sylvie vanished and well before her body was found. Mabel always knew …" Cassia shook her head. "She's always known Sylvie was dead." She waited a beat. "No comment?"

"Not really." He couldn't imagine the pain caused by the loss of a sibling; he was an only child. The concept of siblings wasn't exactly a known element for him. But he could imagine a strong bond forged by family. "They were twins, weren't they? From what I hear, that is a relationship only those lucky enough to share it understand."

"They definitely had a unique connection." Cassia looked at him for a good while, her expression unreadable. "Sylvie saved Mabel's life that night up in the hills."

Mitch frowned. "Excuse me?" Hadn't Sylvie Reynolds been missing for … seven or was it eight years before her remains were discovered?

"Down in those tunnels beneath the building, Mabel swears Sylvie guided her out, led her to the graves. It sounds crazy, I know."

Crazy, yes, Mitch thought. But also plausible. He might veer toward the logical, but he also wasn't so arrogant as to not consider the possibility there was more beyond this life than simple corporeal existence. "You and I have experienced enough crazy to know that doesn't discount anything as possible."

"Huh." Cassia's smile brightened the edges of his day. "Look at you, proving me right. You know, when we first met, I thought of you as a hybrid of Mulder and Scully. The truth is out there, but there should be some logic to the explanations."

"Logic doesn't preclude the extraordinary." He'd seen enough miracles in his life not to discount them. Finding Cassia alive had been one of them. Even if, in the end, it had cost him her love.

"Always the good guy, aren't you?"

"I try to be." He smothered a yawn, felt his eyes getting heavy. "Sorry. Elliot makes for a stellar weighted blanket."

"Food will be ready in about ten," Cassia said. "Close your eyes if you want."

"Yeah?" Even as he asked his eyes drifted shut. "Okay. Just for a few minutes."

A second later, he was out.

# CHAPTER SEVEN

OF all the ways Cass considered how the evening might progress, Mitch falling asleep on her floor with her dog as a blanket hadn't cracked the top one hundred.

She'd called him twice for dinner, assuming his FBI trained brain would respond immediately to the sound of her voice even as he slept. Instead, he didn't move and, until she walked over to check on him, she wasn't entirely convinced he was breathing.

Standing over him, she met Elliot's soulful gaze, as if making sure she understood that Mitch, along with Cass, was his person.

Uncertainty and relief swirled inside of her.

Mitch was … different. It wasn't the beard or the that he'd clearly lost a good twenty pounds. He'd always been in shape, to the point that when he'd been "protecting" her in New York, she'd surrendered to his not-so-subtle hint she should consider getting a treadmill for her apartment. But that ferocity was nowhere on display; instead, he seemed more serene. Calm.

Introspective and less impulsive.

He'd said he'd stopped drinking. Considering he'd been a one, maybe two beer a night kind of guy, he must have gone down a dark path in the aftermath of what they'd been through in the warehouse. She could empathize.

Sometimes, when she allowed herself, in the quietest moments, she could hear the shot.

Cass turned her head away, as if she could simply look around the past trying to sneak around her set-in-stone defenses.

The Mitch Keaton who had shown up at her door was almost a reflection of the man she'd fallen in love with. The man who, despite making choices that had nearly cost her her life, had always put others, put her first.

He still was that man. Otherwise, he never would have made the trip out.

"Okay, Elliot. Leave him be." She coaxed the dog over to his bed where he curled up with a sigh. Cass expected the sudden lack of warmth would wake Mitch up, but he continued to sleep, his hands resting on the gentle rise and fall of his chest. Flat out on the floor. "He'll need a chalk outline pretty soon."

She went to the sofa and lifted up the hinged seat at the end, pulled out one of the many weighted blankets she owned. For a long while, they were the only things that helped her sleep. She grabbed one of the sofa cushions, lifted his head gently to place it, then covered him up.

He slept on.

She touched a hand to his shoulder, allowing herself the brief moment of contact. A moment of memory of another time. When they'd been unable to be more than a few feet away from one another. The quiet, secretive, promising smiles they shared even when in a crowd. Promises of what the alone hours for them would be like.

"Thank you." It was a whisper of gratitude she wanted to seep into his subconscious, on the off chance her speaking the words to his face hadn't sunk in.

She returned to the kitchen, finished fixing her plate, set a plate with lasagna in the oven to keep warm for when he did wake up, and forced herself to eat something of actual substance. It acted as a distraction as she alternated between checking on Mitch and the computer she'd disassembled over the past couple of hours before he'd come back.

It was stupid to think some kind of device or technology had been planted in her CPU. She had no doubt there was something on the market that would have given Whittaker the capability of accessing her account, but that wouldn't explain how he obtained the specific details of her email.

It was more likely she'd opened or clicked on something that opened a door he'd left for her to find.

That rational logic, however, had not stopped her from ripping the guts out of the machine not once, but twice. Peace of mind often came at a high cost.

Part of her therapy had been to confront all the details involved in her experience with the Whittaker brothers. Jonathan, the older of the Whittaker brothers, the architect of their crimes, had tested off the genius scale when he'd been only thirteen. Graduating from MIT two years later and earning his doctorate before he was twenty had been considered an astonishing feat considering his background. It stood to reason that even now, if he wanted something, he'd find a way to make it happen.

Even inside one of the most secure prisons in the world.

The more she thought about it, the more it made sense. Somehow, some way, he was working an angle inside The Nest. But without proof, she had no case to make.

What she did know was that the man had charisma to spare. It was how he'd coerced his younger brother Gavin into joining his misguided revenge crusade against Cass after her testimony was partially responsible for sending their father to prison for the torture and murder of three teenage girls. The prosecution had felt her expert testimony in explaining and confirming the processed evidence was the final nail in Whittaker senior's coffin.

And, it turned out, almost her own.

Jonathan had vowed revenge on everyone involved in the prosecution, holding them all responsible for his father's conviction, his multiple life sentences, and his subsequent death at the hands of his fellow inmates.

Cass had no regrets over her participation; she'd done what she always did: examine and present the evidence in the best scientific but also practical way possible that left no room for doubt in a jury's mind. She'd rarely if ever considered the actual person accused. For her, DNA, genetics, and blood told the story far more clearly than examining the personalities and behavior of the individual.

As Mitch was a behavioral analyst, this had been one topic they'd often discussed and disagreed over. But …

Cass glanced over as she took another bite of salad.

Mitch was a damned good profiler. Despite her misgivings about the science behind profiling, she'd recognized his talent in human behavior immediately upon their first meeting. He'd fascinated her with his way of looking at the world, examining criminals and crimes, putting the pieces of a mind together the way she assembled microscope slides or ran a centrifuge.

He'd seen her more clearly than anyone ever had before. It made him especially appealing, not to mention terrifying. And tempting. There was no hiding from Mitch, especially when he was convinced he was right. It was that tenacity, more than anything, that connected them. It was that tenacity she needed now.

She needed the man who had done whatever it took to find her in that abandoned warehouse in New York.

The man who had dissected and invaded the mind of Jonathan Whittaker across an interview table for hours on end, listening for the smallest, tiniest clue as to where she was being kept.

The man who, she later found out, had spent more than fifteen minutes in that interview room, without any camera rolling, in order to get what he needed. Fifteen minutes that had not been addressed or mentioned in any report. How she'd learned about it didn't matter. But she knew.

Her mind shifted and focused on The Circle.

There was a reason people rolled their eyes and dismissed the idea of secret societies. Yes, they were intriguing, but historically groups like the Illuminati or even the Masons, wielded an incredible amount of power and influence on their members while striking fear and obedience against those outside their organizations. History had shined a light on them, along with numerous other groups.

The Circle, with its still suspected propensity for abuse, kidnapping, and ritualistic murder, hovered on the precipice of being added to those footnotes. If someone could finally break through the walls of protection they'd built around themselves. Walls held in place by their followers and, more importantly, those granted power and prestige in exchange for their support.

"A maniacal fraternity."

She didn't doubt the Circle's existence. Or the power it wielded.

They were out there. Lurking. Waiting. Planning no doubt. They'd already tried to silence Riley and Mabel. One more reason Cass felt grateful for her self-built fortress of solitude. They'd find it nigh impossible to get to Cass.

Another reason that adding Mitch to her arsenal of weaponry was necessary. He was necessary for their success in exposing the Circle and its crimes once and for all.

Even if bringing him out here may very well risk the one thing she couldn't afford to lose again: her heart.

*

"Namaste, my butt!"

Mitch's eyes popped open. He blinked up at the unfamiliar brass tile ceiling, his mind racing as the continued muttering echoed from another room. The voice was familiar, but it took his mind a moment to catch up with yesterday's events.

Cassia.

His pulse kick started as if it had been in a four-year coma.

He sat up, shoving the unfamiliar weighted blanket off.

Elliot immediately padded over, the clicking of his nails across the hardwood floor loud against the steady hum of electrical equipment. The dog pushed his head under Mitch's chin in a silent plea for reassurance and affection.

"It's okay, boy." He grasped the dog's head and pressed his forehead against his for a perfect moment of comfort.

Mitch checked his watch, glanced out the window into pre-dawn light struggling through the tall narrow windows.

"Sweet silent suffering!"

Wait. Mitch frowned. Was that a … gong?

He shoved to his feet, his body protesting as he tangled with Elliot. "Hang on, boy." Cassia's continued mumblings guided him past her desk to a narrow doorway. He stopped short of stepping inside the claustrophobic space. It was beautifully decorated with serene green and blue paint, dim lighting and a collection of eclectic spiritual items that apparently did absolutely nothing when it came to bringing Cassia a sense of peace.

"Damn you, downward dog."

Mitch crossed his arms over his chest and leaned a shoulder against the doorframe, unable to stop a smile from forming. Tilting his head to the side, he watched, hypnotized as she dropped her knees to the floor in a less than gentle way. She threw back her head and blew the hair out of her eyes.

Eyes that narrowed the instant she saw him.

His smile widened. God, he'd missed her. "Morning."

"You're awake."

Well, he was now. Seeing her in a pair of figure-hugging leggings and an oversized t-shirt with splashes of neon color made her look like an 80's circuit board was as effective as an IV of caffeine. "Hard to sleep through the yoga."

She snorted and sat back on her heels. Reaching for a bright pink water tumbler she took a long drink. "I promised Laurel and Sutton I'd give daily yoga a shot for at least a month." She winced, drank some more. "I'm only on day six and I think I'm the anti-Yogi. It stresses me out."

"Holy humming bowls, Batwoman."

She stood up, grabbed the mallet and struck it against her meditation bowl with enough force to make Elliot whine.

"I think your pitch is off."

"My something is." She walked over and stood in front of him, met his gaze without hesitation. There was the woman he'd been expecting to see yesterday. That calm, steady demeanor she possessed despite her inability to turn her mind off for anything.

Well. Almost anything.

He could feel the warmth of frustration and exertion radiating off her. Her hair and skin smelled faintly of the ocean, bringing to mind sandy summer beaches and tumbling waves. He'd never quite understood what insatiable meant before they'd met. But being with Cassia had only made him want her more. More of her, more of them. More of everything.

"Mitch?" She tilted her head, lifted her tumbler as her hair fell over one shoulder.

"Yes?" His fingers flexed and once again he resisted the urge to touch her.

"Move, please." Her brown eyes darkened and for a split second he saw the silent plea for him not to grab hold of the past and drag it back to the surface.

He stepped back so she could pass. He looked down at Elliot, shrugged at the dog's confused expression then followed her into the kitchen.

"You sleep okay?" She asked in an unusual display of conversation.

"Apparently." He rolled his shoulders. "I think I might have aged out of slumber parties, though. I'm too old for the floor. What about you?"

"What about me, what?" She grabbed a scarred Star Trek mug and a travel tumbler out of an overhead cabinet and set the coffee pod machine to brewing.

"Did you get any sleep?" The instant, intoxicating aroma of coffee filled the air.

She faced him again, a different kind of surprise lighting her eyes. "I did, actually."

"Good." What else was he going to say? That she looked better this morning? Rested? Put together? Raring to go? Even though there was nowhere for her to get to? "Do you think—?"

"Linnea and her team usually get to the site by—"

"Seven, yeah." Mitch glanced at his watch. He couldn't blame her getting back to business. He hated small talk as much as she did. "I'll give her a call when I'm on my way." He scrubbed a hand across the back of his neck. "Would it be okay if I grabbed a—?"

"Shower? Yes, but this might suit you better." She grabbed something off the counter and tossed it to him. He snatched it out of the air and looked down at the key in his palm.

"What's this to?"

"Apartment 3D." She gestured to the floor above them. "Laurel talked to Riley last night and Blake dropped that off after you crashed. It's just a studio, but it's partially furnished and nice. We all agreed it doesn't make any sense for you to stay in some crappy motel when there's an empty apartment here. It'll keep you closer in touch with the case and make you easier to find if we need you. Plus, it's safe here." She rolled her eyes. "Unless you count Mrs. Yan in which case … don't."

"Noted." He squeezed his hand around the key. Whatever the reason, she wanted him close by. He'd take it. "Thanks."

Her smile was quick. "If there's anything you need, ask Blake. There are storage units in the basement with tons of … what Riley calls crap. Furniture and other stuff former tenants left behind or that Riley's grandfather never got rid of. The tenants just moved out—"

"Yesterday. Yeah, Estie and Heather."

Her brows rose. Tiny diamond studs sparkled on her ears and he remembered her telling him the stones had once been part of her late mother's engagement ring.

"They were packing up their car when I was here earlier." He slid the key into the back pocket of his jeans. "My spine definitely thanks all of you. Trust me, I won't overstay my welcome."

She flinched, the color draining out of her face before she turned her back on him.

"What?"

"Nothing." But she was too quick with the answer and far too fidgety doing nothing.

"What did I say?" With everything that had happened before, he didn't like the idea of having said something that triggered her. "Cassia. We need to be honest with each other." Even if they couldn't talk about the herd of invisible pachyderms standing between them.

"It's stupid." She tried to laugh it off but stopped herself. "It's just … the last time you said 'trust me' I walked out of my apartment in New York straight into …" She trailed off as if the rest of her statement had been abducted by ghosts. "See?" She lifted her hands in the air. "Stupid. I'm sorry."

"You never owe me an apology." But he felt the need to offer one himself. It hadn't occurred to him to couch his words, that something so innocuous as "trust me" could be upsetting.

"You must be starving." She yanked open the refrigerator. "I've got a couple containers of lasagna from last night. And some cake over there." She gestured behind her. "You can take them with you—"

"Cassia." He walked around the kitchen island, covered her hand with his where she gripped the fridge handle. He could feel the tension in her fingers, the same tension that shifted through her entire body. "I'm the one who's sorry. About everything."

She still didn't look at him and instead squeezed her eyes shut. "I still don't want to talk about it, Mitch."

"We're going to have to at some point," he pressed for the first time since his arrival. She wasn't the only one who needed a verbal purging of the past. He'd been dragging it along like an anchor around his neck for the past four years. Now, finally, he was with the only person who could help him cast it away. "We can't avoid it forever."

He saw her lips twitch. "I can try."

Elliot stuck his nose in and wedged himself between them. As far as distractions went, Mitch thought, the dog had spectacular timing.

Cassia looked down, her gaze flitting quickly to his before she stooped down to pull Elliot into a hug. "He saved my life, you know." She buried her face in his coat and held on. "Since you gave him to me, that means you saved it, too. Twice over." Only now did she meet his eyes with a gaze filled with both sadness and gratitude. "That's all that matters now. You gave me something to focus on so I could move forward; leave what happened behind me."

"Forgive me for saying." Part of him wanted to snatch the rest of the thought back, but it was too late. "It doesn't look as if you've left anything behind."

She looked up at him. "That's your opinion." Her flinch was barely perceptible.

"Talking about it—" He stopped at the flash of anger in her eyes, held up both hands. Frustration shifted through him.

They'd never talked about it. She'd never shared with him what those hours had been like, trapped in a glass coffin smeared with the blood of victims. Being forced to listen not only to the shrieks of a young woman she'd been unable to help. The deafening whirring of the bone saw. Her own screams.

The only thing sharper than the truth was speaking it. The truth cut deeper and more painfully than any lie, but it was dealing with it that had been key to him moving on from the guilt and belief he deserved to be punished for failing her.

"I'm here for you, Cassia. Anytime you want to talk about it."

She shook her head, gave Elliot another pat and stood back up. "I didn't want to talk about it with that first FBI recommended therapist four years ago, and I definitely don't want to talk about it with you now."

"First therapist?" Oddly, it felt like a topic he could gently tease her about. "How many have you gone through?" Not enough considering she'd locked herself away in Temple House since she'd walked out of his life.

"Three." She narrowed her eyes in challenge.

"Amateur," he scoffed and held up four fingers.

"Huh." Her brows went up. "Wow."

"Is that an impressed wow or a you're-more-messed-up-than-me wow?"

Her lips twitched. "I don't think you're in danger of winning that battle." Her hands shook as she rearranged the containers of food.

"Hey." He reached out and covered her hand with his. Her skin was cold, and the trembling of her fingers reawakened that protective instinct he'd had to learn to control. "I won't push. For now," he added at her glare of skepticism. "I just know that once I finally stopped fighting it and gave up, let it all out, that's when I finally was able to start to move on. That and remembering that Gavin Whittaker is dead and his puppeteer of a big brother is locked up where he can't hurt anyone ever again."

"Right." He saw her swallow hard before she looked down at their touching hands. "He's locked up." She pulled free. "I think that's a far enough walk down memory lane for today, yeah?"

Their gazes met just long enough for him to see the longing he'd been coping with surge to the surface of those fathomless eyes of hers. Eyes he would never stop thinking about. Eyes that he would happily drown in, given half the chance. "I've missed you, Cassia."

It felt like a new knife to the heart, seeing the fear rise before she slipped her mask back in place. He wanted, more than anything, to hear she felt the same. That she thought about him. Maybe even still loved him.

Instead, all he got was a desperate silence.

He pointed to the fridge before he embarrassed himself further. "Okay if I grab a fizzy water to go?"

"Right. Sure. Fizzy water." She wrapped her arms around her torso, hands clutching her elbows as if folding in on herself. It was, he thought as his jaw clenched, the most un-Cassia action he'd ever seen her make. She pulled out a knife and sliced off a chunk of chocolate cake and place it into another container for him.

"Did Sutton bake the cake, too?" Mitch asked.

"She's a good neighbor and friend to have," Cassia admitted.

Elliot sat up straighter and whined.

"I don't feed him from the table." Cass gently shooed him away. "I won't have a pest for a dog. And remember," she warned Mitch. "He can't have chocolate."

"Poor pooch." Mitch stuck his finger into the frosting and took a taste. The explosion of flavor zinged through his system. He'd probably scarf the cake down the second he was out of the shower. *Carb overload, here I come.* "I'm going to grab that shower and head up to the site. You okay alone?"

"Always." After placing the containers into a reusable shopping bag, she followed him to the door.

He picked up his duffel and headed to the door, opening it.

"Mitch?" She set the bag of food on the nearest desk.

"Yeah?" She walked over to him. She was close. So close. Maybe too close. Every cell in his body reignited as if they'd been in hibernation for the past four years. She touched his arm, her fingers flexing against his skin. "Cassia—"

She looked at him with a mixture of uncertainty and awe. "I've missed you, too."

"Yeah?" His spirits lifted. "You sure about that?"

She rose up, rested a hand against his chest. Her fingers felt hot, like a branding iron against his heart. "I'm sure." She pressed her mouth to his.

He didn't want to over-analyze the kiss, nor could he allow himself to surrender to the urge to wrap her in his arms and carry her to wherever they could spend endless hours reuniting. But the timid touch of her lips showed him she was testing the boundaries of her own mindset. Of what might be possible.

He lifted a hand, cupped her elbow and pulled her closer, closer still. He took a step back, drawing her with him, then another, smiling against her mouth as she pressed herself more fully against him, slinked an arm around his neck. Kissing her again, tasting her again, feeling her again, smoothed the sharp edges of pain they'd both been carrying around for too long. Pain neither of them knew how to completely exorcise.

When she pulled away and sank back on her heels, Mitch continued to hold onto her, his hand grasping her arm.

"Cassia?"

"Yes?" She blinked up at him and he saw a flash of the woman he'd loved before. Wild and free, tempting and flirty, brainy, compassionate, and capable.

"Don't get mad."

"About what?" She touched a finger to his cheek, a bemused smile curving her delicious lips.

"Look where you are."

"What?" She frowned, as if needing to process his request. He watched, half-holding his breath as she looked to one side, then the other, only to find herself standing out in the hall. *Outside* her door.

Her apartment a good three feet behind her.

Her body tensed. He could all but feel her breathing halt, but he maintained his hold on her returned gaze, sent every bit of energy he possessed into her, through his fingertips, in the hopes it would shock the fear out of her. But the fear quickly abated and was replaced—he suspected—by wonder.

"It's okay." He lifted a hand to her face, to her hair and she trembled. "You're okay, Cassia. You're safe. Wherever you are, no one is going to hurt you ever again. I promise." He pressed his forehead against hers. "Especially me."

Not wanting to press his luck, he gently turned her around. She walked to the door, halted, jerky steps like a one-year-old just learning to walk. Once she was inside, she set the bag with his food outside. He stepped back again, waiting for her to close the door.

"I'll wait until you're secure," he told her, uncertain what to think about the dazed expression on her face. "Go on."

She held his gaze. "Have a good day, Mitch." She closed the door.

He waited for the trio of locks to engage; heard one click into place.

"You, too." He counted to ten. To thirty. To sixty. "Only one lock," he murmured to himself as he headed for the stairs. "I'd definitely call that progress."

# CHAPTER EIGHT

"WHAT'S that there? By your left hand?" Cass pointed to the unidentifiable debris displayed on the center large screen above her desk. Stupid, she chided herself. He couldn't see her. They were miles apart with him up in the hills and her back at Temple House.

The souped-up video glasses should be the perfect solution to proving the higher-ups wrong. She'd found a way to get real time eyes on the ground. Instead of making her feel more connected and involved as her role as site supervisor, her entire body itched with frustration. She may as well be standing on a hill of fire ants.

"Cassia—"

"Seriously, Mitch." She stepped closer, narrowed her eyes. "What is that?"

He sighed, a sound she'd become all too familiar with the past eight hours. "You mean this?" Brush in hand, Mitch pointed to a twisty, woody rope that had wrapped itself around the now exposed skeletal remains. It weaved in and around not only the ribcage, but the femur as well. "It's another eucalyptus root from that tree over there." Her head spun when he whipped his gaze to the left. "Cassia—"

"Oh, right." She recalled reading in Linnea's notes about the number of tree and shrub roots they'd been encountering as the excavation process continued. It made sense given the flora dense location. "Sorry. It didn't look—"

"Hey, Mimi?" Mitch waved one of the other two team members working the site. Frizzy red hair and blue eyes magnified behind heavy spectacles, graduate student Mimi DuPont left her own assigned grave to join Mitch. "I'll be back in a few. Can you finish exposing the remains so we can get them into the evidence tent for transport?"

"Yeah, sure." Mimi nodded, leaned over to wave into his glasses before he turned away. "Hi, Dr. Davis!"

"She says hi, back," Mitch lied.

Frustrated, Cass crossed her arms over her chest, listening to the ever-so-faint sound of Mitch's boots striking the compact dirt with each step. As he walked away from the trio of unearthed graves they hoped to have completed by tomorrow's end of shift, Cass moved back and forth, side to side, as if she could get a better look at things despite her two-dimensional view. It was odd, seeing the site in full color after all her previous observation had come through the pair of black and white cameras, or static photographs sent to her from the team.

Her mind couldn't help but dwell on the advantages she'd have by walking the site herself. Normally those kinds of thoughts she had to push aside before they triggered another anxiety attack, but today?

Today the frustration overrode the panic and she actually found herself rationalizing the idea as ... possible. She wanted this case over and done, before she and Mitch stepped too close to the fire of the past. She couldn't afford to be burned again.

"Amazing what one kiss can do."

"What was that?" Mitch asked in that distracted tone she recognized from his meticulous ability to focus. He was definitely thinking ... something.

"Nothing." Her cheeks went lava hot. She was so used to talking to herself she'd forgotten he was there. She rolled her eyes, shook her head as if to dislodge the thought. As if that were possible.

He was here to help her keep control of the case, not erode her confidence in her decision. But there she was, beginning to regret, or maybe resent, his presence. Not because he wasn't of benefit, but because he was making her far more envious than she had a right to feel.

Blaming him for a situation of mostly her own making was utterly ridiculous.

Didn't mean she could stop herself though.

She dropped her arms to her side and shook out her hands to stop the nervous tingles. As Mitch made his way to the evidence tent and office, she could see the third member of the weekend crew emerging with coffee before returning to where Mitch had left Mimi.

Ugh. Her hands fisted hard. She should be up there herself!

"Where are you going?" She demanded then bit the inside of her cheek when he pulled open the door to one of the two portable bathrooms. "Oh. Sorry. Maybe you should turn off the camera before—oh." She blinked when Mitch stepped up to the sink and stared into the mirror, straight at her. Huh. The scientist in her roared to attention. The resolution in the examination glasses was really impressive. "Hi."

"Hi." He inclined his head, but all she could see was the irritation in his stark blue dark eyes. He lifted a hand and tapped the back right temple tip of the glasses. The red recording button on the bottom of her screen went dark. "This isn't working."

"The glasses? They seem to be doing just fi—"

"Not the glasses. This. Us. You." His voice carried that strained patience she'd heard him previously use with suspects and difficult witnesses. "You in my head. The running commentary makes it difficult to hear my own thoughts. Or am I not supposed to have them?"

She straightened. "Of course you're supposed to have them."

"I'm good at my job, Cassia. Maybe not as good as you—"

"I didn't say anything like that." But even as she protested, she realized that's exactly how she was coming across by micromanaging his time at the site. She certainly wouldn't have done that with Linnea. "Okay." Thankfully he couldn't see her bow her head and flinch. "Okay, you're right."

She did not like being wrong; she liked being called on it even less.

Elliot walked over and stood beside her, leaned against her leg as if wanting her to understand she wasn't completely alone. It didn't help that that damned beard of Mitch's had gone and done the impossible in making him even more appealing than he'd been without it.

"I'm sorry," she added reluctantly. "I didn't think I could feel any more useless than before you got here." She was also looking for a distraction. Not that she was about to admit that kissing him had fried the part of her brain that normally allowed her to maintain complete concentration on whatever task she was working on. Yet again, her frustration and discomfort were her own damned fault.

She pressed her fingers into her eyes. What had she been thinking, kissing him like that?

It was such unprofessional behavior, especially after the way she'd insisted that he was only out here to work. The last thing either of them needed was to re-tangle themselves around one another to the point neither of them could objectively do their job. In that moment, she'd kissed him believing that they just needed to get it over with and out of their systems. To close the door on that part of their past once and for all.

Instead, she pretty much detonated emotional C-4 and blown them completely into the unknown. And literally *through* a door.

She rolled her shoulders. At least she knew how to manage a panic attack. But this discombobulation made her feel like a probie on her first crime scene.

"I mean it, Mitch. I'm sorry." She looked back at Mitch's image in the mirror fast enough to see a hint of self-satisfaction slip into his gaze. "It's just … it all feels so close now. Closer than I've been in a very long time. It wasn't a judgement on your work, but frustration that I wasn't doing the work myself." Her hands flexed again. She wanted, more than anything, to be out there, hands in the dirt, recovering the victims who had been put in her care.

Instead, her brain, her mind, her memories kept her trapped, not only in her apartment, but in the past.

"You want to come out here?" Mitch asked with neither expectation nor frustration. "I'm happy to come get you. Better yet, I'm betting Blake would be happy to drive you up."

"Not funny." That familiar aggravation and anger twisted into a ball in the center of her chest and sat there like cement. Did he not understand? "I can't do that."

"I'm not joking. The Cassia I know can do anything," he said easily and without, she was surprised to her, judgment. "I'm not saying today or even tomorrow, but I think we can both agree that after the past …"—he checked his watch—"eight-plus hours of you muttering and running play-by-plays in my ear, this is where you belong."

*Not anymore.*

But for the first time, the very idea didn't leave her cowering in the corner unable to breathe. Her lungs burned. A bit. But his words struck a much more receptive Cass and gave her something she hadn't felt in a very long time: hope.

"The glasses are part of my taking control of the site," Cass tried to explain, but the words came out a little curt. "I'm meant to oversee." She needed to prove she was in control.

"Then oversee," Mitch said. "Silently. If I have a question or need to point something out, I will. I just need to also be alone with my thoughts to examine. To profile. You said you trusted me, Cassia. Please do that. I know what's at stake."

Possibly her entire future. She couldn't afford to be taken off this case. Not if she was going to maintain her status in the forensics community. The second she was deemed ill-equipped for one case, the rest would tumble down like uneven Dominoes. And if she didn't have her job, she didn't have anything.

"Yeah." It irked her that he wasn't wrong. Again. "I'll activate the part of the software that puts communication entirely in your control." She walked around to her computer, tapped in a few keys after accessing the glasses monitoring system. "Better?"

"We'll see." He didn't sound entirely convinced. "I'm going to grab something to eat. And the glasses need to recharge. I'll check back in about an hour." He killed the feed.

"Well." She scrunched her mouth. Now what?

She stared at her computer screen for a long, silent moment. She hadn't been able to sit at her desk since she'd looked into Jonathan Whittaker's face. Even now, she shivered at the thought of a replay. "Suck it up," she ordered herself. Whittaker had taken enough from her. No more.

Her unanswered questions as to how he'd gained access to a computer while in prison let alone her private email aside, she had to focus on the here and now. She'd already gone down multiple rabbit holes of websites dedicated to the intricacies of the prison system. There was no one quick answer or fix. If anything, her inquiries only raised more questions.

Most prison systems available to inmates were seriously outdated which Whittaker, once given access, could have easily exploited. He knew computers and technology as well as she understood a crime scene. The only difference being that Whitaker's DNA had a good dose of sociopathy. Murder turned out to be the family business, resulting in Jonathan receiving the same life-in-prison sentence his father had.

Cass squeezed her eyes shut so tight they hurt.

How many times would she wish herself back to the days before she ever heard of the Whittaker family; before she'd agreed to examine and testify as to the validity of the evidence against Jonathan's father. If only she hadn't answered that phone call. If only …

She took a long, slow breath. So much would have been different. Everything would be different. Most importantly, she wouldn't be in the situation she was in now, locked away from the world because her fears overwhelmed her reason.

"The flip side," she murmured to herself like a mantra. "Focus on the flip side." Whatever regrets she had, they paled in comparison to what she'd gained. Not to mention, had she refused the case she never would have met—or fallen in love with—Mitch. Add to that, had she not accepted the consultation, she wouldn't have found what she'd needed most: Temple House. Her new home. A fresh start.

A family.

Despite her life not including the man she loved, she had everything else she'd ever wanted. Didn't she?

Cass's cell phone chimed in the dedicated tone she'd assigned to her food delivery app. Shaking off the past—and as much as Jonathan Whittaker as she could—Cass snatched her phone off her desk.

She stared down at the alert and scowled. "What the hell? Cancelled?" She tapped through the app, looking for the details. But other than her name and account information, the standing order she'd had in place for going on two years was gone. Not just future orders, but all of them.

A quick glance at the overhead screen said Mitch was still on his break, so she quickly called customer service.

Ten minutes later she was on representative number three and explaining the situation all over again to the young man on the other end of the call.

"I don't understand how this happened," she insisted. "I was due to get my weekly delivery about an hour ago." She checked her watch. "It's been set up for more than two years. Is there a way to reactivate or retrieve it?"

"I'm afraid not, ma'am." The forced patience made her grind her teeth. "It was completely deleted from our system."

"By whom?" Cass demanded in a less than conciliatory voice.

After a short, uncomfortable pause, "You, Dr. Davis. Or at least someone who has access to your account."

That didn't make any sense either. "The only other person who has my info is on vacation." And Nox would never have changed anything without checking with Cass first. Cass pinched the bridge of her nose. "Can you at least tell me what time the cancellation occurred?"

"I'm showing yesterday around noon."

"But I didn't receive any notification."

She heard keys tapping in the background. "I apologize, Dr. Davis. I don't have any information on that. As far as I can see there was a cancelation confirmation sent at twelve-ten yesterday."

Cass's mind raced back. That time yesterday she'd been caught up in a severe panic attack that had left her almost unable to breathe, let alone maneuver through the convoluted, customer un-friendly app.

"Is there anything else I can assist you with, Dr. Davis?"

"No."

"Of course you're welcome to place another order with us—"

Cass hung up.

It wasn't a huge deal. She wouldn't starve, but the schedule and routine she had locked in place kept her in check. Her monthly order always arrived by ten on the morning of the twenty-second. These days there were plenty of other stores offering delivery, and she could always set her order up again, but still …. Unease trickled down her back. "Seems like everyone's got glitchy equipment these days."

Outside, grey clouds moved in and darkened the sky to match her mood.

Great. A storm. She looked out her window, lifted her eyes to the sky. Rain was a crime scene's worst enemy.

Mother Nature could be ruthless when it came to destroying evidence not yet collected. The only bright side to California's ongoing drought issues had been the efficiency with which outdoor crime scenes could be processed. Rain brought everything to a standstill and this would be yet another delay.

Only this one was at the hands of something none of them could control or fight back against.

She scribbled a note to herself, then grabbed her remote to turn on the additional screens on either side of the main one dedicated to Mitch and the burial site. Either he hadn't seen the clouds move in or he didn't want to talk to her about procedure for securing the site.

Either way, she needed to do what she'd brought him out here to do. She needed to trust him.

While the center screen remained on standby mode, the others flashed once, pixilating in the upper right corners before settling in to display a collection of dossiers. Each screen connected to a different dedicated file filled with the names and information she'd gathered on potential identities connected to the bodies found at the burial site. The program tweaking Nox had performed on the software had turned the advanced LCD screens into their own processing systems that allowed her to use the remote to access information without going through her desktop.

She'd created a search algorithm weeks ago in the hopes of culling through reports of missing women who fit specific criteria that put them at risk of falling victim to The Circle. It had taken some time tweaking the program, but they'd ended up with nearly seventy cases that fit. Close to the number of bodies currently being recovered. These were cases that put faces to names.

A bright red line flashed across both screens before the images settled back in place. "Glitchy," she muttered. "Everything if fucking glitchy." She really needed to talk to Riley about power utilization. She suspected all her new servers were overloading the current capacities of Temple House.

She smacked the remote control as if that could fix any issues. When the doorbell chimed, she tossed it back onto the desk and headed for the door. A quick glance at the video camera aimed at the hall had her snapping the lock open.

"Hey, Blake. What's going on?"

He handed her a substantial box then bent down to pick up the soft-sided toolbox that was practically an extra appendage at this point. "The Aegis SecureLock Seven." When she merely blinked, he added, "For your front door."

"Okay." She arched a brow at the box as if it were a bomb about to go off.

"Includes biometric-multi-scan," he continued as she clicked on lights. "A dynamic encryption code and is made from reinforced material developed with aerospace tech for military outposts and embassy safe rooms."

She eyed him with both suspicion and admiration. "It's also restricted in its use outside of diplomatic or military projects." She'd been reading about Aegis technology for years. They'd earned their reputation as one of the most reliable security experts not only in the country, but in the world.

She caught her lower lip in her teeth. Was this really what her life had come to? A military grade security lock on her door inside an already secured building?

Unexpected resentment worked its way in around acceptance.

She was happy with her setup. It was old-fashioned perhaps, but her deadbolts got the job done keeping people out.

Which was of course the problem Blake and Sutton had pointed out yesterday when they hadn't been able to get to her. Her life would be so much easier if she didn't keep finding new ways to lock herself away.

When, deep down, all she wanted to do was fling open every door in her path and take her life back.

That said, this system would be next level safety. Accepting it felt like surrender, but as long as she wasn't willing to take the steps to break free from her situation, she couldn't very well argue Blake's point.

"How'd you get this, anyway?"

"I've got connections," Blake said. "And a lot of outstanding favors."

"Owed to you by the same person who got you access to Hawk-Eye?" She hadn't thanked him properly for the tracking program that not only kept an eye on Addie, Lucas, and Keeley, but had played a vital role in locating Mabel after her abduction. The man knew his security systems, that's for sure.

"Tangentially connected," Blake admitted. "We can set up as many or as few people as you want to have access. There's also a silent distress code setting in case you get into trouble inside and a hidden override mechanism I'd suggest only one or two people know about."

"I have a cell phone for when I'm in distress," she grumbled.

"Cell phones fail."

"So do biometric locks." She could argue with him about electronics forever and it would always come out a draw. But he kept her on her technology toes.

She waved him inside in partial surrender. "Come on in and convince me. I'm fixing myself some leftover lasagna. You want some?" She didn't wait for an answer before she grabbed two containers out of the fridge and stuck them in the microwave. "I've got chocolate cake, too."

"Sutton's chocolate cake?"

She wondered if he heard how his tone gentled when he said Sutton's name. Heaven help her, she sounded like Riley.

"Well I certainly didn't bake it," she teased.

Blake took a seat at the breakfast bar, grabbed the box and used a utility knife to slice through the security tape.

Cass glared at him over her shoulder. "I haven't said yes yet."

"You will." There was no pretense with Blake. "I asked my friend what he'd use for his own family if he had his pick of locks. He didn't hesitate."

"Then you can send it to him."

Blake removed some of the packing material. "I'm not one to force things on people—"

"Sure you are," Cass snorted and grabbed him a fizzy water. "When you're convinced you're right."

"Being locked inside doesn't always mean you're safe," Blake said easily as he pulled out the extensive instruction pamphlet and flipped it open.

"How about we just create a safe word or something. For when I'm in distress or need help?" She paused, then snapped her fingers. "I can just tell you my fridge needs defrosting."

He glanced up, his brow furrowed. "Do fridges even … oh." He nodded. "Got it. Clever. But no. I mean, we can do that, too, but you're getting the new lock."

She pouted. "What if I don't want it?"

"Then I'll have this conversation with Riley and she'll come down and tell you why you're wrong." There was no smile on his face, only simple straight-forward acceptance. "You want me to call her down?"

"No, I don't want you to call her," she mumbled. "Fine."

"You need to make a list of who you want to give access to."

The microwave beeped. Cass grabbed forks out of the drawer and, after pulling the steaming containers out, slid one in front of him. "Play later." She pulled the box away. "I don't want Sutton's food going to waste and she made enough for an army."

"It's her way of giving comfort." Blake stuck his fork into the pasta. "She's also good at it. One might consider it a calling."

"Upping everyone's fiber intake is her calling," Cass laughed.

"That, too," Blake agreed. "I like Mitch," he said a few bites later. "I can see why you two were a thing."

Cass had to focus on swallowing. "Who said we were a thing?"

"My eyes." If Blake ever took offense to anything, he certainly never showed it. "And there's this … tension between you. Susan could always pick up on it. I learned to pay attention to it from her."

"Susan was your wife?" Cass wanted to tread carefully. She could count on one hand the references he'd made to his family. "You've never really mentioned her before. Or your son."

"No." He waited a beat and an all too familiar melancholy settled over them. "I suppose I haven't."

"How long since you lost them?"

"Going on four years. Ricky would have been ten this summer."

Ten. Cass swallowed hard. The same age as Sutton's nephew Lucas.

"Susan would have loved it here. In Temple House." Blake looked around Cass's apartment with something akin to approval in his eyes. "She'd have appreciated the community you all have built. She grew up a Navy kid, so she spent pretty much her entire life moving from place to place. That didn't stop when she married me. It's why …" he caught himself, as if surprised he'd continued speaking. "She wanted our son to have stability with his schooling, with his friends. We fought about it. Argued. I didn't want to be away from them, but my transfer to Spain was meant to be my final push for promotion. We agreed once I made captain, I'd put in for transfer home. I was ten months shy when they died in the fire."

None of this information was particularly new to her; she'd done her own background check on him after Riley had hired him. Hearing it firsthand, however, twisted a knife she hadn't realized she'd been stabbed with. A knife she suspected he lived with every day.

"I'm sorry you lost them." It was the only thing Cass could think to say.

"Me, too." He finished his lasagna and turned his attention back to the lock.

"You want cake now?" She lifted the lid on the dish.

"After I get this thing installed." Blake got to his feet. "It'll be my reward. Thanks, Cass."

"For what?"

"For listening."

She simply smiled, wishing she could be as open with, well, everyone. "It's what friends are for."

# CHAPTER NINE

AFTER disconnecting from Cassia, it took Mitch all of ten minutes to scarf down the cold lasagna he'd brought for lunch. The cake, as expected, had been scarfed down in record time minutes after he'd climbed out of the surprisingly luxurious shower.

In between silently praising Sutton for the culinary genius that she was and feeling slightly guilty over having challenged Cassia's observation technique, he'd found a sweet spot of competence. With the glasses charging in the office, he returned to work. Being back out in the field in any capacity, but especially with a forensics team, made him feel far more useful than he had in a long time. It helped that this team, in particular, suited his way of doing things.

Had Cassia considered that when she'd called? He wouldn't imagine so.

He'd gotten used to simply running tests and providing results these past few years. Initially, he'd craved the isolation of working one-on-one with machines and lab results. But he also quickly learned that the expected mundane of routine and repetition kept him on the edge. Being out here now, in the fresh air, felt like a good compromise between the thrill of the unexpected and the stability of habit.

Upon returning to the remains he'd been working with prior to his break, Mimi was finishing up exposing the bones. Next was taking the photographs, identifying any other items in the grave, and gathering soil samples that had been in direct contact with the bones.

How decomposed the remains were dictated how they removed them. In this instance, the decomposition was severe, so he and Mimi gently recovered the bones one by one with detailed documentation.

After carrying the remains to the evidence tent, they made quick work of placing them into sturdy body bags that provided rigid support for transport to the lab. DNA samples and tests would be run once there, the results of which would come through not only the lab's records, but Cassia's as well.

Mimi and Kian completed the chain of custody documents as well as the labeling of additional evidence recovered from the grave. Kian was chattier than the shy Mimi, but his upbeat mood kept things light despite the gloom that hovered over the sight.

The gloom was definitely increasing along with the storm-filled cloud cover. Mitch could feel the weather shifting.

While Mimi and Kian moved the body bags into the van for transport, Mitch stepped out of the evidence tent and returned to the grave he could now mark as complete. GPR hadn't detected detect any more bodies beneath the surface in this particular grid, but it would take weeks before the entirety of the site was completed.

Or ... longer.

His ribs grew tight when he glanced up at the darkening clouds. Just when he was finding his footing, Mother Nature had other plans. Normally the contingencies built into Linnea and Cassia's schedule would have offset time lost due to weather issues, but the break-in the other evening had already eaten into that buffer. But that, he reminded himself, was not his responsibility.

He knew the case was on a certain timetable, but another delay would give him the opportunity to catch up on some sleep and recharge. Jetlag was no joke and made him feel like he was working under partial power.

He found himself increasingly grateful for the small but comfortable space Riley Temple had granted him for the time being. He'd only been in the studio apartment long enough to grab a shower, change clothes, and eat something, but he was looking forward to acclimating to his new, however temporary, home.

Mitch removed the yellow flags from the corners of the grave, replaced them with the red ones signifying they could move on.

The temperature continued to dip along with the sun, casting a chilly haze over the hills. Earthquake weather, his mother had called it; when the clouds moved in with their promise of a deluge even as the sun struggled to shine from behind.

Crouching, he assessed the area, mentally mapped out plans for their next full day. The surrounding woods beyond the fence line was dense in some places, thinner in others. Unattended and overgrown. The perfect camouflage for nefarious activity. Whoever had chosen this area for their private, gruesome graveyard knew what they were doing.

Mitch started to stand.

A twig snapped in the distance.

He froze.

His ears perked but he stopped himself from glancing up, making a show of brushing off his jeans and hands as his heart skipped a beat.

The silence in the area had been noticeable and palpable, at times pounding against his ears as loudly as a bass guitar ripping through a speaker. He glanced behind him toward the evidence tent. Kian and Mimi were occupied and too far away to be responsible. Which only left …

He looked toward the trees beyond the fence.

Even the rustling leaves seemed to have gone silent against the increasing wind. When he stood up the rest of the way, he gazed down into the unearthed grave. Momentarily, he dropped his mind into what might have been.

Had the victims screamed? Or were they already dead when they'd been dropped into the earth. Was he hearing things? Or had that sound merely been a ghost on a haunting jaunt around the property?

The hair on his arms stood up as if answering. He turned in a slow circle. The back of his neck prickled as he drew his gaze back to the trees.

*There!*

Something flickered in the distance, at the other end of the cordoned off area. In the thickness of tree trunks and overgrown shrubs there was flash of light. Almost like a mirror reflecting against the cloud-banked sun.

Pressure built in his chest.

Someone was out there. Watching. He could feel them. Hot eyes monitoring his every move.

Watching. Waiting.

But for what?

Flags forgotten, he walked forward, toes pinching in his boots as if his feet were telling him to stop.

He'd have thought it was only his imagination playing tricks on him had the light not flashed again. Then, one more time, just as he turned away.

He wasn't imagining things.

One flash was something to dismiss. Maybe even two. But three?

He ducked back down, finished with the flags as the training he thought long forgotten kicked back in. Whether it was the same people responsible for the break in, or someone new, didn't matter. The site had to be protected.

That said, whoever was out there, they'd be long gone by the time he made an approach.  Didn't mean he wasn't going to, thought.

Feigning ignorance in the hope of offering a false sense of security to his observer, he tempered the adrenaline surge and headed back to the tent.

He remembered this feeling, that rush of endorphins that could easily erode common sense. It had been trained out of him for the most part during his time as a field agent. Mostly.

This building of energy, the erosion of exhaustion … the last time he'd felt this way had been moments before stepping into his worst nightmare.

He couldn't afford to lose control this time.

Mitch checked the weather app on his phone as he made his way back to the evidence tent. "Storm's moving in," he told Kian and Mimi as they zipped up the last body bag. "Where are the tarps?"

"Ah, right." Kian spun one way, then the other, his eyes a bit frantic. "In the office. Back closet."

"I'll get them." Mimi hurried off.

"Discarded soil goes back to the lab, right, Kian?" Mitch asked to confirm.

"Yeah." Kian indicated the stack of polyethylene bags in the corner. "We use these."

"I'll take care of the dirt. You and Mimi start laying the tarps and protecting the untouched grids, yeah?"

"On it," Kian assured him.

Mitch went to retrieve a stack of the bags along with the plastic bin containing waterproof labels and markers, all the while keeping one ear on his surroundings.

When it came to a case this potentially explosive, even something as innocuous as discarded dirt was given care. It would remain as part of the collected evidence until the case was concluded and the hollowed-out graves would be refilled with fresh soil once their job was done.

He grabbed a shovel and returned to the just finished grave, keeping one ear on the area beyond the fence line. Thunder rumbled in the distance. Fat raindrops exploded like tiny water bombs against the ground.

It took some juggling, but as he filled each bag, Mitch completed the waterproof label with the case number, grid location, as well as the depth level, date of collection, and his initials. If anyone opened the bag after this, their initials would replace and override his.

By the time he'd taken multiple trips to haul four full bags into the evidence tent, he was wet, tired, and longing for a hot shower. Pulling out his phone, he gave brief consideration to calling Linnea, but at the last second, he changed his mind and dialed someone else.

"Burton."

"It's Mitch." He paused, turned, and looked out the clear plastic window into the hills surrounding the site. "Someone's up here."

"Who's with you?" Mitch could hear the other man moving around.

"I've got two of the forensics team. I'm going to send them home early." Mitch wanted them out of the way. More importantly, he wanted Kian and Mimi safe. It could be just some crass paparazzo or blogger hoping to get a look at the site. Or some ghoul wanting photographs of the graves. Wouldn't that be oddly lucky.

"I'm on my way," Quinn said. "Fifteen, twenty minutes max given the rain."

Mitch let him know where he will later lie in wait for a probable intruder, banked his concern, and returned to help Kian and Mimi lock down the final two tarps. "Storm is expected to last through tomorrow," he told them.

"That means we get Sunday off." Kian bent to straighten and tighten and knock the stakes further into the ground. "We're out of overtime for the month."

Mitch gnashed his back teeth together. Cassia was right to be concerned. When a case was getting national headlines, funds and budgets should be expanded, not restricted.

The weather continued to play with them, casting shadows between the sun's rays as it surrendered its hold on the day. The wind began to howl through the trees. The entire area shifted from eerie to menacing.

"I think that's as good as we can do." Mitch gestured back to the tent. "Let's get under cover." Rain fell heavier, hitting the tarps in a macabre symphony when it struck the white plastic. Once the remains, dirt, and additional bagged evidence were loaded into the van, Mitch slammed the sliding door and turned to his charges. "I want you two to head out."

Kian frowned. "But we've got—"

"Weather's turning and we're losing light." He pointed to the van. "This needs to get taken in."

"We aren't supposed to leave without completing our end of day check list." Mimi flinched, clearly uncomfortable arguing with her supervisor. "Sir, I'm sorry, but—"

"I'm no one's sir," Mitch countered easily. "And Linnea made me well aware of the list. I'll take care of it." He turned his gaze on Kian. "You good driving the evidence to the lab?"

"Yeah." Kian didn't look entirely convinced but unlike his co-worker, didn't seem inclined to argue. He glanced at Mimi. "You're my ride home."

"Then she can follow you out." Mitch waved them off. "You guys did really good work today. We make a good team."

"We do, don't we?" Mimi beamed then glanced around uncertainly. "You sure you'll be okay here alone?"

"He's an FBI agent," Kian said before Mitch could respond. "He'll be fine."

Mitch busied himself tidying up the evidence tent, wiping down the tables, setting all the items used during the day back into their labeled containers. He recognized Cassia's meticulous list of tasks, no doubt edited and clarified by Linnea.

He hadn't been blowing smoke when he said he, Kian, and Mimi made a good team. He'd had his doubts with there only being three of them for the day, but Linnea had trained her people well. There was no handholding or babysitting required and they each had excellent instincts for the work. Plus the vibe was positive and productive. Not remotely competitive like with some cases Mitch had worked while earning his certification from the American Board of Criminalists. He hadn't had time for that one-upmanship bullshit. Maybe that was because of his age. Thirty-eight was pretty old for a new career path. Or maybe he didn't have the patience for pettiness because he'd seen and done things his fellow students couldn't have conceived of.

He'd just wanted to focus on the work.

It felt good, to belong. Even if it was only temporary.

That said, he wasn't about to allow himself to get complacent. Or comfortable.

He was only here as long as Cassia needed him.

By the time Kian drove off with the van, Mimi's blue Prius riding his taillights, darkness had settled in. Mitch ducked into the back of his SUV to grab his FBI windbreaker and pulled it on against the wind and rain.

Tension eroded the ache of a good day's work as he returned to the evidence tent and turned on one of the two telescoping masts to bathe the area in white light. He went to the trailer office where he set the coffee machine to brewing, completed the daily action report while he glugged it down, made notes for the incoming shift's responsibilities, and unplugged the recharged surveillance glasses which he stashed in his jacket pocket.

All while he waited for the sensation of being watched to abate.

It didn't. If anything, there was a new charge in the air. Excitement maybe? Or anticipation.

He returned to the tarps to double check the drainage in the area. Kian had already addressed that issue, but it gave Mitch the chance to eye the strained crime scene tape that had been looped around the cut fence rungs from the other night. The line of barbed wire along the length of the fence acted as a kind of arrow to this already subverted entrance. Unless they'd cut through some other area they hadn't noticed.

The rain began to fall in earnest and Mitch finished closing everything down. Office door locked. Freezer storage locked. Locks secured on the containers housing their tools and equipment.

Mitch turned off the flood light and headed to his vehicle, making a show of appearing to lock the padlock on the chain around the fence entrance on his way out.

He climbed into his vehicle, started the engine, and quickly made a half U-turn. He drove far enough that he rounded a curve before he killed the headlights. Pulling into a shallow grove of bushes, he parked.

Far ahead, a pair of headlights turned in and headed up the hill.

Branches scraped the back of the SUV when he popped the back to retrieve the duffel bag he'd repacked after his shower. He slung it over his shoulder, closed up the car and hiked back to the site.

He was careful unwinding the chain and opened the squeaky gate wide enough to squeeze through. Rather than returning to the tent, he made his way through the shrubs and branches, grateful for the noise of the storm as he approached the abandoned production studio building.

The single-story structure sagged against the elements. Broken windows and peeling stucco painted a rusty iron red spoke of asbestos and toxicity as Mitch approached the plywood enclosed front door.

Memory surged like a tidal wave as he shifted the covering aside. A whoosh of stale, frigid air sent him careening into the past. Nausea rolled in his stomach, threatening to choke him, but he swallowed hard and took a deep breath, pulling himself free before the memories swallowed him whole.

He took comfort in the silence, preferring it to soul-throbbing death metal that eroded the spirit and blurred the mind.

His wet boots sent dust and dirt pluming as he walked through the darkness, the scarred wood floors all but surrendering and groaning against his weight. Moonlight streamed through the broken window frames. Desks, filing cabinets, and chairs sat askew and toppled, coated in inches of years of dust, dirt, and grime.

The wind whistled as the cool storm air sank into his bones. He moved left, to where he knew one of the windows would overlook the clear area between the evidence tent and trailer. It would give him the perfect line of sight to the yellow taped fence rungs.

He dropped his bag and crouched, digging around inside. His fingers tingled as he wrapped his hand around the butt of the Glock-19 he'd bought in Vegas. It felt heavy—heavier than the weapon he'd carried as a field agent. He'd surrendered that weapon when he'd changed career paths and while he had a carry permit, he had yet to buy a personal weapon. There was no need as the firing range at Quantico allowed for a stress-relieving therapy session whenever he felt it necessary.

The knot that tightened in his chest drove the air from his lungs. He had to switch the gun into his left hand for a moment, flex his right fingers in an effort to remind them that they had a job to do.

His breath came in short, even pants.

It had been four years since he'd shot at anything other than a paper target. But as he'd learned long ago, you never picked up a gun unless you were willing to use it.

A clap of thunder sounded like a gunshot overhead.

"Get it together, man." He changed hands again. Logic wasn't going to cut through the borderline panic. But remembering Cassia had asked for his help did more to steady his nerves.

Shimmery moonlight pushing through the rain and into the building helped his eyes to adjust. He dropped the ten-round clip free, checked it, slammed it back into place, and loaded the chamber. He confirmed the safety was in place before shoving the weapon into the back waistband of his jeans. He grabbed one more item from his bag before he stood back up.

He aimed the pair of night vision binoculars out the window. Adjusting the setting, he scanned the green-tinted view laid out before him with more patience than he thought he possessed. All the while his heart beat like a jackhammer on overdrive.

Nothing yet. He drew the binoculars slowly across the perimeter looking for anything out of the ordinary. Trees swayed in the wind, their branches heavy with water, dipping and dragging. Leaves rustled as the storm pushed them around like negligible dust bunnies.

Footsteps sounded behind him. His ears perked.

"It was a dark and stormy night."

Mood lightened, Mitch grinned at Quinn's Vincent Price impression. "Sorry to call you out in this."

Detective Quinn Burton joined Mitch at the window; held out his hand for the binoculars. "What do we have?"

Quinn's jacket was thicker than Mitch's. Warmer too, he'd bet. "There. Just beyond the tape." He pointed to the previous entry point highlighted by the crime scene tape. "Hill goes up pretty steep, but the shrubbery's pretty thick. Good place to hole up and wait."

Quinn didn't respond, but Mitch felt instantly better having someone at his back. Times like this, he missed his partner.

"Probably thinks we wouldn't expect them to come back through that way," Mitch went on. "I've spent most of the day looking for another way in. Barbed wire means they can't go over the fence. Soil's too rocky to go under and everything is in the line of sight. Only way in is through where it's already cut."

"You think that's the plan?" Quinn asked. "To come back?"

"I have no idea what anyone's plan is about any of this." Despite Cassia's Cliff's Notes version of this Circle thing along with the basic rundown of the events over the past few months, he really didn't have a clear picture what they were dealing with beyond the job he was brought here to do. "LAPD on alert?"

"Two patrol vehicles for the overnight shift," Quinn said. "I spoke to Officer Yarrow and his partner on the way in. They're ready for when we need them."

"Any other officers in the area?"

"I might have made a call or two on my drive up. Don't worry. We'll be covered. Gotta admit"—Quinn continued to scan the area, turning back and forth—"it would be nice to get ahead of these guys for a change." He shook his head. "I'm not seeing anything."

"Me either." Mitch winced. "It was more of a feeling."

Quinn snorted. "Whatever you do, don't let Riley know you got me out of bed because of a feeling."

"Bed?" Mitch glanced at his watch. "It's only eight … oh." He cringed and shot an apologetic look at the detective. "Sorry about that."

"Whatever," Quinn muttered. "If someone's lurking out there, they have to be pretty desperate to be sitting out there in this storm."

Desperate, stupid, or determined. Any one of the three could make someone, anyone, dangerous.

As if taking Quinn's observation as a personal challenge, thunder boomed again. The deluge that followed made it almost impossible to hear anything else.

"Hold up." Quinn leaned in, all but pushing the binoculars out of the empty window as he zoomed in. "Okay. I think I see what caught your attention." He handed back the binoculars. "Three o'clock. Coming at us. Same path as before. Son of a bitch."

"What?" Mitch demanded.

"There's two of them."

Mitch immediately spotted the pair of dark figures moving down the rain-slicked hill. "I bet you five bucks one of them wipes out in the mud."

"Sucker's bet. Just be careful we don't."

Mitch felt like a panther ready to pounce. All that pent up anxiety and energy could have jump started his car. "How long do we wait?"

Quinn reached into his jacket, pulled out his weapon. "We don't." He spun around and headed out the way he'd come in.

Mitch dropped the binoculars and as he raced to catch up, pulled out the surveillance glasses and shoved them on his face. Cassia wanted to see the beating these things could take. They were about to find out. He tapped the smaller button on the right earpiece. "Cassia?" She didn't respond right away as he picked up his pace. "Cassia, you there?"

For a moment, Mitch wondered if she'd forgotten about him and turned the system off completely.

"Yeah, Mitch. Sorry. I'm here." Her voice sounded like sunshine in the darkness. The rain pelted down as he nipped at Quinn's heels. "Feed just blinked on. I figured you'd be headed back with the rain. You're still up there?"

"You recording?"

"Ah." Another pause. "Yeah, why. Why is everything jumpy?"

"Because I'm moving fast. We've got two more intruders. Sorry," he muttered at Quinn who shot him a glare essentially telling him to shut up.

Mitch pulled his own weapon, held it up against his chest.

Quinn stopped at the corner of the production building, leaned out and over. Mitch moved in behind him.

"Mitch, I'm going to need more than that." He could hear the nerves in Cassia's voice. "I'm looking at the security camera feed now and not seeing anything."

"That's all we've got. Could be the same ones as before. No idea. Going silent."

"Mitch?" The scientist vanished beneath worry and concern and provided him a modicum of warmth. "Be careful."

"Yeah."

"I've got left." Quinn swiped water out of his eyes and pointed in that direction. "I'll go out and around. You go right and we'll block them in."

"On it." Mitch waited for the detective to move to the far perimeter before he made his own way behind the evidence tent.

His boots squelched in the mud. A few times he slipped and almost lost his balance, but he bent his knees to shift his center of gravity. Gun held at the ready, safety now off, he pressed his finger against the side of the trigger. He made quick work closing the distance toward the exposed section of fence.

Two hooded dark figures moved in. The smaller of the two cut across the grids and graves, heading for the open gate entrance. Mitch straightened as the second figure came straight at him.

Mitch flattened himself against the paneling, waiting for Quinn to circle around. His heart hammered painfully.

Mitch dropped his head back, closed his eyes for a brief moment as he took a deep breath.

His hands shook around the gun. The cold, he told himself.

It was the cold and nothing else. He could do this.

"Freeze! LAPD!"

Mitch snapped to attention at Quinn's shout.

The first man actually yelped and jumped straight into the air. When he landed, his feet flew straight out from under him and he hit with a loud, squelching plop.

Mitch moved in, weapon trained on the second figure spinning around and racing off. He skidded and tripped in the mud.

"I've got him!" Mitch's feet barely touched the ground as he gave chase.

"Mitch, wait!" Quinn's voice vanished in the wind.

Arms pumping, Mitch ran full out, dodging the small red flags snapping in the wind. His target dropped to the ground in front of the yellow tape and scrambled like a lizard through the cut chain link.

The rain cut like razors against Mitch's face.

He shoved his weapon back into his waistband before he dived forward. He hit the ground hard. Air whooshed out of his lungs. Mud and water splashed up and over him, soaking him instantly. His fingers caught an ankle, but he twisted away when the man's other foot kicked back at his head. The heavy boot clanged against the fence.

Mitch lost his grip. He waited a beat, blinking his vision clear before he pushed himself through the pried opened fence. He swiped a hand over the glasses, trying to clear the mud and grime.

"Mitch, he's not worth it!" Cassia's voice erupted in his head.

His jacket caught in the sharp tines. He wrestled free of the fabric and shoved himself through.

He heard Quinn's voice behind him. Far behind him. Too far. Mitch couldn't be certain if he was yelling at him or calling for backup.

His lungs burned. His body pulsed with pent-up energy. The man stumbled ahead of him, just out of reach. He clawed his way up the muddied and slippery hill, feet flying as if he were caught on a runaway treadmill.

Rocks and mud came flying at Mitch's face. He kept his focus pinned squarely on the retreating man's back.

"Mitch, if he's armed—"

"Not now!"

All his effort was focused on getting enough traction to propel himself forward. He just needed to bring him down. Mitch gained some distance. Instead of feet ahead, the man was now only inches away.

Mitch pushed harder, breathed harder, climbed faster. His legs ached, screaming at him to stop.

The top of the hill loomed within reach. He could hear the other man huffing in panic. He was losing steam. Advantage, Mitch.

He slowed, forcing himself to take deliberate steps to make up ground. When the man reached the top of the hill, he paused long enough to look over his shoulder. Lightning cracked across the treetops.

In that instant, he saw the panic. The fear. The terror in the other man's eyes.

"There's nowhere to go!" Mitch yelled.

The man threw himself forward and out of sight.

"Dammit!" Mitch raced the rest of the way up and crested in time to see his shadowy form rolling head over heels like a drenched tumbleweed.

"Mitch, don't you dare!" Cassia yelled.

Too late.

He took a step over the edge. His foot sank into the mud.

The undergrowth from the trees twisted around him down the steep path. He struggled for balance. He reached out to grab branches or shrubs, doing his best to slow himself down even as he tried to keep the man in sight.

In the distance, the thick woods opened and jutted out in multiple directions.

But … that was all he saw.

Defeat sank through him. The heat of success drained away. He'd lost him.

He couldn't stop the downward skid he'd started at the top of the hill. He stretched out an arm behind him, as if attempting to control a muddied surfboard.

Water exploded up, drenching his already soaked clothes and shoes. Mud seeped in over the tops of his boots, coating his feet with sludge. The cold seeped into his marrow.

Momentum took over and his balance vanished. He pulled his gaze away from the path at his feet, searching for where the man had disappeared to. Too late, he realized he should have paid more attention to what lay ahead.

He hit a bump, his boots catching and he went flying, somersaulting twice before he caught himself. Arms and legs splayed, he landed face first on the non-existent path.

Energy spiking, adrenaline pumping, he shoved himself up. His hands sunk into the drenched earth as he twisted on his knees one way, then the other. He sputtered, spitting mud and dirt as the storm and forest coated his mouth.

He blinked against the rain, swiped a hand across his face. "Shit!"

The glasses were gone.

Cassia was gone.

It took a moment for his eyes to refocus. The darkness and haze of the storm obscured his vision. Holding an arm across his aching ribs, he sank back on his heels, nearly tipped over and caught himself with his free hand.

He gasped, scrambled away and turned, looking down at what could only be an arm protruding from the mud. He dragged his gaze up to the shape of a shoulder and the silver hair draped over it in long, wet ropes.

Flashlight beams arced in the distance, over the rise of the hill he'd tumbled down.

"Mitch!" Quinn's voice roared over the storm. "Mitch!"

"Here!" He called out, uncertain if his voice had any power. "Down here!" He moved his hands back and forth, feeling, hoping, needing to find those glasses. "Careful!" he yelled as Quinn stepped into sight. "I need light!"

Two more flashlights shined down from the hands of uniformed officers flanking the detective. Instead of them being helpful, the glare had him squinting.

"Watch where you step," he told Quinn as he approached. "I lost my glasses."

"I don't give a flying fuck about your glasses," Quinn spat.

"They're Cassia's," Mitch clarified and hoped that would be enough to convey their importance. "They record."

Quinn swore again and grabbed hold of a branch to stop from skidding the rest of the way on his ass.

"You get the other guy?" Mitch asked weakly as pain began to shift in around the cold numbness. Quinn bent his knees and made his way closer, stopping and scooping something up before he stood upright again.

"He's cuffed and in custody," Quinn told him. He shined his light down.

Mitch shielded his eyes before the beam shifted in front of him. "Double shit." He hadn't tripped over a rock.

The man he'd been chasing had come to a neck-breaking halt thanks to a ground splitting tree root. His open, dead eyes were filled with shock as they stared up into the stormy star-filled night. His body lay twisted like the vines of weeds and cover encircling him.

"Son of a bitch probably saved your life," Quinn muttered as he moved around the body toward Mitch. He gestured behind them to the rocky creek sitting only feet away at the bottom of the hill. The water level rose as it greedily accepted the rain. "You okay?"

"I will be." Once he thawed out.

"Here." Quinn held out a muddied hand.

Mitch grabbed for the glasses, relief swamping him as he shoved them back on his face. Even before he had them straight, he could hear Cassia's voice echoing through the earpiece.

"Mitch? What the hell is going on? What's happening? Are you—?"

"I'm here." He struggled around the air catching in his lungs. "Hang on." He wiped his hand across the lenses. They might have been waterproof, but mud proof? Not so much. "Can you see what I'm looking at? Are these still working?"

"Are you all right?" The breathy quality in her voice told him something he felt certain she'd be unhappy about. She still cared. She cared a lot.

"Cassia, can you see?"

"I don't care if I can see," she snapped and almost brought a smile to his face.

"Can. You. See?" Her concern was as warming as a roaring fire, but they had more important things to deal with. "The glasses. Are they still recording?"

There was a moment of silence. "I'll check." Those two words snapped through the storm.

He concentrated on taking deep breaths despite the stabbing pain they caused. Bruised ribs. He'd bet on it.

Quinn shifted around but Mitch held up a hand, stopping him as the two uniformed officers slid carefully down the hill.

"Call for a bus," Quinn called, referring to the ME's office vehicles. "We've got a dead body."

"Mitch?" Cassia's voice sounded almost detached. "It's recording."

"Good. Look at this." He shifted to his knees, scooted back and aimed his gaze down. He didn't want to disturb the area any more than the storm already had. Water spilled in and around the shallow grave. The hint of flowered fabric eked out beneath the mud. The silver hair.

Mitch reached out, touched a hand to the wrinkled skin of the body lying beneath the surface. "You seeing this?" He asked Cassia.

"Yeah," Cassia murmured quietly. "I see it."

"See what?" Quinn crouched and shined the light down.

"Have them send two busses," Mitch told him. "We've got another body."

# CHAPTER TEN

THE worst of the storm had passed.

Or maybe, Mitch thought as he stood crouched beside the body of the man he'd been pursuing, he'd simply gotten used to the rain.

Staring down at the body beneath the yellow tarp he held in one frigid hand, he realized he'd never seen a dead man look quite so shocked before.

He was younger than Mitch expected. Mid-to-late twenties, maybe, and on the hefty side. With spiky black hair tempered by the weather and the edges of a skull-and-bones tattoo peeking out from under the worn collar of a blue t-shirt, he looked both unique and like every other kid roaming the streets of LA.

Mitch had overheard enough to know that there had been no ID found on the body, which meant they'd be waiting on prints once he was taken to the morgue. If that didn't get any results, they'd do a DNA test, and they'd release his picture to the public and hope, pray even, that whoever he was, whoever he'd been, someone was out there missing him.

Mitch dropped the covering back in place and shoved to his feet He sucked in a sharp breath and grabbed hold of his chest when his ribs protested.

"You sure you don't want to get that checked out?" Quinn called from where he stood by the second body with Officers Yarrow and Deacon.

"Quinn's right." Cassia's voice echoed gently in his ear. "You should—"

"Are you still recording?" Mitch swallowed hard. The last thing he wanted to hear right now was sympathy.

"No." After a beat, "Mitch—"

"I'll check in with you later." He snatched the glasses off his face and pocketed them. Rude? Probably. But he had enough on his mind without having Cassia's doubting voice in his head.

He walked away from one body to approach the other.

From a distance he could see the bright flowered fabric of her clothing shining in the barely-there streams of moonlight. The coroner had already come and gone, releasing both bodies and thus the site to the crime scene investigators. Cameras snapped and lights flashed as the area was documented and mapped out. Additional officers milled about, providing support and assistance when needed. The tone and mood were as subdued and professional as any he'd ever seen.

Head lamps and battery-operated lights brought in on foot cut through the night, rain, and dank.

What an absolutely shitty night.

Quinn tried again. "If you want to go to the ER—"

"They aren't broken." That didn't mean his ribs didn't hurt like a son of a bitch. "They won't do anything other than give me meds I won't take. I'm fine. Where's the other guy?" Whatever they'd been up to certainly hadn't been worth risking their lives.

"He's in custody." Quinn checked his watch. "I'll let him get dried off and warmed up and question him in the morning."

Mitch wasn't in any position to feel disappointed at not being invited to at least observe, but then he worked for Cassia, not the LAPD. He indicated the newly unearthed victim. "Can I see her?"

"Sure." Quinn nodded to Officer Deacon who bent over to lift the corner of the tarp.

"No ID. Coroner thinks she's in her late sixties, early seventies," Quinn said as Mitch bent down. He winced into the darkness and Officer Yarrow called over one of the techs for some light. "She's frail, but that's probably age. Beyond that, we won't know anything until he gets her on the table. The question is what in the hell is she doing out here?"

Whatever answer Mitch might have offered stalled behind suddenly stiff lips.

He blinked, staring as the light banked the shadows and the old woman's face came into clear focus. The deep-set wrinkles stretching across her forehead, the large age spots stark against the crepey skin of her neck. Brittle, straw-like silver hair. Cold, empty and all too familiar green eyes.

His cold body flushed with sudden heat. It couldn't be ...

Could it?

His chest tightened. Hands flexing, he swallowed hard as his mind raced.

"Mitch?" Quinn asked. "Something wrong? You recognize her?"

"No." It didn't occur to him not to lie. Mitch shook his head, not just to clarify his answer but to try to clear his thoughts. "Just wondering if she's connected to ..." He looked over his shoulder to the hill. "You think she's connected to them?"

"Not sure how," Quinn admitted. "I'd be surprised if she is, though. As far as we know all those victims were under thirty. But is it possible?" He shrugged. "I've learned not to discount anything."

"Coroner thinks she's been dead no more than seventy-two hours," Officer Deacon said.

It was less, Mitch thought. Much less. He shivered and glanced up, trying to connect the officer's voice with the words she spoke, but he couldn't shake the fog from his mind.

His skin felt clammy and hot at the same time. Nausea rolled in his belly. Or was that dread? He nearly pitched forward until Officer Yarrow steadied him with a hand on his shoulder. "Thanks. Sorry." He shifted back to his feet, head spinning. He planted his hands on his knees and bent over. "Guess maybe tonight took more out of me than I thought."

"I can have them drive you back to Temple House," Quinn offered.

"No. Thanks." Mitch shook his head. "I'm good. Is this going to stop us from working the site once the weather passes?"

"Hard to say." Quinn shrugged again. "Paul's due back tomorrow. If the mayor or DA tries to use this as an excuse, he'll do what he can to push back. That said, a recent death is going to take precedent over bodies that have been buried for years."

Mitch couldn't argue with that reasoning. No matter how much he wanted to.

"In the meantime," Quinn went on, "I suggest we handle this as just another case."

Mitch heard the doubt in the detective's voice. "You don't believe it's just another case, do you?"

"No," Quinn said quietly as Officer Deacon replaced the tarp and they moved off. "I definitely do not."

*

The last time Cass spent the night curled up in an office chair had been the night before her PhD dissertation on microtrace biosignatures. Somehow the months she'd spent researching and theorizing the potential uses for nanotechnology seemed a lifetime away from a stormy night spent watching security camera feeds.

Arms curled around updrawn knees, Cass's gaze was locked on the center space of the four screens, giving her peripheral line of sight for when Mitch finally walked through the lobby doors of Temple House.

Every muscle in her body had tightened to the point of pain. She had the feeling the second she tried to move she may very well snap apart.

There had been something particularly horrific about standing in the middle of her apartment, eyes glued to the center screen, watching Mitch throw himself into the storm-tossed hills in pursuit of a known subject. There was no thrill to the chase, no detached TV script standing between reality and fantasy. Anything she'd yelled— and she'd yelled a lot—had fallen on deaf ears.

When he'd flown forward and tumbled into darkness, she'd dived at the screen, hands stretched out as if she could catch him.

Instead, her screen had gone black. The apartment, silent.

Her heart had all but stopped in those endless moments. She didn't remember breathing until she heard his voice again. She'd had to cover her mouth to stop the anger and fear from spilling out in a tirade chastising his reckless and impulsive behavior.

159

The same behavior that had changed both their lives forever.

He wasn't an agent anymore! What had he been thinking?

But she knew the answer to her own question. He hadn't been thinking; he'd acted on instinct. Because deep down, despite his job change, despite the four years that had passed, he was an FBI field agent at heart.

The fear had subsided, replaced with an irritation she couldn't explain when he'd refused medical attention. He'd tripped over a dead body, wiped out face first in the forest and his plan was to walk it off.

"Typical man." It was better she focus on that aspect rather than have to accept the reality of her feelings.

While everything else might have changed in the past four years, one thing had not.

She still cared about him. She still …

Cass closed her eyes before the admission could fully form in her mind. In his bed against the wall, Elliot's gentle doggie snores lulled her into an unexpected calm. Her eyes drifted closed, only to snap open when movement streaked across one of the screens.

She sat up straighter, wincing as her spine popped. She watched Mitch walk through the lobby doors. As the ancient, creaking elevator didn't operate between ten p.m. and six a.m., he headed for the stairs.

Cass checked her watch. Her heart skipped a beat. She unwound herself and dived out of the chair, startling Elliot awake as she raced to the door.

Her hand reached for the deadbolts that were no longer in place. It took her a moment to remember she needed to enter the four-digit passcode on the keypad beside the door then press her thumb into the biometric scanner near the handle.

The lock disengaged. She yanked the door open just as Mitch rounded the landing.

He stopped for a moment, hand tightening around the banister before he took the final set of stairs. "It's one in the morning, Cassia." His voice was low, his clothes wrecked, his face bruised. "I just want to take a hot shower and get some sleep."

"But—" She stepped into the hall, bare toes tingling against the cool tile floor. She almost tripped, her mind and feet arguing over who had the most control at the moment. Cass gave in to her feet and, since he didn't seem inclined to approach her, walked to him.

It was an odd defeat she saw in his eyes, a haunting of sorts displayed by the drawn tightness of his mud-caked face. She couldn't stop herself. She touched his cheek. Not until this moment did she truly believe he was, for the most part, unharmed.

He closed his eyes as if her touch caused him pain.

"You're sure you're okay?" It was one question among dozens that hovered behind her pursed lips. "Your ribs—"

"I'm fine." He caught her hand, pushed it away, but instead of letting go of her completely, twined his fingers through hers. "I just really want to get into a hot shower and crash for a few hours. I'll call you when I'm coherent."

"Yeah, sure." She nodded, waiting for that punch of panic to strike and send her scrambling back into her apartment like a frenetic squirrel. "Mitch—"

"We'll talk later." He squeezed her hand before he released it and pulled himself up the stairs and out of sight.

A long-ignored longing swept over her. It had been so long since she'd held him in her arms. So long since there had been anything but the past standing between them. But in this moment, for this breath, all she wanted was to be with him.

Hands shaking, she reached for the banister and gave in to the overwhelming urge to follow.

"I don't know him well." Cass spun around to find Laurel lounging in the open door of her own apartment. "But I feel safe in saying it's best you leave him alone, Cass." She tilted her head, sending her dark wavy hair cascading over the shoulder of one of her cozy sweaters. "Amped up?"

"Maybe." Was that what this feeling was? She felt like an overclocked computer processor with too many windows open. "You heard?"

"About them finding another body up on the hill? Yeah. Riley texted a few hours ago." She stretched out a hand, her long red nails glistening in the dim light of the hall. "Come on. I think we could both do with some company."

Cass glanced back at her apartment door as Elliot nosed his way out.

"You, too," Laurel called to him. "I've got treats." Elliot immediately trotted over and disappeared into Laurel's apartment. "Go close your door," she instructed gently. "I'll wait here."

Cass swallowed hard. The last two days had been a mishmash of activity and emotions, the latter of which didn't feel solid enough to fully identify, let alone embrace and process.

Feeling a bit like a zombie, she walked back to her door, reached for the knob. And pulled it shut.

The gentle click loosened something inside of her and her legs felt lighter when she returned to Laurel.

"How'd that feel?"

"Liberating." It was, Cass thought, the only word that came close to the truth.

"Wine, chocolate, or popcorn?"

"Um." As much as she would love a glass of wine, she didn't like drinking when she wasn't certain when her next dose of anxiety meds might be necessary. "I'll take bachelors two and three."

"On it."

It wasn't until she was sitting on Laurel's plush deep-seated sectional that complimented the gold and white elegant décor that Cass was even inclined to panic. But that inclination was quickly swamped by exhaustion. She simply didn't have the energy to feel anxious right now.

Instead, she focused on how comfortable her friend's home was. How welcome she felt. How much she missed a life lived outside the cage she'd built for herself.

Cass loved the loft-style plan that was open and spacious and, despite Laurel's success working for some of the most powerful people in the entertainment industry, completely unpretentious. Quality over bling. The same could be said of the woman herself.

Cass sank back into soft cushions that felt like giant marshmallows. The flat screen television on the opposite wall rivaled those of a movie theater and currently displayed a rather gruesome swamp creature frozen on pause.

Elliot, finished with his promised treats, curled up at her feet.

"Question," she called.

"Shoot." Laurel rummaged through her cabinets and packages.

"What is it with you and horror movies?" The woman watched them on a loop and was at least partially responsible for Keeley's rabid interest in both scary films and novels.

"They're a reminder."

Cass twisted around, grabbed the back of the sofa and watched her friend sort through a selection of chocolate candy. "A reminder of what?"

"That no matter how bad things get, they can always be worse." She flashed a smile that didn't come close to reaching her dark eyes. "And they remind me of my dad."

Cass curled her legs in. "He was a diplomat, wasn't he?"

"Mmmm." Laurel came over to retrieve her empty wine glass off the coffee table. "Of a sort. He was a Consul General, first in Hong Kong, then in Dubai." At Cass's blank stare, she added, "He was their main business negotiator, primarily in trade deals."

"Oh. That sounds"—What was the word?—"tense."

"It was a lot of things." Laurel ripped open a bag of mini M&Ms and added them to a bowl filled with "healthy" popcorn. "I lived in hotels pretty much until college. He was always working, but he wanted me with him." She poured another glass of wine, grabbed a bottle of water out of the fridge, and headed over. "Before my mom died, he promised her he'd never leave me behind. Or alone." She handed Cass the bottle and bowl and sank into the space beside her. "He kept one of those promises at least. Wasn't his fault he couldn't keep the other." She popped a handful of popcorn into her mouth.

Cass was familiar enough with grief to recognize it, even when it was carefully concealed.

"I remember reading about the terrorist attack when it happened," Cass said. "Wasn't the group responsible called the Crimson Dawn or something like that?"

"There's that computer brain of yours at work." Laurel sipped wine, seemed content to look anywhere other than at Cass. "I was supposed to be with him that weekend. I begged off at the last minute. I'd just started college and didn't want to make the trip out. He was relieved, actually. There was this big merger he was working on and he needed to focus. We agreed to spend a few weeks the next summer in Paris. That's where they were both from but with his work, we never really spent much time there as a family." Her smile was quick. "The bombing happened two days later."

Cass's attention drifted to the collection of framed photos lining a side table beneath a window. "When did you finally go to Paris?"

"That summer." In pure Laurel fashion, little emotion sneaked into her voice. "The company he'd been working for paid out a huge settlement to the families. They'd ignored the threats and refused to hire extra security. I used some of what I got to take the trip we'd always wanted, scattered some of my mother's ashes in the Sienne, then came back and went to law school. It's what he hoped I'd do, and I wasn't about to disappoint him, even after he was gone."

"You're good at it." Cass couldn't imagine doing better.

"I'm my father's daughter," Laurel confirmed. "On the few nights we'd have together, we'd watch horror movies non-stop. We'd get the jumps and the giggles and," she shrugged, "it was home for me. So. That's why horror movies. But speaking of horror ..." She ate more popcorn as Cass plucked out a handful of yellow M&Ms. "Mitch being back going okay for you, so far? I mean, other than tonight?"

"We haven't spent that much time together. It's hard to say how things are going."

"Then let me say, considering what I saw out in the hallway. You're doing just fine. Surprised you two didn't start a five-alarm fire."

"Please." Cass rolled her eyes. "I don't think—"

"Good," Laurel cut her off. "You think too much. Sometimes you just need to feel and go with the flow."

"Remind me, when was the last time you went with the flow?" Cass tossed a popcorn kernel at her face and earned a smile.

"We aren't talking about me and besides, I'm picky." Laurel inclined her head, narrowed her eyes. "Come to think of it, I did go out with this hedge fund manager a few months ago. Really didn't think I could be bored talking about money but listening to this guy talk about his ever-growing portfolio was just ... ick." She shuddered.

"You need to be challenged," Cass observed. "Someone as ambitious as you are."

"Good luck finding them. And you changed the subject."

"Nothing gets by you, counselor."

"Mmmm. True." She ate more salt and sugar. "Tell me about Mitch. The short version, if that's easier," Laurel added at Cass's wary expression. "You're going to have to come clean with us at some point. We've let you get away with keeping things to yourself for four years, but I think it's safe to say your streak is over. And we're done waiting. Especially now that your mystery man is actually here."

"I wouldn't even know where to start." It wasn't a lie. Exactly. Other than with her therapists, she'd never talked about that time with Mitch. With anyone.

"Start with how you two met." Laurel pushed. "That has to be fairly easy to answer."

"You'd think." Cass laughed a little as the past loomed. Maybe it was time. If she ever wanted to get her life back, if she ever wanted to take an actual step out of Temple House, it was going to have to start with her shoving herself out of protective mode.

"A little background first." She thought it might be easier, but as she started to speak, she could feel that tension pull at her chest. "There was this case I testified as an expert witness in a number of years ago. I was asked to explain, in layman's terms, what the evidentiary results were so the jury could understand them."

"What kind of case?" Laurel asked.

"A fifty-six-year-old man was accused of killing three teenage girls. It was … as nasty as you'd imagine. Both the case and the trial. The victims' families were a mess and the accused's were delusional in their belief in his innocence, despite a documented history of violence in the home. At one point during the trial, the man's younger son was banned not only from the courtroom, but the courthouse for shouting threats. And their mother …" Even now she could see Irene Whittaker's unwavering, evil-eyed stare while Cass had pounded the last nail in the prosecution's coffin. "That woman could have been standing in the middle of an inferno and still been frozen solid."

"Years of abuse and violence does that. You're right," Laurel agreed. "It doesn't get much nastier."

"The man was eventually found guilty and sentenced to life in prison. He didn't last six months before he was killed by other inmates."

"Natural selection at work," Laurel toasted with her wine.

"Hmmm." It almost felt as if Cass was telling someone else's story. "That brings us to a little over four years ago in New York. Two of the jurors from that trial went missing and were found dead days later. They suffered violent, awful deaths." That haunting bone saw whirred in the back of Cass's mind. "It took authorities until victim number four—the judge who oversaw the trial—to put the pieces together, and even then it was an FBI profiler who presented his suspicions." She glanced at her friend. "Mitch."

"Ah."

"He was one of the FBI's brightest rising stars at the time." So bright he'd been offered a teaching position at Quantico shortly before everything went to shit. "After the judge was murdered, the prosecutor was killed. The list of who was being targeted got pretty small. Obviously I was on it." The detachment she felt from the exposition should have disturbed her more than it did.

"Shit." Laurel's eyes sharpened.

"Mitch and his partner were assigned as my protection detail. He and I …" She shrugged. "Clicked."

"Sounds like the beginnings of one of Sutton's steamy romance novels."

"Things definitely got steamy," Cass admitted. "And I'll admit it— he was a great distraction. I didn't do well, locked up in my apartment for weeks on end. Not being able to live my life, work my own cases. The killings stopped. We found we had some breathing room and we filled it up." With one another. "It was—well, it was lust at first sight." But the love had followed. It had also lingered. "Mitch was different from anyone else I'd ever met. To be honest, it was nice not having to pretend to be something I wasn't. To stroke his ego or make him feel adored or important." That was what she'd loved most about him. He hadn't been intimidated by her intellect, nor did he buy into the weaker sex bullshit she and so many other women had to deal with. He'd simply loved her for her. "This probably isn't surprising, but I've always found relationships to be—"

"Challenging?" Laurel suggested with over-wide eyes.

"Touché." It was as good a word as any. "Nothing rattled him. He took everything in stride. Seriously, unshakable. Even with the most inhumane and gruesome things he's seen. We worked together as partners in all ways, me with the crime scene evidence and him with his profiling, something that until I saw it in action, I wasn't convinced would work. We finally found what we needed to bring in a suspect. The older son of the man I'd testified against." She took a deep breath. "Jonathan Whittaker."

Laurel's expression didn't change. "You say that name as if I should know who he is."

"Be glad you don't." Relief had Cass blowing out a slow breath. The FBI's guardrails on the case continued to hold and for that, she was grateful. "He's not someone you want living in your head."

*It's almost time. Can't wait to see you.*

Cass shuddered.

"I'm assuming something went wrong," Laurel pressed.

"Everything. Everything went wrong," Cass admitted out loud for what felt like the first time. "Mitch assumed Jonathan's sociopathic tendencies made him incapable of working with a partner. He was wrong." So very, very wrong.

"Let me guess," Laurel said. "The whackadoo brother. Following in daddy's footsteps."

Cass reached out and took Laurel's wine glass, took a healthy swallow so she could finish.

"Once Jonathan was in custody, Mitch called to tell me the threat was over. You can imagine how thrilled I was to be out from under lock and key. The first thing I did was walk out of my apartment to get a coffee from this shop near my apartment." Her throat threatened to close around the faint memory she had of that day. That intoxicating, cold metal, exhaust-fume-tinged New York air. The winter chill had coated her lungs. A suffocating terror descending when that arm had locked around her throat before the pinch of a needle hit her neck.

She didn't remember being dragged back and into a van.

She only remembered waking up surrounded by blood.

Cass cleared her throat. "Gavin was waiting for me."

"The brother, right? Jesus Christ." Laurel shifted closer and took her wine glass back. "Why in the hell didn't you ever tell us any of this?"

"Tell you what exactly?" Cass asked. "That I was kidnapped by a spree killer? That I was held and tortured and forced to watch him kill a young woman who had done nothing other than serve on a jury that convicted a guilty man? That I was drugged and ...” The screams. Even now she could hear those screams ricocheting through her head. She could almost push them out of her mind. But not completely. Never completely.

The trembling returned. She fisted her hand around the edge of the ceramic popcorn bowl. “It's bad enough I have to live with what happened, Laurel. I didn't want you all saddled with it as well. I didn't want you to, to ... pity me. To only see my trauma.”

“We're your friends,” Laurel argued gently. “We're your family, Cass. If you can't trust us—”

“Trust has nothing to do with it, Laurel.” It had everything to do with trauma. Trauma she hadn't wanted to voice. Trauma she'd never intended to voice. “The only reason I'm telling anyone now is because Mitch is here, and, honestly? I don't have the bandwidth to censor myself when we have work to do. He could have died tonight because of our case. Because of me.”

“Not because of you.”

Cass shook her head. “I called him here.” She paused, tried to explain. “He brings back emotions I've tried to bury, but also all the horror of that time I want to forget.”

“How long?” Laurel's question snapped Cass back into detached mode. “How long did he have you?”

“Eleven hours, twelve minutes.” Twenty-nine seconds. Not that she'd counted. “What is happening now has nothing to do with what happened then,” she insisted.

“That might have been true before Mitch got here,” Laurel argued. “He has a lot to do with both now.”

“I'm working on compartmentalizing,” Cass admitted. “My head is anything but clear when he's around, but ...” She couldn't explain it. Maybe didn't want to. Because the truth was, she'd missed him. And ... she did want him around. “I can't afford to let the past get in the way. Not if we're going to get the answers we need and the victims the justice they deserve.” She took a long, slow breath. “Not if we're going to have any chance of going up against The Circle.”

“The Circle.” Laurel may as well have spat out a curse. “Maybe they've gone into hibernation. Or they disbanded after coming after

Riley then Mabel. Wouldn't that be nice? I mean, no women have gone missing since Eve Hudson, so that has to be good."

"I've never known you to be delusional." Cass had no doubt the group was still out there, either biding their time or making plans to prevent their exposure. An organization didn't survive for decades without having contingencies in place. She'd learned enough from Mitch to suspect The Circle going seemingly dormant only meant they were regrouping. And planning.

"I'll lean into whatever delusion means we can stop obsessing over these people." Laurel shook her head. "Listen to me. Like we don't even have any names or faces to tie to the Circle. All we've got so far are their victims, a bunch of rumors, and some swanky gentleman's club that updates their website about as often as I buy knockoff shoes."

Cass glanced down at Laurel's feet currently encased in Gucci slippers.

Laurel was quiet for a moment. "I'm going to suggest something you aren't going to like. But I want you to seriously consider it."

Drained, Cass didn't know if she had the energy to even think about arguing. "Okay."

"You need to tell the others what you've told me. All of it, Cass. About what happened to you and with what happened with Mitch." She paused, frowned. "Hang on." She reached out and touched Cass's arm. "What *did* happen with Mitch?"

Then again, maybe there was some energy in reserve. "Not tonight. Please, Laurel," she added when Laurel opened her mouth. "Not tonight." It was bad enough she'd had to walk back through the details of her abduction. She wasn't in any frame of mind to dissect what had happened with Mitch after …

After.

"All right." Laurel smoothed her hand down Cass's arm. "Sorry. You're right. It's the lawyer in me. I always have questions."

Cass's smile was weak.

"But I'm right about you sharing this with the others. I can't be the only one who knows, Cass," Laurel insisted. "You're right that what happened then isn't about *now*, but *then* is affecting you. Otherwise, you wouldn't have spent the last four years locked inside Temple House. Just like you were locked up for that month in New York."

It was a comparison that hadn't escaped Cass's notice.

"Do you know how many conversations we've had trying to figure out the best way to help you?" Laurel asked. "How many scenarios we came up with that could have caused … this? What kind of exposure therapy might shock you out of your refusal to walk back into the world? What you've told me explains so much, Cass. Riley and Sutton and Mabel, they deserve to hear this truth. They've been at your side through it all. Trust me on this," she said in that lawyer-y tone she picked up when making a final argument. "Get it out. So we can deal with it. Together." She tightened her grip on Cass's hand. "And the sooner the better."

Tears blurred Cass's vision. "I don't want to." It was bad enough Laurel now knew, but Cass's defenses had been lowered enough that her resistance was threadbare. Laurel was the strongest of all of them. She'd dealt with some pretty nasty clients and cases over the years. There was very little that could surprise her. "I don't want to be pitied, Laurel. Can you imagine what Sutton will think? Or—oh my God." Cass pressed a palm into her left eye. "Jesus, Laurel. This means I have to tell Nox."

"*We* will tell Nox," Laurel said softly and shifted so she could wrap an arm around Cass's shoulders. "That's something you're going to have to get used to because I'm done walking on eggshells around you. You aren't alone. You never have been, but it's time for you to remember that. You've got this, Cass. I—we'll—make sure you do."

She made it sound so easy, but how was Cass supposed to believe her when she couldn't trust herself?

Cass rested her head on Laurel's shoulder and sighed. "If I agree, will you shut up about it?"

"For tonight." Laurel gave her a squeeze and finished her wine. "Right now I'm thinking tomorrow is the perfect time to restart mimosa yoga."

"It'll be raining," Cass murmured as exhaustion crept over her.

"The important word in that statement is mimosa," Laurel said softly. "You get some sleep." She tightened her hold on Cass and whispered over her head. "I'll take care of everything."

# CHAPTER ELEVEN

"YOU were abducted?!" Riley Temple's voice carried the shocked disbelief Cass pretty much predicted. "By. A. Serial. Killer."

"Technically Gavin Whittaker would be considered a spree killer," Cass corrected in a tone Mitch would have been proud of.

"What's the difference?" Sutton leaned over and picked up her second mimosa of their spur-of-the-moment brunch.

"What's the—?" Riley gaped, irritation filling her narrowed eyes. "*That's* the question you want to ask?"

"I'm sure we all have questions we'd like to ask." Laurel reached for the empty pitcher, pushed out of Cass's sofa, and went into the kitchen for a refill. "And perhaps we can save them all for our next margarita night. But for now, Riley's correct. This isn't the time to argue semantics about certain psychopathic members of society."

Cass smiled in relief. Laurel was keeping her promise to take care of things. It wasn't the only reason she felt grateful this morning. She'd had one of the best night's sleep she'd had in months. One thing Laurel always managed to do was make people, especially the people she cared about, feel safe. As for how she wrangled their mutual circle of friends, had Laurel the inclination, she could make just as much money as a mediator.

With the grey clouds and intermittent wind and rain, Cass couldn't have picked a better day to blow up the rest of her life. But that was the fear of uncertainty talking. She had to—no, she needed to—keep the faith that her friends would understand the secrets she'd been keeping. The secrets she hadn't let herself completely process for more than four years.

"Yes, please. Let's save that for another brunch." The edge in Sutton's voice had Cass shifting into defensive mode.

Cass knew that disappointed tone. Secrets hurt the most when you finally came clean about them. How many times had Sutton offered to listen, that she wouldn't judge or comment only to have Cass insist she didn't need to unburden herself of the past. It had been, Cass realized now, a lie.

"You could have told us before," Sutton accused less gently than was the norm.

Cass met her friend's concerned gaze. "No, actually," she admitted and felt another brick in that wall she'd built break free, "I couldn't. And I'm going to be honest." She took a deep breath. Here was the difficult part. "I didn't want to say anything now, but Mitch being here has brought up a lot of stuff I can't afford to ignore anymore."

Riley snorted. "I'll bet."

"No," Cass pinned her friend with a look. "Don't do that, Ry. I meant what I said the other day. Mitch is a good guy. After I got back, we were just caught up in something neither one of us was emotionally equipped to handle." Something Cass wasn't willing to handle.

"And this is where we pick up from last night," Laurel called from across the room.

"There's more?" Sutton set her half-eaten vanilla scone aside as if it had turned rotten.

Cass had been debating sharing the details of her rescue all morning. It wasn't that she didn't trust her friends, or even that she wasn't ready for the tidal wave of emotions that came along with her admission. "I'm not entirely sure of the details as to how Mitch and Lynda found me. I know he was left in the interview room alone with Jonathan Whittaker and that when he came out, he had the location." She winced.

She didn't want to give voice to what she'd thought he'd done in those fifteen minutes. It was easier for her to dwell on those hours she'd spent in that glass coffin than to entertain the idea he'd compromised his integrity and perhaps violated his oath as an agent by coercing, intimidating, or maybe torturing a suspect because of her. That was, she'd accepted years ago, a line too far.

"But they did find me and I'm here and alive and Jonathan Whittaker is where he belongs." Her voice almost broke with doubt she still couldn't shake on that front.

Riley snorted. "You know you look at Elliot when you're lying, right?"

"What?" Cass went wide-eyed as Laurel returned with a full pitcher and a plate of iced-lemon cookies Sutton had grabbed out of her freezer this morning. "I'm not … I do not!"

"It's your tell. One of them, anyway." Riley held up her empty champagne flute and earned an annoyed glare from Laurel. "You have other ones when you don't want to talk about something."

"Or when she changes the subject," Sutton added.

"Again," Laurel said calmly. "Veering off topic. If you don't want to tell us any more, I'm more than happy to have Nox conduct a deep dive on the case once they're back," she told Cass. "So there's your out. This either comes from you or the official report."

Cass shook her head. "Nox would need to break into the secure FBI records system to … oh." She scrunched her mouth. She saw the trap immediately. Nox wouldn't care how many laws they might be breaking if they thought it would help Cass.

"Either way," Sutton said, "Nox's going to be brought up to speed once they're back tomorrow."

As Cass expected, her past was barreling toward all of them like a steam engine without breaks.

"After all this time, I would imagine sharing this can't be easy for you," Mabel spoke for the first time in a while. The giddy "I just got back from a trip with my sexy boyfriend" glee had vanished as soon as Cass had begun sharing with them what she'd told Laurel hours before. "But I bet you feel better for having done it. Don't you?"

"Maybe." Cass frowned. It would explain her sleeping so soundly. Clearly Mabel's group therapy sessions for victims of violence were doing some good. "Are you going to judge me in some weird way every time I look at my dog from now on?" Elliot's ears perked up and he immediately jumped onto the sofa beside her, heaved a sigh and rested his head in her lap. She stroked his fur, the uncertainty that had been circling settling into a dull ache in her chest.

"We aren't judging you, Cass," Sutton assured her, but there was still a ghost of pain in her eyes. "I think we're all disappointed you felt that you couldn't trust us."

"It doesn't have anything to do with trust," Laurel echoed Cass's sentiment from last night. "She wasn't ready. She's still not," she added and snatched up a cookie. "Otherwise, she wouldn't be stalling. I'd rather not put my lawyer hat on and start asking you questions, but I will if it'll help." She curled back up on the sofa on the other side of Elliot, draping his tail over her legs.

"Mitch gave him to me." The statement came out of nowhere.

"Who? Elliot?" Riley's brows shot up. "You're serious?"

"About a week after I got … out." When was she going to find a better way to describe those days? "I was spinning, trying to get back to my old life, pretending as if nothing had really happened. I was alive. I was safe. He suggested therapy but as you can imagine I wasn't particularly receptive to that idea. Then the nightmares started." Nightmares that occasionally still reared up when exhaustion pushed her over the edge. "He begged me to talk to him, but every time I looked at him …" she didn't want to go back to those days. "The next thing I knew, he walked in my front door carrying this guy." She stroked Elliot's head. "He'd flunked out of cadaver school and needed a home." She smiled down as Elliot whimpered. "He saved me. They both did. That's all that matters."

"He loved you," Laurel said. "He still does, Cass. It's written all over his face whenever he looks at you."

"Not anymore," she whispered, desperately pushing that balloon of hope that swelled inside of her back down. "I'm not the same woman I was before the warehouse."

"I'd imagine he's not the same man," Sutton said.

Cass's heart tripped. She knew for a fact he wasn't. How could he be after …

"Laurel's right," Sutton went on. "Mitch dropped everything to come out here when you called. Circumstances might have changed for the two of you, and other things, too, but the core of your bond is still there. Plus, he's responsible for this bundle of love." She reached over and gave Elliot a pet. "The man earns serious cred for that alone."

The dog sat up, as if surprised and more than eager to be the center of attention.

"It was bad, wasn't it?" Laurel prodded. "Those hours you were held."

"I don't remember most of it." Thankfully the scopolamine they'd found in her system after had done its job and blocked the most heinous memories from ever settling. She got impressions, flashes. Feelings. But solid, grab-hold-of-to-deal-with recollections? "I do remember being trapped in that bloody box." She held up a hand as if touching it to the glass, the same way she had that day. Her fingertips burned with memory. "I remember Mitch standing over me, pressing his hand down. His voice was muffled, like I was stuck underwater." The drug again. The distortion of sense and feeling was one of the major side effects. It was also what made someone incredibly docile and malleable. "I screamed." She felt Laurel's hand on her arm. "My throat hurt so much, I didn't think I'd ever be able to speak again. I just screamed and Mitch was telling me to be quiet. *Be quiet. Please be quiet, baby.*" Tears blurred her vision.

"Cass—" Sutton's whisper skimmed the edges of Cass's consciousness and she heard Laurel shush her.

"There was this buzzing sound. He used a bone saw on the victims. I had to watch as he carved up ..." She sucked in a breath, sobbing as her hand flexed against glass that wasn't there. "There was blood everywhere. And then the saw went dead and Mitch's partner yelled and ..." She blinked and tears coursed down her cheeks.

"Cass?" Laurel pushed. "What happened next?"

"Mitch shot him." Bang! She jerked as if hearing the shot once more. "He kept one hand on mine above the glass, he turned around and shot him. Point blank." She pressed her index finger to her forehead. She shook her head. "Then he was dead. That's ..." she shrugged herself out of the past, dragged in air to her starving lungs. "I remember waking up in the hospital a few days later and everyone telling me it was over. But it wasn't." She swallowed a new wave of tears. "It's never been over. He killed him. For me," she whispered brokenly as the last of the truth broke free.

"Something I'd bet you've been punishing yourself for ever since," Laurel murmured as Elliot whined and tried to snuggle closer. "Dammit, Cass."

Sutton shifted closer and wrapped an arm around Cass, drew her close.

Cass counted. *One, two, three, four* … desperate to find her footing again. It was out. Finally. Most of it, at least. Why? Why hadn't she done this earlier? Why hadn't she … trusted them?

"Well,"—Riley cleared her throat and looked into her glass—"I don't know about you all, but as soon as I see FBI special Agent Mitch Keaton, I'm giving him one great big juicy kiss. Hell, maybe I'll even throw in a lap dance."

"Riley." Mabel shook her head, but then she started laughing. She covered her mouth, her eyes wide in horror as she looked to Cass then Laurel. "I'm so sorry. That's … it's nothing to laugh over."

"No, it's not," Laurel agreed as Sutton stroked Cass's hair until they all lost their composure.

The sound of laughter broke through the misery of memory and shone a light over all of them. Her friends. Her family.

"For once, I'm going to say Riley has the right idea." Laurel leaned over and plucked up her glass, motioned for the others to do the same. "To Mitch Keaton." She toasted him. "If not for him, we might never have found each other. And for that, we owe him an eternity of gratitude. But that's all." She eyed Riley with warning.

"To Mitch," Sutton murmured into Cass's hair. "Thank God he saved you."

Fresh, clear tears swam in Cass's eyes.

"I can't wait to meet him," Mabel echoed.

"To sisters!" Riley added.

They leaned in and clinked glasses.

An unfamiliar and most welcome peace washed over Cass. "To sisters," she whispered, and stepped free from the past.

*

Mitch awoke to a drizzly, overcast day, sore ribs, and the dread of living on borrowed time.

176

The anxiety he'd escaped by soaking his head under a hot shower and sleeping deeper than he had in weeks returned full force. Soft grey walls, white trim, and beautifully polished hardwood floors surrounded him in home-away-from-home comfort. A pair of framed Zeigfeld girls movie posters hung on one wall and a small flat screen television on the other.

The sparse furnishings suited him. He'd never been one to clutter his life up with items. The only thing missing, necessity wise, was coffee and he could get that downstairs in the lobby.

He lay in the queen bed and stared up at the ceiling.

Someone else was dead because of him. *Partly* because of him, Mitch corrected himself in the same way one of his therapists might have. There was enough of a difference to prevent the guilt from manifesting fully. Still.

Whether he was responsible or not, Mitch did not like carrying the weight of another death on his shoulders. Especially when he had so many unanswered questions about last night.

Last night, however, could very well be the least of his concerns.

He needed to figure out his next move, but any move he made was complicated by the fact that he'd flat-out lied to Quinn.

His stomach clenched. Mitch knew precisely who the old dead woman was.

Which meant it was only a matter of time before her identity was uncovered and his connection to her exposed.

So, yeah. He sighed. Definitely borrowed time.

"You made a deal with the devil," he reminded himself as regret surged. He'd already paid for that mistake with his career. It appeared as if he might be paying again, only this time he wouldn't have the FBI protecting the public from the details.

Everything he'd put in place four years ago was unraveling.

He shoved his hands into his hair.

What in the ever-living *fuck* was he going to do?

He dropped an arm over his eyes, thoughts swimming like a shark around blood.

Except a shark had far more options than he did. He knew what to do. What he had to do. He just didn't want to do it.

The only way to get ahead of this was to come clean, beginning with the main person who mattered. "And sooner than later."

He swung his legs over the side of the bed, dragged his hands through his hair before checking his phone for the time. The souped-up glasses sat on the nightstand, charging away.

Scrolling through his text messages, he played the "not going to answer that one, or that one—definitely not that one" game. The only one he paused to read was the one from Linnea that confirmed the burial site was shut down for the day because of the storm; possibly into next week depending on how the wind was blowing with the DA's office.

"Shit." He nearly chucked the phone across the room. He wouldn't even have work to distract him.

If he'd known answering one phone call from Cassia would throw the entirety of his life into chaos …

Who in the hell was he kidding? He wouldn't have done anything differently. He'd made her a promise and after everything that had happened between and to them, nothing in this world or the next would have prevented him from keeping it.

Speaking of Cassia …

Not a message, missed call, or voice mail in sight.

Probably for the best.

He carefully and cautiously got up and went into the surprisingly spacious black-and-white tiled bathroom. He already knew the waterfall shower was glorious and offered water pressure a longtime New York apartment dweller had only dream of. Not to mention, there was a small stackable washer and dryer behind the folding doors. After last night's mud-surfing session, laundry definitely made sense. He picked up the mud-caked clothes he'd left on the floor last night and got them running.

He lifted his shirt, checking the growing bruising on his chest in the mirror above the sink. The purple splotches across his skin proved he'd told Quinn the truth at least once last night: he'd definitely had worse.

Mitch popped some OTC painkillers, dragged on fresh jeans, a clean shirt and, after grabbing his cell and keys, headed downstairs to the lobby.

He had half a cup drunk and a second one brewing when the glass door was pulled opened.

Keeley and Barksy, along with a tall, athletically slender man entered, the latter carrying two paper bags soaked with what Mitch suspected was a mixture of rain and grease. He was tall and on the slender side, with intense eyes and dark blond hair that could have put him on the top of any casting director's leading-man list. He wore dark slacks with a white t-shirt beneath a windbreaker and sneakers fit for walking.

Keeley shoved the hood of her raindrop-covered jacket off her head, her face splitting into a molar-exposing smile. She waved. "Hi, Mitch!"

Looking at her, it was impossible not to feel a mood elevation. "Hey, Keeley."

"My mom and dad are back!" She pointed to the man.

"Mitch?" the man said, his dancing eyes turning serious. "Mitch Keaton?"

"That's me." Mitch extended his hand when Paul came over. "Paul Flynn, I take it?"

"Good to finally meet you." The handshake was firm and quick. "Kee? Do me a favor?" Paul asked.

"I know." Keeley dropped her head back and let out a long sigh and accepted one of the bags Paul held out. "Take these up to mom and change Barksy's water bowl." She stomped off, Barksy at her side. "Mom's not even in the apartment," she called over her shoulder. "She's drinking mimosas with Aunt Cass."

"Mimosa yoga Sundays," Paul told Mitch. "Normally they have it up on the roof but when it's crap weather—"

"They just drink the mimosas and talk about yoga," Keeley yelled from the upper landing.

Mitch could do with a mimosa about now. Or twelve.

Instead, he scrounged through the snacks and fruit that were constantly refilled for the tenants.

"Hungry?" Paul walked around the counter to brew his own coffee when Mitch grabbed his second cup.

"Starved." Sutton's leftover lasagna had been forever ago and the idea of nacho cheese chips or a granola bar did not particularly appeal.

"Grab one of the sandwiches in the bag," Paul said. "There's a bodega—nope, sorry. That's my New York talking. There's a convenience store a few blocks away that has this sandwich counter in the back. They make amazing avocado bacon breakfast torta. I always get two."

"Don't judge me for not saying I'm fine with an apple." Mitch all but dived into the bag and pulled out one of the warm wrapped sandwiches. "Thanks."

"Not a problem." Paul filled one of the larger cups while Mitch walked around and sat in one of the high upholstered stools at the counter. "So …" He took a long drink, eyed Mitch over the rim. "You found yourself another body."

"Lucky me." Mitch was hungry enough to be able to ignore the way his stomach pitched at the turn of conversation. "I haven't heard anything yet. Is there any news?"

"I talked to Quinn on our ride in from the airport."

Mitch's heart beat double time. It took all his focus to keep his voice even. "Have they identified the woman yet?"

Paul shook his head. "They're running her prints and looking at missing persons reports."

"What about the kid Quinn arrested?"

"Nelson Pritchard. Turns out he's not shy or particularly smart." Paul leaned back against the coffee counter. "Kid hasn't stopped talking and never once asked for a lawyer. He was told they were paid to break into the site, cause as much damage as possible and leave the way they came in."

"Leave the way they …" Mitch stopped unfolding the sopping parchment paper and looked at Paul. "That's an oddly specific instruction."

"Quinn thought so, too." Paul retrieved the second sandwich from the bag. "Nelson's friend was the one who was hired. Nelson was supposed to get paid once they were back at the friend's place. But then the friend went and snapped his neck trying to run down a hill of mud and …" Paul shrugged.

The guilt wasn't quite as sharp, but it also wasn't going away. "He'd still be alive if I hadn't chased him."

"We don't know that," Paul said. "You did what you were trained to do."

180

"I'm a lab rat now, not an agent."

"From what I've heard, there's no such thing as a former agent. Eat." He pointed at the sandwich sitting in front of Mitch. "It'll make your brain work better."

Not a bad pep talk coming from a former prosecutor.

Mitch lifted the sandwich and bit into crisp, toasty bread, creamy avocado topped with bacon and scrambled eggs. The salsa added a nice spicy kick. "Okay, I'm going to need to know where this place is," he told Paul. "This is delicious. Sorry." He took another bite. "What do we know about Nelson's friend?"

"Carlton Tinkerton." Paul started eating. "Twenty-two. Juvie record as tall as Kee; one felony strike last year for aggravated burglary. This could have put him in some serious trouble, which could explain why he ran."

"Kid may as well have had jet packs on his shoes," Mitch said. "He knew the area. He knew where he was going." Of that much Mitch was certain. He just hadn't counted on the darkness, the rain, or Mitch.

"You're thinking he's the one who broke in the first time?"

Mitch shrugged. "I'm not thinking anything without any evidence. I don't know why he'd have come back. They got away with enough equipment, he shouldn't have needed more cash—unless he was a junkie."

"No indication of him being involved with drugs, "Paul said.

"What did Nelson say about the second break in?"

"Nothing," Paul said. "If Carlton came in the first time, he did it without Nelson. Quinn got Carlton's address. They found one of the microscopes under his bed when they searched the place. He lives with an older brother who wasn't around. We've got officers looking for him for a notification."

"What about a cell phone?"

"We found his main one and a bunch of burners," Paul confirmed. "Techs are working on them. Guess we're in wait-and-see mode for now."

Mitch was perfectly happy remaining there. "Cassia filled me in on a few things that weren't in the files you sent me." He finished his sandwich and wiped his hands, drank some more coffee. Finally, he was feeling slightly more human. "About The Circle."

"Did she?" Paul's face was a blank mask. "And what exactly did she tell you?"

"That you all suspect there's a secret society operating in modern day Los Angeles. One with a history going back decades."

"Close to a century actually." He waved his fingers toward himself. "Keep going."

"You suspect they have connections to high reaching individuals in both politics and the business world."

"The film industry, in particular," Paul added.

"Most importantly," Mitch chose his words carefully, "she's convinced this group is behind the murders of these women, that they're responsible for their being buried on that hill, and that they're somehow manipulating how the case is proceeding."

"She's told you a lot. Did she happen to mention we've started building a list of people who are likely compromised, beginning with Johanna Eichorn?"

"The Los Angeles DA?"

"She's made some moves that put my investigation, and that of a good friend, in jeopardy."

"Jeff Chambers," Mitch filled in before Paul could say. "He was hurt in an explosion last month, wasn't he?"

"Nearly killed." Paul's appetite appeared to wane. "Serious head and spine injuries, but he'd doing okay. Better than they expected."

"I'm sorry." Mitch knew better than anyone, that words meant nothing. "He have a family?"

"A wife and son. I'm heading over to visit Jeff later this afternoon." Paul's eyes darkened. "He sent them away to stay with her parents until … well. Until we get a line on the people responsible for the bombing."

"You and Jeff weren't working together then?"

"No. He was digging into the conviction of Dean Samuels. He's—"

"The vanishing prisoner," Mitch said.

"Cass said she trusted you." Paul paused a beat. "Are you buying into any of it?"

An interesting and unexpected question. "Cass believes it," he said. "I'd like to see some of the evidence myself before I fully commit."

"Exactly the response I'd expect from a crime scene tech." Paul glanced away, eyes narrowing as if his mind were working overtime. "What does the behaviorist think?"

"That he hasn't been one for quite a while and therefore his opinion—"

"Is more than valid with me," Paul cut him off. "This is crazy Hollywood-script level shit, Mitch. We need all the help we can get, but if you don't think there's any validity—"

"Don't put words in my mouth."

"Okay." Paul grinned. "Okay. I like the attitude. You're open to the possibility that what you've heard is true."

"Why do you think it's true?"

"Because I don't believe in coincidences and we're falling over way too many of them, the more we dig. And every time we pull a string, it leads us to Touchstone Productions, the Tenado estate—"

"Where Riley attacked. There's some kind of dungeon in the basement, isn't there?"

"There was." Paul nodded. "That's where the women's photographs were found. Including one of Mabel's twin sister."

"Sylvie."

Paul smiled a little, ducked his head. "You have no idea how many points you'd earn from Mabel by remembering that."

"I remember every victim of every case I've ever worked." Both as an agent and as a lab tech. He'd also memorized the list of names of all the suspected missing women, including those they might not be unearthing up in the hills.

"And then there's Young and Fairbanks." Paul paused again, clearly waiting for a response.

"The law firm with more dead clients than live ones." Mitch earned an impressed nod for that comment.

"You are up to speed." He sat back, looked at Mitch for a good long moment. "It isn't my place to ask, but I'm going to anyway because I think you'd be of use to us. Do you want in?"

"I'm already in," Mitch said. "That's why I'm here."

"You're here because the FBI sent you out at Cass's request."

Mitch did his best not to flinch. He really didn't like lying to these people. Especially Cassia.

"I'm not talking about your forensic work with Linnea and her team," Paul said. "I'm asking if you want to help us take on The Circle."

"Oh." Mitch blinked. "Is there an official—"

"No," Paul said immediately. "There's nothing official. We're addressing it here, in Temple House. Cass is leading the way, collecting all the information we've gathered so far. What names we know about, what businesses we suspect they're involved in. What their motives might be in continuing to exist. Other than cold-blooded murder."

Mitch pressed his lips together and glanced away.

"What?" Paul asked. "What's that look?"

"I can't really comment—"

"Sure you can. This isn't an official conversation," Paul said. "It's just two men debating the existence of a murderous secret society that may or may not be operating in the shadows of Los Angeles and Hollywood. Come on." He waved his hand again. "You're thinking something. Out with it."

"I've seen the list of missing women. I know the number of bodies that are up on that hill. I know about the lily connection."

Paul's left eye twitched.

"You're looking at more than a secret society, Paul. What you're looking for is a cult."

"A ... cult." Paul frowned, but in a way that showed Mitch he was considering it.

"There are similarities among the victims. Ages, professions, the way they disappeared. What they were found with?" Like the remains of an exotic flower that had become commercially available only a few decades ago. "How they were killed."

"We think they were all drowned. They found specific diatoms in the bone marrow of some of the remains. They match algae that came from the underground pool at the Tenado estate." Paul stopped short. "Where Riley was almost drowned last year. The woman responsible said something about a sacrifice needing to be made."

That tracked. "Beth Tompkin. She was what, thirty something?" Mitch posited. "Serial killers aren't generational. At least, we've never had one that we know of. This is organized, to the point it remained secret until Riley came across that undeveloped roll of film in an old pawn shop. If she hadn't developed that film, no one would be any the wiser as to their existence. Except those involved. Yes, that's essentially the definition of a secret society. But, if they're continuing to earn devotees who would rather throw themselves off highway overpasses so as not to be taken into custody, you're definitely looking at a—"

"Cult. Well." Paul blinked, clearly processing information. "Shit."

"Pretty much. I don't know that the distinction helps with your investigation or not."

"It's definitely a track we hadn't considered before." His gaze sharpened. "Do you want in?"

"I, uh …" He had to admit, the investigation sounded far more interesting than anything he had going in his life. That said, he wasn't exactly walking around with a stellar record. "You don't want to take some time to think about asking me? Maybe do a deep dive into my background?"

"You mean, am I okay working with the man who killed Gavin Whittaker after he and his brother murdered six people? Yeah," Paul's tone left no room for doubt, "I'm more than okay with that."

"How did you—"

"I've made a lot of friends over the years," Paul said. "And those friends have a lot of connections. You want in, you're in. I think we could use your help. If you're up for it."

"I'm up for it, for sure." But would Cassia be?

That was the big question.

# CHAPTER TWELVE

"JUST tell her the truth." Mitch muttered to himself as he descended the stairs to her second-floor apartment. His conversation with Paul Flynn had both answered a lot of questions and presented new ones. But questions didn't interest him in the moment. Answers did. Answers that evaded him when he returned to the apartment on the third floor to retrieve Cass's special glasses. He didn't want the responsibility of them, if he wasn't going to be using them.

"Tell her the truth about everything," he said again. Sure, it could all blow up in his face and she'd throw him out on his ass, but he knew one thing for certain.

There was no moving forward until he came clean.

"Huh." He stopped at her door, hand raised toward the bell. "That's new." He'd seen similar specs at security companies when it came to biometric door locks, but this went beyond any technology he'd been able to get his hands on. "Blake." This had to be Blake's doing.

The door swung open before Mitch got the chance to ring the bell. He spine instantly stiffened when he found himself staring into not one, not two, but four very female sets of eyes that had him pinned in their sights.

The furies strike again.

"Ladies." He forced a smile. "I was hoping to talk to Cassia."

"You!"

In his more than ten years as an FBI field agent, he'd faced down killers, deactivated bombs, and one time chased a trio of suspected terrorists through the New York subway system. Yet it was the sight of Riley Temple stepping out of Cassia's apartment and heading straight for him that made him back away.

Tall and curvy, with an apparent affection for classic rock t-shirts and practicality, her pretty face was outlined by dark brown hair pulled back into a severe ponytail.

"You!" She said again and grabbed him by the shoulders. "You are one very special agent, Mitch Keaton."

"Uh—"

She kissed him. Full on the mouth, lip-to-lip kissed him! "Thank you."

He could taste bubbles and orange juice on his lips when she released him. "Ah ... you're welcome?"

"She's slightly toasted," Laurel explained as she scooted out behind her friend. Mitch took another step back and earned a wicked smile from the defense attorney. "Don't worry. You're safe. Unless ... Riley?" She caught her friend's hand and tugged her close. "What about that lap dance you wanted to give him?"

Mitch's face went fire hot.

"Mmmm." Riley tilted her head. "I might need to puke first."

"Right. And on that note ..." Mabel Reynolds joined them, offering a quick wave and gentle smile to Mitch. "Sorry about her. She's just expressing the gratitude we all have for you in protecting and saving our friend." She patted a hand against her heart and fluttered her mimosa-laced lashes. "You are a good man, sir."

"Thanks?" He backed away as the women filed out, Sutton taking anchor position as Mabel dragged Riley's arm around her shoulders so she and Laurel could help her upstairs. "You aren't going to kiss me, too, are you?"

"No." But she did touch a hand to his arm. "She told us. About the warehouse. About ... what you did. And about Elliot."

"Oh." He frowned. She hadn't told them before now? "Just doing my—"

"No." Sutton shook her head. "It was more than your job. For the record, we're on your side." She nudged him toward the open door. "I think you've got a shot at a second chance," she whispered before she moved off to the stairs. "Don't blow it."

"Right." If only Mitch was so talented as to not blow up his life for a second—or was it a third?—time.

"Anyone else in here?" He called when he stuck his head in the door.

"Mitch." Cass stopped in front of her sofa, her hands filled with empty mimosa glasses. "Come on in."

"You sure it's safe? No one else in here that's going to kiss me?"

"Kiss—oh." Her face broke into a smile that lightened his mood. "Yeah, Riley always does what she says she will. If she offers you a lap dance—"

"I think Laurel headed that one off for me."

Elliot let out a gentle woof and hopped off the sofa, coming straight over for some pets.

"How are you?" The glasses rattled as she set them in the sink.

It was, he thought, the most normal he'd seen her behave since he'd arrived.

"Fine. I brought these back." He set the glasses on the counter. "They took a beating last night so you might want to give them a good once over."

"Thanks." She turned on the water, eyed him over her shoulder. "You didn't get your ribs checked out, did you?"

"No, listen …" He stepped all the way in and closed the door. Elliot offered a pitiful whine, looked up at his leash before returning to his bed by the bank of computers. "I'd like to talk to you about something."

"Sure." She continued washing. "Help yourself to some cookies and scones. Sorry, we polished off the last of the chocolate …" She stopped when she found him watching her. "What is it?" Cassia grabbed a towel, shut off the water and dried off her hands. "Something wrong?"

*Nothing. Everything.* He should have rehearsed how to start this conversation. Telling her he knew who the body they'd discovered last night belonged to seemed so easy moments ago. If only he could come right out with it, but the instant she heard the name, it wouldn't be long before she discovered what he'd had to do to save her life.

"Hey." She tossed the towel down and came over to him. "You're sure you're okay?" She took his hand.

"I don't even know where to start." He'd dreamed about touching her again. Every night, for months, years even. He'd imagined a moment like this, when the two of them could block out the rest of the world. How did one even cope with the rebirth of a dream he'd long ago given up hope on? "You just told them, about New York." He gestured to the door.

"I did." And she seemed lighter for it. "Laurel convinced me they had a right to know, especially after all this time. I'm sorry if I should have checked with you—"

"You don't owe me an apology." He twined his fingers through hers. "Let alone an explanation. I'm surprised it took you this long."

"Yeah, well." She flashed a nervous smile. "That I will blame on you. It was easy to push it all away and pretend none of it happened when I moved out here. Seeing you again—"

He flinched.

"No." She lifted her hands, cupped his face in his palms. "No, don't do that. I'm glad you're here. You've got me to where I should have gone myself." She rose up until their mouths were even, until he couldn't look anywhere but into her beautiful brown eyes. "Where I was too afraid to go alone."

"Cassia." There were no words. He'd spent the past four years banking a love that had nowhere to go. What she hadn't taken with her when she'd left, he'd simply had to push aside. "I don't know where we go with this." Nothing in his mind made sense right now. All of his thoughts, all of his senses, were filled with her. "There's too much …"

Too much what? Too much of the past standing between them? Too much longing? Too much looming that could derail the promise of them being together again.

"Too much to talk about?" She summarized in her typical, efficient way. "I know." She rose up on her toes, the movement slow and hypnotizing. She pressed her mouth to his. Briefly. Tenderly. Her fingers flexed against the sides of his face. "I'm sorry," she whispered and kissed him again. "I'm sorry I left you. I'm sorry I ran." He could see in her eyes the statement surprised her, too. "I couldn't see a way through. I should have given us time to adjust and cope. Most of all,"—another kiss—"I'm sorry I left us both with regrets."

He inclined his head, gazing at her lips before he claimed them, kissing her the way he'd wanted to every day for the past four years.

"The only regret I have," he murmured when she softened in his embrace and leaned into him. "Is letting you go."

Tears sprung into her eyes and she smiled. "Is there maybe a way I can help you get over that regret?" She stroked his face, her fingers soft against his beard.

"I can think of a thing or two." Every cell in his body tightened with desire. It was as if she'd re-stoked a long burned-out fire, breathing on the embers of his affection with one, warm breath. But even as promise hovered on the brink of fulfillment, he couldn't quite let himself believe. "Nothing can change the past, Cassia. You know that, right?" It was important to him that she understood where his head was. Most of it anyway. Even now, he could feel the blood draining straight to his groin. "If we do this, it's to move forward. Not to cling to what was."

Or to what might have been.

She nipped at his chin, rubbed her cheek against his. "I can agree to that. Mmm." She pressed closer. Her breasts flattened against his chest as she wound her arms around his neck. The pain in his chest and ribs subsided. Or maybe her touch was as effective as the most powerful of painkillers. "I like the beard."

"Yeah?" All the trepidation, all the worry and concern he had over what was to come, drained away in her embrace. "My brother calls it my coping mechanism." Something more to hide behind.

"It's sexy, whatever else it might be." She nuzzled closer and drained the last of his logical thought-based resistance.

He ducked his head and kissed her, taking what she offered.

His lips slid over hers, pressing open her willing mouth. Their tongues danced, teased one another. Tempted one another. His hands slid down her back, his arms moving around her waist to pull her higher against him as he sank in and deepened the kiss.

The rounded curves of her hips nearly drove him over the edge before they even got started. His fingers gripped her flesh, flexing

190

into her as his mind soared ahead of his body in anticipation of sinking into her once more.

Sinking ...

Shit! He drew back, wincing when her fingers tightened at the back of his neck. "Wait." He tried to take a deep breath, but it was nearly impossible with every inch of her was pressed so firmly against him.

"What's wrong?" She sank back on her heels, confusion filling her passion-tinted eyes. "I know I'm different—"

He silenced her with a kiss intended to push whatever protest she'd been about to make completely out of her head. "You're perfect," he whispered when she relaxed again. "I don't have any condoms."

It took a moment for understanding to register, but when it did, she smiled and lit up the darkest hours of his life. "Condoms plural?"

Her sense of humor had improved these last years.

"If history is any indication, definitely plural." He flattened his hand against the base of her spine and pressed her forward where there was no ignoring his intentions. "There's a drugstore a couple of blocks—"

"I don't think you should go out in public, given your current state." She stepped back, that smile shifting to a grin filled with temptation and mischief. "Give me a sec." Cassia laughed when he tried to keep hold of her hand to stop her from leaving him. "I promise I will be back."

She hurried across the room and disappeared down the hallway on the other side of Nox's desk space.

There wasn't a part of him that wasn't tingling, but he banked it and left the comfort and space of the living room for the small doorway nestled in the corner of her apartment. The barn door stood open. The space on the other side was barely big enough for a bed, a nightstand and a closet at the far end.

He clicked on the small table lamp to keep the shadows at bay. Two picture frames sat beneath it, one of Cassia and the parents she'd lost shortly before she'd graduated college, and the other ....
He picked it up, chuckling as he looked at the five faces of Cassia and her friends.

ANNA J. STEWART

It was an outside photograph and they were bunched together like clinging grapes. Behind them he could see the faintest hint of the Hollywood sign that was visible from her window.

"You're happy here," he said when he heard her move behind him.

She stepped close, rested her head on his arm. "I was."

"I didn't just mean in the picture. You're happy here. In Temple House." It wasn't until this moment that he understood the relief that brought him. "Moving here was good for you."

"Yes," she agreed. "As much as I loved New York, this is where I belong."

"When was the last time you actually saw the city?" He knew the answer thanks to Blake.

"On the drive in from the airport." She reached around him and took the frame from his hand, set it back on the nightstand and shimmied in front of him so her back was to the bed. "Do you mind if we save the conversation for later?" She dropped a handful of condom foil packets onto the stand and smoothed her hands up his chest. "I've got about four years of pent-up frustration I'm dying to work out."

"Four years, huh? That's quite a dry spell."

"I wouldn't get too cocky if I were you," she warned with a teasing glint in her eyes. "You've had some serious competition thanks to my lifetime supply of batteries." Her smile was quick. "Think you're up to it?"

He pulled her hard against him once more and watched her eyes darken. "More than."

She reached up and sank her hands into his hair, pulled his mouth toward hers. When she kissed him, the years melted away. His head spun as she drank him in, pulling every thought from him once more as all he could feel, all he could process, was her.

Mitch nipped at her lips, pulling his mouth free to trail hot, moist kisses down the side of her neck. Her hands slipped beneath his shirt, her nails scraping against his flesh.

He shivered. "Cassia."

"Four years, Mitch." She curled her fingers against his skin and set him to groaning. "Talk later."

Taking his time to savor this moment was clearly out of the question. Her hands shifted to his back, drawing his shirt up as he

192

fell into a Cassia-triggered trance. He lifted his arms, flinching at the pain that coursed through his system as she pulled his shirt off.

She gasped, pushed him slightly away and drew her fingertips across his torso to the bruises developing across his body. "Mitch." His name sounded like a prayer on his lips.

"It's fine." He wasn't about to let a few bruised ribs stop him from loving her once more. "I'm fine." He caught her hands in his, lifted them to his lips. "I barely feel it." What was one more lie at this point? The fire of her touch burned the pain out of his system. "Might need a little help with some things, however. If you're up to it."

Her brow arched. "That sounds like fun. Challenge accepted."

She reached down for the hem of her shirt, but he stopped her, shook his head. "This I can do." He pulled it over her head, dropped it to the floor on top of his. His hands immediately cupped her full breasts within the front-clasp sports bra.

"Haven't had much use for pretty underwear," she told him before she moaned and dropped her head back. That perfect exposure of her throat had him locking his mouth to her pulse, gently sinking his teeth into her neck. "Jesus." She trembled, her breath tumbling out of her on a laugh when he made quick work of the hooks. "You haven't been dormant for four years, have you?"

What he'd been doing was dreaming of this moment. Every scenario. Every intoxicating move. He drew the straps down her shoulders, flicked the fabric away. Over thinking was out of the question when his brain's current blood supply couldn't have filled a thimble. He nudged her back, his eyes greedily drinking in every curvaceous inch of her.

She ducked down to catch his gaze before she sat down on the bed, unknotted her hair and stretched out. Cassia held out her hand.

As tempting as her hold was, he curled his fingers around the waistband of her yoga slacks and drew them all the way down past her pink-painted toes. His ribs protested when he stood back up, but the sight of her laying there, completely exposed to him, dulled any ache.

He slid a knee onto the bed between her knees, slowly moved forward only to freeze when her hands went to the button and zipper on his jeans.

"Fair play," she muttered, frowning in frustration when she had trouble working the zipper around his erection.

"Careful," he murmured, feeling both the bliss and pain of torture. "Don't want this to end before we get going."

"Then I might have to cut these damned things off … ah!" She lifted her triumphant gaze to his and inched the zipper down. "There we go. Commando, huh?" The wicked grin of hers remained in place as she shoved his jeans down to his thighs. Before he could shove them free the rest of the way, she wrapped her hands around him and encased him in her warmth.

"Cassia." He sucked in a breath so hard his entire body vibrated. He bit back a groan. He'd never been this hard before. Never this entranced. This …

She sat up, ducked her head and drew her tongue up the length of his shaft. Her hand squeezed and moved, up and down—gently, torturously—before drawing the tip of him into her mouth.

"Too much," he whispered as he moved against his own wishes. Her tongue swirled as her lips pursed. He looked down, touched the back of her head with fingers that felt as if they'd been touched by the sun. "Cassia …" It was too much. He could feel the pressure building, that desire for release taking over what little reason he continued to possess. "Not this way," he murmured and pulled himself free.

He couldn't bring himself to look at her as he reached for one of the foil packets and ripped it open.

"Want some help?" She touched a finger to her lips and drew a bead of his pre-release into her mouth.

Jesus!

His fingers couldn't move fast enough as he covered himself. She shifted further back on the bed, turned to lie back on the pile of pillows beneath her head. The creaminess of her pale flesh glowed in the dim light of the windowless room.

He lay down beside her, began to shift over her, only for his chest to constrict and his ribs to protest. He tried to stop the gasp of pain from escaping.

"Stop," she ordered gently. Cassia placed a hand on his chest, her hair spilling around her shoulders when she sat up and gently, carefully, pressed him back onto the mattress. "Let me."

She shifted, straddled his hips and sank onto him in so effortless and fluid a movement he thought he'd gone to heaven. She stretched around him, drawing him deep before she lifted herself, rotated her hips in a way that caused him to surge up and into her.

He groaned, arched his back as she gasped and continued to move, her hands reaching for his. Fingers tangling, they found their rhythm. He could see the control in her face, the held-at-bay passion that built as her breath quickened. Her breasts strained, begging for his touch. His mouth. His caress, but she straightened her arms and kept him in place.

Next time, he promised himself, as the promise of release built once more. Next time he was going to feast on her flesh before she drew him in. But now …. Now he forced himself to keep his eyes open, to watch as she began to crest over him.

She threw her head back, her back arching as her pace quickened. As their pace increased. He could feel her gently gripping him, drawing his release with hers as she gasped and panted. Her knees tightened at his hips. She drew their linked hands up and drew her head forward, opening her glistening, passion-filled eyes to his as she let the orgasm overtake her. Her cry of passion drew him up as he spilled himself into her, locking his mouth to hers.

She sank forward, gasping even as she came over the peak she'd driven them to.

He drew her down, tightened his hold even as he let go of her hands. "No," he whispered when she tried to move off of him. She was perfect. Wrapped around him in every way imaginable, she was absolutely perfect. He stroked a hand down her back, closing his eyes against the sweet pain of her short breaths pounding out against his heartbeat. A heart that beat only for her.

He loved her.

He always had.

Mitch tucked her head under his chin, pressed his lips to the top of her head and enveloped her completely.

He always would.

# CHAPTER THIRTEEN

CASS awoke alone to the silence.

She wasn't sure why it surprised her. She'd been waking up alone every day for years. And the silence was certainly nothing new. Reaching for her phone, she checked the time. She blinked, trying to comprehend exactly when she'd lost the majority of the day.

Just like back in New York, the time spent in Mitch's arms made the world—and time itself—fade away.

She climbed out of bed and after dragging on some underwear, slipped back into the shirt Mitch had placed over the end of the bed when he'd reclaimed his own clothing. Scrubbing her hands through her tousled hair, she left the bedroom only to find the apartment empty.

"Mitch?" She wandered around to the area by Nox's desk, checked what she laughingly called the guest bedroom and bath—rooms that were pretty much Nox's when they preferred not to go home. Yep. Just as she thought. She scrunched her face and looked to Elliot's empty bed. Of course, she thought. He'd taken Elliot for a walk.

That said, it wasn't exactly an ego boost to find him having left without a goodbye. But she supposed it was sweet, him not waking her up on his way out.

Instead of dwelling, she chose to embrace the loose, relaxed sensation coursing through her body. Nothing like a tension relieving bout of seriously good sex to work out the kinks and frustration.

She woke up her computer, and, after only a brief hesitation as to what she might find in her inbox, accessed her email. She was not, she vowed, going to spend another moment cowering in fear.

If Jonathan Whittaker had sent her another email ...

Cass blew out a slow, controlled breath upon finding only one message from Linnea. As unwelcome as the news was that work at the site was officially on hold until the preliminary reports were in about the new body found in the vicinity, it would give them time to connect the dots.

She wasn't entirely sure how they were going to prove one way or the other that the new victim wasn't in some way connected to the others. Logically she couldn't fathom how, but given how the past few months had gone and the insanity that had descended upon them since they'd begun their investigation into The Circle, she wasn't in a position to dismiss any possibility.

Besides, the rumor mill was going to run the coincidences into the ground. Suspicion would be there from now until the end of time. No doubt that idea had contributed to the decision the killer made to make the body dump at that location. Muddy the investigative waters, on both this new case and the buried women.

It was, she had to admit, part genius. Conspiracy theorists and obsessive bloggers were going to go bat-crap crazy zinging their out of the butt ideas and accusations about cover ups and secret agendas. Ironically, some of those ideas weren't exactly far-fetched now, were they?

That said, bat crap crazy would always win, especially when there was rumor, innuendo, and hidden agendas more than willing to provide some peripheral backup.

Besides, neither Cass nor any of her friends were in any position to counter the argument, were they?

It felt odd, running through her usual daily routine of website checks and busy work when nothing about the day felt ... normal. She caught up on her other cases, none of which needed single-minded devoted attention.

She shook out her tingling hands. She felt oddly electrified and antsy, and not in that anxious, fearful way that had plagued her for so long. Confined, she realized with a frown. It was almost as if she could feel the walls closing in around her. In the one place she'd always felt safe.

She activated the daily systems check on her equipment. She wanted to be ready to hit the ground running when the latest round of blood samples hit the system. Something to check in with Linnea about. They needed to make some progress.

And yet, it was progress that was being stifled by multiple forces. In the meantime …

On the security screens, she could see Blake restocking the lobby drink and snack bar, waving to tenants as they came in and out while on their Sunday jaunts. The smiling faces, the bags from shopping, the friendships built on shared bakery love and perfect weekend outings …

Cass pressed a hand against her unexpected envious heart.

She … missed that. She missed having a life.

She missed living.

While she was tempted to return to work and carve out more detailed contingency plans for moving forward with the case, impulse had her grabbing her jeans and shoes. When she stood at the door, she found herself resenting the Fort Knox-lite security it now displayed.

Instead of throwing caution to the wind, she simply picked it up and carried it with her out into the corridor. Her heart hammered at an unsteady beat, but it was one she could still move to.

*One, two, three, four …*

She made it as far as the staircase before she had to grab hold of something. But she stood and waited until her breathing evened out and she took a step down. Then another and another. Until she found herself on the first-floor landing.

Pride had her smiling as she took a seat. She wrapped her arms around her knees as she waited, impatiently for Mitch and Elliot to return.

She had to admit, the looks of surprise on people's faces as they walked up and down the stairs acted as a courage booster. "Hi, Liz. Hi, Randy." She waved at the couple who ran a costume shop in downtown LA, specializing in period wear geared toward renaissance faire attendees.

"Cass." Liz's voluptuous figure was on full bosom-heaving display, as was the flamingo tattoo peeking out from beneath the shoulder of her tavern-style dress. "Wow. How are you?" She tucked her dark hair behind her ear and shot a surprised grin at her boyfriend who was trying to keep his sword from knocking into the railings.

"Doing okay, thanks." Cass waited for the panic to surge, but it barely ticked the anxiety meter. That alone had her doing an internal boogie. "It's almost faire season, isn't it?"

"First one's in a few weeks," Liz confirmed. "Hopefully we're over the worst of the weather."

"Hate wearing chainmail in the rain," Randy added. He touched a hand to the base of Liz's back. "Good to see you!"

"You, too." Cass rested her chin on her knees.

Mitch rounded the corner a few minutes later and stopped short, a slow smile spreading across his full lips. "Didn't expect a welcoming committee when we got back." Elliot immediately leapt at Cass and shoved his head into her hands for kisses and pets. "Today's just full of all kinds of surprises." He shifted one of two bags of groceries to balance them out. "I went to raid your fridge and found it rather bare."

"Yeah, sorry about that. My weekly order got screwed up and I forgot to make other arrangements." She shoved to her feet, held her hand out for Elliot's lead. "Thanks for shopping."

"Happy to help." He walked behind her as they returned to her apartment. "You're doing okay." It was more a statement than a question, one that bolstered her already boosted confidence.

At the door, she keyed in her code, pressed her finger onto the pad and looked over her shoulder. "I'll have Blake set you up with a code for access."

He simply smiled. "Okay."

While they were unloading groceries, Elliot circled around his bed, walked back and forth and let out that low whine that had Cass sighing. "I wish he'd stop that."

Mitch left Cass to load the fridge with containers of deli salads, sliced meats and cheeses, along with a few heat-up side dishes, and walked over to Elliot's bed. Elliot plopped his butt down, tail wagging back and forth. He barked once. And looked back at the wall.

"That's alert behavior." Mitch rested his hand on the dog's back.

"Even for a cadaver school dropout?"

"Elliot didn't deal well with the dead," Mitch told her. "Doesn't mean the rest of his training was wasted. Is it that weird hum that's bugging him?"

Cass shrugged. "I barely hear it." She tapped a hand against her ear. "Tinnitus."

"Still listening to your ear pods on full blast?" His smile was quick and cursory. And more than a little accusing.

"No lectures today, please." She'd much prefer to enjoy their post coital honeymoon phase of whatever relationship they were rebuilding. Sure, she was happy about the sex. Even happier that her memories had indeed proved accurate where Mitch's abilities were concerned. But that didn't mean she was ready to step all the way back into the real world.

But she could be, she thought as the idea made her tingle all over. She definitely could be soon.

"What is it you hear?" Mitch asked Elliot, who barked once, louder and more sharply than normal.

Cass was about to tease him about expecting an answer, but Elliot walked closer to the wall and pressed his nose against the brick.

"That isn't vet worthy behavior." Mitch took a quick look out the window. "I'll work with him. See what might be going on. Could be he's feeling as cooped up as you." When he stood up, he found her watching him. "What?"

She shook her head, trying to dislodge the instant desire simply looking at him triggered. "I was just thinking that maybe you missed your calling, switching to forensics." She hoped it wasn't as touchy a subject as she feared. She set aside the sandwich fixings he'd bought. "You should have gone into K-9 training." Elliot looked over his shoulder and chuffed. "See?" She gestured to the dog to break any possible tension. "Elliot agrees."

"It was on the list of possibilities," Mitch said. "But so far, I prefer the lab. Mostly. Hungry?" He teased as she ripped open a bag of Cheetos.

She shoved a handful into her mouth. "I love these," she said around them.

"I remember. I also remember finding cheesy fingerprints in the most interesting of places." He walked over, reached across the counter and took her hand.

She watched, mesmerized, the blood rushing to her cheeks as he drew one finger into his mouth and sucked gently.

"Do not start something you're not intending to finish," she warned.

"Okay." He smiled and paid the same attention to the rest of her fingers. "Still hungry? Or can you wait?"

She stretched her arm across the counter as she walked around, putting up no resistance when he tugged her forward and tumbled her into his arms.

"I can wait as long as it takes," she said as he lowered his head and took possession of her mouth. And soul.

\*

Mitch awoke early on Monday morning feeling certain of two things.

One, the old adage about certain relationships being better the second time around appeared to be true. And, two? He was willing to do whatever it took to make sure he didn't lose Cassia again.

Which meant he had to tell Cassia the truth about the woman buried up on the hill.

It would take work, he reminded himself as he carefully slid out of her hold and out of bed. But it was work that would be well worth it. If he could find his way around the potholes he'd left behind him.

Behind, around, in front of. He tugged on his jeans and t-shirt, walked into the kitchen to get the coffee brewing and refill Elliot's water bowl. He was in the middle of scrambling up a batch of eggs when the front door clicked.

"I'll get you set up with full access," Blake's voice was low as he pushed open the door. "I thought Cass would have texted you about the updated lock."

A new-to-Mitch voice responded. "I was under strict instructions not to answer my phone unless the world was on fire."

Mitch flipped off the gas and set the eggs aside. He turned around as a multi-colored pixie-short-haired individual came to an abrupt stop at the edge of the sitting room. "You must be Nox."

"Huh." They inclined their head, eyes filling with surprise and understanding. They were on the short side and wearing baggy cargo pants, and an oversized shirt with a rainbow printed "Love is Love" across their chest. "I'd have thought you'd qualify as an inferno." Their smile was warm as they approached, pulling a long-strapped messenger bag over their head. "FBI guy?"

"Mitch Keaton." He offered a wave. "Nice to meet you."

"Uh-huh." They pursed their lips, looked back at Blake who held up his hands.

"None of my business," was all he said as he backed out of the apartment and closed the door.

"Hungry?" Mitch asked with a quick glance out the window. The weather was clearing, and while he was more than happy to spend another day in bed with Cassia, he'd had to get back to work.

"I could eat." Nox set their bag down at their desk, stopped to give Elliot a good morning pet, then perched themselves in one of the bar stools. "So, does this mean you and Cass have worked things out?"

"I'd say we're a work in progress." He knew a loaded question when he heard it. "Toast?"

"Yeah, thanks." Nox nodded and Mitch set a mug of coffee in front of them. "Good weekend?"

"Pretty good." For the most part. "You?"

They took a long drink of coffee, eyeing him as if trying to decide if he passed inspection. "Pretty good. How are things coming at the burial site?"

As Mitch wasn't certain it was his place to fill Nox in on the events of the last few days, he played coy. "Interesting."

Nox's dark eyes narrowed. "What happened?"

Mitch shook his head. "I don't know what—"

They indicated the silently humming machines. "No new IDs have come in, have they? Otherwise those things would be spitting out results and Cass would have her ass glued to her spiny chair." They leaned back as if they could peer into Cass's bedroom. "There's never been a morning when she hasn't been up before the sun already halfway through her day by the time I got in. So"—they pinned

Mitch with an unwavering and slightly unnerving stare—"what's going on? And don't think about censoring yourself. I've read your FBI file," Nox added. "You've a reputation for being a straight shooter." Their eyes narrowed again. "In more ways than one."

Mitch took a long drink of coffee. Given what Cassia had told him about her assistant, he shouldn't be at all surprised about their wealth of knowledge. Especially knowledge that wasn't commonplace. He dished out breakfast, couching his words. "She doesn't think you know what happened in the warehouse."

"I know what's in the report." Nox accepted the fork and plate he offered. "I know you saved her life."

"That report was never made public."

"No," Nox said easily. The toaster popped behind him. "It wasn't."

"I don't suppose you'd like to tell me how—"

"No," Cassia said from the bedroom doorway. "They wouldn't." Her attention was pinned on her assistant. "I'd planned to tell you everything, Nox."

Nox shrugged. "I figured you'd tell me when you were ready. Or when you needed to." Nox pointed to her eggs. "These are good."

"Butter," Mitch murmured. "My secret ingredient."

Cassia approached, her dark t-shirt hiking up to her thighs when she wrapped an arm around his waist, but her attention was still on Nox. "How long have you known?"

"About New York? Since about a week after I started working for you," Nox admitted without a hint of guilt or reservation. "I worked out the timeline, your … situation." They gestured around the room that had become Cassia's entire world after leaving New York. "Went on a bit of an information hunt."

"You never said anything," Cassia said. "You never even hinted—" She shook her head. "I don't know what to say."

"There's nothing to say." Nox shrugged again. "The way I saw it, I was doing my job and part of my job is keeping you safe. No one gets past me, remember?" They eyed Mitch in a way that made Laurel's protective instincts seem negligible. "No one."

"You couldn't have found any place safer if you'd move into Fort Knox," Mitch murmured before pressing a kiss to Cassia's temple. "Sit down and eat something."

Nox watched as Cassia moved around and into the stool beside them.

"What?" Cassia asked when Mitch slid a plate in front of her.

"Just never seen you sit still long enough to consume a crumb let alone a full plate of food before noon." Nox finished their own breakfast. "New lock, old boyfriend, eating at the kitchen counter. That's a lot of change for one weekend."

"Speaking of weekends," Cassia said. "How was yours with Wally?"

Mitch busied himself with the food, eating his own meal while cleaning up and listening to the two of them chat about Nox's food-truck centric trip to San Diego with Quinn's detective partner. When he got out of the shower, Nox was at their desk booting up their dormant computer system while Cassia washed their dishes.

"Thought I'd head up to the site," Mitch told her after putting on his shoes. "Maybe check out the—"

Cass's doorbell rang.

"Hold that thought." She went to the door, glancing quickly at the video monitor before she pulled it open. "Quinn. Paul." She stepped back and waved them inside. "To what do I owe the early morning visit?"

When they looked immediately to him, Mitch's stomach dropped all the way to the lobby. Shit.

"We need to talk to Mitch." The friendliness Mitch was used to seeing on Quinn's face was nowhere to be seen.

"Well, he's right there." Cassia waved at him. "Have at it."

"Not here," Paul said in what Mitch could only describe as his prosecutor's voice. "Down at the station."

Cassia snorted. "Yeah, right."

Nox rose up from their seat. "What's going on?"

"They're joking," Cassia stated.

"No, Cass," Quinn said. "We're not." He met Mitch's gaze. "Do you want to tell her?"

"Tell me what?" Cassia looked between them, disbelief rising slowly in her eyes. "What's this about?"

"The ID came through on the woman we found buried up on the hill," Paul said.

"What woman?" Nox asked.

"Long story." Cassia held up her hand. "I'll fill you in later. Well?" She looked back to Paul and Quinn. "Who is she?" Neither man seemed in a rush to tell her, something that clearly annoyed Cassia, but before Mitch could come with the words, Quinn continued.

"The woman's name is Irene Whittaker," Quinn said.

"Irene …" Cassia's voice faded into disbelief and ghosts rose in her gaze.

"She was reported missing from her nursing home in Las Vegas late Thursday night." He turned his gaze back to Mitch. "About an hour after you signed the visitors log when you visited. There's video of you arriving, Mitch."

Of course there was.

"Whittaker." Cassia spun around, her face draining of color. "What …? What the hell, Mitch?" But he saw the instant the truth dawned on her. She was putting together pieces he'd hoped she hadn't seen. "You knew." She blew out a long, controlled breath. "Oh, my God. You recognized her as soon as you saw her face, didn't you?"

"I can explain." Could he though? Even as he said it, he wasn't convinced. "She was perfectly fine when I left," he told the detective and special investigator. "And if I had done something, I certainly wouldn't have signed my name in the guest book."

"Exactly what I expected you to say." But Quinn didn't sound entirely convinced. "We still need to get all this on the record."

"On the record? Are you serious?" Cassia was looking between them like she was caught up in a maniacal tennis match. "Why? You don't think …. You can't think he killed her. Quinn! That's ridiculous!"

"It might be," Paul cut in. "But the time of death lines up to when Mitch landed in Vegas and arrived in Los Angeles. Plus he had access to the scene beginning on Friday and he sent his co-workers home early on Saturday night."

"Around the time they believe the body was buried," Quinn added.

Mitch pressed his lips into a thin, numb line. It all fit perfectly, didn't it?

Quinn looked at Mitch. "I'm sorry."

"Yeah." It was, Mitch knew, what he'd be doing in the detective's place. "Let me get my—"

"No!" Cassia's sharp order cut through the static buzzing through his head. "No, you're not going to do this. Paul. Quinn. Please."

"Cass, we don't have a choice," Quinn said. "The DA's already been alerted and given Mitch's involvement with your case, we can't just let this slide. We have to follow procedure."

"You're honestly going to take him in as a suspect?" She cut Quinn off. "Have you talked to Riley? Did she tell you—?"

"About Jonathan and Gavin Whittaker?" Paul said. "Yeah. We know what happened, Cass."

"And we get it," Quinn said. "But I'm sure you can also see where this would give Mitch a motive."

Yeah. Because the best way to avenge Cassia's abduction four years ago was to kill Jonathan Whittaker's mother. "Cassia, it's okay." Mitch stepped close and touched a hand to her shoulder, but she flinched and moved away even as she stared at him. What he wouldn't give to erase that helpless panic shining in her eyes. "I need to go."

"He didn't do this," she spat at her friends. "Shame on you for even thinking it's possible."

"Cass." Quinn shook his head.

"They know my record, Cassia," Mitch reminded her. "And because they do, they know what I'm capable of. They know it's possible I did it."

"That's bullshit!" Cass blasted. "Just because you—" She caught herself before saying anything that could very well be strengthen the case against him. Her eyes filled not with tears, but with rage. "I'll take care of this. I'll call—"

He pressed his lips to her forehead. "I'll be fine." He waited until she lifted her gaze to his. "I promise." He retrieved his cell phone from her bedroom, grabbed his non-FBI jacket. "Let's go," he told them and followed them out.

"I am sorry," Quinn said when they were out in the hall. "Cass, I—"

"Don't be sorry," she snapped, holding the edge of the door in a white-knuckled death grip. "Do your damned job."

She slammed the door in their faces.

# CHAPTER FOURTEEN

"WE have a problem."

Cass looked up from her own computer screen and found a nervous Nox staring at her across the room.

She could not, for the life of her, come up with any rational explanation as to what Mitch had been doing in Las Vegas, let alone why he'd have visited Irene Whittaker.

Jonathan and Gavin's mother had been diagnosed with severe dementia a few months after her husband's conviction and subsequent death. Irene had been in the Las Vegas care facility for years before Mitch had even considered questioning her in regards to her son's murder spree. As far as Cass knew, Irene wasn't even aware of the circumstance surrounding her younger son's death or her older one's incarceration.

She was, quite simply, a shell.

None of that negated the fact Mitch had indeed flown from Virginia to Las Vegas. Or that he'd landed at three on the day Irene had been reported as missing.

"Cass?" Nox said again.

"I heard you." Cass blinked herself free of frustration. "What's the problem?" She could only hope it was one.

"I can't find any record of Mitch flying from Vegas to LA."

"Yeah." Cass was looking at her own computer screen. "I know."

Nox frowned and walked around Cass's desk. "I thought you asked me to look into his flights."

"I did." But that didn't stop her from wanting, from needing to do something herself. Other than make one phone call after Mitch had been taken in, she'd spent the hours since spinning her proverbial wheels. "I'm sorry."

"Me, too." Nox sounded uncertain. "I don't know where else to look. Or what to look for."

Cass heard her own desperation in her assistant's voice. "You believe him. Don't you?"

"That he didn't kill Whittaker's mother? Yes." No hesitation. No hint of doubt in their voice.

Relief and gratitude surged through her to the point she could barely breathe around it. "Okay." Cass shoved herself up, squeezed Nox's arm, and went to pour a fresh mug of coffee. "Okay, let's look at this from Mitch's perspective. Whatever the hell that might be." He had a hell of a lot of explaining to do once she got her hands on him again. "He didn't deny visiting Irene. That isn't something he would have done out of the blue."

"Would he have visited her before? Why?"

Cass couldn't imagine why. "Is there a way to check?"

"If they've digitized their visitors logs and banked their security recordings." But Nox didn't move.

"Another problem?" Cass asked.

"Not for me," Nox hedged. "I'm just wondering if there are any guardrails on my search." That was Nox code letting Cass know they were about to put their black hacker hat back on.

Cass clenched her fists. She was finally getting her life back on track. Her real life. Not the sequestered, isolated one she'd been existing in for the past four years. She could see hope and a very small light at the end of her self-created prison. "I want him back." Cass's statement felt like a declaration of independence. "Whatever it takes, Nox. I want him back and out from under suspicion."

"Understood." They zoomed back to their desk.

Elliot walked over to Cass, pushed his head up against her leg.

"I know." Cass reached down to touch his head. "We're working on it."

The doorbell rang.

"What the ever-loving fuck is going on with today?" She stalked over, sloshing coffee over the rim as she jabbed a finger against the video button. "Yeah? Oh." Her anger evaporated and shifted immediately into surprise.

"Cass?" The familiar female voice sounded before the front door camera fizzled into focus. "It's Lynda Prince." Mitch's former partner held up her badge.

"Lynda." What on earth? Then a light bulb blinked on in her head. "Are you here about Mitch?"

"Mitch? No." She frowned, glanced over her shoulder. "You requested an FBI presence on the field work you're supervising." She tilted her head. "Sorry I'm late, but I had another case to close before I could get out here."

*Another case ...*

Cass's temper might have caught if confusion hadn't squeezed in around it. "But ..." They weren't going to get anywhere talking over the speaker. "Yeah, come on up."

She hit the buzzer.

Nox leaned around the corner. "Another FBI agent?"

"Mitch's former partner," Cass said. "But I'm guessing you knew that."

Nox's wide-eyed silence confirmed more than denied. "Want me to get out of here? Take Elliot for a w-a-l-k?"

Elliot trotted over, barked once and went to sit beneath his collection of leashes.

"Apparently it isn't up to me." Cass pulled open the door while Nox leashed Elliot up. It didn't dawn on her until Lynda stepped onto the second-floor landing that she'd done so without any hesitation or ... fear. "Lynda, this is my assistant Nox."

"Hey." Nox offered a quick wave. "I've got that preliminary program running that'll take a while." They shot Cass a look that showed some concern, but they moved on down the stairs.

"Thanks, Nox." She turned to Lynda. "Come on in."

The FBI agent stepped in and to the side, waiting for Cass to close the door and lead her the rest of the way. Unlike Mitch, Cass saw no hint that Lynda had changed one iota since they'd last met. She was as tall and slender as Cass recalled, and wore her very long dark hair in a smoothed ponytail that hung more than halfway down her back. She wore black slacks, a black blazer and a sharp-collared white button-down shirt that, to Cass at least, looked as close to an FBI uniform as anything.

"Can I get you something to drink?"

"I'd kill for some actual coffee." Lynda set her cell phone and sunglasses on the kitchen counter. "I swear the local FBI office only makes weak bean water. Nice setup." Her low-heeled boots clunked dully against the hardwood floor as she strode over to the window. "Excellent view. I like the neighborhood."

"You're as bad at small talk as your former partner." Cass pushed the brew button. "It's good to see you again, but I'm a little confused as to why you're here."

"Did some wires get crossed?" Lynda strode over to the counter. "I was told you requested federal assistance."

"I, yeah, I did." Cass pulled the mug free and slid it toward her guest. "But Mitch got here on Friday. I only need one of you."

Lynda's hand froze halfway to her mouth. For a flash of a moment, her confusion seemed to mirror Cass's, before her gaze narrowed. "Mitch is here now? In Los Angeles? Here in your apartment?"

"Not right at the moment, no," Cass admitted. Having his former partner bust in while Mitch was being interviewed as a murder suspect probably wouldn't earn either of them any points.

The doubt in Lynda's voice, however, left Cass wondering if they were having the same conversation. She motioned for Lynda to join her on the sofa. "I called him as soon as the mayor threatened to remove me from the case unless I brought in the FBI. I wanted to make certain he was amenable to coming out here before I made the official request."

"And obviously he was."

Cass faced Lynda when she sat on the edge of the cushion and set her mug down with a clack. "I'm surprised he didn't tell you."

"Don't be." Lynda smirked. "If he had, I'd have had to remind him he's no longer a field agent."

"Well, yeah." Cass shrugged. "The bureau took care of that when they demoted him after ... Whittaker." She detested how her voice automatically dropped into a whisper whenever she spoke his name.

"The bureau didn't demote Mitch, Cass." Lynda sat back and faced her. "Hell, they bent over backwards to try to keep him in the field. We all did."

"What are you talking about?" Cass's mind raced around the un-expected information, but those oddities—his lack of a rental car, the hotel booking issue—now seemed to mean something more. He'd never once mentioned his work or his move to Virginia, other than to mention it in passing. "When he didn't get the teaching position at the academy, I just assumed ..."

"I won't lie," Lynda said rather deliberately. "The FBI had some qualms about his abilities after Whittaker, but that's what the six-month suspension was for. Along with the mandatory therapy."

At least he'd been honest about her with that.

"You really don't know what happened after you left, do you?"

"No." And maybe that was her fault. "I ..." Obviously it was time to be honest not only with Lynda but with herself. "I wanted a clean break. No ... reminders." And maybe, she told herself, that had been part of her problem. Despite her own therapy sessions, she'd done what she always did with uncomfortable topics and events; she compartmentalized and pretended they didn't happen rather than dealing with.

Just like Mitch, she thought. Complete avoidance.

No wonder she'd become paralyzed. "I'm sor—"

"You don't owe anyone an apology about how you chose to pro-tect yourself," Lynda stated firmly. "You went through hell in those hours Gavin Whittaker held you captive. You coped how you coped. And so did Mitch. It's not up to anyone to judge that."

"He probably could have coped better if he'd landed that job teaching at Quantico." There was no keeping the accusation out of her voice.

"Strike two." Lynda leaned over for her coffee. "Mitch is the one who took himself out of consideration for the position before his suspension. Then after, he turned in his badge and gun."

Mitch had ... what? Cass's stomach pitched. Being an FBI agent had been all Mitch had ever dreamed of being, ever since he was a kid and he and his father would watch procedurals together. It was one of the things about him she'd first fallen for. His absolute dedication to a long-held dream he'd worked hard to achieve. This didn't make sense. Or … did it?

"So his going to work in the lab at Quantico—?"

"Was entirely his decision. And before you ask"—Lynda cut Cass off before she could get a response out—"he didn't talk to me about any of this beforehand. One day I've got a solid partnership, and the next I'm having to break in a newbie." Irritation clouded her eyes for a moment. "Worked out okay, in the end. But ever since with Mitch, it's been 'how's it going' or 'what are the kids up to these days' rather than shop talk."

"So he's been lying to me—saying he was assigned to this case." She wanted to be more surprised, more hurt even. But instead it was the confusion that lingered.

"I doubt it he sees it that way." Lynda reached for her coffee. "But he'd feel justified if it got him the only thing that mattered."

"And what's that?" Cass scoffed.

"The chance to see you again." She arched a brow as if Cass shouldn't have had to ask the question. "So you being sidelined by the mayor. Does that have to do with …" she waved a hand around the apartment. "I spoke with some of my colleagues in forensics before my flight this morning. You don't stray from home much, do you?"

"Much? At all." Cass caught herself falling into her usual coping mechanism of playing off her anxiety issues with a joke. "I've found it difficult to step outside my comfort zone." She rested her cheek in her hand. "Most days that zone is the apartment. On others …" Her nerves began to buzz and hum. "Others I can make it all the way to the roof before I lose it. Classic PTSS with a side of agoraphobia."

"PTSS I get," Lynda said. "Agoraphobia? You had at least one foot out in the hallway when I came up the stairs. I'd say that's an overreach."

"Oh, would you?" Cass actually grinned, surprised that she didn't take offense. "Get your doctorate in psychiatry since I last saw you?"

"My husband's one. PTSS is his specialty. I've picked up a lot over the years." She sipped her coffee. "Did one of your therapists diagnose you or is this more of a self-exploration conclusion kind of thing."

Cass tucked her legs in under her. "I can't answer that without sounding like an ass."

"Here's what I see," Lynda said. "I see a clear-eyed, focused woman recovering from a trauma most people can't begin to relate to. I think it's easier for you to cope if you can put a name to what you're feeling. An unanswered issue would drive you nuts so"—she shrugged—

"Agoraphobia. When was the last time you left your apartment?"

"A few nights ago," Cass said easily. "My friend Laurel lives across the hall—"

"And the last time you had a panic attack?"

"The day before that." Cass thought back. "It was the first one I'd had in months. I went on lockdown after Christmas. We had an intruder in the building and it freaked me out." Enough that she hadn't left her apartment in weeks.

"But you've been out since."

"If you can call the roof out."

"My husband specializes in anxiety disorders. I'd be happy to put you in touch with him if you want to really nail down what's going on. In the meantime, what triggered this last panic attack?"

Cass opened her mouth, then snapped it shut again.

"Not talking about these things is why you're still feeling trapped. If you don't talk, you won't get out."

"Are you sure you didn't get a doctorate by proxy?" Cass tapped restless fingers on her leg. "Let's take my panic attack out of it." She was adamantly adverse to coincidences, but she couldn't help but think Lynda's arrival was perfectly timed. "I need to tell someone about this and I guess you're it. But I don't want this to turn into a therapy session."

Lynda's brow went up.

"Anymore than it already is," Cass clarified. After a moment of debate, she got up, went over to her desk and retrieved the plastic bag containing the postcards she'd been receiving. "These started arriving about six weeks ago. A couple every few days. I get crank stuff all the time. Forensics fans can be a bit obsessive. Most of the time, I trash the emails or letters."

"But these you considered special enough to keep," Lynda murmured as she accepted the bag.

"Don't know if special is the right word. They gave me the creeps. And I have a pretty high threshold for creep."

Lynda moved them around in the bag, flipped it over, then back again. "Short and to the point. Messages could be interpreted in a few ways, but the threat is apparent." She frowned. "Utah. New York. Los Angeles." Her sharp gaze locked on Cass's. "Whittaker?"

"He's supposed to be on lockdown," Cass rationalized. "No visitors. Nothing in or out."

"Prisons leak far more than most people would be comfortable with. They can become enterprises unto themselves. Even super max ones like The Nest. Whittaker comes from money," Lynda went on. "He had a lot of disposable income even after the fortune he spent on his lawyer. That would earn him some prestige as a high-profile prisoner."

"What about buying himself out?" It sounded borderline stupid now that she said it out loud.

"Out of prison?" Lynda frowned. "No. Whittaker might have tested off the charts on the genius scale, but even he couldn't bribe his way out of The Nest. It's easy enough for him to pay someone to get him these postcards, though. And just as easy to have someone mail them. Prison guards are paid crap. They're human. A lot of them are fallible."

"It's happened before, hasn't it? Prisoners going missing." It had happened with Dean Samuels after he'd pled guilty to murdering Melanie Dennings; a murder Cass and her friends were convinced had been committed by members of The Circle.

"Only in episodes of *Supernatural*," Lynda tried to joke. "You're hedging. There's something else behind this conversation, isn't there?"

Doubt nearly silenced her. "It's going to sound crazy."

"I make a living with crazy," Lynda reminded her. "If you're worried I'll tell Mitch—"

"Not worried exactly." But it seemed as though they were more similar than Cass had realized. He had his secrets, just as she'd been keeping her own. "I just haven't confided in him about this, but he can't exactly get upset about it given his lack of forthrightness the past few days." She shoved herself up and walked over to her desk. "I got an email the other day. I thought it was from my assistant, so I opened it. It was a video message. From Whittaker."

"That's ..." Lynda blinked quickly. "That's not possible. He's under strict lockdown without access to ..."

"You just said yourself, money talks. Some guards would be susceptible to bribery or payoffs. And Whittaker is smart enough to figure out which ones he could use to his benefit."

"This is Hollywood movie level shit, Cass. Not the real world."

"Yeah, well, believe me, this video felt very real world." Replaying it in her head over and over was worse than any horror movie she'd ever seen. "He was wearing normal clothes and there wasn't anything around him that indicated he was in prison."

"Backgrounds and clothing and details are easily manipulated these days thanks to AI. People can make it seem like they're anywhere. Or like anyone."

"Yeah, but this didn't feel fake." How did she make her understand. "I looked into his eyes, Lynda. I know those eyes. They stared at me the entire time I was testifying against his father. You cannot fake or re-create that level of loathing." Or madness.

"I assume there's a reason why you aren't showing me the video."

"It disappeared as soon as it was over."

"Of course it did. What did he say?" Cool, calm, rational Lynda. Nothing ever fazed her. "What were his exact words?"

Reciting the words made her shiver. "That it was almost time and that he couldn't wait to see me again. I'm telling you, Lynda, I swear—"

Lynda held up a hand, dismissing her plea. "I believe you got the email, Cass. I'm just questioning your supposition that he did it from outside prison."

"Yeah. I know." She pinched the bridge of her nose. "That's why I called the warden. I demanded to see live footage of Whittaker in his cell. Then I spoke with three of the guards to confirm he was where he was meant to be." She shook her head. "Can't believe I did that. I'm sure Warden Taggart thought I was a few ants short of a picnic."

"Should I even ask how you got the number for the direct line to The Nest's warden?"

"My assistant might be the computer genius, but I've got game." She'd known where to look.

"The warden and guards didn't convince you, did they?"

"I don't know." And that's what she couldn't shake. "I don't know if I can trust my own judgment with this. And I don't have the video. It's just this big question mark hanging over my head. If he's out—"

"Don't get ahead of yourself," Lynda said. "My brother-in-law works for the Bureau of Prisons at the Justice Department. Let me make a call. Utah is only a couple hours by plane." She shrugged. "Can't hurt to make an unannounced visit."

"Yeah?" Relief surged. Just the fact Lynda hadn't thought her crazy was almost enough to completely ease Cass's mind.

"I'm in standby mode at this point anyway." Lynda reached into her blazer pocket and pulled out her cell and opened her contacts list. "Earliest I can get into the excavation site is in, what? A couple of days. No sense wasting the taxpayer's money with me sitting around. Yeah, hi. I'm calling for Charlie Prince. Tell him it's his sister-in-law, Lynda. Yes, I'll hold. Don't worry," she murmured and touched Cass's arm. "I've got this."

*

"Here." Quinn closed the interrogation room door behind him. Florescent lights hummed and flickered, casting the small space in a silvery-grey light that reflected off the stained linoleum tile.

Mitch stopped pacing long enough to look down at the paper cup of steaming coffee Quinn set in front of him and gave a cursory glance to the file Quinn placed beside it. Even after two hours of waiting, Mitch wasn't remotely interested in any coffee produced inside a law enforcement building. The air smelled stale, carrying the distinct aroma of body odor, disinfectant, and more than a little guilt.

"Relax, Mitch." Quinn sat in a metal chair at the scarred table. "This is just a conversation. You'll be out of here in no time."

"Do you know how many times I've said that to a suspect?" He didn't want to admit that it felt like a low blow that Quinn and Paul had seen fit to bring him into the LAPD Hollywood Division offices in order to continue their conversation. But he knew, perhaps better than most, that friendship, especially fledgling friendships, had their limits. "I didn't kill Irene Whittaker."

"We know."

"You could have fooled me." But it felt good to hear, nonetheless. "I take it my word wasn't enough to convince you, so what did?"

"As Cass is so fond of saying, the evidence. You don't wear a ring, do you?" Quinn looked down at Mitch's hands. "Not even your FBI class ring."

"I couldn't even tell you where that is," Mitch admitted. He'd probably tossed it when he'd moved to Virginia. "And no. I'm not the jewelry kind of … ah." The light dawned. A bit too slow for his liking.

Quinn pushed the file across the table.

Mitch flipped open to reveal the graphic autopsy photos. The old woman looked anything but at peace. Her sallow, wrinkled skin sagged against death. Her silver hair, free of the mud that had caked it. He flipped through to a close-up of the back of Irene Whittaker's neck. The imprint of a band to what was undoubtedly a thick ring stood out from the bruising. "She was strangled then." He winced. "It wouldn't have taken much. She was … frail." Even more frail than the pictures indicated. "Doesn't rule me out completely though, does it?"

"You visited her on Friday afternoon," Quinn pressed.

"Yes."

"But that wasn't the first time, was it?" Quinn's questions came across, at least to Mitch, as ones designed to make it clear to anyone who might see the recording that he wasn't responsible.

"No."

"How many times would you say you visited her in the past few years?"

Mitch swallowed hard as the truth began to emerge. He glanced at the two-way mirror on the wall across from him. "Paul can come in and join the party," he said. "I'd rather not go over this again—"

The door opened and a young detective with slicked back dark hair and a god-awful blue tie poked his head in. "Quinn?"

"Yeah?" Quinn tilted his chair onto its back feet and looked behind him. "Detective Wallace Osterman, FBI Special Agent Mitch Keaton."

"Nox's boyfriend," Mitch said before he thought better of it. "Nice to meet you. Heard you two had a pretty good weekend." He was happy to talk about anything other than Irene Whittaker's murder.

"Ah." Wallace looked to his partner as a flush crept up his round face. "Yeah, actually. We did. Quinn, we've got a—"

"I'm not a problem, Wally. Not yet anyway." Laurel Fontaine, dressed in a power navy suit and wearing deadly spiked matching heels, swept in behind him and Wallace quickly danced out of her way to push the door open completely. She carried a soft-sided briefcase, showed off a collection of thin gold chains around her throat, and pinned Quinn and his partner with a look that had Mitch withering in sympathy.

"Let me guess ..." Quinn dropped his chair forward with a thunk and cast a "help me" look at the mirror. "Cass called you."

"About two seconds after you carted him off in your prison mobile."

"Oh, come on, Laurel," Quinn groaned. "I told Cass this was simply routine."

"LAPD *routine* pays my rent. Come on." She waved her hand as Paul approached the door. "Nope." Her palm went flat like a stop sign when he started to come in. "I need to speak with my client. Did they mirandize you?"

Mitch shook his head, only to remember she was looking at Paul. "No." Given Quinn and Paul's sterling reputations, he had to assume that oversight was on purpose.

"Out." Laurel stood her ground as Quinn stepped around her. "Seriously. You could have talked to him at Temple House. This didn't have to become nasty."

"There are a lot of moving parts to this one, Laurel," Paul said. "We have to be careful what—"

She snapped the door closed, waited a beat then walked over to the camera installed in the far corner of the ceiling. She stood there, not moving, until the red light blinked off. She walked to the table, her spiked heels sounding like gunshots in the small space.

"I didn't kill her."

"No shit." Laurel set her bag down on the floor and took the seat Quinn had vacated. "Sit. Breathe. Then talk."

He sat, but he was at a loss as to what to say. "What do you want to know?"

"Smartest response ever." Her left brow arched ever so slightly. "Let's start with Irene Whittaker. No way that name is a coincidence."

"It's not. She's Jonathan and Gavin Whittaker's mother."

"The mother of the one man you killed and the other you locked away for life. Fabulous." Laurel leaned over, pulled out a yellow legal pad, clicked open a pen and began writing. "And what, may I ask, would have you traveling across the entire country to visit the incapacitated mother of two murderers?"

He got what she was trying to do, but it wasn't going to work. "I can't afford you."

"No, you can't." Her smile was quick. "But I give all my friends at least one freebie. Most of them wait a few years to use it. Why did you stop in Las Vegas to visit Irene Whittaker?"

"Because." He paused, trying to grab hold of any excuse not to answer. "Because I made a promise." He was in this deep. Time to start paddling. "And because I needed a gun before I got to LA."

He gave her credit. She didn't give anything away. The only sound he could hear, other than his own pulse hammering in his ears, was her fountain pen scraping against the paper.

"You're an FBI agent," she said without looking up. "You don't have a backup piece you travel with?"

"I'm an FBI technician," he corrected and earned a glance this time. "I'm no longer a full-fledged agent so ... no. I didn't want to deal with the hassle of checking a bag, which is the only way I could have brought a sidearm from Virginia to California. Not to mention the paperwork."

"And Las Vegas was your solution." He could hear the insult loud and clear.

"I've got a friend who's a private pilot with a fleet of aircraft."

"So, fly into Vegas, buy a gun, have your buddy fly you to California and you're armed and raring to go."

"Pretty much." It had made sense to him at the time.

"Thank God she wasn't shot," Laurel muttered. "You left out the part where you stopped at a nursing home to visit the mother of the murderer you killed."

He didn't humor her with a reply.

She stopped writing, set her pen down. "You haven't done anything illegal, so why the subterfuge? And think carefully before you answer because we both know Quinn and Paul don't believe you killed her anymore than Cass or I do." She pointed at the mirror. "What is it you don't want them to know?"

He didn't give a rat's ass what Quinn or Paul knew or didn't. "It's not them I'm thinking about."

She looked him dead in the eye. "It's always about Cass for you, isn't it?" There was the barest flash of something akin to gratitude in her gaze.

Did she expect him to deny it?

"Well." She folded her hands on top of her tablet. "Then you've got a problem because if you want to walk away from being a murder suspect, you're going to have to come clean. With them. And with Cass."

"And you."

"Obviously," she scoffed. "Time's ticking and I've got meetings today. So let's speed it up. Out with it."

She was right. There wasn't any way out of this without help and right now, Laurel—and maybe Quinn and Paul—were his only options. "We might want to back up to where you said I haven't done anything illegal. That's not entirely true." He took a deep breath and surrendered. "For the past few days I've been impersonating a federal officer."

Both of her brows went up this time.

"Is that a good place to start?"

"Yeah." She clicked open her pen again. "It is. Now back up." She held up her perfectly manicured index finger. "And start at the beginning."

# CHAPTER 15

"YOU need to eat something." Sutton's gentle order fell on deaf ears.

Cass was too amped up, too worried, to do anything but wonder what was going on down at the LAPD. Lynda had left shortly after Nox's return with a promise she'd call in a few hours with an update.

Mitch's former partner probably wouldn't appreciate hearing second hand about his being taken in for questioning, but that was a worry for another time.

Ironic, Cass thought, as she hadn't received a call of her own and it had been hours since Mitch had left with Paul and Quinn. Endless hours that felt like years ticking her life away. She had just enough optimism left to believe that no news was good news.

But when it came down to it, it was time to accept a new, harsh reality. Mitch had lied to her. By omission, to protect her, to protect himself. Didn't matter the reason. A lie was a lie, and it only fed that deep, shadowy fear that trusting him was dangerous. Especially to her heart.

Across the apartment, Nox's fingers flew over keys and clicked on windows, an increasing frown on their face.

"Did you do something to the system when I was away?" Nox called as Sutton nudged a peanut butter protein cookie in Cass's direction. "Make any changes? Run updates? Start playing that online battle game you used to like?"

"No. Why?" Cass asked almost absently.

"Because it's not working right." They shook their head. "I need to reboot." The stood up, pointed at Cass's desk. "We need to reboot everything."

It wasn't until Nox passed by that Cass's brain kicked into gear. "What do you mean it isn't working right?"

"There's a delay in processing speed that should not be happening," Nox said. "I don't know it's almost like …"

"Almost like what?" So she hadn't been imagining things.

"Like something is drawing power away. I used to get more business as a programmer and technician when a system had been invaded."

"Invaded like with a virus?" Sutton asked.

That ball of anxiety shifted back into its usual spot in Cass's chest, only this time it actually hurt.

"Pretty much," Nox confirmed. "There are all kinds of virus-type programs. The one I'm talking about is more subversive. It's planted deep into the system's programming and kind of sits and waits until whoever sent it activates it. That's how they get in to control things." Nox woke up Cass's machine, powered it off, then unplugged it. "It'll take me a little while to—"

"Can that have happened through an email?" Cass's entire body went cold. "Like a video file maybe?"

"Well, yeah. I guess." Nox shrugged. "But neither of us is stupid enough to open an unknown attachment or file."

How Nox overestimated her. Even someone as smart as Cass could be tricked. "What if I thought the email had come from you?"

"From me?" Nox's pixie-like face shifted into an expression of alertness. "Did someone spoof my address? The one I have dedicated to you? No, wait. That isn't possible. I've got layers of protection on everything we do."

"Drink." Sutton pressed a glass of something thick and green into Cass's hand. "Nox, how would someone go about getting that information?"

"I mean …" Nox looked completely baffled. "This isn't Grand Central Station. No one comes in here, so it couldn't be hardware

222

based. If someone wanted to get that deep into the system to break through my protection levels, they'd have to ride in electronically. Through our WiFi or some unsecured device. Wait. My question didn't come as a surprise, did it?"

Cass winced, partially because she loathed kale. "There was an … incident on Friday just after you left." She glanced at Sutton. "Before my panic attack. It's actually what caused the attack."

"You had a panic attack?"

"Not the point right now," Sutton told Nox. "What happened, Cass?"

"There was an email from you," she told Nox. "At least, I thought it was from you. About updating the VR program we've been working on."

"I don't send my ideas in an email," Nox countered which only made Cass feel more stupid. "You know that. You're sure it was my address?"

A question she'd asked herself a dozen times. "I wouldn't have opened it otherwise."

Nox returned to Cass's desktop, tapping restless fingers as the rebooting finished.

"There's no use looking for it," Cass admitted. "It's not there anymore. The email vanished as soon as I watched it. Or, well … as soon as it played. Believe me, I looked for the damned thing. I even pulled the computer apart."

Nox looked at Cass as if she'd lost her mind. "That wouldn't have done anything."

"Yes, I know." But at the time it was something to do.

"Don't keep us in suspense," Sutton said. "What was the video? And don't say porn because porn doesn't cause panic attacks."

If there was one universal truth about secrets, it was that they always came out. Especially when one didn't want them to.

"It was Jonathan Whittaker," she admitted and saw the shock rise in both their gazes. "He just wanted to scare me."

"Well it worked," Sutton said. "He did. What did he say?"

She did not want this maniac back in her life. She didn't want his name even spoken in Temple House. And yet here they were. When things were finally beginning to turn around.

But the fear she saw in Sutton's eyes, the notion that Whittaker, in contacting Cass here at Temple House, could very well put Sutton and her family in danger.

"He told me that it was almost time and that"—she swallowed hard—"he can't wait to see me." The timing of this couldn't be worse, could it? She was barely clinging to her professional reputation. Adding Whittaker into the mix now was just ... her mind picked up speed and siphoned through the probabilities. "Nox, I'm sorry. I didn't think—"

"It's fine." Nox was in distracted mode now, focused entirely on Cass's system. "I'll find it."

"I don't think you will." Cass shook her head. "Whittaker was a—"

"Computer programmer, yeah." Nox finished for her. "You weren't the only one I read up on when you hired me. He was good, too. But"—they yanked Cass's chair over and sat down—"he's not as good as me. Everything leaves at least the barest of a trace. And that's here in the system. I just have to find it. And the best way to do that is to sneak in behind and ..."They opened a new screen that back-doored into Cass's programming.

Elliot jumped to his feet, spun in circles and barked at the wall.

Cass pressed a hand against her right ear. "Okay, now I'm definitely hearing something."

"Yeah." Sutton winced as they watched Elliot. "Me, too."

Cass pushed past Sutton to where her dog began to paw at the brick. Something flickered outside her window. Above the high-pitched screech, she heard a faint whizzing, a mechanical click. She pressed her forehead to the glass, turned her head. "What in the hell is that?"

Nox reached Cass before Sutton did. They not so gently pushed Cass aside, tried to get a look, but gave up. "I'll be back."They grabbed the glasses Mitch had brought back from his time at the burial site and ran out the front door.

Sutton opened the camera app on her phone, flipped it to take a selfie and pressed the camera against the window. She had to angle it in different ways, but then she stopped.

"You see something?" Cass came in to look over her shoulder.

"Reminds me of a giant plastic spider." Sutton took a couple of pictures. "Like something Lucas would build with his Legos. Kinda creepy."

With all the buzzing and clacking, it was definitely a machine of some kind. Blinking red lights on its underbelly. Strange suction cups on its arms that were bent at odd angles that kept it attached to the wall. "Keep an eye on it." Cass retrieved her remote and clicked on the center overhead monitor, rummaged through her messy desk to find her Bluetooth headset.

She tapped a nervous finger against her teeth, waiting for the glasses feed to connect. "Nox?"

The screen fizzled and went snowy before it connected. "Not sure if the zoom is going to be powerful enough," Nox's voice came through loud and clear as the image went in and out.

"What's going on?" Blake pushed the front door in that Nox had left open. "Nox just blasted out the front door like they were on fire."

"Someone got into my system and I'm betting they used that"— she pointed to the screen—"to do it. What do you think?"

Blake cast a quick look to Sutton before stopping at Cass's back.

"Nox, slow down the focus and come in slower." It was forty feet up from ground level. They'd be lucky to get a fraction of resolution … "There! Stop!" She looked over her shoulder at Blake. "Drone?"

"Yeah." He nodded. "A sophisticated one by the looks of it."

"Can we shoot it down?" Cass asked.

"No!" Both Blake and Nox said at the same time, but Nox's voice carried a tinge of panic.

"I think we've had enough police activity in the building for one day," Blake said. "Firing off a gun is only going to cause panic."

"And possibly lower property values." Sutton's attempt at a joke had both Cass and Blake looking at her. "Right. Sorry." She held up both hands in surrender.

"I want this thing in one piece," Nox demanded. "I want its insides. Hold on. What's it … shit. I think it's powering up!"

"It's wiggling around," Sutton called from the window. "A lot."

"Tell Nox I'm headed down," Blake ordered and ran out.

"We need to jam whatever signal is controlling it," Nox said. "Cass?"

"Yeah." Cass reached for her phone and fed the Bluetooth through her speaker. "Tell me what to do."

"Okay, you'll need my password first off." They rattled off the fifteen digit and symbol code and Cass typed it in. "Click on security, then open the file called Wave tracer."

"Yeah." Sutton moved in behind her as Cass sat down. The screen filled with a bunch of wavy moving lines. "Is this radio traffic?" It would look meditatively peaceful if it wasn't quite so intimidating.

"Yeah. We need to isolate the control signal from the drone. They usually operate at 2.4 or 5.8 gigahertz. We'll start there. Click the filter tab and narrow the scan to address those bands."

Cass's hands were far steadier than she felt. "Okay."

"WiFi traffic is random, but drone signals pulse in a steady rhythm. Watch for a repeating spike very couple of milliseconds."

"Like a heartbeat." Sutton pointed at the screen. "There. That could be it."

"Yeah." Cass watched for a precious few seconds. "It's at four point seven, spiking every half-second."

"We want to jam it, not fry it," Nox said. "Go back to my programs and locate the Destructo file."

"I'm never watching Wargames again," Sutton mumbled.

"I'm seeing a bunch of sliders and graphs," Cass's eyes flew back and forth across the large screen.

"We're going to lock in on the data coming through that signal. Did you find it?"

"Yep." Cass clicked the mouse on various boxes. Outside the drone's mechanisms ratcheted up.

"It's taking off," Sutton told them. "Nox?"

"We're almost there. Cass? Hit the execute button."

Cass clicked it. Hard. She spun the chair around.

Sutton gasped and rose up on her toes to get a better look.

Cass looked back to the screen. The drone plummeted straight down. When it landed, fragments of its arms shattered and spun off. Nox moved over it, bent down and the image enlarged on the screen. They flipped the machine over and hit a switch on its underside.

The lights on the drone went dead.

"We've got it. Now"—Nox picked it up, turned it over—"let's see if we can figure out where you came from."

\*

"Round trip service," Mitch said to Quinn after they parked in the small, gated lot behind Temple House. "Thanks."

Quinn didn't respond. He sat there, arms resting on the steering wheel of his SUV, starting out into the dimming light of the late afternoon. "Someone's setting you up."

226

"For murder? Yeah. Got that much." Mitch wasn't in any particular rush to head upstairs. He knew it was time to come clean with Cass; he'd have done that anyway even if Laurel hadn't threatened him with masculine specific bodily harm if he didn't follow through. "They aimed true though. I don't believe in coincidences in the best of circumstances."

"And these are definitely not the best of circumstances."

Before his trip out to LA, there had been no reason to burden Cassia with the truth about the last four years. But now that he was poised to gain an unexpected second chance he wasn't about to blow, he found himself out of options.

"Any idea why someone has it in for you?"

"Funny," Mitch said feeling anything but amused. "I was stuck more on the who."

"One answer might get us to the other," Quinn suggested. "So let's start with the who."

"There's only one case I worked that was personal enough to warrant this much backlash," Mitch said. "And Jonathan Whittaker is locked up in a maximum-security prison in Utah. Even if he was going to frame me for someone's death, he would not have chosen his mother."

Quinn glanced at him. "Given what you told us back at the station, I agree," he said slowly. "So what about Cass?"

"She's going to be pissed, but I don't think she—"

"No," Mitch cut him off. "I mean what if someone's using you to get to Cass. That could be the answer to the why."

Mitch shook his head. "They'd have to know our history to try to pull that off and neither one of us has been particularly chatty about our previous involvement." Plus he'd gone above and beyond to keep her name from being mentioned back in New York.

"Doesn't mean someone doesn't know about the two of you." He paused. "Or a group of someones."

"As much as I love to dance," Mitch lied, "How about you come out with it and tell me what you're thinking."

"Think about it. The pushback we've gotten since discovering those bodies from higher-ups, refusing to use LAPD officers for security, hiring it out instead to a private firm with a less-than-stellar record. The break-ins are looking more and more like it was a hired-out job. Now Irene Whittaker being found exactly where you've been working. Someone really doesn't want us digging up those bodies."

"You're thinking it's this Circle thing Cass and Paul told me about." Mitch would be lying again if he said the thought hadn't crossed his mind—before it crossed right out. What an absolutely convenient and ridiculous idea. And yet it made entirely too much sense. "That's a lot of effort to go to in order to stop an exhumation."

"It is. But Cass isn't easy to dissuade, is she?" Quinn looked at him. "She's also not easy to get to. Riley and Mabel were softer targets. They move around the city as easily as anyone, but not Cass. If the Circle's agenda is to stop the investigation into the murders, an investigation that could lead directly to exposing them, then it stands to reason they'd use whatever methods they could. Including targeting you as someone Cass cares about. That's how they get to her."

Circular reasoning, Mitch thought. Not all together out of the question, but definitely circling left field. "I'm trying to find a delicate way to point out that you're being paranoid about a supposed secret society that may or may not exist."

"They exist." Quinn's voice shook with anger. "You haven't been up there, have you? To the Tenado estate? Where the women were held. Where Riley …. You haven't seen the scratches or broken nails left in the walls. Or the blood each victim shed trying to get out. The Circle exists, Mitch." He grabbed the door handle and shoved. "They're out there and they're waiting. Watching. And I'm of the growing belief that you need to accept that before they hit you with something you can't alibi your way out of."

Mitch had to admit, despite Quinn and Paul both believing his protests of innocence, it was Laurel who had locked in his alibi by contacting his pilot friend to confirm Mitch's post-weapon-buy flight to LA. One that put him in the air with not only the pilot, but two other passengers in the hours well before Irene Whittaker's disappearance.

Another reason Jonathan Whittaker wasn't responsible, Mitch thought. Jonathan would have paid close attention to details like possible alibis. He wouldn't have left any potential thread dangling.

Mitch followed Quinn down the block to the apartment building's entrance. Finding Cassia's apartment door standing open was an unexpected surprise, but when he walked in, he found Cass, Nox, Sutton, and Blake all standing around her coffee table looking down at a mangled and battered drone.

"This isn't some kind of mock funeral for my reputation, is it?"

Cassia's head snapped up. He saw happiness and relief in her eyes first, before the doubt and annoyance set in.

"Surprise," he tried to joke. "I'm innocent."

"Of murder, at least." Quinn stuck his head in the door far enough to say that. "They need to talk," he told the others. "Now. You, too, Nox. Please."

Mitch glared at him over his shoulder. "Subtle."

"Effective," Quinn corrected as Nox looked to Cassia.

"Take Elliot," Cassia murmured and closed the door behind them. She turned, crossed her arms over her chest and locked him down with a blank expression. "Laurel didn't call."

"I asked her not to," Mitch admitted. "I wanted to talk to you first."

"So"—she still didn't move—"was it an alibi or your charming personality that set you free?"

"Alibi." She had every right to make him pay for this. "One I need to explain." But instead of sitting down and diving in, he went into the kitchen to make himself a sandwich. "What's with the drone?"

"Oh, that ..." She shrugged dismissively and took a seat at the counter. "Someone's been spying on me. Hacked through Nox's uber-security who knows when and got access to my system. It's why Elliot's been acting wonky. He heard it."

"I'm sorry?" He couldn't tell at first if she was joking.

"Oh, those details can wait." She tilted her head as if considering the situation from a different angle. "I'd rather hear all about your day in police custody, but I can wait." She motioned for him to finish. "You're going to need sustenance before I'm through with you, no longer special agent Keaton."

His hand almost got caught in the mayonnaise jar. Laurel never would have violated attorney client privilege, which meant someone else had entered the picture. "Did you call the FBI direct?"

"Close. Your old partner stopped by," Cassia said with unnerving accuracy when it came to reading his mind. She watched, silently, as he finished building a substantial turkey and cheese. "Turns out she's who the FBI actually assigned to help me oversee the burial site, so, yeah. She's taking care of a few things before we get down to business." She reached over and snagged a piece of sliced cheese. "Proceed."

"Not sure I'm that hungry anymore." He sliced through the thick sourdough and tossed the knife in the sink. When he turned around, she'd snagged half his sandwich.

"I didn't eat either," She mumbled as she chewed. "I was rather pre-occupied thinking about not only that you were a murder suspect, but that you've been lying to me from the second you walked in that door. Mmm." She toasted him with the food. "This is good."

Whatever anger he'd picked up on earlier seemed to have dissipated.

He pulled some paper towels out to use as a napkin. "You don't sound particularly mad."

"I was." She led him over to the couch. "I probably still am, but I'm also just over the edge of caring. Do you want to just blurt it all out, or should I question you?"

There was something unintentionally sexy about her offer. "Ask what you need to ask." He wasn't entirely sure volunteering information was the best course of action.

"I will on one condition," she replied. "No lies. About anything. One lie and I'm done with you, Mitch." There was an intensity in her voice that shook him. "I need you to believe that. It'll be for good this time, so promise me." The edgy playfulness he'd seen in her eyes died back and was replaced with a determination he hadn't seen since he'd been here. "Only the truth."

Not entirely sure he could speak, he simply nodded.

"Why were you visiting Irene Whittaker?"

Not the question he expected her to start off with. But, it was the biggie, wasn't it?

The answer, however, wasn't cut and dried.

With his stomach at least partially satiated, he chose his first words carefully. The rest would simply … come. "You once asked me how we found you that day in the warehouse. I never told you." He couldn't drag his gaze from hers. "But you've had your suspicions, haven't you?"

She set her food aside, scrubbed her hands down her jean-clad thighs. "I figured you did what you thought you had to do."

He ducked his head for a moment. He supposed he understood her thinking he was capable of forcing a suspect to talk. Considering what she'd seen him do in the warehouse. "I know you were given access to the unredacted report, so you know that the cameras in the interview room were deactivated for fifteen minutes after I went back in alone to question Jonathan Whittaker."

He saw the answer in her eyes.

"I didn't hurt him, Cassia. I wanted to. I was ready to." There were still times he regretted not doing so. "But then I heard your voice in my head and I knew …" Dammit, why was this so hard? "I knew if I crossed that line then I wouldn't be able to look you in the eye again. Because … I wouldn't be the man you loved. And so, I did the only thing I could do." He took a deep breath and confessed his sin. "After I took the death penalty off the table, I asked Whittaker what he wanted in exchange for giving up his brother and your location."

"You offered Jonathan Whittaker a deal." He could already see that she hadn't been expecting this explanation.

He'd promised not to lie, but he didn't think she needed to know that Mitch had been pretty much convinced she was already dead. In that moment, he'd been negotiating for her body, not her life. Maybe that was why …

"He only asked for one thing." It seemed strange *then*, Mitch thought. It felt even stranger in hindsight. "That every six weeks I visit his mother in that care facility. That I spend time with her, talk with her, listen to her talk about their lives as a family."

"No one would have held you to that." Cassia reached out, touched her fingers to the back of his hand. "Why on earth would you subject yourself to—?"

Mitch shook his head. "You already know the answer to that question."

"Jesus, Mitch." Sympathy, and more than a touch of frustration eked into her tone. "This honor code of yours is going to get you killed one day. You went through with it, didn't you? You agreed."

231

"Yeah." It hadn't dawned on him until after the first visit what Whittaker's motivations had been. "Didn't take me more than one visit to understand why that was Whittaker's offer. He knew that with every flight, every trip I took, every time I walked through the sliding glass doors of the Oasis Springs Assisted Living, that I'd be reminded of what I'd lost."

Her hand caught his and she scooted closer. "But you didn't lose me."

His smile was one of grief and acceptance. "Didn't I?" He turned his hand over, slipped his fingers through hers and hung on. "On the bright side, I guess I don't have to go to Vegas anymore."

"Oh, yay, a silver lining," she muttered. "You should have told me."

"Why? When?" The statement honestly baffled him. "Cassia, you shut me out from the second I carried you out of that warehouse. It didn't matter what I said or did in those weeks that followed, I couldn't reach you."

"Except with Elliot," she reminded him.

Thankfully his final idea had had been the best one.

"You still should have told me," she insisted.

"There was no reason to." Nor had he wanted to. "I got what I wanted. We found you in time. You were alive. That was all that mattered." He paused. "It still is."

"Why did you lie to me?" She drew his arm over her head and leaned into him. "About still working for the bureau."

"I didn't lie exactly. I avoided the specifics."

"Semantics may be the death of me," she said. "Lynda said you didn't have to resign from the bureau. That they still wanted you to teach."

He was trying to decide if his former partner had the best or worst timing possible. "Lynda's wrong. I did have to leave." And now, finally, the truth spilled forth. "I couldn't trust myself after what happened with Gavin Whittaker. Taking that shot ..." He could still hear it echoing in his mind, if he let himself.

"It's hard to take any life, Mitch. Even one as deranged as—"

"You don't get it." Because he wasn't explaining it well. Or because she couldn't imagine what he was trying to say. "I couldn't be an agent anymore because I didn't care that I killed him." His arm tightened around her and he turned his head, so he didn't have to look at her. "I still don't."

"You don't mean that," she whispered.

"I promised to tell you the truth." His arm tightened around her shoulders and he turned his head so he didn't have to see the affection fade from her eyes. "I need you to believe me. I have not had one moment of regret or guilt. Not one bit. I'd do it all again in exactly the same way. I'd kill him again. That is not the kind of person you can trust with a badge of any kind, let alone a federal one."

"Mitch," she whispered in a forgiving tone.

"If I couldn't trust myself anymore, I couldn't ask my partner to trust me. And I sure as hell shouldn't be teaching new recruits."

"I would think that makes you uniquely qualified." She shifted closer. Her hand moved to his chest, her fingers resting over his thundering heart.

"Cassia."

Anything else he might have said vanished as she moved over him, straddled his hips. She caught his face between her hands.

"That's all there is," he promised. "No more lies. I came because you called. I promised to help you when you asked for it, and I am. I'm here. Badge or no, I'm here." He rested his hands on her hips, flexed his fingers into her flesh and tilted his head back to look into her darkening eyes. "I'll understand if you can't forgive me."

She pressed her forehead to his, squeezed her eyes shut. "There's nothing to forgive." Her murmur of acceptance jump-started his stuttering heart. "I'm still ticked that you lied, but I'll get past that. I love you, Mitch. I always have. I'm sorry I didn't tell you that one last time before I left." She kissed him, smiled against his stiff lips as he processed the words. "Maybe you made the right move quitting the bureau, if you didn't see that coming, Mr. Profiler."

His hand moved up her side, over her back, until he cupped the back of her neck. "Say it again?" Just so he knew he wasn't dreaming.

"No." She nipped at his chin. "Not until you say it."

He couldn't have resisted her request if he'd wanted to. "I love you, Cassia." Uttering the words felt like breaking the final link of the chain locked around his heart. He'd thought it every day for the past four years. Saying it now felt like the ultimate freedom.

"I'm sorry I didn't stay," she murmured against his softening lips. "I should have."

"No." He pulled back ever so slightly. "We needed to become who we are now to accept what we've always known." The question hovered, plaguing him. "Does this mean we're officially trying again?"

She drew her arm down between them, pressed her hand against his crotch and grinned against his lips. "All answers point to yes."

It was all he needed to hear.

*

"You're hovering."

"Sorry." Cass flinched and backed away from Nox's workstation. It was just the two of them this evening. Mitch had gone out for a run and probably, if she knew him as well as she suspected, an exploration of the local markets. But not before he and Blake had added his biometrics and personal four-digit code to her front lock. "Anything yet?"

"I'd have said something if there was." Nox didn't pull their eyes away from the largest of their three computer screens as they typed at a superhuman rate. "The drone's operating system is encrypted which means … ah! Dammit!" They slammed back into their chair and glared at the screen. "Wormhole."

Cass saw the junk mail images reflecting in the window. "Sorry."

"Not your fault."

But something was. "What's going on, Nox?"

"Nothing apparently."

"Nox …"

"You'd tell me if I needed to get another job, right?" For an instant, Nox looked every bit their very young twenty-one. Insecurity Cass had never seen before rose in their eyes for the flash of a moment they looked up.

"Do you want another job?" It was the only question she could think to ask.

"No. But I thought maybe now that Mitch is here and that you've been …" She gestured to the front door. "You can go out more than you used to. And I was just thinking maybe you won't need me anymore."

"Nox." Cass walked around to sit on the edge of Nox's desk. "I didn't hire you because I've locked myself away. I hired you because you're brilliant and I need someone I can trust working with me. This drone thing?" She pointed to the machine that had its stomach ripped out and was hooked up like an old game of Operation, right down to the blinking nose. "This is beyond me. Doesn't matter who else might enter the picture. I have no intention of letting you go anywhere."

"Oh." It was as if Cass had suddenly lifted a thousand pounds off Nox's shoulders.

"We're a team," Cass assured them. "How long that lasts is entirely up to you. Okay?"

Elliot whined and joined them, bopping Nox's arm with his nose as if adding his own opinion. Nox flipped off their main screen.

"When you need a break, I've got something new for you to do."

"Oh?" Nox shooed them away from their desk, an action that instantly improved Cass's mood.

"Can you put together a complete folder of all the information we've compiled on The Circle? Official files, the victim profiles, all my notes. I want to ask Mitch to take a look at it all with his profiler mind."

Nox frowned. "You think he'll see something we haven't?"

"I'd bet on it," Cass confirmed. "He looks at things differently. Not necessarily better, just different." She snapped her fingers. "That reminds me. I forgot to give Laurel that research file on Granger Powell."

"I've got all the surveillance camera footage from that nursing home in Vegas," Nox called when Cass returned to her own desk. Laurel was old school when it came to her research. She liked paper over screens. "Want me to start going through it?"

"How far did their archive go?"

"Officially?" Nox shrugged. "Six months."

"Unofficially?" Cass prodded.

"Longer."

"Why don't you shoot it over to me and I'll—" Her video bell rang. "I think at this point," she muttered to herself as she headed to the door, "it might be easier to give everyone access to that blasted lock. Hey, Riley." She jumped back when Riley plowed inside.

"Turn on the news." She beelined for the coffee table where the remote control usually was.

"What?" Cass retrieved it from where she'd left it on the kitchen counter. "What's going on?"

Nox came around to join them as Cass clicked on the local evening news.

"Repeating our top story once again. Former FBI agent Mitch Keaton was taken in for questioning yesterday regarding the discovery of a body up in the Hollywood Hills. The body has since been identified as Irene Whittaker, the mother of convicted murderer Jonathan Whittaker. A source inside the DA's office confirmed that Keaton, the agent responsible for Jonathan Whittaker's arrest, is considered their chief suspect."

Mitch's official FBI portrait flashed onto the screen.

"Shit," Cass muttered as her thoughts raced. "Where the fuck is this information coming from?" Outing an agent, even a former one, wasn't business as usual.

"The most reliable source there is," Nox said. "An anonymous one."

"Keaton," the reporter continued. "who was the agent responsible for Whittaker's arrest, was released from police custody at the behest of his lawyer, attorney to the stars, Laurel Fontaine. Neither Ms. Fontaine nor Mr. Keaton could be reached for comment."

"Please," Riley snorted. "I doubt they even tried to call for a comment."

"Laurel wouldn't have given one," Cass said.

"They're not done." Nox pointed to the screen.

"Former agent Mitch Keaton was recently brought in as a special consultant to Dr. Cassia Davis, who's supervision of the exhumation of the mass grave found in the same area, is being called into question due to her rumored fragile mental state. Although unconfirmed at this time, it's believed Dr. Davis's instability is the result of her being the victim of a violent abduction when she was working as a consultant in New York. The then Special Agent Keaton who rescued Dr. Davis after killing her assailant."

Cass felt the color drain from her face. Her hands shook until Riley grabbed hold and squeezed. "It's out," she whispered as her nightmare scenario unfolded. "It's all coming out." And yet …

She could still breathe. She pressed a hand to her heart, waiting, expecting it to explode beneath her touch. Instead, all she felt was a cool, detached determination that was quickly twisting into anger.

"Not quite all of it," Riley reassured her. "Some of the details are missing."

"A spokesperson for the mayor's office confirmed that they are taking steps and looking into alternate specialists to ensure the remaining exhumations are completed without any conflict or bias. The question that needs to be answered is whether Dr. Davis is fully capable of overseeing this case to bring justice to the families and to ensure the victims can finally rest in peace. To recap—"

Cass shut off the TV. "So that's their next move," Cass murmured as if from outside her own body. "It's good cover, taking Mitch's questioning public." Not to mention her history that she'd kept under wraps for four years. "Putting the focus on us shifts attention away from what matters: those victims on the hill. I'll show them fragile mental state, my ass."

"You need to give Mitch a head's up," Riley said.

"Right." She located her cell phone and called him.

No answer. Straight to voice mail. "Mitch, call—"

Her own phone rang. Mitch's name flashed across the screen. She clicked over, breathed a sigh of relief. "Mitch, I was just—"

"He shouldn't have touched my mother."

Cass gasped. She spun around, looking frantically looking to her friends. "Whittaker." She waved a hand to Nox, then her phone. Nox scrambled back to their desk and began typing furiously. Cass tapped speaker, held out her cell. Her hand shook. "Where are you?"

"I made some lovely friends while I've been away, Cassia. They've been very helpful in helping me ... relocate."

"I don't believe you." Her voice shook.

"Yes, you do." She could practically hear him smile.

"Where's Mitch?"

Riley moved in, grabbed her hand again and squeezed, steadying her.

"He broke his promise." Whittaker's voice was cold. Controlled. "He was supposed to keep my mother safe. Instead he killed her, just like he killed my brother."

"Mitch didn't hurt your mother." Cass clung to calm. Anything else was futile. "Where is he? Where are you?" She looked to Nox, who shook their head.

No lock.

"I'm closer than you think. You aren't safe, Cassia. Especially now." She felt like a mouse after being cornered by a particularly vicious cat. "Neither of you are safe. Be ready, Cassia. What my brother did to you will pale in comparison for what I have planned."

"Please—"

The call went dead. She stared helplessly down at the phone in her hand.

"Mitch." She could feel the panic closing in. Her chest closing up, but she focused on drawing in long, deep breaths. The darkness abated before it could overtake her completely. She squeezed her eyes shut. Focused. Breathed.

The idea of Mitch being in the hands of the brother of the man he'd killed was as bone-marrow terrifying as anything she'd ever been through herself. She could feel synapses reconnecting and firing after dormancy had left them numb.

Maybe she was wrong. It was possible he was still locked up and this was just some new form of torture he was inflicting on her.

"That's it." Riley's voice was soothing as she stroked Cass's hair. "Breathe in and out. In and out. I've got you, Cass. We've got you."

"He's got Mitch," Cass whispered. "Nox?"

Nox shook their head. "He spoofed Mitch's number. I couldn't get a trace on it. I'm sorry."

Cass could only nod.

"How the hell would that psycho get Mitch's number?"

"How did he get mine?"

The front door buzzed. "I've got it," Riley said and pushed the Intercom button. The small black-and-white screen flashed awake. "Hello?"

"It's Lynda."

"Mitch's old partner," Cass said and rushed to the camera. "I've been waiting for your call. When did you get back?"

"Better let me up, Cass." Lynda flinched into the camera. "You need to hear this face to face."

# CHAPTER SIXTEEN

MITCH was well aware of the irony of hitting a bakery after finishing a five-mile run, but after his less than cordial conversation with his boss back at Quantico, he'd needed to clear his head. And ingest an unhealthy amount of sugar.

His shiny new access code for Temple House felt like a badge of honor. He buzzed himself in just as the sun began to dip into its nightly bed. He suspected the éclairs and cannoli wouldn't hold a candle to Sutton's chocolate cake, but they'd been end-of-the-day special and he couldn't resist. Besides, Cassia had been more than understanding about his casual relationship with the truth where his job was concerned. He looked forward to putting a non-carnal smile on her face.

He avoided the elevator which, with its gear whining and creaking, simply did not appeal. Mitch took the stairs two at a time and landed at Cass's door in record time. His hand flexed before he keyed in his code, pressed his thumb into the biometric scanner.

The lock clicked.

He pushed open the door. "Hey, sorry I missed your call—Whoa!" He barely had time to toss the box onto the hall table before his arms were filled with a trembling Cassia. She wrapped her arms around his neck and squeezed so tight he had trouble breathing. "What's this? What's going on?" He looked over her head to where Riley, Nox, and his former partner sat on the circular sofa. "Hey, Lynda."

It wasn't often his partner looked anything other than controlled and stoic. The abject relief he saw on her face was beyond cause for concern. "Okay. Cassia, let go." He reached up, grabbed her wrists and pulled them from around his neck. Her tear-streaked cheeks left him with only one conclusion. "Who died?"

"We thought you did." Riley ignored Cass's gasp of horror and walked over, a light akin to sympathy shining in her pessimistic gaze. "Glad to see you're all right." She picked up the box. "I'll just take this …" She jerked a thumb toward the kitchen.

"I'll help!" Nox jumped to their feet.

Mitch guided Cassia back to the sofa, pushed her into the cushions, and looked to his former partner. "Explain."

"Nice to see you, too."

"Yeah, sorry. Hi." He swiped a hand through his wind-tousled hair. "How are you? How are the kids?"

Cassia actually laughed and Lynda grinned. "You're predictable, at least. You're going to want to sit down."

"If this is about you taking over—"

"It's not about that." Lynda picked up a file folder from the coffee table. "Cass and I had a chat yesterday about some postcards she's been receiving the past few weeks."

"Postcards?" This was the first he was hearing about them. Mitch accepted the folder, flipped it open.

"Sixteen in all," Lynda said. "As you can see, they're from very specific states."

"Including Utah." He turned the plastic evidence bag over, scanned the messages. The endorphins he'd worked up drained in an instant. "This is Jonathan Whittaker's writing."

"Confirmed," Lynda said.

Cassia winced.

"Why didn't you tell me about these?" He dropped the folder and the cards onto the sofa.

"I should have," Cassia admitted. "I was hoping it was nothing."

"Isn't it?" Mitch questioned. "Prisons are notorious for what inmates can get out. But you should have had these turned in for evidence. They could have stopped it."

"Woulda, shoulda, coulda," Cassia said quietly.

"They were followed up with what seems to be a self-destructing email," Lynda informed him.

"A what now?" Matt sank onto the back of the sofa, rested his hand on Cassia's shoulder. He was confident in the answer, but he still asked, "From …?"

"It was Whittaker," Cassia said. "It was a video telling me he couldn't wait to see me again. I reacted, for want of a better word, badly."

"In what way?" He stopped, replaying that day he'd arrived. His stomach pitched. "The panic attack. That's what caused it? This email? And not—"

"It wasn't you," Cassia admitted. "I'm sorry I let you think that it was. I wasn't"—she tapped a finger against her forehead—"I wasn't thinking straight. I probably wasn't thinking at all." He could see the remorse in her eyes. And the fear.

There was a little hurt that she hadn't confided any of this information in him, but then there had been a lot to deal with since he'd gotten to Los Angeles. "How did Whittaker gain access to a computer system? He was supposed to be on lockdown."

"He's out, Mitch." Cassia looked up at him, the shell-shocked look in her eyes cutting through his disbelief. "He's been out for weeks."

"He's what? They let him out? Was it some technicality?" He would have begun to pace, but right now all he wanted to do was keep a steadying, comforting hand on Cass's shoulder. As terrifying as Whittaker being out was to him, he couldn't begin to fathom what she was thinking. Or feeling. "Why weren't we notified? Was it because I'm not an agent anymore?"

"You know better than that," Lynda chided softly. "He wasn't released. It was some kind of secret prisoner swap that meant he pretty much walked out and disappeared."

"Just like Dean Samuels." Cassia said pointedly.

"The hell you say," Mitch said. "People don't just walk out of prison."

"No one knew until today," Lynda said. "After talking with Cass I made a few calls, got in to see Whittaker for myself. I'll admit I was expecting to prove her wrong. Then I got there and realized there was a lot off about the place."

"I knew there was something about that warden I didn't like," Cass said. "I called the prison, after the email. I asked Warden Taggart to show me the security video feed of Whittaker in his cell. And he did. I even talked to three of the guards to confirm he was still in custody." She shook her head, let out a little laugh. "I know they thought I'd lost my mind. But they humored me. He disappeared. Inside or outside the prison, he just went poof." She glanced up at Mitch, that knowing gleam in her eye.

Mitch struggled against accepting the far-fetched notion that Whittaker would be remotely connected to Dean Samuels. There was more than two decades between the cases, not to mention they were utterly and completely different. But with this many coincidences …

"I was given special access to the cellblock where Whittaker was housed." Lynda picked the folder back up, handed him a pair of photographs. "I took these myself of the man incarcerated in Whittaker's cell. Under Whittaker's name. Wearing Whittaker's ID bracelet."

Mitch looked closely. The build and height were right. The shorn hair required of all inmates would have definitely changed his appearance. But it was the eyes … Mitch had been haunted by the piercing evil he'd seen in Whittaker's eyes. "That's not Whittaker." He looked back to Lynda. "Who is he?"

"No idea. Prints aren't in the system and he's not talking. Guy may as well be a mime for all the information we got out of him. DOJ's got him in custody now in a secure location."

"So where's Whittaker?" Mitch demanded.

"He's here," Cassia said quietly. "In Los Angeles. The last postcard," she added. "It was sent less than a week ago."

"And this warden Cassia talked to?" He asked Lynda. "What did he have to say?

"Here we go." Cassia rubbed her temple as if she had a migraine. "Turns out the Warden Taggart I spoke to was a senior prison guard who had recently transferred in. The actual warden was on vacation until yesterday."

"We're going through Taggart's employee file now," Lynda said. "But one thing of note: His primary reference came from a senior partner at a Los Angeles based security firm. Axiom Security."

"Son of a bitch," Mitch muttered. Quinn hadn't been paranoid or delusional after all. "The same security company the city hired to guard the burial site."

"One and the same," Cassia confirmed.

"When I asked to speak with Taggart," Lynda said. "I was informed he left work after taking Cassia's call on Friday and he hasn't been back since. I checked the address on file, had local officers check it out. It's empty. He's gone. I've put out an all-points on him."

"He probably high-tailed it straight to Mexico."

"If he did, he made one stop first." Riley came over, half a cannoli in her hand. "Nox?"

"Right. Center screen," Nox said. "We've been going through the security footage at the Silver Age Retirement home, where Irene Whittaker lived."

"You have?" Mitch frowned, standing up.

"Just locking down your alibi," Nox said. "You're on camera leaving a good hour before." They clicked a remote and stopped the video footage, zoomed in. "Then this guy arrives."

Mitch looked at the tall, rather burly looking man wearing black cargo pants and shirt. Definitely looked like the security type. "Zoom in at the bottom right quadrant, Nox." Mitch walked around the sofa, moved closer to the screen. Nox hit a few buttons and the screen rotated down, lowering as the picture focused in. "There." He pointed to the man's right hand. "That's a ring, isn't it?"

"Hang on." Nox closed the video, opened another that showed the man approaching the desk and picking up a pen to sign into the visitor's log. "You can see it there a lot more clearly."

"Quinn showed me the autopsy photos. Whoever killed Whittaker's mother wore a thick ring. He strangled her so hard his fingers imprinted." Overkill, Mitch thought.

"Hey, Nox." Cass stood up to stand beside Mitch. "Can you use one of your pixilation programs to extrapolate an estimation on the ring's pattern?"

"It'll take me a few minutes." But they got to work, tapping away on their keyboard. Riley drew Lynda away with the promise of some actual non-sugar laced food.

Mitch stood beside Cassia, trying to find the right words. He was working on banking the frustration he felt over her confiding

in Lynda before she told him about the email and postcards and …
phone call. Anger got him nowhere and he wasn't particularly justified where that emotion was concerned. It was going to take time
for her to completely trust him again. If he tried to rush her, it would
only put more distance between them.

"Any more secrets I need to know about?" He finally asked.

"Well, it's not so much a secret as a new development." She tilted
her head back. "We were headline news tonight. Your being taken
in for questioning, my fragile mental state. The subtext of which was
that neither of us has any business working on those graves."

"Awesome." He sighed. "That explains my contract coming up for
renewal sooner than anticipated."

"Your contract with Quantico? Is that what your call with your
boss was about?"

It was funny. He could very well be out of a job, but that seemed
completely negligible at the moment given the abject terror attempting to wrap itself around his entire being.

Whittaker being in custody these past years had at least brought
Mitch some sense of peace. Enough that he could sleep at night. But
if Whittaker really was out there, hunting, stalking them … would
either of them ever be safe again?

Didn't seem as if unemployment particularly mattered by comparison.

"I don't care about any of that right now."

"Okay, I think this is working." Nox's call to attention had Mitch
refocusing on the image on screen. It was like he was being tested for
glasses, with the blurry edges coming into focus. The screen looked as
if nano-bots had taken over and were reforming the outline of the ring.

"Shit," Riley muttered as she joined them, her eyes glued to the screen.

Mitch narrowed his gaze. It took a moment for his brain to process. "It's a flower of some kind."

"Not just any flower." Riley looked to Cassia.

"That's a lily."

\*

"It's late," Cass said to Nox as they gathered their belongings to head
out. "Why don't you just stay in the guest room tonight?"

244

Nox couldn't have looked more dubious if they tried. "And listen to you to going at it all night like a couple of teenagers?" They rolled their eyes even as they grinned at Cass's flushed cheeks. "No thanks. I'm taking these." Nox held up the observation glasses Mitch had barely returned in one piece. "I need to do an evaluation on how they performed."

"Recordings are on the server," Cass said. "I know you run on caffeine and adrenaline, but take some time to decompress, yeah?"

"Sure. Oh. I might be a little late tomorrow. I'm meeting Wally for breakfast at the new coffee bar near his place."

It was nice to see Nox happy despite the frenzy of the past few days. "Take the whole morning," she told them. "You deserve it. You did really good work today. Thank you for having my back."

"Pfffth." Nox dismissed her appreciation. "Like you always say, we're family. I put all those files and documents on a laptop for Mitch like you wanted." They handed over one of their old machines covered in a plethora of snarky stickers. "It's nothing fancy, but I'm guessing he didn't bring one out with him."

"He'll appreciate it, I'm sure. I know I do."

"Yeah, well, he might as well go all in on the crazy that is The Circle with the rest of us," Nox said. "See you tomorrow. Night, Elliot. Night, Mitch!"

Elliot barked once before settling back into his bed.

"Nox turned you down about staying overnight?" Mitch emerged from Cass's bedroom.

"They're a little unnerved by the idea of us having sex."

"Yeah?" Mitch actually grinned. "I'm not." He approached as she turned to pick up the laptop. She pushed it into his stomach when he reached for her. "Ooof. What's this?"

"A gift of sorts." She considered him. A tension-relieving bout of sex did sound incredibly appealing at the moment. "It's everything we've put together the past few months on The Circle. I'd like you to read through it with your profiler brain activated."

He looked like she'd just kicked his puppy. "Fun." He set the laptop aside. "I'll look at it later." He grabbed her by the hand, tugged gently and she tumbled into his arms. "How are you doing with all this?"

"All this?" She slid her hands up his arms, curled her fingers and scraped gently. "You mean the man who stalked me walking out of prison with the help of a sociopathic secret society we can't definitively prove exists?" She looked up at him. "Better than I should be."

With Riley promising to update Blake about the developments with Whittaker, Cass had the utmost faith that her friends would do whatever it took to continue to keep Temple House, and thus her, safe. It was, she realized, the one life preserver other than Mitch that felt solid enough to cling to.

"Just do me a favor and stay close to home until those reinforcements Lynda's going to ask for arrive." Lynda was also planning on meeting with Linnea tomorrow to get a rundown on the case in the hopes that her presence would allow work to begin again at the site.

At this point, doing so would all but be an act of defiance.

Cass touched his face, traced his lips with her fingertip. The four years separating them had long ago evaporated, but she wasn't so naïve to think they were remotely out of the woods. Whittaker being out should have been concern enough. Add The Circle on top of that and ... "I don't know what I'd do if something happened to you."

He rested his forehead against hers. "Same."

"Yeah, well, I'm not one to go jaunting around the city, am I?" She wanted to laugh, but all she could think was that she'd finally come around to considering leaving Temple House; to finally break her self-imposed isolation and step back into her own life. Now she wasn't so certain that would ever be possible. "So are you staying over, or do you want to go back to your place?"

"Let's start here." He dipped his head and captured her lips. "Then see where we end up."

# CHAPTER SEVENTEEN

MITCH didn't know how Cassia did it.

Only a few hours into their ode-to-a-psychotic-murderer lockdown and already the need to crawl out of his own skin was overwhelming.

That said? He continued scrolling through the impressive collection of documents and reports and photographs all supposedly connected to The Circle of the Red Lily.

It was, he'd realized shortly after seven a.m., an utterly fascinating read. One that made for a far more believable crime thriller than suspected reality. This town was the perfect centralized location for an inner circle of elites. What went on behind closed doors was no doubt appealing to those looking to surrender to temptations that would otherwise be considered taboo or even illegal. Participating in such activities would create a loyal membership, either out of fear of their activities being made public, or to continue to build their own power.

What had Blake said? This town was borderline incestuous with its intermingling among every business that kept the movie industry afloat.

Except Mitch would be very surprised if The Circle's reach didn't extend well beyond the boundaries of the film world. A group like this could wield influence across the spectrum, which could, unfortunately, mean they were looking at a bigger organization than they'd considered.

That would definitely give The Circle, and its members, reason to stop anyone from exposing them.

He clicked back and forth to the various reports and gathered evidence. The black and white portraits of women were chilling, yet beautifully macabre to look at. An ode to talent of days gone by, with even the most recent victims made up to look like starlets from the pinnacle of the film age. The attention to detail where the make-up was concerned, and the hairstyling—the photography itself was highly stylized despite its simplicity.

But it was the vacant expressions, the hollow, dark eyes looking at him as if from beyond the grave that truly left an impact.

Riley Temple had made her own observations on that front, dissecting the kind of film, development methods, and lighting techniques she suspected had been used. Her late grandfather had been a renowned studio photographer back in the day, but it was one of her grandfather's friends, a Clinton Bryant, who had been revealed as the photographer for a good number of the early shots. It was his photographs of Melanie Dennings that had opened up the entire can of worms Cassia and her friends were now dealing with. A photograph that contained the ever-so-faint shadow of a newspaper that called the accused killer's innocence into question.

Murder wasn't remotely out of the range of possibility when it came to cults like this. It was, Mitch thought, one of the easiest way to control members. Once you were involved in some way, there was rarely a way out. And with each new member they recruited, their circle—pun intended—grew larger.

"Incestuous indeed."

He'd read through everything fully, but there was one thing that had caught his attention that he wanted to check again.

"Morning." Cassia wandered out of her bedroom wearing one of her oversized t-shirts. She walked behind him, trailed light fingertips across his back as she circled around to the one true object of her desire: the coffee machine. "FYI, you're far better for my sleep habits than any prescription."

His smile was faint. "Thanks."

"Been up long?"

"Since about three." His brain had been way too overactive to get anymore sleep. After reading through everything they'd compiled, he was worried he might never sleep again.

"You want a refill?" She popped open the bakery box to peer inside and plucked out one of the remaining éclairs. Elliot trotted over and eyed his food container with something akin to relish.

"Sure." He pushed his mug toward her.

"Did all that exceed your very limited expectations and conclusions?" She scooped food into Elliot's bowl then retrieved a couple of treats to add to the mix.

"I hadn't reached any conclusions," he argued. "I was just having trouble buying into it."

"Hmmm." She glanced at him. "And now?"

"As I share Quinn's and your aversion to coincidences, I'd say your suppositions about this group make sense. There's a particular psychopathy that takes place when an organization has been around for as long as it looks like The Circle has been."

She rolled her eyes. "In other words …?"

"Consider me convinced." What the hell they could do about it, however, remained a big question. "It's hard to wrap my head around the idea they've been around since what? The nineteen forties?"

"Ish." Cassia leaned on the counter and rested her chin in her hand. "It's one reason we've been debating about talking to Moxie about her experiences back then. She probably knows some details that can help us fill in some blanks."

"The notes say she has a kind of mark on her neck? Not a tattoo, but a brand?"

"I haven't seen it myself," Cassia said. "Riley and Quinn both have, but she had a major freak out when Riley asked about it. They also saw the same mark on the back of Joyce DePalma's neck. Poor thing had a panic attack when they asked about it. Much," she mused as if she just thought of it, "like Moxie."

It would fall in line with the misogynistic, sexist, abusive vibe he was getting off The Circle's behavior. Women had been one of—if not the biggest—bought and sold commodity in Hollywood's heyday. One could assume they'd look at branding certain "property" as no worse than branding cattle before a sale. "Joyce is a resident up at the Golden Age Retirement Home." Mitch said. "Isn't that where Sutton works?"

"Yeah." Cassia stood up straight and stretched. "Last she heard, Joyce was in a comatose state. She hasn't said a word to anyone since Quinn and Riley visited with her in December." She tapped fingers on the counter. "Riley asked if I'd be willing to talk to Moxie about that mark. How she got it. She thought I might be the best suited for it. Would you be willing to help me with that?"

"I'm not a therapist or psychiatrist," Mitch argued.

"I'm not either. But you understand the effects a group like The Circle might have on someone, especially in the long term. That might make the conversation easier."

He considered the idea. "I'd want to do some research first," he said. "I wouldn't want to cause any more harm or damage than she's already been through."

Cassia's expression softened. "You really are a good guy, Mitch Keaton."

He hid an embarrassed smile. "I did have some questions about Eva Hudson. Mabel was the one who interacted with her, correct?"

"Yeah." Cassia filled both their mugs and handed his back to him. "Up until recently, Mabel volunteered as a rape victim advocate. She was called to speak with Eva when she was brought into the hospital earlier this year."

Eva had been one of the millions who had come to Los Angeles looking for fame and stardom, only to find herself used, beaten, raped, and thrown out of a car on a hiking trail near the Hollywood reservoir. A few days later, she was abducted from the hospital and killed by Orson Berwick. The same man responsible for setting off a bomb in Echo Park and kidnapping Mabel Reynolds.

Mitch had found himself staring for quite a while at the raw, red brand on the back of Eva's neck; the same lily image they'd seen hours ago on a certain senior prison guard's ring.

Definitely incestuous.

"I was reading through Mabel's notes about her conversations with Eva. She mentioned a stuffed rabbit a few times."

"Benedict Cumberbunny." Cassia grinned into her mug. "It's a female thing. What about the rabbit?"

"It was the only thing Eva specifically told Mabel she wanted. Not the laptop Paul found under her bed, not even the invitations to that private club ..." He scrolled through another document. "Scheherazade. Not any of her other belongings. She just wanted the rabbit."

"And you think that means something."

"I think it's a detail that sounds out of place. Do you have it?"

"The rabbit? I don't."

Mitch felt himself deflate a bit.

"But Keeley does. Mabel let her keep it."

"I need to see that rabbit." He checked his watch, got to his feet. "What time does Keeley leave for school?"

"Pretty soon. Give me a second to get dressed and I'll go up with you."

She grabbed her mug and disappeared into the bedroom before he could erase the surprise from his face. That offer seemed almost— what was the word?—normal.

She'd spent the past four years petrified of her own shadow, while the man responsible for her abduction and torture was behind bars. Now, Whittaker was out and instead of closing herself off even more, she seemed ready to bust out of Temple House's seams.

Burst might have been an overstatement, however. Walking up the stairs, Cassia seemed to be thinking about each and every step she took. But she kept moving. Kept her head up and her gaze pinned ahead. He could hear her breathing become a bit more labored when they approached Mabel's apartment door. But she took a shaky breath, shot him a quick, tremulous smile and knocked.

The door was yanked open. "Cass." Paul Flynn's shock was almost comical against the stark pristineness of his dark slacks, white shirt, and power blue tie. "Hi. What brings you—?"

"Who is it?" Mabel called before popping into view. "Cass?"

"Don't go throwing me a parade." Cass's voice sounded tense. "Mitch had some questions for you about Eve Hudson. And Benedict Cumberbunny."

"Ah, sure." She waved them inside and into the open kitchen area where Keeley was having a stare down contest with a rather healthy-looking bowl of oatmeal.

251

"What are the black bugs?" she asked Paul.

"Chia seeds. They're good for you." He touched a hand to the top of her head.

Keeley wrinkled her nose. "Can't I have Lucky Charms?"

"Oatmeal once a week," Mabel said in the same disapproving tone as her daughter. "We agreed. Add some more honey."

"Morning, Keeley." Mitch pulled out the chair next to her and sat down. "I understand you've been given custody of Benedict Cumberbunny."

"Uh-huh." She nodded and stuck her spoon in her bowl. "Do you like oatmeal?"

"Sometimes." He leaned over, lowered his voice. "I like mine with chocolate chips."

She lit up immediately. "Mom!"

Mabel glanced at Paul, who didn't look too eager to fight.

"Keeley, would it be okay if I took a look at the rabbit?"

Keeley shrugged. "Sure. I keep him on a special shelf in my room. Want me to get him?"

"Please." Mitch nodded as Mabel dug around in one of her kitchen cabinets.

"Mitch spent the morning reading our Circle dossier," Cassia told them. "I think we've converted him."

"Awesome word," Mabel muttered. "So appropriate. Ah! Here they are." She pulled out a package of baking chips, turned annoyed eyes on Paul. "Sugar free? Seriously?"

Paul shrugged. "Small steps." He walked over, kissed her upturned mouth, and took the package from her.

"I'm marrying a health food nut," Mabel grumbled, then seemed to realize what she'd said. "Oops." She covered her mouth and only then did Mitch—and clearly Cassia—see the ring. "Surprise. It happened in New York."

"Oh, my gosh." Cassia raced over, grabbed Mabel's hand. "Way to bury the lead! Why didn't you say anything? You weren't wearing this at my place the other day."

"We wanted to wait to announce until after he talked to Keeley," Mabel said as her daughter returned, uniform skirt flouncing around her knees, a big stuffed white and worn rabbit in her arms. "I just told Cass our news."

"We're getting married!" Keeley announced. "And I'm getting adopted!"

Cass spun around and Mitch found it hard to remember a time she'd looked happier. "It's all official?"

"It's all official," Paul confirmed. "I downloaded the paperwork yesterday." That earned him a very enthusiastic hug from Cass.

Mitch felt a bit proud at witnessing what was clearly a family celebration. A family that included Cassia.

"This is Benny." Keeley held out the rabbit to Mitch.

"Benny the bunny," Mitch repeated as he accepted the rabbit. "Nice to meet you, Benny." The stuffed animal had definitely seen better days. It was soft and well-loved with eyes that had been sewn back in place and one ear that flopped at an angle. He squeezed his hands, feeling around the fabric. The feet. The hands (did rabbits have hands?), the head. He felt something hard just behind the left eye. He checked the rest of the body before he asked, "Keeley, I think there's something inside the bunny's head. Is it okay if I try to get it out? I'll be careful."

Her eyes went wide. "You think it's a treasure?"

Following a hunch, he said, "I think as investigators, we're obligated to find out."

"Kee, go get grandma's sewing scissors out of the knitting box." Mabel cleared a space at the table. "What made you come looking for the rabbit?"

"In your notes, you said this was the only thing Eva specifically asked for when she was in the hospital."

"Yeah. After she was kidnapped, I found it wedged under her hospital bed."

Wedged, Mitch thought. Not dropped. Wedged.

"Here." Keeley set the scissors on the dining room table, but she ignored her oatmeal despite the addition of chocolate. "Can I watch?"

"You can help. Can you hold him for me?" He slid the point of the scissors beneath the crooked stitch around the rabbit's eye. "Am I the only one who suffers from Toy Story syndrome?"

"Is that condition listed as an official malady?" Cass teased as she came to stand beside him.

"Don't tell me you didn't think your toys came to life at night and played while you slept."

"I think that might be a you thing," she teased back.

For the second time that morning, he marveled at the magic that had re-awakened the woman he'd fallen in love with back in New York.

Mitch snipped the threads and pulled the black-and-pink felt free. He stuck his finger into the small opening, then dug deeper. He pulled out a bright pink jump drive.

"What's on it?" Keeley whispered.

"Not sure yet," Mitch said. "Thank you for taking care of Benny the bunny, Keeley."

"Mom? Can you sew his eye back on?"

"That's okay. I got it," Mitch said as he handed off the drive to Cassia. "I just need some needle and thread, if you have it. We'll have him fixed up in no time."

"I know where there's some!" Keeley ran off again.

"A jump drive is pretty old school these days," Paul said when Keeley was out of earshot. "Cloud storage—"

"Can be hacked," Cassia said. "We'll dig into it as soon as we get back downstairs."

"You want something to eat while you wait for Geppetto to stitch Benny back together?" Mabel asked.

"Sure. Ah,"—Cassia looked uncomfortably to the bowl of oatmeal—"can I have Lucky Charms instead?"

\*

"Big build up, little show," Cass muttered as she and Mitch stared at the encrypted file. It had taken them more than an hour after returning from Mabel and Paul's to even get this far. The drive itself wouldn't open and the transfer took forever.

"Whatever is on the drive, we aren't going to see it anytime soon." Mitch closed the laptop and sat back. "I'd call that a dead end."

"A temporary one," Cass countered. "We need Nox." She checked her watch. "I picked a bad day to tell them they could be late." This had been a nice distraction while it lasted. There wasn't any doubt in Cass's mind that the drive was important, otherwise Eva Hudson wouldn't have gone to so much trouble to hide it. Unless Mitch could do some kind of afterlife profile of her, guessing the password necessary to even run the encryption program would be next to impossible.

But, Eva had inadvertently put that drive into Mabel's hands. There must be some workaround that would make the information accessible in an emergency.

"How about we take Elliot for a walk?"

For an instant, Mitch's suggestion sounded perfect. The very idea of feeling the sun on her face, feeling the breeze against her skin was as tempting as the man sitting beside her. But that door she thought she'd started to open slammed shut once more.

"Go ahead." She turned her back on him, not wanting to see the disappointment in his eyes. Her progress-not-perfection mantra was beginning to fail her.

Mitch caught her hand, tugged her back. "How about you walk us down to the lobby? You can check in with Blake. See what, if any added security measures there are he thinks we should take."

She wondered if he was somehow onto her "I can do anything if it was work related" mentality. Going to Mabel's had been one thing. Making her way to actual entrance into Temple House was another. Coming that close to the outside world … she wasn't entirely sure she was ready. But she wanted to be.

Oh, how she wanted that.

"Small steps," he urged before pressing his mouth to hers. "You're already taking them."

She nodded. "Okay. Downstairs." She'd almost made it down to the lobby before. She could take the extra steps today.

Elliot jumped and hopped his way over to his leash and, after Mitch offered his hand, Cass took it and stepped out.

Her knees trembled a bit as they headed down, but that was as far as her anxiety reached. She couldn't stop the tears from filling her eyes when she rounded the landing and saw the lobby of Temple House for the first time since she'd arrived four years ago.

"Land's sakes, look who's out and about!"

Cass shifted closer to Mitch as Moxie Temple headed down the short hall from the lobby theater. Along with her movie memorabilia collection, the old-fashioned screening room had always been Moxie's pride and joy. She took immense pleasure in rotating out the Hollywood artifacts that occupied glass cases on the walls. She changed out movie posters depending on the time of year or her personal fancy.

"Hi, Moxie."

Cass lifted a nervous hand in greeting as the older woman came over to give her a hug. Moxie stood just about Cass's height and wore her hair in various styles, but always in her trademark Sally Tate red. The blinding yellow tracksuit added more than a pop of color to the white marble and gold accented décor of the lobby. Her makeup was subdued today, with her perfectly outlined brows and bright pink blushed cheeks. She looked both the entirety of her eighty-plus years but also as young as she'd once been when she'd graced the silver screen.

Moxie stepped back and lifted her hands to Cass's shoulders. "It's good to see you out and about, young lady. And hello, Elliot." Moxie beamed when the dog gave her a bark in return.

"Moxie, this is Mitch Keaton." Introducing Mitch felt a bit like a coming out party.

"Mr. New York." Moxie's mouth widened in a brilliant smile. "DSP told me all about you. You're FBI, aren't you?"

"Ah, mostly," Mitch admitted. "It's a pleasure to meet you, Ms. Temple. I'm a big fan of your films."

"Are you now?" Moxie sidled closer and turned her beaming face up at him. "Which is your favorite?"

"It's hard to choose." Mitch frowned for a moment. "It would be between Death on the Night Shift and Blueprints for Murder."

"Oh, Blueprints!" Moxie wrapped her arms around Mitch's. "You know, that was supposed to co-star James Craig, but he had to drop out at the last minute because of some western with John Wayne." She wrinkled her nose. "Never could bring myself to call him The Duke."

"Well, John Hodiak was a much better fit for that role," Mitch countered. "He had unexpected gravitas."

"Gravitas, yes!" Moxie patted his chest with her hand. "Hodiack definitely had that. And handsome. So handsome!"

Elliot whined and dropped his butt onto the ground.

"I need to get this guy outside," Mitch said. "Moxie, I would love to chat movies and your career with you some more, if that would be okay?" He glanced at Cass in a way that told her he was laying the groundwork for their plan to talk to her about The Circle and what connection she might have to them.

"Oh, yes, dear. That would be lovely. Cassia?" She held out her hand as Mitch stepped back. "Blake's up in 4B taking care of some bathroom issues. Would you be a dear and help me in the theater for a bit?"

What Cass really wanted to do was scramble back up the stairs and back into her apartment. "Sure. I'll wait for you down here," she told Mitch as he and Elliot headed to the door.

Moxie tucked her manicured hand through Cass's arm and nudged her down past Blake's building manager apartment toward the double doors on the left at the end of the hall.

This was one of the few areas in Temple House that wasn't covered by security cameras. With only one way in and out, it didn't seem prudent to Cass to observe and, given it was Moxie's personal sanctorum, had felt a bit invasive. Not that Moxie would have protested. She and Riley had been more than amenable to Cass's protection-focused proclivities.

Three dozen swanky velvet covered chairs filled the room, with additional seating stored in a back closet. Wide arms and cushions allowed for comfort as well as a throwback style that more than suited the former screen queen. A snack bar filled with a selection of sweet movie treats sat at the back, along with an old-fashioned popcorn machine that displayed instructions on how to get things popping. But it was the custom nine-by-sixteen-foot screen accented by a gold-tasseled red curtain pulled back at the sides that literally stole the show in the room.

Cass had helped Riley order the various types of machinery necessary to be able to showcase all kinds of films, from streaming service applications, to playing any of the thousands of DVDs that filled the shelves along one wall, to historic projector reels that, from time to time, Moxie was able to borrow from various studios.

The cozy atmosphere felt a bit dreamlike, which is probably why Cass didn't feel nearly as overwhelmed or out of place as she expected.

"You've never been in here," Moxie declared as she went over to an open box near the popcorn machine. "I know Riley's tried to get you to come down to join in the fun." She had a bit of a twinkle in her eye when she waved Cass over. "Maybe you just needed the right person to give you a nudge."

"Maybe," Cass agreed. "What can I help you with?"

"Well, I've been in a bit of a cowboy mood these days." She bent over and pulled out one of two packages. "I had Riley ask the warehouse to send a few things over from my collection." She made quick work of the wrapping. Inside the plastic display case sat a distinct and familiar black hat with a dark band.

"Is that?" Cass lifted a hand, but didn't dare touch. "Is that Redford's hat from Butch and Sundance?" Even after all this time, she was still amazed at the magical feeling items like this could evoke. Moxie set the case on the back counter and went back in. "Don't tell me the other one is—"

"Yep. This one was Paul Newman's." Moxie lifted the second one as if it were the Holy Grail itself. "That man was one serious heartbreaker. Do you know, I was in the cast of Picnic on Broadway when he and Joanne Woodward met? You want to talk about flying sparks? Those two may as well have opened a fireworks factory." She shook her head in amazement at the tan hat. "Prized possessions for sure." She motioned for Cass to pick up the other box. "I want them up over here." The custom boxes were equipped with hooks that settled nicely into the dedicated spaces around the room. "Just there, please."

Cass situated her case at eye level, then did the same with the other while Moxie stood back to assess. "That's perfect." She clapped her hands together. "Thank you, Cass."

"You didn't really need my help, did you, Moxie?" Cass asked.

"Course not." Moxie waved off the idea. "I just thought it would be nice to spend some time with you. Don't get to see you very often. Oh! Do you know, I remember you liked these the last time I ordered. Come on." She took Cass's hand and drew her back to the candy station. "Sno-Caps." She pointed to the collection of boxes. "They're your favorite, aren't they? I seem to remember you saying."

"They are," Cass confirmed, touched that Moxie had remembered. It had been a cursory conversation years ago when Moxie had been deciding how to fill out her candy station. "My grandmother used to buy them for me when we went to the show." She hadn't thought about those days in a very long time.

"That's what the movies are all about," Moxie agreed. "The memories they bring back. The magic. Do you know, Edgar's had another call from Granger Powell."

"Has he?" Edgar was Moxie's long-time agent who, despite his advanced years, still had quite the connections in the business. Granger Powell, on the other hand, seemed to be Los Angeles's version of a dog with a very big bone. "What did Mr. Powell have to say?"

"He wants me to come to the studio for a tour and lunch. Now don't get that look, young lady," Moxie chided. "I'm no pushover. I know what he's really after."

Temple House, Cass was tempted to say. The man was after Temple House.

"Well, I hope if you go, you take someone with you. Laurel perhaps," Cass suggested. "I bet she'd love to have a sit down with Mr. Powell."

"What a lovely idea." Moxie seemed entertained with the notion. "Do you know, I'll do that."

They put the moving box away and closed up the theater. Cass felt much calmer when they returned to the lobby, and she was about to ask Moxie if she'd like to sit and chat while they waited for Mitch when someone keyed in a code and pulled open the lobby door.

"Wally. This is a surprise." Her smile faded when he turned concerned eyes on her. "What's wrong?"

"I was going to ask you that." Wally straightened his already straight tie. "Nox was supposed to meet me this morning for coffee, but they never showed. I thought maybe they got tied up with work."

"I gave Nox the morning off," Cass told him. "Have you tried calling?"

"Yeah." He pulled out his cell and turned it so she could see. "At least a dozen times. They aren't answering."

"And you guys didn't have a disagreement or a fight?" Stupid question, Cass thought. Nox was far more likely to confront than avoid.

"No. Everything's going great. So they're not here?" The panic rose like a tide in his eyes at about the same rate as it rose inside Cass's chest.

"Don't worry. We'll find them. Moxie, I'm sorry."

"No—go, go." Moxie waved them away. "Nox'll turn up. I'm sure they're fine."

Cass patted her back pocket and only then remembered she didn't have her cell. "Come on." She had Wally follow her upstairs and into her apartment. She'd hoped that maybe she'd missed Nox coming in, but the apartment was as empty as she and Mitch had left it. "Okay. Let me try calling them."

Her hands shook around her cell. Her heart struggling to keep up with the rapidly vanishing air escaping her lungs. Don't panic. Nothing to panic about. "Wally, check their desk. See if there's any note about a meeting or something."

"Yeah." Wally ran a restless hand through his hair. "Yeah, I'll do that."

On the other end, Nox's phone rang and rang and … voicemail.

She swallowed hard, pressed her phone against her chest. *One, two, three, four.*

"Cassia?" Mitch strode back in and unsnapped Elliot's collar. "Moxie said something's going on with Nox. Wallace." He stopped short when he saw the detective. "What's going on?"

"Nox didn't turn up for our date," Wally said. "They're never late. And they always call if there's a problem." He turned fearful eyes on Cass. "Always."

Cass felt frozen. That white noise whooshing through her ears felt like a tide threatening to drag her under.

Her phone rang. The sound cut through the silence of the apartment. She let out a relieved sob when she saw Nox's name.

"Nox! Where the hell are you?"

"Are they okay?" Wally moved in as Mitch stood behind her.

"Cass?" Nox's voice was strained. Overly calm. Tense. But it was Nox. "I'm sorry. I'm so sorry!"

"What for?" She tapped speaker phone on. "Nox, what's—?"

"I warned you." Jonathan Whittaker's voice overtook Nox's. "I told you you couldn't keep them safe."

Wally's eyes filled with horror. "Is that—?"

"Yes," Whittaker said.

"Let me talk to them," Cass demanded, a cold resolve sinking through her. Wally spun away and pulled out his phone, leaving the apartment so as not to be heard. "They've nothing to do with this," Cass told Whittaker. "Nothing to do with us."

She couldn't, no matter how hard she tried, block out the imagined images of what he was capable of doing to someone. Gavin might have carried out their plan, but the plan had been devised by Jonathan. He was the mastermind behind Cass's pain. And now …

Cass drew in a shallow breath. Now he had Nox.

"You took what mattered most to me." Whittaker's voice was dead. Flat. Emotionless. "My mother was all I had left. She was the only thing left that mattered. And he took her from me."

"No, he did—"

"That's right, Whittaker," Mitch grabbed the phone out of Cass's hand. "I killed her. Which means your fight is with me. Not Nox. Let them go."

Silence was the only response.

"Whittaker?" Mitch said again and took Cass's hand. She saw the apology in his beautiful eyes even as her ultimate nightmare began to play out in slow motion. "You want another deal? Name your price."

Tears blurred Cass's vision. She shook her head, knowing nothing she said or did would stop him.

"Whatever you want." Mitch's gaze locked on Cass's. "One last time. Promise me you'll let Nox go and you'll have it."

"A trade," Whittaker finally said. "You. I want you. Come alone. No backup. No FBI. None of your new cop friends. Just you."

Cass grabbed for him, a silent scream caught in her throat. There had to be another way. She couldn't lose him again, but … Nox. Her heart was going to shatter into a million pieces.

And this time there would be no putting it back together.

She tried to swallow as Mitch's hand locked around hers and squeezed.

"Tell me when and where," Mitch said. "I'll be there."

# CHAPTER EIGHTEEN

MITCH tightened the Velcro on his FBI-issued flak jacket. He tried to force a smile of thanks when Lynda handed him a back-up piece that he bent to strap to his ankle. The silence in Cassia's apartment was beyond eerie considering the number of people standing around.

"Just like old times." Lynda smacked his arm. "I'll be close, but not so close that Whittaker will spot us. Don't get dead."

"I'll do my best." Mitch checked his cell phone. Ten minutes until Whittaker was due to call. Ten minutes until he walked back into the hell he'd tried to leave behind for four years.

One way or the other, Whittaker's obsession was going to end.

There was no other option.

Mitch looked to where Cassia stood surrounded by her friends. Something inside of him broke free watching Riley, Sutton, Mabel, and Laurel, in subdued moods, offering quiet comfort and support. He could feel their affection all the way across Cassia's apartment. The furies united. It was, he thought with a touch of regret, a beautiful sight to take with him.

Whatever else happened from here on, he went knowing she'd be taken care of.

Cassia was going to be okay.

The ferocity of her gaze, however, felt a bit scorching. Cassia had shifted from terrified to furious in the space of seconds. She was definitely not pleased with his handling of the situation.

He wasn't particularly thrilled with it himself, but he had to take the chance if there was any hope of getting Nox home.

Nox.

Mitch looked to Wally, standing at the window, staring out into nothing other than the haunting hills that were partially responsible for their current situation.

"Mitch—" Lynda said, but he held up a hand.

"Give me a sec." He joined Wally at the window. Despair and fear radiated out from the control the young man was trying desperately to hold on to. "I've been where you are." He didn't say it lightly. Bringing up the memories was the absolute worst thing he could do for his own state of mind. "I know the thoughts that are going through your head. The worst-case scenarios. Wondering if they're even still alive."

Wally's jaw tensed. "I keep thinking if I'd been there—"

"Whittaker probably would have killed you." Mitch wasn't about to couch his words. "You're negligible, Wally. Nox is useful. They're getting him what he wants. Me. And I'm going in there knowing he's capable of anything." He paused, glancing back at Cassia who had her eyes on them. "I'll get Nox home to you, Wally. I promise. And you can ask Cassia. I don't make promises I can't keep."

"I want to go with you."

"I need you here," Mitch countered. "I need you waiting for when Nox comes back."

Wally nodded, but Mitch could see the struggle to keep the tears of terror at bay. "Lean on your friends. The other people who care about Nox as much as you do. I didn't have that, Wally." He rested a hand on the detective's shoulder. "You do."

"Mitch?" Quinn called.

"Yeah. Okay?" He checked one last time with Wally before rejoining Quinn. "He wants to come with me."

"Of course he does." But the steel in Quinn's eyes told Mitch Wally wouldn't be going anywhere. "I've got LAPD standing by as backup. We'll liaise with Lynda, let her take the lead," Quinn went on. "Blake's pulling his SUV around now. You'll take that."

"I got insurance on the rental," Mitch attempted to joke.

"You'll take that," Quinn repeated. "We've added some special equipment you'll be needing. No argument."

"Right." He wasn't going to turn down anything that could give him an advantage.

"You're sure he's going to set the meet at a warehouse?" Paul asked. There was a cool acceptance about the prosecutor that eased some of Mitch's nerves. Levelheaded in a crisis. He'd have made a good agent.

"I'm sure," Mitch said. "It'll be abandoned and outside the city proper. Near water, probably. Whittaker's father worked in a warehouse like that all his life. He hated it there. Took out his frustrations on his family."

"Except this isn't about his father anymore," Cassia chimed in, proving she could eavesdrop from half a room away. "This is about his mother. The mother he thinks you killed."

"Details may shift but he can't change his psychopathy," Mitch said. "He is what he is and what he is a man who spent years planning revenge on the people who he held responsible for their deaths. First his father. Then Gavin. Now his mother. Even with a shorter reaction time, Whittaker won't be able to pivot." He ducked his head before he added, "Trust me, Cassia."

He found a silent plea in her eyes when he finally looked at her again. So much for making her mad.

The middle screen over Cassia's desk flickered to life.

"What the hell?" Cassia moved away from her friends, heading for her desk, only to yelp and jump back when Nox came into focus. "Nox?"

Mitch moved in, rested a hand on Cassia's hip as their friends gathered. Mitch glanced back to find Quinn standing beside his partner who looked as if he'd just been shot.

"Are they okay?" Wally asked in a hoarse voice.

"They are fine." Whittaker's voice boomed over Cass's computer system. "Nice glasses, Cassia. They tried to get me to give them to them." The lenses flipped around and for a quick moment Nox was replaced by Jonathan Whittaker's dead-eyed stare. "Figured they had to be special for them to push so hard. Very nice."

"Jonathan," Cassia said. "Please. Just let them—"

Mitch squeezed his fingers into a fist. She covered his hand with hers.

"Before I give you the location of our meeting," Whittaker said. "I thought you'd appreciate a preview of what you can expect, Agent Keaton." He put the glasses back on and stepped back.

Mitch's eyes scanned the screen, taking in Nox, standing in the center of a very narrow glass box. Their hands were pressed against the sides, unable to stretch their arms out completely. They turned in circles, obviously yelling, but only the faintest, dullest echo of their voice reached through the feed.

"Forgot one extra detail." Whittaker held out a remote and pushed a button. Thick red liquid trickled down from the top of the box.

Rivulets of blood dripped and cascaded down, pooling on the ground beneath the base. Filling the glass box in small, terrifying increments.

"Jesus," Paul whispered as Nox screamed.

Mitch looked back to Wally. The young man's body had tightened to the point of snapping. The rage in his eyes, both understandable and disheartening.

"Killing Nox won't get you what you want," Mitch reminded Whittaker.

"This won't kill them. Not right away. But you're right." Whittaker hit the button again.

The cascade stopped.

"I'd rather you watch this in person. Port of Los Angeles. Berth forty-seven. You've got one hour before I turn it back on and walk away."

He clicked the glasses off.

Lynda turned away to convey the information to her team.

Mitch waited a beat before speaking. "You heard him. One hour." He pulled Cassia close, wrapped an arm around her as she clung to him. "You'll be okay," he whispered. "I'll get Nox back to you. I promise."

She shook her head. "You can't promise that."

He stepped back. "I promised Wally and I'm promising you." He kissed her. Not the way he wanted to, but how he needed to. Mitch looked to Riley, then to Laurel—the latter of whom offered an understanding nod despite the stark reality he saw in her gaze. "I'm ready." He let go of Cassia and followed Lynda out the door.

It felt odd, Mitch thought as they descended the stairs with Quinn right on his heels. It wasn't dread that accompanied him. It was more of a certainty that he was doing the right thing. No doubt. No hesitation. Simple, clear resolve. He followed Lynda to the double glass lobby doors.

He'd felt that for a brief moment back in New York. Despite fearing the worst, there had been a small part of him that believed, that hoped, he'd find Cassia alive.

He had that same hope now for Nox. It was enough. For now.

Lynda pulled open the door.

"Wait!" Cassia raced down the stairs. "I'm coming with you."

"The hell you are." Mitch couldn't believe what he was hearing. Or seeing.

Where was the panicked woman who couldn't leave her apartment? The woman who had been so terrified about the outside world she hadn't been able to step out into it for years?

Cassia pulled on a jacket she'd brought with her, shoved something into her pocket. "I was wrong." She pulled him aside, her hand locking around his forearm. "All this time I thought work was the only thing that allowed me to leave, but this isn't work. This is family." There was such strength in her voice, he found himself wavering. "Nox needs me. I'm the only person in the world who knows what they're going through. And you need me, too."

"Cassia—"

But there was no stopping her. "You want to throw Whittaker off? Have both of us walk into that warehouse. Make him have to look both of us in the eye." She stood in front of him, nose to chin, tilted her head up with that defiance he adored shining brighter than the summer sky. "He'll be thrown off his game. Not completely. But maybe enough."

How could he possibly be considering this. He looked to Lynda, then to Quinn. They both offered shrugs of "it's up to you," although he could see the worry in Quinn's eyes. "Cassia—"

"Don't leave me behind, Mitch," she pleaded. "I have to do this. I *need* to. Please." She took a deep breath. "This is how I break his hold on me. This is how I get my life back." She touched his face. "A life with you."

It went against every protective instinct he possessed, but he was also looking at the woman he'd fallen in love with in New York. No longer a shell of her former self. She was somehow, inexplicably, back. "I'm not turning around if you change your mind," he told her even as he called himself foolish. "Once we walk out those doors, we don't walk back in until this is done. You understand that?"

"I understand." She nodded and only then did he see the flicker of doubt. Of fear. Before it was gone again. "I'll be with you." She gripped his hand. "I'll be fine."

"Okay then." He squeezed her fingers. "You go first."

She stared at the doors. Walked up the three steps. She looked at Lynda holding open the door.

And stepped outside.

*

She had a plan.

An unexpected bubble of hysteria popped inside her throat and she covered her mouth with one hand. It was a ridiculous, impulsive plan that even now hadn't fully formed. But it had enough for her to grab hold of the idea of success.

They'd climbed into Blake's SUV that was parked right outside Temple House without any sign of Blake. She was a bit disappointed in that, but it meant she wouldn't have to hear his two cents about her decision to come along.

To meet with a killer.

God almighty, what was she thinking?!

She felt like she was spinning, caught on an out-of-control carousel fun-house hybrid, mirrors circling around her in a way that left her questioning reality.

The pressure built, slowly, steadily, as if letting her get ahead of the panic that rose with each passing moment. Her lungs struggled to expand as the consequences of her actions—consequences Mitch had reminded her of himself—became clear.

She'd walked right out of her meticulously built sanctuary with nothing other than Mitch for a safety net.

It was, she realized as she focused on her breathing, the best-case scenario of her worst nightmare. A nightmare she'd chosen to walk in to.

"I'm not going to ask if you're okay." Mitch took a right turn and pressed his foot harder on the gas. "Because neither of us are. I can't believe I agreed to this ridiculous idea."

"I've got it under control," Cassia lied. "It'll be fine."

"Cut the crap. You're already on sensory overload."

She sensed concern beneath the anger. "We need to catch him off guard," she repeated. "You taught me how to profile and you said yourself he can't change his nature. Divide his attention, make him question his end game. Those seconds are seconds Nox needs. God." She squeezed her eyes shut, but all she could see were those trickles of blood streaming down the glass. Blood that reminded her …

"This isn't your fault." Mitch reached over and grabbed her hand. "You hear me? No one is responsible for this other than Whittaker. You remember that."

She nodded, still shaky. There was no point in wishing she was back in her apartment. Back with Elliot. With her friends. She'd made her choice. She dipped her right hand into her pocket, gripped the USB drive so tight her fingers went numb. So much of her plan relied on such a tiny thing.

There was no going back now.

Cass spotted Lynda's black SUV four cars behind. Another unmarked vehicle sped past them, taking the turnoff before theirs and vanishing into the twilight.

"He said no backup," Cassia said.

"Whittaker knows me as well as I know him," Mitch said. "He knows I'd never walk into a trap without backup. Cassia, I need you to promise, if I tell you to do something, you do it. No questions asked."

"I—"

Bringing you with me goes against all of my training, not to mention my instincts. I don't want you here."

"I know." She didn't want to be here, either. "They're my family, Mitch." She squeezed his hand. "So are you."

"Yeah, well, after we get home, you and I are going to have a delayed discussion. We've already lost four years. I do not plan on losing one minute more."

The idea would have thrilled her if she could see beyond the now. "Sounds like appropriate motivation walking into a death trap." She squeezed her eyes shut again, hating the speed with which they zoomed past the derelict buildings and properties. Nausea churned in her stomach. "Probably shouldn't have gone from zero to a thousand miles an hour in the one decision." From solitude to one of the biggest cities in the western hemisphere. She hadn't really thought this through, had she?

"What's that?" Mitch hit his turn signal and veered left.

"Nothing." Something was keeping her together. Whether it was Mitch, the thought of getting to Nox, or the idea of helping put Whittaker away once and for all, she couldn't be certain. Maybe the three had combined into some kind of magic spell that made her feel capable of doing anything.

Mitch slowed the SUV down as they followed the signs to the port. They scanned the tops of buildings for the grey, abandoned warehouse numbers. "Forty-six, forty-seven."

He pulled to a stop near the only door that wasn't padlocked shut.

He pulled out his weapon, checked the clip, chambered a round, released the safety. "You can still wait here," he said. "That would be better for both of us."

"Not better for me." The warehouse loomed like an oversized tomb in the growing darkness. Darkness she refused to surrender to.

Cass took a deep breath and shoved opened her door.

Mitch climbed out, came around to meet her. "You stay close. You do what I say, when I say."

"I heard you the first time." She tugged her jacket tighter at her throat, shivering against the cold.

He lifted his weapon, aimed it at the door. He took one step forward and tested the knob. It twisted easily. Mitch pushed open the door.

Cassia turned her face away from the blast of cool air that whooshed out. The smell. She covered her mouth, her gag reflexes kicking in. Decay and mildew mingled into a toxic stench that burned her eyes. Chemicals must have been stored here. Or something virulent had died in the vicinity.

The light evaporated when they stepped into the shadows. She tried to keep her eyes on the ground, stepping where he did, but the walls closed in. She lifted her head, focusing instead on Mitch and his assuredness as they moved.

He had both hands on his weapon now. Tension radiated off him in waves. She didn't want to be a distraction but could see in the way he kept glancing back that she was. But she didn't have a choice.

There wasn't any other way to see her plan through.

She squeezed her arms into her sides, trying to shrink away from the cobwebs, dust, and filthy walls. It was how she imagined the warehouse in New York had been. She didn't know for sure. She'd never seen anything beyond the room in which she'd been held. The second Mitch had lifted her free of that glass coffin, she'd closed her eyes.

She hadn't opened them again until she heard the doors of the ambulance slam shut.

Cassia shivered.

God! What had she been thinking? She couldn't do this. Even as she placed one foot in front of the other, the doubts mounted. Along with the terror clawing its way into her throat. Impulse may very well be the death of her.

"Cassia?"

Mitch's voice floated over her like a cleansing rain.

"I'm okay." It was, she realized, the biggest lie she'd ever told in her life.

A light swung back and forth in the distance. A solitary bulb arcing against the darkness. An end to their wanderings through corridors of hallways and broken interior windows.

"You made good time." Whittaker's voice shot out at them like bullets.

Mitch stopped, held his left arm out to make sure she did the same.

Ahead of them, Jonathan Whittaker stepped out of the gloom. "I have to admit, you impress me, Cassia."

Cass had no voice. He looked exactly as he had in the email. But the most terrifying thing about him wasn't the remote in his hand. Or the gleam in his eye.

It was the idea he'd walked right out of a maximum-security prison weeks ago and no one had known.

Not entirely true, she thought as her mind began to clear out of the shock.

The Circle knew. They'd planned it. Arranged it.

They'd used him as a weapon to bury her in paralyzing fear to stop their secrets from coming out.

It was that knowledge that had made walking out the lobby doors of Temple House possible.

He was … less impressive than she expected. She tried to see him through her analytical rather than emotional mind. She saw the dull but crazed light in his eyes. Grief perhaps, or at least his version of it. She held no sympathy for him, but she did understand.

"Where's Nox?" Cassia's voice shook despite her best efforts.

"Waiting for you." Whittaker motioned them forward toward the broken table holding a laptop computer and the remnants of various food and drink containers. Close by, a generator hummed, powering a pair of low intensity tower lamps that shined in their eyes. The same kind of lighting used at crime scenes.

Not ten feet away stood the glass box, now completely covered in blood.

Nox's shadowy form was barely visible.

Cass's head spun. She could smell that throat-clenching metallic odor wafting over her. She had to swallow hard to stop from vomiting. That throbbing in her head intensified. For a moment, the room pitched. She took a deep breath, bringing it all into herself rather than shying away.

She didn't have the luxury of surrendering. Nox needed her.

The only way to the other side, the only way to a future with Mitch, was to push, shove, and break her way through.

"I'm here."

Was Mitch talking to Whittaker, Cass wondered? Or was he reminding her?

Mitch held one hand back to keep her at bay, lifted the other with his weapon before he bent down to set it on the ground. "This is what you wanted, Whittaker. Let Nox go."

Whittaker smirked and pressed the remote.

The blood flowed faster now. Thicker.

Screams erupted from inside the box.

Cassia's feet were frozen to the spot. Her legs refused to obey, even as her mind demanded they move.

Her mind. She needed to get her mind under control. "They lied to you," she said, too quietly at first because Whittaker hadn't heard. Mitch looked back at her, shook his head. He hadn't expected her to talk.

But she had to. She had to have her say.

"They lied to you!" She shouted it this time. Her voice echoed off the steel-enforced walls. Keep him away from his computer. Away from the monitors he'd surely set in place. He'd known she was there before he'd seen her walk in.

They needed to stall and give Lynda and her team time to get into place.

"Mitch didn't kill your mother," Cass called. "But I know who did."

Had Whittaker not been standing within the light's glow, she wouldn't have caught the surprise on his face. He dialed up the remote.

The blood poured down faster. It pooled at the base. The level within the box slowly rose. One inch. Two inches. Three …

Nox's screams turned into whimpers as they banged against the glass.

"Nox!" Cassia called out. "We're here!" She moved closer to Mitch, stepped to his side even as he hissed out a sharp breath.

She took a step forward. Away from him. Toward Whittaker.

"Cassia."

She had to ignore Mitch's plea.

"Do you want to know who killed your mother, Jonathan?" She took another step, dazedly surprised at how easy the next one was. "Because I can tell you." She reached into her pocket, pulled out the flash drive she'd loaded before racing to catch up with Mitch. "I can show you."

Her fingers felt frozen.

He looked tempted for a moment, then shook his head, but he set the remote down—only to exchange it for a gun. He lifted the weapon, aimed it first at Mitch, then at her.

He released the safety. Cass tried to swallow, but her mouth was desert dry.

Whittaker frowned. He was confused, she thought. Conflicted. Exactly as she'd predicted.

"You'd say or do anything to convince me he's innocent." But Whittaker's voice shook ever so slightly. Just enough to have hope building inside of her once more.

"You know me, Jonathan." God how she hoped that was true. "You know that the only thing I ever look at is the evidence. I believe what that shows me. What that tells me. It was the evidence that convicted your father. Not me. But you blamed me because how do you make lab results pay?"

She took the fact he was listening as a win. But she also knew that her feelings, her trust in Mitch, wouldn't matter to him one bit.

"Mitch has an alibi," she said more quietly now. "The police have confirmed it. He was on a plane when your mother was taken out of the retirement home. He didn't do it, Jonathan. Someone else took her. Someone else killed her. But they wanted you to believe he did." She took one more step. "They loaded you like a weapon and aimed you at the one thing they needed to be rid of. Me. And Mitch."

She could hear his breathing shift now. His pulse was racing. And hopefully, so was his mind. "They set you up. They got you out, but they killed your mother so you'd come after us." She lifted the drive higher. "It's all right here. I'll give you the evidence. Just let us—let all of us—go."

"You can't talk him down, Cassia," Mitch said, but he remained where he was, crouched, with his hands up. "He isn't interested in the truth. He only sees what he wants."

"And I see the man who murdered my brother." Whittaker swung his weapon on Mitch. "That's one murder you did commit."

"I've never denied it," Mitch said and made Cass flinch. "But you can't blame me for that without blaming yourself. You spent your life protecting him from your father only to turn Gavin into a killer yourself. If you need to punish me for stopping him, you need to think about the role you played in setting him up. You gave him to me. That's something you can't walk away from. You're as responsible for his death as I am."

Now who was trying to talk him down?

"Let Nox out," Cass plead yet again. "Let them out and I'll show you the face of the man who killed your mother."

"You wouldn't do that," Whittaker scoffed. "You know what I'd do to him."

It was, Cass thought, the one thing that had caused her a moment's doubt. "She was your mother. Your family." She looked to the box. "Just like Nox is mine. We do anything to protect our family, don't we?" Even face their greatest fears.

Whittaker flinched. His gaze dropped to the drive she held out.

He snatched up the remote and hit a button.

Blood released in a flood. "No!" Cass screamed even as she turned to the glass box.

Just as it popped open. Blood spilled out over the cold cement floor.

Nox crawled out on all fours, coated and covered in blood, sobbing and crying, swiping at their face and eyes.

"Take it!" Cass stretched out her arm as Whittaker spun toward her. "A deal's a deal."

Her body shook and vibrated like an overloaded circuit.

He took one step toward her. She met his dead-eyed gaze with ice in her spine. She would not cower. Not anymore.

Not to him.

He snatched the drive out of her fingers.

Cass didn't wait. She didn't think. She turned and dived toward Nox. Grabbed for them. Hauled them away from the box as the thick, metallic smelling liquid continued to spill forth, coating Cass's hands as she hugged her assistant tight. She covered Nox with her own body as Whittaker shifted toward them.

"No more!" Cass held out a hand, feeling stronger and more terrified than she ever had before.

Mitch picked up his weapon, fired one shot high.

The sound shot Whittaker out of his trance-like state. He took a few steps back, offered a slow, maniacal smile before he turned his back on them.

And disappeared into the darkness.

Cass let out a shuddering breath, tightened her hold on Nox. "You're okay," she whispered. "You're going to be okay."

"I'm sorry," Nox sobbed as Cass rocked them back and forth. "I should have been more careful. I should have realized ..."

"Stop!" Cass grabbed their face in her hands and looked them straight in the eye even as blood smeared beneath her fingers. "You did nothing wrong. Absolutely nothing. This is not your fault, do you hear me?" She hugged them again. "Not your fault."

Mitch swung the lights around, caught a flash of Whittaker as he disappeared out one of the side doors.

"Cassia." Mitch's voice sounded odd. Cautious. Disbelieving. Terrified. "You and Nox get out of here. Now!"

Cass swung around on her knees, still holding Nox.

The light arced across the back wall.

Her pulse slowed as she recognized the yellow detonator cord strung across its expanse.

Before connecting to chunks of grey, molded clay. C4. Her breath caught. "Mitch?"

A timer popped up on the laptop, ticking seconds down. Cass shoved to her feet, caught a glimpse of the countdown. "Forty seconds!" She shouted at Mitch as he started after Whittaker. "Let him go! They'll get him. Nox!" Cass held out her hand.

Nox flew at her, grabbed hold. *Thirty-five, thirty-four, thirty-three—*

Sirens blasted in the distance. An engine roared.

Cass looked back and nearly sobbed in relief to see Mitch running toward them.

The south wall exploded in.

Blake's SUV plowed inside. It braked hard, feet away from Cass, tires screeching.

Blake stuck his head out the driver's side window. "Get in! Now!"

Cass wrenched open the door and shoved Nox into the back seat. She jumped in after them as Mitch threw himself into the passenger side. "Twenty seconds. Go go go!"

"Hold on!" Blake slammed the car into reverse, turned and braced his arm across the back of Mitch's seat. He hit the gas.

They soared backward, out of the building. He pulled hard on the wheel as he braked. Tires squealed as the car spun.

"Lynda, get your people clear!" Mitch shouted into the earpiece he'd been wearing.

She couldn't help but continue the countdown in her head. *Ten, nine, eight—*

Cass pulled Nox down and covered their body with hers.

*Three, two, one—*

The explosion blew the warehouse apart.

She yelped and ducked. The car sped up.

Fireballs and burning debris rained down, clattering onto the roof as Blake drove them clear.

He didn't stop for half a mile. When he did, Mitch jumped out of the car before it completely stopped. He yanked open the back door, caught Nox's arms and pulled them up. "Are you okay?" He held their face, the same panic Cass had been feeling from the moment they knew Nox had been taken evident on his face.

Cass watched as Nox's eyes filled with tears. They nodded. And began to shake.

"It's okay." Mitch hauled them into his arms, held them close and closed his eyes.

When he opened them, he held out a hand to Cass. She grabbed hold and silently swore never to let go.

"Let me guess," Mitch said to Blake when the other man sat back with a heavy sigh. "You're the special equipment Quinn said I'd need?"

"Something like that." Blake looked back at Cass, then at Nox. "Okay?"

Nox nodded but continued to cling to Mitch.

"Cass?" Blake asked.

"I'm good," Cassia said and watched the warehouse continue to burn. "Yeah." She actually smiled. "I'm really good."

*

"Nox is sleeping in the guest room tonight," Cass told Mitch as she closed her bedroom door. "Wally, too."

"Wallace," Mitch corrected her. "Kid got a good dose of just how dangerous the job can get. Not just for himself, but for the people he cares about."

"Yeah."

He reached for her when she slid into bed. "For the record, I intend to sleep until noon. I suggest you do the same." He pulled her into his arms. It wasn't the embrace of passion, but of comfort and relief and …

Love, she thought with a secretive smile. So much love.

She snuggled against him but suddenly couldn't hold onto him tightly enough. The adrenaline that had been coursing through her system at heart-damaging speed was finally beginning to drain. "Everyone's mad at me."

"Yep." Mitch kissed her forehead, stroked her hair. "Definitely mad. Sutton especially."

Cass flinched. "If I'd told them I was going with you, they'd have locked me up."

"I understand the temptation." He smoothed a hand down her hair. "Go to sleep, please. I'm tired."

"I'm not." She rose up and rested her cheek on her hand, gazing down at him.

"Awesome. Try anyway." He threw an arm over his eyes.

She lay her head on his chest, listened to his heartbeat. Tried oh so hard to push everything aside and recharge.

Lynda Prince had taken charge of the scene once the firefighters were done putting out the flames. Cass had watched everything happen like an overwrought movie of the week, answering questions, giving statements, standing by Nox's side while they did the same.

It felt as if it had taken hours to finally return to Temple House.

At least they were home. Back where they belonged.

She'd tended to Nox first, helping them in the shower to scrub the blood off their skin, out of their hair. Wally had stayed close by, retrieving Nox's clothes and bringing them fresh ones from their apartment. An apartment he was pushing her not to return to.

Cass needed to talk to him about that.

Nox needed to get through this in whatever way worked best for them. That was the benefit to working for a woman who had been through what they had. Cass knew the road they needed to walk, and Cass would make certain they didn't stray too far.

Beginning with not making rash and impulsive decisions about their future.

As for Cass, she'd taken her own never-ending shower, but there was no washing the blood or the memories out of her mind. She would ... eventually, because she knew now to use the support system she had in place.

A system that began with the man trying to sleep beside her.

She held out her hand, waited for it to shake.

"What are you doing?"

"Checking something." Anxiety level stable. She smirked. Now that was a surprise. "Oh. Do you have plans for Saturday?" She turned her head and smiled at him when he lifted his weary head.

"I do not."

"Great. It's Keeley's birthday party." And she had no intention of missing it. "I've already got Keeley's present." She sat up and kissed him quick and hard. "I'll sign your name to it."

"Cool." He closed his eyes again.

"Mitch?" Cass waited until he looked at her. "They didn't find him, did they?" It was the one question she was trying not to dwell on.

"Who?"

She narrowed her eyes and rested her hand on his stomach. "No lying, remember? I know Lynda stopped by while I was in the shower."

"Laurel has a big mouth."

"Yes, she does," Cass agreed. "Whittaker made it out, didn't he?"

"I told you. The man always has a plan." He looked at her with concerned eyes. "How are you feeling about that?"

She swallowed hard. "Not great." But she couldn't quite find the energy to be afraid. "He has more important targets in mind than the two of us now."

Mitch lifted his arm behind his head. "You really gave him the picture of Taggart?"

"I really did." If for no other reason than she didn't want Whittaker coming back to focus on the two of them. Or Nox.

"Risky," Mitch said. "He's going to kill him, you know."

"Maybe I'll feel bad about that at some point." But she doubted it. The sooner the former prison guard landed in the morgue, the better for everyone. "That wasn't the only thing on the USB drive."

Mitch frowned, stroked his other hand down her back. "No?"

She flinched. "I might have given him a copy of the dossier we've built on The Circle." She knew it was a gray area, morality wise, but she couldn't quite bring herself to care.

His hand stilled. "You gave him *what*?"

"They sicced a serial killer on us," Cass said, as if that explained everything. "I see it as returning the favor. They set him up and that was a mistake. He'll be a good distraction for them while he starts hunting them down."

"Jesus, Cassia." He pulled her back across his chest, his hold tightening. "That's next level lethal."

"Maybe. I'll be anxious to see how they deal with the monster they set free. And who knows,"—she shrugged a little—"maybe he'll end up returning the favor with whatever information he finds."

"Yeah," Mitch murmured before he sighed. "Maybe. But I doubt it. Can we get some sleep now?"

She drew her hand down his chest. Down his stomach. Lower. "I might need to burn off some energy first. If you're up to it." She grasped him, smiled when he groaned, gripped her hips, and flipped her onto her back. He lowered his mouth to her throat. "I'll take that as a yes."

*

"Oh, wow, thanks, Aunt Cass!" Keeley, wearing a new Taylor Swift sweatshirt and a smile as wide as her face, stared down at the boxed telescope with exactly the awed expression Cass had hoped for. The patio was filled with family and friends, plenty of tacos and a birthday cake decorated with big pink frosting roses and lots of glitter. "This is so cool! Will you help me learn how to use it?"

"Of course." Cass had already scoped out the perfect spot on the roof of Temple House in order for the budding scientist to begin exploring the stars.

Today was, she thought as she stayed a bit out of the fray, a good start to the next part of her life. Hers and Mitch's.

A newly unemployed Mitch, seeing as he'd resigned from Quantico two days ago. He needed a break, a new start. One he intended to begin with her.

It was, Cass thought even now, the best ending she ever could have hoped for. The only question was … how was he going to fit into her apartment?

The days following Nox's abduction had been a bit of a roller coaster. Cass's impulsiveness resulted in a bit of a setback anxiety wise. She'd had a whopper of an attack the day after they'd rescued Nox but, for the first time, she'd gotten through it far more quickly and easily thanks to Mitch's calming attention. Well, his and Elliot's.

Even her friends had come around to forgiving her. Now, if they'd only stop watching her as if she were a time bomb ready to explode. She offered Laurel, Sutton, Mabel, and Riley a fingertip wave and a smile when the four of them kept looking over to where she and Mitch stood in the back corner.

As the gifts were opened and the cake was served, Cass glanced through the patio window as the lobby door swung open.

"Hey." She nudged Mitch as he took a giant bite of chocolate cake. "Lynda's here."

"Right." He finished his piece and grabbed his half-finished can of sparkling mango water and took Cass's hand. They made their way out, quietly closing the door behind them for some privacy.

"Just in time for some cake," Mitch motioned his former partner over to a small bank of tables by the bar.

"Thanks, but I'm actually here to clarify a few things." Lynda looked to Cass. "This morning I was notified that you requested the FBI officially take over the excavation of the bodies on the hill." She inclined her head. "Is that true?"

"It is. My only caveat was that you be the lead agent on the project. That, and you keep my original team."

"Yeah, I got all that," Lynda waved off her explanation. "The mayor and DA's office both released public statements of support for you."

"I bet that hurt, too." Cass flashed a somewhat irritated smile.

"Only fitting since they tried to publicly humiliate her," Mitch muttered.

"Me stepping down is the right thing to do." Didn't mean it didn't hurt though. It had taken a lot of discussion and a lot of self-evaluation to make the decision. "My job is to make sure the victims have a voice. That the job gets done right and without any scandal or perceived bias. I don't want any kind of cloud over those graves."

"I'll be honest." Lynda sat forward, her hands clasped between her knees. The frown on her face had her forehead wrinkling against her tight hairline. "I think you're making a mistake stepping down."

"Noted," Cass said. "And appreciated."

"Don't appreciate me just yet." Lynda looked to Mitch. Then back to Cass. "I agreed to accept the assignment with my own caveat. I want you to remain on board as a special consultant. You, too," she said to Mitch. "You're both too valuable to put on the sidelines and, if what you've told me about the bigger picture playing out around this case, I'm going to need as much help as I can get from people I can trust. And I think those people are all here. In Temple House."

Mitch glanced away, but not before Lynda caught the grin on his face.

"What?" She demanded. "What's that look?"

"He just won twenty bucks off me," Cass told her. "He said you'd want to keep me on and that you'd push to make it happen."

"Did he?" Lynda looked impressed. "Glad to see your instincts are still honed. I'm that predictable?"

"You're that reliable," Mitch said. "Any doubt I might have had about Cass stepping down, you just took care of."

"So is that a yes?" Lynda pressed.

Part of Cass wanted to beg off and walk away. But that wouldn't get them very far where The Circle was concerned. This case was the way in—it had to be. "If that's the only way you'll take the case, then I guess I don't have much of a choice, do I?"

"No," Lynda said. "You don't."

Cass's cell phone pinged. She pulled it out of her pocket, glanced down. She shook her head as she texted a response.

"Nox?" Mitch guessed.

"They want us to come up and see what they've found." She hit send. "I told them to come down here and tell us."

Lynda winced in sympathy. "They're having a rough time of it?"

"Comes and goes," Cass said. "But the last thing I'm going to let them do is hide away and hope it goes away." She reached out for Mitch's hand. "They have a life to live. Besides, they should have been at the party an hour ago."

A few seconds later, Nox strode down the stairs, a rather grumpy expression on their face. They'd changed up and dyed their hair again, this time a violent violet that reminded Cass of a Manga character.

Mitch leaned over. "You're late. Wally's been looking for you."

"I take it this is what they call tough love?" Nox's statement might be accusing, but they sounded resigned.

"Yes," Cas confirmed. "What did you find?"

"I broke it."

"Broke what? Your computer?"

"No, not my …ha ha." They rolled their eyes. "The encryption code. On the USB drive Eva Hudson hid in Benny the Bunny."

"And?" Mitch asked patiently, eyes brightening.

A spark jumped into Nox's eyes. "It's a member database. To Scheherazade." They grinned. "Pretty good, huh?"

"Very good," Cass murmured.

"What's Scheherazade?" Lynda asked.

"It's a gentleman's club here in Los Angeles," Mitch said. "A very exclusive one."

"We think it's run by The Circle," Cass added.

Finally, she thought, as she took a deep, steeling breath.

They had a way in.

# EPILOGUE

**BLAKE** pulled his recently scorched SUV up to the telephonic based intercom system outside the gates of the palatial Beverly Hills estate. He powered down his window, hit the connect button.

The box buzzed before a voice answered. "Can I help you?"

"It's Blake. He asked to see me." More like Blake had been summoned. He glared at the gate ahead.

"Of course, Mr. Redford," came the reply. "You're expected."

The gates opened with a silent glide. He drove up the bricked driveway, circled around and parked in his usual spot on the far side of the elegantly landscaped yard.

As far as estates went, it was on the subdued side. It was beautiful but without the ostentatious décor so many of the Hollywood elite put on display.

The two-story mini-mansion had been built back in the late forties by one of Tinsel Town's most powerful families. With its brilliant white paint and elegant scroll work, the architectural design harkened back to classic lines and practical angles. There was artistry in the home that matched its rich history.

The yard was filled with early spring color on the verge of bursting into full bloom. A statute of one of a Greek goddess—Blake had no idea which one—stood at watch over the lush greenery and thick foliage that added depth and beauty to the property. Not a blade of grass overgrown, not a flower that needed pruning.

As perfect as an AI generated movie set.

The left side of the enormous double wooden doors opened. "Good afternoon, Mr. Redford." A uniformed older man wearing a pristine waistcoat Downton Abbey would be proud of, offered a short bow.

"Afternoon, Lyle." Blake stepped into the marble entryway and, as usual, found himself looking toward the pair of curving staircases. "New paint job?" He could smell the telltale hint of turpentine above the scent of the flower arrangement in the center of a circular table.

"Always observant." Lyle shut the door and gestured toward the back yard.

"Uncle Blake!"

Blake glanced up, unable to stop the smile from spreading across his face. "Clara. I didn't know you were home from school."

The fifteen-year-old raced down the stairs, her long blonde hair bouncing against her back. The smattering of freckles across her nose reminded him of her mother who had passed away more than seven years ago.

"It's spring break." She leapt at him for a hug. "Are you here to see Dad or to let me beat you at pickle ball?"

"I never *let* you win at anything." But of course he did. "Everything going okay? How are your classes going this semester?" He wrapped an arm around her shoulder as they walked through the sitting room toward the patio door.

"It's okay. I hate my French teacher. How about you? Anything new and exciting?"

"Absolutely nothing," Blake lied.

They stepped out onto the concrete patio and Clara immediately made her way to the pitcher of fresh lemonade that had been set out on a glass table.

Blake sat down and was about to ask Clara about this French teacher at her private boarding school when the door to the guest cottage opened.

The man who emerged made for an elegant picture in his tennis whites, shocking dark hair sprinkled with grey, and blue eyes that would have put Paul Newman to shame. He was a man who took his health as seriously as he took his business.

And there was nothing Granger Powell took more seriously than his work.

"Sorry to keep you waiting, Blake." Granger's smile was Hollywood bright. "Couldn't get off this conference call about this new series of books we just optioned for film."

"Which series?" Clara asked. "Is it the one I told you about?" She turned to Blake. "There's this awesome one I just finished about this traveling carnival that ..."

"All I'll say is that you might be in the running for a finder's fee. Good to see you, Blake."

"You, too." Blake shook the offered hand.

"Did Clara tell you she's trying to convince me to let her spend the summer at home? And maybe transfer to a private school here in LA?"

"She did not." Blake took his seat again. "I thought you usually go to Italy to see your grandparents, Clara?"

Clara shrugged. "I want to do something different."

"We'll continue our discussion later." Granger gave her a quick hug. "Uncle Blake and I need to talk."

"Yeah, yeah. See you later!" Clara flounced off, lemonade in hand.

"She looks good," Blake said. "Happy."

"Thank God." Granger followed his daughter's lead and poured himself some lemonade. "I heard there was some excitement around Temple House this week."

"That's one way to put it." Blake declined an offered glass. Truth be told, he was anxious to get back to Temple House before Keeley's birthday cake was gone. Plus, he wasn't about to share any details about Jonathan Whittaker's activities of the past few weeks. Funny how the actual details seemed to have been buried by the media in favor of the sensationalism of an escaped serial killer no one could seem to find.

Yeah, Blake thought. He'd keep that information to himself.

"How are things going over there?"

"They're going fine." He knew what Granger expected from him, but Blake had mastered his stalling techniques. Besides, he honestly couldn't give the man what he wanted. Not yet, at least. "I told you I'd be in touch if I had anything new to report."

"You did say that." Granger paid extraordinary attention to his filled glass. "You've been working at Temple House for a few months. I'm anxious to start seeing a return on my investment."

"That'll be difficult considering you aren't paying me anything." His years in the military had more than prepared him for dealing with powerhouses like Granger Powell. The man might operate one of Hollywood's biggest studios and employ some of the biggest names in the business, but that didn't mean he was anything other than a man with stars in his eyes. And an agenda on his mind.

Blake had known the man going on twenty-five years, and well enough for Blake to be named Clara's godfather, although Blake suspected that had been at the behest of Granger's late wife. Probably, he'd realized after losing his own family, to make certain they always stayed connected.

"I don't know how many ways I can try to convince you, Granger," Blake said for what felt like the millionth time. "Riley and Moxie are not going to sell you Temple House. I've seen and heard nothing that comes close to convincing me otherwise. If you're wanting a different response, you're wasting your time."

"I'm having lunch with Moxie in a couple of weeks, actually." Granger took a long, drawn-out drink. "She's asked to bring a guest. Laurel Fontaine."

"Then gird your loins," Blake told him. "She's more protective of Moxie than Riley is."

"Good to know. See?" He toasted Blake. "See, you do have information for me. And you thought your undercover days were behind you."

They were. But his self-loathing ones had definitely arrived. He loved what he was doing at Temple House, but was far from proud about his true intentions. Intentions that were getting more difficult to conceal with the way Granger was pushing.

"I'm not doing you any good there," Blake said. "You wanted me to find a way you can convince them to sell. If offering Moxie a role in the remakes of her movies didn't budge them—"

"I've got other things on my mind other than Temple House these days." Granger's brow furrowed in a way that told Blake he was both confused and concerned. "I've been hearing some strange rumors circulating around Powell Films. Rumors that bring up some rather disturbing history for my family."

Blake did his best to keep his expression passive even as his heart skipped a beat. Granger was one of the most unflappable men he'd ever met. He was ruthless at times, tenacious always, and cautious enough not to show his full hand before he'd calculated the odds.

"Let's set Temple House aside for now," Granger said. "I'd like you to shift your focus to another subject. Something I think some of the residents at Temple House might be able to shine a light on."

"You're starting to sound like a Bond villain, Granger," Blake said. "Spit it out. I've got work to get back to." But even as he said it, he could feel a shift in the air.

A dangerous, unexpected shift.

"All right then." Granger set his glass down, his eyes sparking with ice. "I want you to tell me what you've heard about a group called The Circle."